The Zook Sisters of Lancaster County

Book One

Ruth's Dilemma

By
June Bryan Belfie

Other Books by this author:

Inn Sane–Memoirs of an Innkeeper
All About Grace

E-books:
Moving On
The Landlord
A Special Blessing for Sara
A Long Way to Go
The Inn Game

I am dedicating this book to my first granddaughter, Krista Boorujy Prather, who is not only dear to me, but also a future writer and is like her Nana in more ways than I can count. Even as a toddler Krista had a love for books, which has never lessened. She is also on the cover of this book. Thank you, Krista.

Chapter One

Ruth Zook was aware of Jeremiah Fisher's eyes on her as she tried to emerge from the buggy with a semblance of grace. Her foot slipped and she was headed for the ground when firm hands reached around her waist to steady her. Jeremiah's boyish grin, as he released his grip on her, made her feel even clumsier. A flush reached her cheeks. "*Danki.*"

He gave a slight bow, removed his straw hat from his golden locks, and beamed at her. "You're *willkum*. See you in church, Ruthie."

Ruth's older sister, Emma, jumped down from the buggy, grabbed Ruth's arm, and snatched her away from the smiling group of young men resting against Bishop King's fence. "That was so *deliberate*," Emma whispered. "You knew Jeremiah would grab you in time."

"Don't be silly. Why would I want to look like an oaf? Besides, Ezekiel Schrock was closer." Ruth tucked a loose strand of her shiny brown hair under her *kapp* and quickened her pace.

"Don't get any ideas about Jeremiah Fisher, Ruth. He's far more interested in me."

That thought had never occurred to Ruth. Perhaps he did favor Emma. After all Emma was twenty, the same age as Jeremiah, while Ruth was only eighteen.

"Then I suppose it would have been better if I'd fallen flat on my face?"

Emma rolled her eyes. "Oh, let's forget the whole thing. *Mamm* and Katie are waiting inside for us. Church services should start soon and I want a good seat inside where I can see into the next room and watch Jeremiah."

Ruth sat next to her *mamm*, waiting in silence, for the service to begin. She could see Jeremiah talking to friends as he placed his hat on a wooden peg by the front door. Her heart danced each time she saw him. He always had a strong affect on her and in

Ruth's eyes, he was the most desirable man in the district. That was for sure and for certain. Was what she felt true love, the kind you have for a husband, or was it just girlish infatuation?

Emma had never made it known before how she felt toward Jeremiah. If only Ruth had expressed her feelings sooner–staking her own claim. But then it was only in recent weeks that she realized how much she actually cared for him.

Ruth's older brothers arrived with their families and soon the rooms were filled–women and children in one room and the men seated in an adjoining room. It was cramped in the farmhouse, but since it was early April, it was still too cool to meet in the barn for the service.

Church lasted over three hours. Ruth's favorite part of the service was the music sung from the *Ausbund*. It was poignant as everyone sang in unison. One of the Zook men started the "*Das Loblied*" and everyone in the congregation added their voices. Ruth closed her eyes as she included her soprano voice to the others around her singing praises to the Lord. She could hear Jeremiah Fisher's strong tenor voice from the next room and smiled, visualizing his startling blue eyes as he sang. Someday Jeremiah should be the *vorsinger,* she thought to herself. He could easily lead the singing.

Ruth barely listened to the preacher's words. The sing-song tone of the minister as he spoke in the old German, and his tears as he walked from room to room in the large old farmhouse, unsettled her. It embarrassed her to watch a grown man allow his emotions to show so easily. She was used to her father, Leroy, who never revealed the thoughts which traveled through his head. He had one expression. Somber. Ruth knew he loved her, though words were not spoken. It was his eyes that exposed his tender side. On occasion, she observed a smile as he watched her sisters, Emma and Katie, giggle when they talked about the young gentlemen who flirted with them at the Sings or Frolics.

Her sister, Emma, was not yet betrothed, though several young men tried to get her attention in the past. She seemed indifferent to their obvious interest. Emma had claimed teaching in the one-room schoolhouse near their home was fulfilling enough for her, but that may have changed with her obvious infatuation with Jeremiah.

Katie still had time to think about a marriage proposal, after all she was only sixteen. In the Amish world it was not too early to start thinking about the man one would marry even at her age. Every girl was expected to wed and have a large family. There was old Miss Beiler, who lived with her sister, who remained unmarried. She must be at least fifty. Her sharp tongue and bad breath in all likelihood contributed to her single state.

After the service, tables were brought in from the barn and the men re-arranged the benches for seating as the women set out the casseroles and desserts prepared earlier. Ruth spoke little to the others around her, dwelling instead on her disappointment in Emma's announcement about Jeremiah.

Her friend, Priscilla Miller, a tall, slender girl with auburn hair, came over to her. "I saw Jeremiah catch you as you lost your balance, Ruth. Lucky you! Were his hands as strong as they look?"

"I was so embarrassed, I didn't much notice."

"Oh come on now. How could you not notice Jeremiah's hands around your waist? He can put his hands around me anytime," she said, glancing his way with a glint in her eye.

"At least he kept me from falling, but no man is going to be that personal with me unless it's an emergency situation like before."

"As you please, Ruth. He's so adorable, I can't stand it. See you at the Sing tonight?"

"Maybe."

Priscilla walked away and headed toward the group of young men gathered around the dessert table where she stopped to talk.

After everyone had eaten, the women and girls cleaned up the dishes and when they were done, Ruth nodded to her sisters as a signal to leave.

"Ruth," her mother, Mary, called as the three sisters headed toward the buggies lined up alongside the bishop's large clapboard farm house. "Wait for your brother. Your *daed* and I are staying a while to talk with the others, but Wayne wants to check Prickly. She's about to birth again."

"We'll wait, *Mamm*, but please tell him to hurry."

"I'll send him right out."

Ruth watched as her mother turned and limped towards the King porch to find her youngest son, 15-year-old Wayne. In spite of her physical problem, she was an attractive woman of forty-four. Her hair, pulled back under her kapp, had thinned and was speckled with gray, though with the blonde mixed in, it was barely noticeable.

"Ruth, I saw Josiah watching you," Katie whispered to her sister. "I bet he likes you."

"Well, I don't like him, that's for sure."

"He's cute. What don't you like about him?" The girls spoke softly, checking to make sure their voices wouldn't be heard by the group of young men standing only a few yards away.

"He's boring. I talked with him once and all he talked about was cows."

"He was probably nervous," Emma added as she looked over and smiled faintly at Jeremiah Fisher, who responded with a wide grin creating a dimple in his chin. His curly blonde hair tumbled nearly to his shoulders and he wore his flat straw hat at a rakish angle.

"Where's that brother of ours?" Ruth said tapping her black shoe against the ground as she folded her arms. Her brows furrowed over her brilliant blue eyes.

"Here he comes. He has his friend, Skinny Abner, with him. There's no room for both," Emma added.

Wayne waved his friend off before arriving at the buggy. "Yuck. I have to ride with all three of you."

"You can walk, if you'd rather," Ruth reminded him as she climbed into the driver's seat.

"Can't take the time. I'll live, I guess." Wayne took the front passenger seat as his sisters got in behind them.

"*Mamm* says she thinks we'll get a new kid today," Ruth said.

"*Jah*. Prickly was acting weird this morning. She may be having twins."

"Oh, I hope so," Emma said as she loosened her *kapp*. "It got warm in church today. Too many people in those small rooms."

"I noticed it, too," Ruth joined in. "I thought Fannie looked like she was goin' to faint."

"*Ach*. Bein' in a family way doesn't help," Emma said. "When is the baby expected?"

"I think she said in August. Only four months to go."

"Do ya have to talk about lady things when I'm along?" Wayne asked, blush traveling up his neck.

"It's not a huge deal for a farm boy to hear about babies in the makin', is it?" Ruth asked, grinning.

"*Jah*, when it's my sister-in-law you're discussin', it's a bit too personal. Just talk later."

"Well, we have to hear all about your silly goat," Katie added.

"She's a good milker, that one. You're the silly one, Miss Katie."

"I saw you lookin' at Sadie Yoder. She's pretty cute, *jah*?" Katie teased.

"So, what if I did? She's a *gut* person and she likes to talk about goats."

"Only 'cause you raise 'em." Katie tapped her brother on the head and laughed.

"Girls. All you think about is romance."

"Not true," Katie said pouting her lips. "I think about lots of things."

"Like what?" Wayne turned and grinned at his sister.

"Well...I think about..."

"See? I told you."

"Wait, I'm thinking. Food. Yes, I think about food, a lot."

"It's starting to show, chubby."

"Wayne! Shame on you. Don't say that to your sister," Emma scolded. "She's adorable with a little flesh on her. It makes her dimples stand out."

"That's not all. We may need an addition on the barn pretty soon if–"

"Stop. I'll tell *Daed*," Emma said firmly.

Ruth had been silent long enough. "Can't we even ride five miles without you all getting into an argument?"

"We're not arguing," Emma replied. "But it's cruel to say those things to your sister. *Daed* would be furious."

"It's only a little teasing," Wayne suggested. "You don't take it serious, do you, Katie?"

"I guess not. My dress is getting tight, though. I guess I need to cut back on dessert."

"I did see you take three pieces of shoofly pie, Sis," Emma said softly as she patted her sister's hand. "One would probably do."

"I didn't want to hurt Aunt Becky's feelings. She made them, you know."

"One would do," Emma emphasized with a furrowed brow.

When they pulled up to their home, Wayne jumped out first. "You take care of the buggy, Ruth. I need to go see my goat."

After Ruth took the buggy around the back of the barn, she removed the harness from the horse, and released him to an enclosed pasture. She noticed several crocuses budding and smiled at the thought of spring finally arriving.

As she headed back to the house, another buggy pulled into the long drive. She couldn't make out the visitor. When it got closer, she saw it was Jeremiah driving. He waved to her, pulled over to a wide drive designed for visitors, and climbed out.

"Hi, Ruth. My *Mamm* wanted you to have these rolls she made. She forgot to put them out and she knew how much your *daed* liked them. They have cinnamon in them."
He reached across with a bag.

"*Danki.*" In order to keep him there, she asked the first thing that popped into her mind. "Do you want to stay awhile? My brother is playing mid-wife to a goat in the barn."

"Sure. I'll go join him. Wanna come with me?"

"I guess I can for a couple minutes." Ruth glanced over at the house, hoping Emma hadn't seen the buggy arrive.

They walked together and entered the barn. They spotted Wayne crouched in a corner where the nanny goat was pacing. Ruth frowned and looked over at Jeremiah. "I wonder if she's in trouble. She's makin' a lot of noise. What do you think, Jeremiah?"

He walked over and talked to Prickly, while rubbing his hands across her belly. "Doesn't feel like it should be a problem. I can tell the kid is faced the right way. Takes some gals longer than others."

"Why did you bring my sister with you?"

"Uh, I thought she'd be interested. Are you?" he asked, turning to Ruth.

She glared at her brother. "Not particularly. I'll take the rolls in the house. When you two are done I'll give you some fresh lemonade." Ruth walked abruptly back to the house, annoyed with her brother for his remark. Okay, so watching a goat in labor wasn't her idea of fun but being near handsome Jeremiah was something else. She was surprised he hadn't decided on his future bride yet. He was pursued–quietly and discreetly of course–by many of the females over sixteen. Priscilla was certainly interested.

When she walked into the kitchen she observed her two sisters craning their necks out the kitchen window toward the barn. Emma turned, her eyes wide. "Was that Jeremiah Fisher?"

"The one and only," Ruth answered, trying to avoid exposing her own interest. She placed the bag of rolls on the white enamel table.

"What's in the *toot?*" Katie asked, leaving her station by the sink to open the bag.

"They're really for *Daed,*" Ruth said, "though there are enough for each of us to have one. I told Wayne and Jeremiah to come back here when they're done in the barn and I'd give them some lemonade."

"Ruth," Katie folded her arms and glared at her older sister. "*Mamm* would not like you entertaining a gentleman when she's not even here."

"She'll be home soon. Besides, look at all of us. Do you really think anything wrong would happen with five people sitting around?"

"*Nein,* but it doesn't appear proper."

"Of course Jeremiah knows the whole family," Emma said. Ruth noticed she was far less reluctant to entertain the young man. "He even works with our brother, which should count for something."

"Katie, you help me cut up the lemons," Ruth said.

"All right." Katie moaned and reached in the drawer for a knife.

"I'll be right back," Emma said, as she headed towards the staircase to the second floor.

Katie and Ruth cut up and squeezed a dozen lemons and added water and sugar. Several minutes later, Emma returned. Her hair was slightly looser around her head and her cheeks were a bright pink, obviously pinched, observed Ruth. She was still sorely disappointed that her older sister was enamored of the handsome Jeremiah, since she had recently decided to set her own *kapp* for him. She stirred the pale lemonade. Why hadn't she said something first?

Chapter Two

"What's taking so long?" Emma asked as she paced back and forth from the kitchen to the sitting room. "Ruth, come with me. Something must have gone wrong. That goat should have delivered by now."

"Let's go check," Ruth responded, reaching for her shawl. Emma did the same and they left Katie in charge of placing glasses and cookies on the table.

When they arrived at the barn entrance, Ruth heard the sounds of the new kid. Jeremiah and Wayne were sitting on a bale of hay talking while the nanny goat licked her new infant.

"We were worried something had gone wrong," Emma told the young men, who stood when the girls appeared.

"Nope. Everything's fine. She didn't even need us to be here, but Jeremiah and me wanted to talk about stuff. He thinks they'll need someone in the buggy shop come fall."

Ruth's mouth dropped open. "But *Daed*. What would he say? You need to help him in the fields."

"But this would be something I'd enjoy more. Ya know I like to tinker with things. I get bored farming. But I guess you're right. *Daed* does need me. Thanks for thinking of me, Jeremiah, but I really am needed here."

Jeremiah cleared his throat and looked over at Ruth. "There was nothing definite, anyway. Only thought I'd mention the possibility. Wayne's young enough. He could always change his mind about farming when he's older–maybe after he has boys of his own."

"Jeremiah, you're so nice to think of our brother," Emma said, giving an unusually sweet smile. "You boys deserve a treat after all this. I made cookies yesterday. And we have lemonade."

"We," corrected Ruth.

"We what?" asked Emma.

"*We* made cookies yesterday. The three of us. Remember?"

13

"Oh, right. But I took them out of the oven."

"Sounds good, girls," Jeremiah said grinning. "I'll eat them no matter who made them." He bowed slightly and waved his arm toward the barn door. "After you."

Both girls started out at the same time. Ruth put her arm around her sister and gave her a slight pinch on her upper arm. Emma responded by bumping her younger sister in the hip. Mortified, Ruth heard the stifled laughter of the young men behind her.

After everyone collected lemonade and a napkin with cookies, they went outside and sat on the porch. The boys perched themselves on the steps and the older girls reclined on a squeaking porch glider while Katie plunked herself down on a wooden rocker. Spring was bursting and the scent of fresh soil and budding trees reached Ruth's nostrils. She breathed in deeply and smiled with pleasure at the group around her.

"Good cookies," Jeremiah said with a mouth full.

"I made them yesterday," Katie remarked as she placed a third one in her mouth.

Jeremiah nearly choked on the one he was chewing, as he let out a laugh.

"We, Katie. *We.*" Emma said as she and Ruth glanced at each other. Was even little Katie pushing for Jeremiah's attention?

"Did you have fun during your *Rumschpringe?*" Emma asked Jeremiah.

"*Jah*, it was interesting."

"Did you travel anywhere *gut?*" Wayne asked.

"Not too far. An English friend of mine drove me to New York City once."

"Wow! What was it like?" the wide-eyed boy asked.

Jeremiah smiled at Wayne and rolled his eyes. "Too many people–all in a hurry. They almost run. It's funny. Even ladies with huge high heels raced along like they were being chased."

"Maybe they were," Emma added. "I've heard bad people grab your purse or even push you over for things like sneakers."

"I suppose sometimes it happens, but I didn't see anything like that."

"Did you see anyone get shot?" Wayne asked.

Jeremiah laughed and shook his head. "No. Nothing terrible. Except Broadway. Awful places there."

"Like how?" Wayne asked.

"I don't want to even tell you. Just bad. I was glad to leave there and go to watch a Met's game."

Wayne's eyes were complete circles now. "The baseball team?"

"*Jah.* We took a train from Penn Station."

"A train? Wow! I can't wait till I can go on *Runschpringe.*"

"I have no desire to leave here," Emma announced, folding her arms across her chest. "Everything I need is right here."

"Maybe," Ruth added, "but aren't you even curious about things? I would love to go to Switzerland and see the mountains."

Jeremiah smiled over at Ruth. "I hope to see the ocean someday."

"Oh, *jah*, the ocean. That would be exciting."

Emma shook her head. "There's too much temptation when you travel and surround yourself with other people like that. We know first-hand how some never come back."

"True. *Mamm*'s sister left the Amish," Ruth added.

"Most do return though," Jeremiah added. "You can't be afraid to think about the other way."

Emma let out a sigh. "A true Amish woman finds her fulfillment in marriage and bearing children. I will make a *gut* wife for someone. I love to cook and sew and I want a dozen children."

Jeremiah smiled at her. "*Jah*, you'll make a fine wife for some lucky fellow."

Ruth wanted to cry. So he did like her sister, after all.

"What about you, Ruthie?" Wayne asked. "Is that what you want? To be a wife and mother?"

"Of course. As Emma says, every *gut* Amish woman wants a family, but it doesn't mean you can't enjoy other things for a while. I would love to travel and go to concerts and shop in big stores. I'd even like to wear prettier clothes and not be afraid to wear my hair loose. I don't know why it is so wrong to do some of those things."

"Because they lead to vanity and other things," Emma said with authority. "Next you'd wear short skirts and tight clothes and end up like the others. Like being a tramp."

"Nonsense! There's no way I'd go that far and look–"

"Ladies, stop. I'm sorry if I started something. Everyone has to make up their own mind about their lives. Living outside our world briefly didn't destroy my love for my people or my way of life here, but I wasn't afraid to explore the outside world. I think there are groups of Amish now who are more relaxed in their rules and yet still remain true to the old ways."

"Look, here come *Mamm* and *Daed*," Katie announced pointing to a buggy making a turn at the drive. After a few pleasant exchanges, Jeremiah excused himself and headed for his buggy. Emma followed right behind with a paper plate filled with additional cookies. She and Jeremiah chatted for several minutes before he left. Ruth watched for signals–anything. Did he prefer her older sister to her? Was his smile a bit too broad when he looked into Emma's eyes? Once he glanced back at Ruth and she thought he nodded at her, but she quickly averted her eyes so he wouldn't think her too forward.

That night as they prepared for bed, Katie went to her own room and Emma and Ruth, who shared a room, took turns brushing each other's long hair. Emma sat cross-legged on the bed with Ruth kneeling behind her. "Ouch! You're pulling too hard," Emma complained.

"Sorry. You have snarls."

"I can't help it. You know how curly my hair is. It always snarls up when I unbraid it. So, what do you think of Jeremiah?"

"What's to think? He seems nice. Why are you asking?"

"Just wondered what you thought. I'm sure he likes me, don't you agree? He didn't seem in any rush to leave."

"He liked our cookies."

"Ruth, don't be silly. It was more than the cookies. He kept looking at me and smiling. Didn't you notice?"

"He smiled at Katie, too. It doesn't mean he's crazy in love to smile at someone."

"Oh, you know what I mean. He smiled a certain way. Like this." Emma turned and gave a long languishing smile with half-closed eyes.

Ruth let out a giggle and shook her head. "Goodness, I never saw him make a face like that. He'd look pretty stupid if he smiled that way."

"Forget it! I'll do your hair now. Get in front."

Ruth moved in front of her sister and pulled her golden brown hair down from her bun, letting it flow behind her. Emma moved the brush harshly through her sister's hair.

"Stop! I'll do it myself. If you think Jeremiah is so madly in love with you, go ahead and think it. I think you made a fool out of yourself–first pretending you made the cookies all by yourself and next parading outside with a whole plateful, chasing after him. He's going to think you're boy crazy!"

"You're jealous because he looked at me more than at you!"

"He did not!"

"Did to!"

"Girls! Girls! What's all this about?" *Mamm* came through the doorway, placing her finger to her lips. "*Daed* heard you up here. Why were you yelling at each other?"

"Um, just a disagreement," Ruth responded, trying to avoid her mother's scrutiny.

"We won't have arguing in this house. You know the rules. If there is disagreement, discuss it calmly and if you can't work it out, come to one of us and we'll try to help sort it out. You're sisters."

How well I know, Ruth thought. "Okay, *Mamm*. We're done talking about it now."

"Do you want to explain what it was about, so I can help?"

Ruth looked over at Emma who shrugged. "No, we're done."

"Well, say your prayers and get a good night's sleep. Tomorrow Emma has to teach and you and me are goin' to plant some more herb seeds, Ruth."

Ruth sighed and walked over to kiss her mother goodnight. "Sorry, we had everyone upset. Emma and I love each other. We just have spats once in a while."

"I know. My youngest sister and I didn't always agree. I realize that. *Gut nacht,* girls."

"*Gut nacht, Mamm.*"

After they were left alone, Ruth leaned on her elbow and called across to her sister. "Before we *outen* the light, I want to say sorry. I didn't mean to yell at you."

Emma turned her head and smiled at her sister. "I know. Me, either. I was being prideful. Of course, Jeremiah wouldn't choose me over you. You're a much better person."

"Not true. I'm sure he was showing more attention to you, now when I think about it. See you in the morning. *Gut nacht.*"

Now if only she could get him out of her mind. No matter how hard she tried, she couldn't remove the picture of his smile or the sound of his laughter from her mind. As was her custom, Ruth hummed one of her favorite hymns in her mind before losing herself in sleep.

Chapter Three

Spring was rainy and the crops were late in being planted. Ruth's father, Leroy, worked most of the daylight hours with his son at his side. The tilling had to wait until the sun partially dried the rich soil in order to spare the horses. Since the tractor had been banned for use by the Amish back in 1923, the horses did all the hard labor, though the farmers were allowed to use diesel-operated equipment if they continued to have them horse-drawn. So much depended upon the weather.

Seedlings for their vegetable garden were started in cold frames by the women. Ruth, her mother, and Katie, spent hours each spring, cleaning and washing the household bedding after the long winter's use. Everyone worked hard but it was not looked upon as unpleasant. The rewards were many as they worked as a unit.

One Saturday afternoon, when the sun finally made its appearance, Jeremiah pulled up in his buggy and Emma ran out to greet him. Ruth watched from the front window and felt a lump in her throat. Why hadn't she made her interest in him known before her sister made it plain she wanted him to court her? There was no one else she was even remotely interested in.

Instead of coming back in the house, they walked around the herb garden. Ruth could see her sister pointing out the different herbs. She watched as Emma smiled up at Jeremiah and he returned the smile. Yes, he did appear interested. There'd be other men for herself. Maybe in a different region. Perhaps at the next auction she'd find the love of her life.

"Ruth, why are you so quiet all of a sudden?" Her *mamm* asked as she popped the early peas from their pods into a pot.

"Was I? I didn't realize. Just quiet I guess."

"*Jah*. Just quiet. Mmm. So it looks like your big sister is enjoyin' the attention of a young man. Do you approve?"

I'm sick over it. I wanted so much to have him smile at me. "He seems alright."

Katie was grinding meat for dinner and looked up. "Alright? He's marvelous. I wish I was older, I'd have him crooning over me."

Mamm laughed at her youngest daughter's enthusiasm. "Wait your turn, little *wootzer.*"

"*Mamm*, don't call me 'little piggy.' I hate that."

"Sorry, sweetie. It's only a nickname."

"But it's awful. *Daed* started it. Please tell him to stop."

"*Jah.* You're right. I'll tell him myself. Now, make the meat into a loaf. I have old bread in the bowl with the dishtowel. Ruth, have you checked for eggs today?"

"I thought that was Emma's job on Saturdays."

"*Jah,* but you see she's busy falling in love." Mary smiled at her daughter. "Go check. We could use a couple more for the meatloaf."

Ruth reluctantly changed her apron to a fresh one and headed out to the chicken coop with a basket. On the way she met up with Jeremiah and Emma, who was holding a barn kitten in her arms. "Look, Ruth. Isn't he adorable?"

Jeremiah is adorable, that's just a cat, Ruth thought to herself. "Cute."

"*Hallo*, Ruth. You don't like cats?"

"I do. I'm real busy, is all. I have to check for eggs."

"I did check already and there aren't any new ones. Jeremiah and I searched everywhere."

"Well, I guess I can go back then. There's lots of work to do."

"Oh, I guess I should be leaving," Jeremiah said hesitantly. "I don't want to interfere with your chores, Emma."

Emma glared over at her sister. "I *did* my chores. Let's walk over to the barn and look at the new goat. He's getting big. You were here the day he was born, remember?"

Jeremiah glanced over at Ruth and cleared his throat. "Uh, *jah*, I was there. Let's go see him. See you later, Ruth."

"Maybe," she answered and turned quickly before the tear forming behind her eye made a formal appearance. *Ridiculous. Emma is older than I am. She should marry first.*

"No eggs, *Mamm*. Emma checked."

"Well, use the ones we have. I think there are four. They will have to do. Did you know we're celebrating your *Oma's* seventieth birthday next week-end after church?"

"But it's not for another ten days."

"*Jah*, but we want everyone to help celebrate, so we're going to give her a cake after services. That way all our friends can help make it special."

"I can't believe my *grossmammi* is seventy. She looks so young."

Mary nodded in agreement. "And here she has six living children and thirty grands. She still seems in good health, too."

"It's amazing that she still works on the farm the way she does. I was hopin' they'd be living with us by now."

"As long as they're able, they want to stay in their own place. I can't blame them, though it would be nice to have them closer."

Ruth heard laughter as her sister and Jeremiah appeared at the screened front door. Emma opened the door and invited Jeremiah to come in. He removed his hat and bowed his head at the others. "You have a fine lookin' billy goat out there."

"*Jah*, Wayne takes *gut* care of his goats. Would you like a glass of juice?"

"I best be goin' since *Mamm* needs help turnin' the mattresses. Oh, I meant to tell you all—here's why I came by today. The family took up a collection and we want to give you twenty-three dollars and seventy-five cents for your *Mamm's* birthday party." He reached into a pocket and took out a wad of bills and three coins.

"Well, that's real nice of everyone. Do you want me to buy something with it or give it to her this way?"

"*Mamm* thought she'd leave it up to you."

"I'll pray about it. I know she loves to sew up new curtains every few years, so maybe I'll buy fabric with it. The ones she has up are lookin' tired."

"That's your decision, ma'am. Well, I best be goin'." He stood an extra moment, turning his hat in his hands and glanced over at Ruth, who was wiping her hands on a cloth. She caught his eyes and quickly looked down.

"I'll walk you out," Emma offered as she gave him a radiant smile. Ruth hadn't seen such a big grin on her sister's face since she came home with all *A*'s in eighth grade.

When she returned, Ruth handed her a dish towel. "We need the pots dried."

Emma took the towel and looked around at the women. "So, what do you think? Is he wonderful or not?"

"Wonderful-*gut!*" Katie emphasized. "Marry him, Emma. I'd love to have him as a brother-in-law."

"Huh. That's a bit premature, isn't it? You hardly know each other," Ruth remarked.

"I've known Jeremiah since I was two years old!"

"Not known him–known him. So we played together in the school yard. That hardly counts." Ruth whipped the cake batter as if her life depended upon it.

"Girls, you're not being nice. Stop right now."

"*Yah Mamm,*" Ruth said as she slowed down her stirring.

Emma walked by and whispered barely loud enough for Ruth to hear, "I think you're jealous."

Ruth drew her lips together and lifted one shoulder, turning away from her sister. Was she? Ruth knew it was wrong to be jealous. She wanted to be happy for Emma. He did seem to be appearing more frequently. Silently, Ruth prayed God would remove any jealous thoughts from her and bring someone else into her life.

"I think I'll take a trip into Bird-in-Hand this week to look for fabric for *Mamm*," Mary said to her daughters.

"Can I go, too?" Katie asked, shoving the pot of shelled peas to the back of the counter.

"No, you must stay and cook for your *Daed* and brother. I'll take Ruth with me. She needs to look for new shoes."

"If you wait for the week-end, I can go, too," Emma suggested.

"Too much traffic. It's a hard enough trip without cars zipping by at a hundred miles an hour."

"Will *Daed* let you go without him?"

"Of course. *Daed* is not like some other men. He wants me to be independent."

Ruth looked over at her sisters and grinned. "Sure, *Mamm*, real independent. As long as his clothes are clean, the house is perfect, his meals are on time...it doesn't leave you much time to be independent."

"Never-the-less, he won't be upset if I take the buggy. Let's go Tuesday, Ruth. You can drive."

"Sounds like fun. Maybe I'll check the fabric, too. I could use a new dress. My Sunday dresses are getting too snug in the bustline."

"I noticed," Emma remarked as she picked up the dishtowel and dried fresh pots.

"As long as the young men don't notice. Keep your aprons loose, Ruth."

"*Yah Mamm*. I try to."

"She doesn't, *Mamm*. I see her parading around sometimes." Emma's eyes fired over at her sister.

"Hush, Emma. That pot's dry enough. Get out the lettuce and make salad for dinner."

"Alright, *Mamm*."

"Katie, you help your sister cut carrots and Ruth, check the pie in the oven. It should be ready."

"I'm goin' to have only one piece today," Katie announced.

Emma glanced over at Ruth and winked. Ruth smiled back. It was hard to stay angry with Emma. They were like twins, often able to guess the other's thoughts and she truly loved her sister.

Chapter Four

Tuesday, Ruth and her mother left around ten in their buggy and headed out the Old Philadelphia Pike toward Bird-in-Hand. Only once were they startled by a truck that came too close. After they hitched the horse to a post outside the fabric store, they went in to do their shopping.

While her mother sorted through the many bolts of fabric, Ruth picked out several yards of pale blue cotton for a new church dress. She became restless while her mother chatted with the owner, who was a distant cousin.

"Excuse me, *Mamm*. I'd like to go for a walk while you're deciding. I'll stay on the sidewalk outside."

"Sure. That's nice. Get some sunshine, Ruth. I'll be a few more minutes. Just catching up with Rachel."

What a gorgeous day. Late April was one of Ruth's favorite times of year. She smiled as she walked along, the warmth of the sun filtering through her bonnet. She thanked God for his creation as she glanced at the budding trees and perky daffodils planted by merchants. Glancing into the shop windows, she came across a poster of the Fulton Opera House in Lancaster City. Debussy. Gershwin. Exciting names. She had never heard a symphony orchestra, but she had caught sounds of a violin as she passed an *Englisher's* home once. It had a haunting sound, lovely to her ears. If only she could just once go to a concert. Was it really so wrong to play a musical instrument?

"Ruth!"

She jumped at the sound of a man's voice and turned to discover Jeremiah standing only six feet away. "Jeremiah, I didn't see you."

"I know. You were much too busy looking at something in the window. What was so interesting that you wouldn't see a friend?" He smiled and looked at the object of her attention. "Ah. A concert."

"Mmm. If only..."

"I've heard them perform. They're wonderful musicians."

"You did? How come?"

"During my *Rumschpringe* days I spent time exploring Lancaster as well as New York."

"I would love to hear them play, but I guess that's not going to happen."

"Why not? You haven't been baptized yet, have you?"

"No, but I plan to be next year. What about you?"

"I haven't yet committed, but probably soon."

"So since I haven't been baptized yet, I could break away for a day or two on my own and not be punished?"Ruth asked.

"You know that's possible. Would you like me to take you? They have a matinee on Saturday."

"Matinee?"

"Daytime concert. See? At three o'clock." He pointed to the schedule. "I'll treat you."

"I wouldn't have to announce it, would I?"

"Uh, maybe just ask your *mamm*. I would need to arrange for a driver. I don't want to use my buggy in Lancaster proper."

"It would be fun. I don't know what to say. Would that be a date?" Ruth's sister came to mind, but if it wasn't a date…

"You can call it anything you want. If you want to keep it secret, we can meet somewhere first. I'm not sure I like that idea, but—"

"I'll do it. I'll go with you, but it's not a real date and we aren't courting and no one must know. Agreed?"

"Sure, if that's the way you want it." Jeremiah gave her a crooked grin and adjusted his hat. "So where should we meet?"

"Down by the bridge north of my farm?"

"Can you be ready by two?"

"Anytime you say."

"Two it is then. And we'll keep it to ourselves. I'd better get back to work or your brother will get upset. I left him by himself and we're real busy."

She was so excited, Ruth wanted to grab and hug him. But she merely nodded and turned toward the fabric shop. "See you then."

Several moments later, she turned and watched him as he walked away, his muscular frame visible under his cotton shirt. When she entered the shop, her mother was paying her cousin for the fabric. "Look what I picked for *Oma*. It has little chicks. Do you think she'll like it?"

"I do. It's really cute."

"You have a nice walk, Ruth?"

"Lovely."

"You're flushed. Is it getting hot?"

"No, it's perfect out."

"We should go see your brother at the buggy shop, don't you think?"

Ruth was afraid something would be said about Saturday by mistake. She rarely did something without telling her parents. But this was okay since she was old enough to do *Rumschpringe* and she reminded herself she had not been baptized. She even knew of girls who drank during their time of freedom. There was no way she'd drink alcohol, but this was just music. Not bad music like she heard from car windows sometimes, but wholesome classical music. What was the difference between singing and playing a violin or something? She couldn't understand the reasoning behind some of the old rules, but she knew when she went through the baptism and joined church, it would be the end of her exploration of the "other" world.

"I'd rather not go over. I know he's very busy this time of year. He told us last time we saw him, remember?"

"*Ach,* you're right. Let's head for the department store and find you a pair of new shoes instead. You can use the ones you have when you work in the barn."

On their way home, Ruth was tormented by her thought of doing anything deceitful. "*Mamm*, I need to tell you something."

"You sound so serious, Ruth. What is it?"

"I'm going to a concert."

"You're what?" Her mother leaned toward her. "A concert?"

"You know I can do things during *Rumschpringe* which normally I wouldn't dream of doing–"

"But a concert. There will be musical instruments, you know."

"*Mamm*, could it be so bad, really? There are no awful lyrics, you know. And it's not like the terrible stuff you hear in people's cars. I love music so much–I just want to hear a symphony once."

"How would you get there? Where is it?"

"Uh, it's in Lancaster City and I'd go with a friend."

"Who? Not Waneta. Her parents would never let her go."

"*Mamm*, it would be Jeremiah Fisher. He offered to take me."

"A date?"

"No, not a date."

"What do you want to call it?"

"I guess a get-together."

"Ruth, you know Emma has her cap set on that young man. She'd be upset if she heard you were getting-together, or whatever you want to call it, with Jeremiah."

"She doesn't have to know."

"But–"

"I wouldn't lie. I just wouldn't say anything."

"She'd want to know where you were going. When is it anyway?"

"This Saturday at three. You're right. She'd ask a million questions."

"Unless you spent Friday night at Aunt Beth's and left from there."

"*Mamm*, you'd do that for me? And *Daed*–would he have to know?"

"I won't lie for you, you know that and you cannot lie, but if no one asks…"

"*Mamm*, you're the best."

"Now watch it–you steered the horse toward the gulley. Good thing he knows to stay on the pavement. I have a confession to make, Ruth. Once when I was your age I bought a regular dress and make-up and went to a movie."

"Really?" Ruth smiled and turned to look at her mother. "What was the movie?"

"It was called *The Sound of Music*, and it was wonderful. I've never regretted it."

"What happened to the dress?"

"I actually still have it somewhere in the attic. It was beautiful. It had pink flowers and lace and a full skirt, which came below my knees. I admit I looked in the mirror and when I put lipstick on, I didn't recognize myself."

"Wow! I can't believe it. I wish you'd show me the dress sometime."

"Maybe."

"Did you feel guilty?"

"At first, but once I was baptized, I haven't thought about doing anything like that again. The music was so beautiful in the movie. They sang and there were a bunch of children and they learned to sing too. So go to your concert, but remember, he's a friend and nothing more. Someday you can tell your sister and you can laugh together."

It will be a long time from now—if ever, Ruth thought to herself.

Chapter Five

Ruth left her aunt's house half an hour early on Saturday since it was a mile to the meeting place. She stood at the bridge scanning the road for a car. Finally, a black Ford pulled up with a driver in front. Jeremiah got out and went to open the back door for Ruth. He smiled broadly and she detected a slight blush.

After she settled in, he asked if she was excited.

"I am! I can't believe I'm actually going to a concert."

"Does anyone know?"

"My *mamm*. I couldn't help it. I had to tell her."

"And she was okay?"

"*Jah*. She went to a movie once and it was all about music."

Jeremiah laughed. "I think if we knew some of the things our parents did when they were our age, we'd be surprised."

"This is the first time I've ridden in an automobile," Ruth confessed, running her hand over the leather seat.

"Really? Well, what do you think?"

"I like my buggy better. But in the winter, I bet this would be warm."

"*Jah*, and in the heat of the summer, they make it cool. There are advantages."

"I know one of my uncles takes a car everyday to work. It seems silly that as long as he doesn't own a car or drive himself, it's okay. So I guess I shouldn't feel guilty about this."

"No. Don't let anything ruin today. It's not a date, so we can be ourselves and relax."

"I like that idea," Ruth said as she smiled broadly. *Oh, he's so handsome. My hands are getting sweaty just looking at him. How I wish it was a date. Oh, Emma, why can't you find someone else?*

"You look nice today, Ruth. Did you do something with your hair?"

"No, it's like always. Tucked under my bonnet."

"So, if you took it down, how long would it be?"

"Down to my waist. It's not curly like Emma's. Her hair is so pretty."

"You're pretty, too."

Oh, my. Did he really say that? Ruth couldn't look him in the eye. She looked out the window. "Oh, I see a magnolia tree in bloom. Look." She pointed to a huge tree about a half mile back from the road.

"*Jah*, that's pretty, too. I didn't mean to upset you, Ruth. I just say the truth sometimes without thinking."

"It's okay. I do the same." She looked over and his face was bright red. She figured he hadn't meant to be so blunt, but down deep, she was delighted he said it.

Ruth's heart pounded as they made their way up the aisle to their seats. They were in the second row of the mezzanine. Ruth looked about her at all the people settling down in their section. She'd never seen so many English at one time. Ruth felt her body heat up as perspiration formed under her arms. Her heart pounded and she wondered if Jeremiah could hear it as it consumed her. She had never been in such a setting before. Her world was so different and predictable. Why had she agreed to come? She moved forward in her cushioned seat and gripped the back of the seat in front of her. Her breath came out in rapid puffs and she felt faint.

"Ruth, are you alright?"

She couldn't answer. She wondered if she was going to black out and then she felt Jeremiah's hand on her shoulder, keeping her steady. He whispered gently in her ear. "Slow your breathing, Ruth. It will be okay. Nothing will happen to you."

She turned and looked into his compassionate eyes. He understood. She didn't, but he did. He touched her cheek with the index finger from his other hand and traced it down to her chin. "You'll be fine. Sit back and try to relax."

She obeyed without thinking and found his hand over hers—strong, yet gentle. She breathed easier and her heart stopped leaping from her chest. She closed her eyes and prayed to be calm, aware of Jeremiah's fingers holding hers.

Ruth finally smiled over at Jeremiah and felt her body relax. A few minutes later, members of the orchestra began filing on stage. They lifted their instruments and tuned them. Some would call it 'strange sound' but Ruth thrilled at the discordant notes. Her attention was drawn to the head violinist, a young woman not much older than she. Jeremiah still had his hand over hers and she didn't try to move it. He was her anchor. She trusted him and she knew she was falling in love.

The conductor, Dr. Gunzenhouser, made his way to the podium and a hush went through the crowd. The lights dimmed and he raised his arms to gain every musician's attention. It began—the most beautiful sound she'd ever heard. A mix of strings, brass and woodwinds, exquisitely blended into a sound she'd not known existed. She leaned forward, moving her hand away, and listened with every inch of her body. Her eyes closed and she pretended it was Heaven. The first movement ended and she was jolted back to the present. Turning towards Jeremiah, she realized he'd been watching her. She must have appeared silly to be so enthralled, but he didn't look amused. It was something else. A bond perhaps. Their eyes met and she had the realization that somewhere inside them was a common bond–a meeting place not everyone would understand. Were they destined to become soul mates or was she merely imagining his response? Then she did something totally out of character. She reached over and touched his hair with her hand. "It was beautiful," she whispered. "Thank you for bringing me."

The music began again and this time it was quick and lilting and touched another part of her. Surely there was no evil in this music and she felt a longing to have it last forever.

Before heading home, Jeremiah took her across the street to Carmen and David's Creamery where they indulged in ice cream sundaes. Jeremiah was a great story teller and soon had Ruth laughing out loud over his experiences on his farm and at the buggy shop.

"I've not heard my brother talk about those people from his shop. I'll have to tease him about that Amos man."

"Then he'll want to know who told you and this is our secret, right?"

"I forgot. Yes, it's our secret. It's been so much fun. I'll dream about it every night."

"Will your dreams include me?"

Ruth took another bite of her sundae. "Perhaps."

"Oh, I forgot. This was not a date. But you can still think of me, right?"

Ruth looked back at her ice cream. "I'll never forget today– no matter what happens."

"Maybe we can have a real date sometime. What do you think, Ruthie?"

I think it would be wonderful-gut!

"I don't know about that."

"But we have such a *gut* time together, *no?*"

"We do. I enjoy your company, but..."

"Well, it was an idea, but if you don't want to, I'll understand. I guess." He looked down at his nearly empty ice cream dish and she could tell by his slumped posture he was disappointed. *Oh, Jeremiah, if only...*

"I told the driver to pick us up at six. It's quarter of, so I guess we'd better finish our sundaes."

"I want to pay for my ticket and this treat. I have my money with me." Ruth began to reach in her apron pocket for the money she had wrapped in a hanky.

"I want to treat, Ruth. Really, I make good money and I have nothing and no one to spend it on, so please let me do it this once."

His eyes implored hers and she hesitated before replacing her money in her pocket. "I guess it's okay, but how will I ever repay you?"

"It's not a debt. You've given me a day to remember. Just watching you enjoy yourself was worth everything. Some people have no desire to listen to music. It's as if their souls are barren. Like they wouldn't even comprehend the meaning of beauty in sound."

"It's sad, really. Since I can't listen to the radio, I confess I like to sing out loud, but I usually wait until I'm in the barn or house alone. I'm embarrassed to sing in front of others. It seems prideful."

"It's not. I've heard you at the Sings. God blessed you with a lovely voice and he wants his people to praise him. Look how beautiful it is on Sunday when we have church. It's difficult not to break down myself when I hear the dozens of voices singing praises to Him."

"You will one day be the leader, Jeremiah. You have the best voice in the whole place."

"No, not really. I don't sing to hear myself, Ruth. Like you, I want to sing to please our Creator."

"We shouldn't hide our light under a basket?"

"Right. He wouldn't want that."

Once the driver came and picked them up they got in the back seat and without even discussing it, they sang verses to the old hymns all the way back to the bridge. When the driver pulled over, Jeremiah got out his side and went around opening the door for Ruth. For a moment, she wondered if he might kiss her, he was so close and his eyes were holding hers with a tender expression, but he stepped back and put his hand out for a handshake. "*Danki*, Ruth, for a nice day. See you in church tomorrow."

"See you tomorrow. *Jah*, it was wonderful-*gut*." Without turning back she headed up the road to her lane. All she thought about was seeing him the next day when all of a sudden she remembered Emma and her spirits fell. *Sisters first and always.* That's the way it had to be and that's the way it was. She made her way back to the farmhouse, music playing over and over in her mind as she walked. Then into the kitchen–back to her Amish life.

Chapter Six

Katie was setting the table when Ruth came in from the concert. Mary was making gravy for the roast chicken. Emma was no where in sight.

"*Hallo* everyone," Ruth said as she took off her cape and went to wash her hands. "What do you need, *Mamm?*"

"I've got it together, Ruth, unless you feel like finishing the biscuits. I haven't cut them yet."

Ruth went over and started cutting out the biscuits with a round tin cutter her *daed* had made. "I'm not real hungry, *Mamm.*"

Mary glanced at her daughter. "Eat what you can. How's your aunt?"

"*Gut*. She said *hallo* to everyone. Where's Emma?"

"She went over to the schoolhouse. She said she'd be late since she had tests to correct, but she should be home soon."

"Want me to get *Daed* and Wayne?"

"Go tell them I'm running a bit late with dinner. Another half hour."

"Let me go, *Mamm*," Katie interrupted. "I haven't been out all day."

"*Jah,* okay. Take a walk, Katie."

"I'll play with the new kittens in the barn." She put on her cape and ran off.

"So, how was the music?" Mary asked Ruth.

"*Mamm*, it was like I died and went to Heaven. It was sooo beautiful."

"*Jah*. I know." Ruth noticed the corners of her mother's mouth droop. She sighed and added, "and Jeremiah, was he polite?"

"Very. He's so nice." Ruth placed the last biscuit on the cookie sheet and headed for the oven with a full pan.

"And just a friend?"

Ruth looked over at her mother, her heart beating quicker. "Just a friend."

"Emma's friend?"

"*Jah, Mamm.* I told you already."

"She'd be hurt though, so we mustn't upset her. I hope she doesn't ask you questions, 'cause you cannot lie."

"I know, *Mamm.* I won't see him again—alone. But it was an experience I won't ever forget. At first, when I went in and saw all those English all dressed up fancy with lipstick and short skirts, I felt overwhelmed. What must they think of me—so plain and homely?"

"You are not of their world, Ruth. What they think doesn't matter."

"You're right, I know, but it still made me wonder."

Emma came up to the kitchen door and called *"hallo"* through the screen. She had a folder and several books in her arms. "Ruth, I missed you last night. I had no one to talk to. Here, grab these papers please. I got mud on my shoes and I want to take them off before *Mamm* has a fit."

"I don't have fits, missy, but *jah,* take them off outside."

Ruth reached for the books and papers and took them over to a card table where her mother paid the bills. "I'll lay them here for you. More tests?"

"No. I'm making out report cards tonight. I thought I'd get everything done at school, but I had a friend stop by."

"Who was it?" Ruth asked as she cleaned off the flour-smeared kitchen table.

"My friend, Abby. Guess what? She thinks she's getting a proposal soon."

"Who? I didn't know she had anyone she was interested in."

"Oh, *jah.* Daniel Schrock."

"He's merely a boy," their mother said, lifting her brows.

"He's seventeen, *Mamm.* Turned seventeen last month."

"That's what I said—just a boy."

"He acts older though," Emma said as she walked toward the staircase in her stocking feet. "I'll be right down."

"I don't remember," Mary said softly to Ruth. "Has Jeremiah been baptized yet?"

"No. He's thinking about it though."

"And you? Are you thinking about it, too?"

"A little. I need more time, *Mamm*. Please don't push."

"*Jah*. You're right. You have to be very sure of your decision. There's no turning back."

Emma skipped down the steps in her Sunday shoes and went to wash up. "How soon before dinner, *Mamm*?"

"Pretty soon. You can mash the potatoes and Ruth, check the beets."

Wayne and his father came in after removing their boots on the porch.

"Ruth. When did you get back?" her father asked as he went to wash his hands.

"A bit ago."

"And your aunt?"

"*Gut*."

Her father nodded and reached for a towel. "Smells good in here, Mary. Chicken?"

"*Jah*. The way you like it. Wayne, scrub those hands *gut*."

"We had to pull a section of broken fence up to replace it. Boy, is it muddy out there in the pasture. Hope the rain is done for a while." Wayne waited until his father moved toward the table before running his hands under the spigot. "Katie's putting milk out for the cats."

"How many do we have now?" Ruth asked as she poured water into a pitcher.

"Can't count that high," Wayne answered grinning. "There are three new litters."

"Keeps the mice down," his father remarked as he sat down at the head of the table to wait for dinner.

"Ruth, taste the potatoes," Emma said. "Do I have enough butter in them?"

Ruth scooped out a spoonful and tested them. "Perfect. You're getting better all the time."

"I always *was* good at cooking," Emma responded with a huff.

"You stank," Wayne remarked with a grin on his face.

"No. I'm better than Ruth and Katie put together."

"Wouldn't be hard," he added.

"So, let's settle down. Your father is tired. He doesn't need your babbling. Come, as soon as Katie gets here, we'll eat."

Katie came through the back entry, muddy shoes and all.

"Katie! Shame on you! Take those shoes off. Look at my floor." Mary reached for a cleaning rag and went over to wipe up the mud.

"Sorry. I forgot. I counted thirty-two cats, *Mamm*." She threw her shoes outside and took the rag from her mother, turned it over and wiped the floor clean.

"Don't put that rag in my sink. Throw it outside. I'll wring it out later."

Katie did as she was told and quickly washed her hands. The family sat together and bowed their heads in silent prayer.

"So, Ruthie, what did you and your aunt do all day?" Ruth looked up at her father and then glanced over at her mother.

"She's chewing, Leroy. Ask later. Now how is the corn coming? With all that rain and now sunshine it should be poppin' pretty good." Ruth thanked her mother with her eyes and made sure she had something in her mouth throughout the entire meal.

"Biscuits?" Emma asked Ruth as she passed the basket to her left.

Ruth nodded and took one, exaggerating her full mouth.

"I'll be glad when school's over this year," Emma said to the family. "I have the Kuhns boy, Mervin, who is always giving me a hard time."

"Why don't you speak to his parents?" Leroy asked as he cut more chicken off the rib cage and placed it on his plate.

"I don't want to get him in more trouble. He's not a happy boy."

"I don't know his family *gut*, but I think his home life ain't great," Leroy suggested. "I heard his *mamm* is in poor health and has a little one to raise."

"They lost two children," *Mamm* added. "It was only three years ago. They both died of the influenza."

37

"*Jah*. I remember that now," Leroy said, nodding. "Very sad. She never got over it, poor lady."

"How old is Mervin?" Ruth asked, quickly popping another biscuit in her mouth.

"He's about eleven. I'll have him again next year. I'll try to be patient with him. I'd forgotten about his losing his two sisters."

The family ate in silence for a few minutes and then Mary reminded them about Sunday. "Now don't forget. This Sunday we're celebrating Oma's birthday. You should make her cards or bake a loaf of bread or something. Nothing fancy. She'd be embarrassed." Mary scraped the last of her potatoes onto her fork.

"I already started a pillow," Emma said. "I'm embroidering it."

"She'll love that." Mary smiled over at her eldest daughter. "Katie, what do you want to do?"

"I'll make tapioca pudding. She loves the way I make it."

"*Gut*. And Wayne? Gonna make a card?"

"*Mamm*, I draw terrible."

"So, you be good at woodwork. How about a shelf?"

"I make her one every Christmas. She'll need new walls."

"*Jah*. True. Maybe make a card without pictures."

Emma turned to Ruth. "What are you going to do for her?"

"I haven't decided yet."

"Well, you can't draw well and you sew like a kindergartener, so maybe you should bake cookies," Emma taunted.

"Oh, so you think I wouldn't poison her with my cookies?" Ruth's eyes spat fire.

"Stop it right now!" Their father laid his fork on his plate and his jaw tightened. "A man needs some peace. You two leave the table if you be actin' like that."

"She started it," Ruth added.

"Enough, girls." Mary nodded over at Katie. "Clear the dirty dishes, Katie, and we'll have dessert."

"I'm not done eating, Mary," her husband said. His fork jabbed a large piece of chicken. "But Ruth and Emma may leave the table and start cleaning the pots."

The girls glared at each other and rose to do as he suggested. They didn't argue with their father. Wayne grinned at Ruth as she removed his empty plate and he reached for the last biscuit in the basket.

Ruth avoided her sister the rest of the evening and went to bed earlier than usual to evade being questioned further about her time away from home. She almost wished she could tell Emma where she'd been–and with whom, to get even for her remarks. When the thought went through her head, she immediately went to prayer. *"Dear God, my feelings are so wrong. Help me to love my sister more…and Jeremiah less."* She felt a tear forming and she shook her head, refusing to admit her thoughts were constantly on the young man.

Tomorrow I'll spend at least an hour in scripture. I need to get right with the Lord and forget about men. I have plenty of time for a man in my life later.

Chapter Seven

Saturday night it was the custom to take a full bath and Ruth enjoyed the sensation of the warm water against her skin as she soaked her long hair. She wondered how often the English bathed in their fancy tile bathrooms and she secretly envied them the luxury of items like deodorant and fancy soaps. She sponge-bathed daily with the pitcher and bowl, but soaking in a full tub of water was something she enjoyed.

Church service was held at Waneta Hershberger's family farmhouse two miles south of Ruth's home. Ruth wore her new pale blue dress, which she had sewn during the week, with a fresh apron and bonnet. Her parents had already left with Wayne in the family's newer buggy.

Ruth's hair shined below the brim of the bonnet as she climbed out of the buggy with her sisters. She glanced surreptitiously at the group of young men standing near the front door. Jeremiah was no where to be seen. Emma leaned over and whispered in Ruth's ear. "I have to talk to Jeremiah today."

"Why? What's so important?"

"I made him a card for his birthday."

"How did you know when it was?"

"He told me himself last week. He stopped by the school one day. Said he found a book, which belonged to the school, but I know he only wanted an excuse to visit with me."

"Oh." A pit formed in Ruth's stomach as she pictured Emma and Jeremiah laughing together–alone.

"There's his buggy pulling in. Tell *Mamm* I'll be right in. Save me a seat, Ruth." She took off nearly in a run. *She's so obvious*, Ruth thought clucking her tongue. She made a point not to turn to watch their encounter. No point in torturing herself further.

"Ruth, I'd like to talk to you after the service," Josiah Stoltz appeared from behind a row of ewes.

"You scared me, Josiah," she scolded. "What do you want to say? I have a couple minutes before I get seated."

"We can talk after. Just wait for me outside. Please."

His appeal was annoying, but she might as well hear him out. He wasn't actually bad to look at–merely boring. Maybe her sister was right. Maybe he talked about cows all night because he was nervous. She decided to give him a chance, especially since Emma had her cap set on the man she really cared about.

The sermon held Ruth's interest. It was all about loving your enemy and forgiveness. If Emma did steal the heart of Jeremiah, she'd need to remind herself of these Biblical truths–often. Once during the singing, she looked over into the section where the men worshipped. Jeremiah was within sight and she caught him watching her once. He looked down quickly and she let out a sigh. Of course Josiah watched her constantly, which drove her crazy. Once she glared at him and he grinned back before turning away.

After the service and clean-up from the meal was accomplished, her mother limped over to Ruth's grandmother and led her by the hand to a rocker in the center of the room. Her grandfather stood smiling.

"*Jah*, what you doin' puttin' me here in the middle?"

"*Mamm*, don't go askin' questions. Close your eyes for a minute."

Ruth's *Oma* obeyed her daughter and rocked slowly back and forth.

Katie carried a big single layer cake covered with candles over to the table next to her grandmother as everyone sang.

"Okay, open your eyes," Mary said.

"Oh my. Look at that. Such a beautiful cake."

"*Jah*. We had to celebrate today. It's the closest service to your real birthday."

"Oh, I don't know what to say. You are all so kind. My dear ones." She dabbed at her eyes with a white hanky and looked around at the well-wishers. There were at least a hundred people remaining for the celebration.

"We made another cake, too, *Mamm*, but no candles on it. Just to take care of all the guests."

Emma and Ruth stood off to the side to observe their grandmother's reaction. Emma looped her arm through Ruth's.

"*Hallo*, ladies," Jeremiah's voice came from behind.

"Oh, Jeremiah!" Emma dropped her sister's arm and turned toward Jeremiah. "I was anxious to see you again. Here is the surprise I told you about. I didn't want to give it to you with all those people standing there." She reached into her pocket and removed a small envelope with her handmade card.

"That's sweet of you, Emma. Thank you."

"It took me a whole afternoon. I wrote a poem, too."

"Should I wait till my birthday on Wednesday?"

"I think so."

Ruth couldn't stand it anymore. "You two are making too much noise. This is *Oma's* celebration." She creased her brows and looked from her sister to Jeremiah.

His mouth dropped open as his eyesbrows arched. "Sorry, Ruth. You're right. Come, Emma, we'll go out so we won't disturb people."

Oh, why did I do that? Now they'll be alone. She watched as they made their way quietly out the kitchen door, un-noticed by all but her. People took turns handing her grandmother homemade goodies and cards, as they said nice things and gave her light kisses. She beamed at the attention. When it was Ruth's turn, she handed her grandmother a small white pitcher intended for cream. She had remembered there was a chip in her grandmother's. She had also baked two dozen peanut butter cookies for her.

"Oh, that's so nice, Ruthie. *Danki.*"

Her mother was last and she handed over a bundle wrapped in white tissue paper with a pink ribbon. *Oma* opened up the curtains and exclaimed, "Exactly what I wanted. *Danki.*" Mary leaned over and kissed her mother on the cheek. "I know you like to sew, but I wanted to make them for you this time. Many of your friends contributed for the fabric and their names are on the card. I'll put the curtains up for you this week sometime. I don't want you on a ladder."

"You treat me like I'm a hundred, but I'll wait for you."
Oma squeezed her daughter's hand.

Ruth and Katie handed out the cake to everyone with the help of Ruth's friend, Waneta. She noticed her brother Wayne was standing three feet from Sadie Yoder, but he didn't even speak to her–just looked at her with adoring eyes.

Emma was no where in sight and neither was Jeremiah. Ruth blinked rapidly to chase the forming tears from her eyes. It would do no good to get teary over something which probably never was.

As she began wiping the crumbs off the dessert plates, she saw Josiah walk over. *May as well get it over with*, she thought, attempting to smile.

"Let me help you, Ruth."

"You're a man, Josiah, you don't have to."

"I know, but I want to help."

"As you please. I scrape the crumbs first in the trash here." He picked up a soiled plate and used the fork to remove the left-over cake remains. His head was inches from Ruth's.

"Ruth, I want to take you to the Sing tonight and afterwards I'll drive you home."

"I'm not sure I'm going to go tonight."

"You always go."

"But not tonight."

"Then next week?"

He was trying so hard. *Oh, why not?*

"Maybe I'll go tonight. *Jah*, I changed my mind. You can pick me up."

His grin spread across his whole face, exposing his even white teeth. She noticed he was clean looking too, which she found pleasing.

"I'll be there by six-thirty."

"If I change my mind, how will I let you know?"

He winked at her. "I guess you can't change your mind, because we don't have phones."

Ruth laughed and turned to see if her mother was ready. She caught Jeremiah's eye as he returned with Emma right beside him. He was not smiling and seemed to disapprove of Ruth's choice of friends. She looked away and reached for soiled cups to return to the sink.

All the way home, Emma talked about Jeremiah. It was nauseating.

"Can't you think of anything else?" Ruth asked, her voice edgy.

"Sorry. I'll try not to bore you again. So what about you? I saw you with Josiah."

"If you must know, I'm going to the Sing tonight with him. He's picking me up in his buggy. I hope that's alright with you, *Daed*."

"*Jah*. He's a nice boy. Comes from a good family. Just don't get home late. Anyone else going with you?"

"We could go too, Ruth. Jeremiah and me."

"He asked you?"

"Well, not exactly, but he said he'd probably see me there tonight."

"Then go with him. I want to go alone with Josiah."

Katie piped up now. "I thought he bored you."

"Maybe that's 'cause he was nervous like Emma said. I'm giving him another chance."

"*Jah? Gut*," her mother said as she nodded approval. "Give the boy a chance."

This was one time Ruth wished they owned a phone. She didn't want to go with Josiah. People might talk and think she was "his girl," meaning other young men would keep their distance. It was an unwritten law. Oh, well, she'd go this one time and if there was any gossip, it would fade away in time. Maybe she wouldn't find him so boring this time. After all, he stood erectly and had good grooming habits. She also knew him to be a talented carpenter. Her father had been on jobs with him. There were a lot of good things about Josiah Stoltz. The only thing he didn't have was Ruth's heart.

Chapter Eight

Ruth moped around most of the day reading while her sisters chatted merrily about church. Even Wayne was in a good mood as he brought in fresh lettuce from the garden.

"Ruth," Mary interrupted her daughter's reading, "don't you feel well?"

"I'm fine."

"You should be excited about going to the Sing later with a young gentleman," her father commented, as he looked over his Amish newspaper, which he rarely found time to read.

"I suppose."

"How about me?" Emma said. "I'm really making headway with Jeremiah. He thinks I'm cute."

"Why would you want to be 'cute'?" Ruth asked as she put her book aside.

"You're jealous I'm getting all his attention."

"That's not nice, Emma. Ruth is getting attention, too. Josiah is a nice fellow–a *gut* catch."

"I'm not trying to catch anyone and I wish people would stop trying to push him on me!" She stood abruptly and headed for the stairs.

"It's almost time for Josiah to pick you up," her mother reminded her. "You daresn't keep him waiting."

"I'll be ready in time. I want to lie down for a few minutes."

"Want company?" Emma asked.

"No." Her voice quivered as she fought off fresh tears and headed for her room.

Ruth slipped her black shoes off and rested on her bed, staring at the ceiling. She thought about the symphony and Jeremiah's hand on hers. His smile and the bond she felt. How could he be flirting with her sister? Had his interest been an act?

She rolled over and cried into her pillow. *Emma deserves him. She's talked about nothing else. Why wouldn't I want her happiness, even if it's above my own? Lord, I need you to help me. Maybe tonight I'll find Josiah interesting and we will enjoy every moment together. He really isn't horrible. He has nice teeth.*

Oh, why not admit it, I'm in love and my feelings are not likely to change. It's obvious it's a one-way relationship. Just because a man smiles at you and puts his hand on yours–after all, he was afraid I might pass out. He needed to give me reassurance. That's the reason he placed his hand on mine. The only reason.

There was a rap on the door. "Ruth, it's me, Emma. Can I come in?"

"*Jah.*" Ruth quickly wiped her tears on her pillowcase and covered it with her quilt.

"Your eyes are all red," Emma stated, as she sat on the bed next to her sister. "Is it your time?"

"No. I'm having a bad day, is all." Ruth tried to smile, but it was a poor effort.

"Ruth, I've been too hard on you lately. I don't know why. Forgive me. I love you." She laid down next to her sister and surrounded Ruth's shoulder with her arm.

"Oh, Emma," Ruth cried out as she began weeping. "I want you to be happy. You're such a *gut* person and a wonderful sister. I've been touchy, too. Let's not let anything or anyone stand between us."

"That would be impossible, Ruthie. You'll always be my sister. Let's not argue again. I'm happy for you to have Josiah interested in you, but if you don't like him, there will be someone else."

Ruth smiled and sniffed back her remaining tears. "I know. I'm not in a rush to marry."

"Girls, it's time to get ready," their mother called up.

"Can you tell I've been crying?" Ruth asked her sister as she climbed off the bed and slipped her high shoes on.

"Well...maybe a little. Put cold water on your eyes and I'll go tell *Mamm* you'll be right down."

"*Danki.*"

"*Mamm* mentioned we'll leave right after you."

The ride over to the Lapp barn lasted fifteen minutes and Josiah talked about the crops and the new calves. Ruth tried to appear interested. She asked appropriate questions and smiled a few times, though she found her mind wondering. She glanced over once and tried to look at him objectively. He did have a nice profile and he smelled good–like a pine forest. She wondered if he cheated and used something from a pharmacy.

About seventy people showed up and the singing began. They used the *Ausbund,* which contained the hymns from the martyrs. Again they were divided, men separate from the women, but since they used a barn when the weather permitted, there were no dividers and many smiles were exchanged between the single teen agers. Only once did Ruth look over at Jeremiah and he was busy reading from the *Ausbund.* When the singing stopped, most of the group stayed and conversed. Emma made her way over to Jeremiah and Ruth walked outside with Josiah, who reached once for her hand, which she placed in her pocket to avoid contact.

After a few minutes Ruth asked Josiah to drive her home. He opened the passenger door for her and drove his buggy carefully along the dark roads toward her home. When they reached the farmhouse, he escorted her to the door. She stayed far enough away from him to avoid any attempt of familiarity.

"*Danki.* See you in a couple weeks at church." Ruth turned the knob on the door.

"Uh, do you want to get together before then?" he asked, arms behind his back.

"I think I'll be too busy."

"*Jah.* Okay. See you at church." He turned and she released a long sigh, made her way into the kitchen and turned up the kerosene lamp. A few minutes later her family returned. Not a word was said about Jeremiah or Josiah, which was the way Ruth preferred it. No salt in the wound.

Late spring and early summer were busy times at the farm. As the crops came to maturity, the family set up a small stand at the end of their drive. It wasn't necessary to man it, as a box was laid on the table with money for customers to make change and people used the honor system. Occasionally, Ruth would help customers if it was necessary to weigh the produce. The family added to their income and nothing went to waste. All four women worked preserving and canning. August was corn and tomatoes. The zucchini they used in breads, desserts and as vegetables done many different ways. There was little entertainment as everyone retired early so they could rise at dawn to attend to their myriad chores.

In August their brother Abram's wife, Fannie, gave birth to another boy and they named him Isaac. It was the hottest August on record and much of the work was done before daybreak. By mid afternoon, everyone was ready for a break. There was little time to think about Jeremiah–the only good thing about the long, humid month.

There was no rain for three weeks straight and some of the crops were delayed in their growth. At last in mid-September they experienced a week of steady, moderate rain which cheered the farmers.

As it got closer to October when the harvesting would take place, rumors abounded as to those couples who would announce their nuptials. Most weddings took place mid-week in November or December, and all their family and friends were invited.

Ruth noticed Emma seemed quieter as late fall approached. One day while she and Emma were working on pickling cucumbers, Ruth mentioned Waneta was to be married to Jacob Mook.

Emma sighed. "Abby and Daniel, too. I'm happy for them."

"You don't sound particularly happy," Ruth said, glancing up as she cut the cucumbers in spears.

"I was hoping that would be me."

"You and Jeremiah?"

"Who else?"

"He may still ask you," Ruth said, wondering if their relationship was even remotely serious on his part.

48

"It's too late to plant celery for the reception anyway."

"Oh, Emma, so what? You can get some from the neighbors."

"But all those traditions are what make it fun. Oh, well, next week school will start up again. Katie wants to help this year. I'm going to have more students. A family with eight kids moved into the Stossel farm and they're all under fourteen.

"Whoa, you will need help. Do you really enjoy teaching?"

"Of course I do. I love my students. Most of them."

"How does *Mamm* feel about having Katie work there?"

"She's okay about it. That leaves you, Ruth. What will you do if you don't marry next year?"

"*Mamm* needs help here and I can work in the field if necessary. I'm in no rush. I always find something that needs doing. Push the crock this way, Emma."

Emma wiped her hands on a cloth and pushed it over to her sister's side where Ruth added the spears after she sliced them.

"Actually, before I go through baptism, I'm thinking about exploring the country a little."

Emma dropped her paring knife and looked at Ruth, her brows drawn together. "That's dangerous. You shouldn't leave the farm."

"I wouldn't live on my own."

"Who would you live with? You can't live with *Englishers*."

"I don't know. Maybe I can stay with the Mennonite family that left here last year."

"They moved to Pittsburgh. Do you have a desire to go there?"

"Oh, Emma, I don't know what I desire. I just feel at sixes and sevens. I know I'm not ready to commit myself to the Old Order yet."

"I can't believe you're saying all this, Ruth. You seem so happy, or you did before this summer, anyway."

"I admit to being restless."

"But to leave all this. There is so much danger out there. Crime and...you know about the stuff that can happen to women."

"I don't know why, but I'm not afraid–I don't think."

Katie burst through the back screen door. "Quick, we have to go to the Schrock's place. Their barn caught fire. Skinny Abner just came by on horseback. He's notifying everyone."

"Where's *Mamm*?" Their father rushed in behind Kate. "Wayne and I are riding our horses over. It will be faster. Tell your mother and Emma, you can bring everyone else over in one of the buggies. Make sure you bring food."

"Be careful, *Daed*," Ruth called after him. "I'll go up and get *Mamm*. She's changing the linens. Emma, you and Katie get the buggy ready."

After wrapping fresh loaves of bread in bags and grabbing several jars of preserves and applesauce, the women made their way to their neighbors. Fire was a dreaded word. So many animals lost their lives in barn fires–and sometimes humans as well. Ruth prayed all the way over.

Chapter Nine

The Schrock farm was approximately three and half miles from their family farm. The four women were silent as they encouraged their faithful horse to move faster. Ruth noticed her palms were sweaty. The building could be replaced, but sometimes…

Half way to their destination, they pulled over to allow two fire trucks to pass.

"*Gut*," Mary said to her daughters. "I hope they got all the animals out in time."

"I keep praying for everyone to be okay, *Mamm*," Ruth said quietly.

"*Jah*. We must all pray."

As they got closer to the Schrock's place, other buggies joined theirs, forming a line as they allowed an ambulance to pass. The siren rang loudly and Ruth placed her trembling hand over her heart.

"Dear God, I hope that was just in case," Emma said tearfully.

"They always send an ambulance to fires," Katie remarked.

"True," Emma replied, nodding. But her eyes spoke of fear. Ruth wished her sister was up front with her as she drove the buggy. She would have patted her hand to let her know she cared. Instead, her mother reached back and touched Emma's knee through her dress.

"We can only pray. Nothing else for us to do yet."

"Look, *Mamm*, I see flames even from here," Katie said.

"We're close now. Look at all the smoke!" As they turned the bend Ruth noticed many buggies parked near the road, their reins secured to a fence. People were walking the long lane to the farmhouse, which fortunately was far enough removed from the burning barn to appear safe.

Each of the women carried a *toot* of food or supplies. When they arrived at the farmhouse, Ruth saw Lovina Schrock standing on the porch, her face expressionless. Her sister had her arm around her and her four young daughters were sitting on the steps, mesmerized by the flames. The two smallest girls were sitting on the laps of their older sisters. No one was crying.

"*Danki,* Mary. You can put everything in the kitchen. My other sisters are in there."

Ruth followed her mother into the kitchen, carrying the rest of the food.

"When did the fire start?" Ruth's mother asked one of the women in the kitchen who reached for her preserves.

"About an hour ago. Daniel dropped a lit cigar on the straw and didn't see the flames until they were too large to control."

"Lovina must be upset. He told her he didn't smoke anymore," Mary remarked.

"She's not happy. They lost two cows. Fortunately, the rest had already been put to pasture. The milking was done."

"Thank God, that's all." Mary nodded to Ruth who was standing next to her. "Ruth, go check to make sure Wayne and your *Daed* are not too close to the fire."

"*Jah, Mamm,* I will."

Emma and Katie were trying to distract the little Schrock girls by drawing pictures of flowers in the dirt with a stick when Ruth went past them toward the barn.

"Ruth, wait for me," Emma called out to her. "Be careful."

"I'll be careful, but *Mamm* is worried about Wayne and *Daed.* You know how Wayne likes to play hero."

"*Jah.* I was wondering about him myself. I want to go, too."

They walked quickly to the back of the barn keeping a safe distance from the building. When they got there Ruth noticed the barn was almost totally consumed by flames. Their father and brother were standing with a large group of Amish observing the firemen as they dragged their huge hoses and equipment closer.

"Girls, you shouldn't be here. You're too close to the flames," *Daed* warned.

"*Mamm* sent us. She was worried about you two."

"We got here too late to do anything. We're just watching."

Ruth looked over at the owner, Daniel, who stood, arms folded, chewing a piece of straw. His eyes were moist, but she knew he would be alright. At least he was able to save nearly all the animals.

A barn cat sat behind them at a distance. The farm equipment had all been moved out before the flames engulfed the side where they were kept. Daniel's five sons ranged from four to sixteen and they stood there alongside their father, quietly observing the devastation. The youngest boy kept wiping his eyes with his sleeve, but he made no sound.

Around four in the afternoon, the fire trucks left. The men sat around on benches or on the ground discussing the plans for the re-building. Ruth, Emma and Wayne stood back and listened. Jeremiah arrived with Ruth's brother, Mark, from their jobs in Bird-in-Hand. They joined the others to discuss the fire. Jeremiah nodded to the girls, but looked grim as he listened to the account of the accident.

"We'll have to wait about a week to make sure it's not too hot. Sometimes the ashes play tricks and start up again," one of the elder Amish men said, speaking from experience. "While we wait, we'll bring in the supplies we need. Brother Daniel, we need you to decide on the size. If you want anything larger, now's the time to tell us. I'll draw up the plans and some of you check it out. Not as good as I used to be with my eyes failing the way they are."

Several men nodded and a couple smiled weakly, but it was a somber group.

Young Sadie Yoder ran over to the group. "We have food out for everyone. *Mamm* said to call you."

"*Jah*, we'll be there," Daniel said. "Couple more minutes."

After Sadie left, Daniel shook his head and looked down at his feet. "Hope the good woman is still speakin' to me."

"It could've happened to anyone of us—a dropped lantern, a young-un with matches. You can't go blamin' yourself, Dan," one of the men said.

"Don't think the woman will see it the same way. Well, I've lived in silence before, it ain't all bad," he said, a slight smile edging along his lips.

His eldest son put his arm around his father's shoulders and everyone started walking back to the yard where the tables were set up. Folding chairs had been brought in from one of the church member's barn. Ruth noticed her mother's limp was more pronounced as she placed cups on the tables.

"*Mamm*, I'll take care of the cups. You go sit," Ruth told her.

"I'll be fine. Tripped over a rock, is all."

When Ruth looked back, Emma was walking beside Jeremiah and they were talking about the fire. He nodded over at Ruth, but she kept working on the table settings. Josiah Stoltz came over and tried to converse with Ruth, but his major concern was the two cows that perished. Ruth rolled her eyes at Katie, who was holding back a grin. Josiah didn't see the exchange and continued discussing the poor animals.

There were not seats for everyone, so the women waited for the men to eat. People had brought cheeses, breads, red beets, jams, sliced bologna, and even soup. There was always plenty of food provided at events like this. The generosity of the neighbors abounded when a friend was in need.

Once the men were done they went back to assay the damage and the women and children sat on the chairs or the ground to fill their stomachs. Only once did Ruth notice tears in Lovina Schrock's eyes. She admired her for her stoicism and courage. Ruth helped herself to more beets and sat back on the ground next to her sisters.

One of the Schrock girls, Anna, who was four, tugged at her sleeve. "Why does your *mamm* walk funny?" she asked.

"She was sick as a little girl. She had polio," Ruth told her.

"I hope I don't get sick like that."

"No, you won't. There is no more polio, so don't you worry."

The child grinned. "I won't," she said and ran off.

Ruth looked over at Emma. "*Mamm* hurt herself today on a rock, but she won't rest. Look at her. Now she's cleaning up. Why can't she wait and let us do it?"

"Cause it's not the way she does things, Ruth. You know *Mamm.* She never stops working."

"That will be us someday, won't it?" Ruth said under her breath. She knew it was a good way to be–constantly thinking of others, but she wondered if she could be so selfless. The English didn't work this hard, for sure and for certain.

"*Jah.* Hopefully, we'll take after *Mamm* in that way. She loves to serve."

Ruth nodded. "Let's go help her. See if she'll sit for you."

Emma shook her head, smiling. "She won't, but I'll try my best. By the way, Jeremiah touched my bonnet. It was crooked and he fixed it." Her face blushed as she spoke and Ruth felt a twinge of jealousy, which she immediately regretted.

"It sounds like he's interested alright. *Gut.*" The girls walked arm and arm over to the kitchen to convince their mother to rest, but after several attempts they gave up and merely joined her in her efforts. That's the Amish way.

Chapter Ten

It took several days for the embers to be fully extinguished before plans were implemented to start the clean-up and rebuild the barn.

"I wish we didn't have to teach school today," Emma remarked to Ruth as she and Katie wrapped sandwiches for their lunch. "I'd rather be helping at the barn raising."

"Come after you close the school. I'm sure the men will be there till it's too dark to work."

"*Jah*, you're right." Katie ran upstairs to get a sweater as Emma leaned over to Ruth. "You keep an eye on Jeremiah for me. I noticed Priscilla trying to get his attention yesterday."

"I'll try, but there's not much I can do. I wouldn't worry about it. The men will be far too busy to be worrying about women-folk. Besides, he's probably not going to get there until afternoon, since he has to work at the buggy shop."

"Last night I heard *Daed* say they're closing the shop till the barn is done."

Katie took the stairs two at a time. "We're going to be late. My first day of teaching and I'll be late!"

"We'll be there in plenty of time. Here, take your lunch and I'll bring a thermos of lemonade. See you later, Ruth. Don't forget what I told you."

Ruth heard them chat as they headed down the lane to walk the mile to the school house. Katie was trying to find out what Emma had told Ruth. Neither sister wanted Katie in on their secrets. Katie was a dear, but she couldn't keep a secret more than a few hours and Emma would be mortified if word got out she was interested in a man who might not be as interested in her.

Ruth had gone from feeling hurt and jealous to hoping it would work out for her sister. Ruth still harbored strong feelings for Jeremiah, but she had learned to control her thought processes–somewhat. She made every effort to concentrate on life around her, even ignoring his frequent glances. In spite of her determination to forget him, her heart was still affected each time she saw him or heard his voice.

The women worked together in the large farm kitchen, talking and laughing and occasionally crying together. Lovina had accepted her loss and showed appreciation for all the efforts of her friends. "I couldn't have gotten through this without you all. I am so blessed to have a community of friends who care." It was the first time Ruth noticed she became emotional, and Lovina's sisters and friends surrounded her, handing her hankies and clucking over her like she was a child.

"We take care of our own," one woman said and Ruth thought how much she would miss if she really did leave this community. She wondered why she had such a strong restless spirit. It had only been the last year she had even considered leaving her family and home. Only since the concert. Was music so important to her? It wasn't as if she could play an instrument herself. Or was she afraid there was more she was missing? She needed to find out for herself. Besides, it was so difficult to be near a certain man and not be able to show her true feelings. Had he felt what she had? It seemed so at the time, but...

"Ruth, please set up the tables with Waneta and Priscilla. They're not getting much done. Here take the napkins. It's a little windy so put the forks on top."

"*Jah*, I will."

Ruth took the napkins and went out, calling the two girls as she headed for the first table.

"So, I plan to invite him to the birthday party," Priscilla was saying to Waneta.

"And who would that be?" Ruth asked as she placed a fork on a folded paper napkin.

"I was telling Waneta I think Jeremiah is paying me special attention and I don't want to discourage him."

"Actually I think he has someone else in mind. Here, do it like this," Ruth added as she handed a stack of napkins and forks to the other two girls.

"Like who, Ruth? You?" She had a crooked smile and it annoyed Ruth to no end. Was that so impossible?

"I have someone else in mind, but I'm not at liberty to name her. I just know he's shown her special attention."

"We'll see." Priscilla had a fair complexion, which set off her auburn hair and dark eyebrows. She was attractive, but pushy. Certainly not the type Jeremiah would be interested in, Ruth thought to herself.

"How about you Waneta? Are you telling us your plans yet?"

"It's out. We're getting married the Thursday before Thanksgiving. I'm so excited."

"Jacob is a good man. I think you'll be very happy with him."

"*Jah,* he's that alright. And a good lookin' fellow, too, don't ya think?"

Actually, Ruth hadn't noticed Jacob's degree of attractiveness. What she had noticed about him was his thick black unruly hair and his constantly runny nose. He seemed nice enough though. For someone else. "He's fine. *Jah,* he's fine," she said heartily.

"Girls, we'll be ready in ten minutes. Time to warn the men. Ruth, you go tell them. Waneta and Priscilla, come in and grab the trays of food. Daresn't put the potato salad in the sun."

Priscilla looked cheated having to stay back and work. Ruth smiled at her and walked over to the men who were removing the last of the charred wood and raking the thick ash piles into metal cans. It smelled of death and decay and she was glad she was a woman, so she wouldn't have to deal with it. "Time to stop for a meal," she told them.

"Just in time," one of her uncles said, "my stomach is growling at me."

"*Ach,* I thought it was you growlin' like a lion," a man teased.

Jeremiah put his rake aside and wiped his face with a handkerchief. The rest of the men started back across the lawns, leaving Ruth alone with him.

"So, Ruth, we haven't seen much of each other."

"I've been busy."

"*Jah.* Me, too. Have you been to any more concerts?"

She shook her head. "Don't I wish. It was wonderful."

"I heard from Emma that you're thinking of leaving the area for a while. Is it true?"

"She told you? I wish she'd keep things to herself." Ruth folded her arms and walked out of the dark remains of the barn to the untouched green of the grass.

"I have a surprise for you."

She turned and cocked her head to one side. "And what would that be?" A smile crossed her mouth.

"Tomorrow. You'll be here?"

"*Jah*, until you're finished, we'll all be here."

"Then I'll show you tomorrow. Come again to call us for food, and I'll hang back."

"You have me curious. Will you give me a hint?"

"Mmm, *no*." He grinned a crooked smile. "I know you'll like it, though."

"You're a tease, Mr. Fisher. You don't want me to sleep tonight."

He laughed and touched the tip of her nose with his finger, accidentally leaving a smudge from the ashes. "Oh, sorry. I need to clean your nose." He turned his handkerchief inside out and found a clean corner. While he concentrated on removing the spot, Ruth could feel his breath on her forehead. She closed her eyes and held her arms tightly across her chest, fighting the emotional sensations crashing through her body.

"There, that's better." He moved his head closer to hers and looked directly into her eyes. "You're eyes are so blue, like a summer sky."

Ruth felt her heart thump in her chest. Surely he would hear it. "No bluer than yours, Jeremiah."

"But I don't have your lovely eyelashes to frame—"

"Here you are," Priscilla scolded from behind them. "It's time to eat. Didn't you know that?"

Ruth tucked a stray hair under her cap. "We're on our way. Jeremiah had to talk to me about something."

"Mmm. The men are eating first, Jeremiah. If you want some of my good cole slaw you'd better hurry. There's a large bucket of clean water for your hands. At least it *was* clean."

"*Danki*. I'll go ahead." He walked quickly toward the long tables where most of the men were already eating.

"I thought you were interested in Josiah Stoltz, Ruth. That's what people are saying."

"We are friends." Ruth started walking back toward the group with Priscilla following two steps behind.

"Just friends?"

Ruth disliked the tone of the question and stopped abruptly. "What Josiah and I have together is no one's business, Pris. I'll let you know if we decide to make it more, okay?"

"Well, you needn't use that voice when you talk to me. I'm only being friendly."

"No, you're being nosy and for your information, I think Jeremiah has a fancy on my sister."

"Really!"

"*Jah*, really. He even arranged her bonnet for her the other day."

"Well, he's still available until he makes his own decision and I for one, am going to make it known to him that I'm still unattached."

"Don't make a fool of yourself over him."

"Ruth, I'd never make a fool of myself over any man. Not like some people I know."

Waneta waved to Ruth to come over to the long serving table. Ruth huffed and went quickly over to see what her friend wanted, leaving Priscilla behind.

"Look, I saved you some macaroni salad from my Aunt Sarah. She makes the best. Ruth, you look funny. Are you upset?"

"I wouldn't go that far, but I'm not real happy."

"Did something happen?"

"Let me get my plate. I don't feel like talking about it." Ruth prayed silently for the Lord to remove her anger. It took a few moments, but eventually she let out a sigh and carried her plate of food over to a table to sit next to her friends.

After the clean-up, several of the women pulled out a quilt they were working on and Ruth joined them. Someone began singing a church song and the others joined in. With the sun filtering through the colorful maple tree they were sitting under and the song of birds overhead, it would be easy to enjoy your day with good friends and a full stomach, but the sight of the devastation to the barn was a reminder that life was unpredictable. How much worse it would be without their strong faith in God, who would always provide for their needs.

Chapter Eleven

Around three thirty, Ruth noticed Emma and Katie pull up in their buggy. They came over to the table where the women were quilting.

"They've done a lot in a short time," Emma said, looking over at the remains of the barn, her arms folded.

"*Jah*, they're hard workers, they are," one of the older women agreed. "Should be ready to start the build-up in a couple days at the rate they're workin'."

"Anyone count how many men are here?" Emma asked.

"No, but probably close to fifty, by the looks of it," she added.

"I think I'll stop for a while," Ruth said. "Maybe the women need help in the kitchen." She put her needle in her case and stretched after rising from her folding chair.

"Let's go closer first, Ruth," Emma suggested. "Katie, go tell *Mamm* we'll be in soon to lend a hand."

Katie nodded. "*Jah*. Maybe they have some cake left from lunch."

Ruth and Emma exchanged glances and smiled. "She has a sweet tooth, that one," Ruth remarked after Katie left them.

"That she does." Once they were half way to the barn, Emma asked about Jeremiah.

"You were right about Priscilla being interested." Ruth told her about their conversation earlier. "But you shouldn't worry about it."

"Actually, I don't see him showing her any interest, do you?"

"No more than anyone else."

"But you agree with me–he does seem to talk to me more, right?"

A pang of guilt ran through Ruth as she remembered how he held her back from leaving in order to speak with her. And tomorrow ... "I guess."

"You *don't* think he does." Emma's forehead crinkled and her eyes looked so sad, Ruth took hold of her hand. "God's will be done, Emma. If he's the man for you, no one will be able to change that."

"You're right, Ruth. I just hope marrying Jeremiah *is* His will for me."

They reached within fifty yards of the work area and stood watching the activity. A couple young men nodded or waved, but their task was demanding and difficult, and there was little talk, even amongst the men as they worked together. Everyone seemed to know his job, having worked in similar situations before.

Ruth spotted Jeremiah who was chopping down a partially burnt beam and she pointed him out to Emma, who shaded the sun from her eyes with her hand. "He's so brave to be up on that framework. It looks dangerous."

"It does, and *Daed* is on the other side. I can't watch. I pray no one gets hurt."

"*Jah*, it's all we can do. That and give them *gut* food for strength. I've seen all I want to, Ruth. Let's go back and help *Mamm*."

After feeding the men supper, the women sat and ate together before clean-up. An hour later, Wayne went home with Leroy in one buggy, and the women followed after they completed their clean-up, in the other one.

Lying in bed, Ruth thought about her exchange with Jeremiah. What on earth was he going to show her? Two more tickets, maybe? No, if he had them, she would not go with him anyway. She could not encourage him knowing how much her sister cared for him. Even staying back to talk with him was probably wrong. She tossed about for another hour, wondering whether she should send someone else over to the barn site rather than speak alone with Jeremiah. Yes, maybe that's what she'd do. Finally she was able to fall asleep, but only because she was tired from working all day and washing dishes for over two hours straight. Her chapped hands still ached from being in the water so long, but at least it was for a good cause.

The next day started out the same way. After Wayne and her *Daed* took care of the animals, they left early with Ruth's older brothers, who came by to pick them up, leaving one buggy for her sisters to take to school and the other for Ruth and her mother to take to the site. Since her *Mamm* tired more easily than other women due to her limp, they left the house around ten. Ruth was concerned her mother had overdone it the day before, since she walked with a more defined limp. "*Mamm*, please let me do the heavy lifting today if no one is around. You look like you're in pain."

"I'll be alright, Ruth. A little rheumatism is all."

"I think you should listen. I heard *Daed* scold you last night for overdoing it."

"When I see how hard he's working, I feel guilty complaining about a little pain. He snored something fierce last night. He does that when he's exhausted."

Ruth laughed. "I heard him. He woke me up once."

"Ruth, I heard you were talking alone to Jeremiah yesterday."

"Who told you?"

"I overheard Priscilla telling someone. It sounded like you two were doin' something wrong in the barn."

"Wrong? Since when is it wrong to be friendly. Jeremiah and I like to talk to each other. We've done nothing to be ashamed of."

"I believe you, *dochder*, but I don't want stories to go around."

"Priscilla is a troublemaker. Always has been."

"Be nice to her. She means well, I'm sure."

"*Mamm*, you think the best of everyone. She's not so *gut*, I'm tellin' you."

"Maybe she needs a friend."

Ruth rolled her eyes and watched for the curve in the road. The farmhouse was just beyond and already the men were laying down the groundwork for the barn sides. Mules had been brought in to do some of the heavy work. The men were too far away to make out individually, but she looked for a young man with long blonde hair.

Priscilla avoided looking at Ruth, but Waneta came right over and hugged her. They began preparing string beans and Ruth found a chair for her mother to use while cutting the ends off.

Ruth's sister-in-law, Fannie, came in with Sammy, her son, who was nearly two now and the new baby, Isaac. Everyone made a fuss over the infant. Fannie placed him in a lined basket so she could help with slicing meat for the meal. Isaac slept soundly even though Sammy bumped the side of the basket several times while playing with a rubber ball.

Ruth looked at the wind-up clock behind the sink, wishing it was lunch time. Finally around noon, she offered to go call the men, completely forgetting her resolve not to be the one to inform them of their lunch break. The food was already on the table and girls were bringing pitchers of lemonade out. It was cooler than it had been, and several of the older women wore shawls over their dresses.

As planned, Jeremiah stayed back as the other men left their chores to go wash up for their dinner. Ruth's *daed* looked over once and waved, but then moved along with Wayne. "Don't wait too long, Jeremiah, you'll lose out on eating," he teased.

"I'll be right there."

Once she knew they were alone, Ruth started the conversation. "So. Here I am. You said you had a surprise."

"*Jah.* I said it and I do. Close your eyes."

She put her hands on her hips and closed them. "Now what?"

He touched her cheek causing her heart to pick up a beat as she felt him place something small in her ear. "Don't look yet," he added softly.

Then she heard it. Music. Beautiful orchestral music. Her eyes popped open and she looked into his eyes. "Where did you get that?" She removed the wire from her ear and looked at the small gadget in her hand. "So that's what English people are doing with those wires on their heads. Listening to music."

Jeremiah let out a laugh. "Most of it doesn't sound like this. Much is terrible music. Bad words even. You wouldn't believe it."

"But this is like the concert. What is the name of it?"

"This is music by Beethoven. Ludvig Von Beethoven."

"*Jah*. I heard of him. German, like our people."

"This is a symphony. His last one, the ninth, and if you listen to the whole thing you will hear singing, too. You can take it home with you, Ruthie, and listen to the entire piece."

"Does it belong to you?"

"*Jah*. I listen to it a lot at night. I know all nine symphonies."

"I can't believe all that sound comes from something so small. I will take it home tonight to listen, but I'll be sure to return it tomorrow."

"You keep it as long as you would like. I want you to enjoy it. Let me show you how to use it." He proceeded to give her instructions and then handed her more batteries wrapped in a paper napkin.

"We'd better go now," Ruth said as she put the items in her apron pocket. "*Danki* for thinking of me."

"I think of you lots."

Ruth pretended she didn't hear his last remark. She turned and began walking over to the group, but she could feel heat rise behind her ears as she flushed crimson red in her cheeks. A true giveaway, she thought. *Now he'll know I feel something special toward him. I knew I shouldn't have come out here. Curiosity got the better of me. Tomorrow I'll return this and it will be over. Completely over.*

Guilt drove Ruth to work twice as hard as normal. She hoped her mind would stay on her chores, but the opposite took place. The repetition of washing pots gave her more time to think. Waneta dried and talked about Jacob the whole time. Jacob this– Jacob that. *Hopefully, I won't ever act so silly,* Ruth thought, but down deep she knew she'd behave the same way if someone she loved, loved her back.

Katie left school with a bad headache so Emma stopped by the Schrock farm before going home to tell her mother they wouldn't be there to help. Ruth was relieved she wouldn't have to watch every word she spoke with her sister.

Since Emma had papers to correct and plans to make for the next day, the sisters merely greeted each other when Ruth and her mother arrived home. Emma didn't even ask about Jeremiah, which surprised and pleased Ruth. It was getting hard not to say something, especially with the music maker lying in her pocket. How would she have a chance to hear the music without the family seeing her? The outhouse was not the right setting, that was for sure.

After everyone went to bed, Ruth tiptoed down the stairs, carrying the IPod with her. Wrapped in a quilt, with only the light of the moon to guide her, she made her way to the sofa and sat to listen to Beethoven. She closed her eyes and allowed the music to encompass her. She felt surrounded by beauty and was able to identify the string section from the brass. She pictured the orchestra in Lancaster as she listened. Subsequently the voices added to the spectacular sound. Oh, to be able to sing with a chorus. How marvelous. *Would it be so wrong*, she wondered. *Is that really a sin?*

The final notes played. She turned off the IPod and headed back to bed. No one stirred and the snores of her father resonated through the hallway as she made her way into the bedroom to catch a few hours of sleep. The notes continued to go through her head as she laid there. At last the music stopped and she dreamt. About music. And heaven. And Jeremiah.

Chapter Twelve

"Pass the butter, Ruth," Emma requested as she salted her scrambled eggs and set toast on her plate.

Ruth passed it over and then asked Emma if she and Katie planned to visit the barn site after school.

"If we're not too tired. Everyone is so busy anyway, what's the point?"

"True," Ruth agreed, somewhat relieved at her answer.

"What time did *Daed* and Wayne leave this morning, *Mamm*?"

"Shorty after dawn. Just before you came down for breakfast. *Daed* thinks they'll get more men today to help put the sides up. They could do it in two days if they get enough men to show up."

"I love to watch them work," Ruth said, as she poured herself more milk.

"*Jah*. It's amazing to see. From trees to barn. All it takes is good folk working together."

"And men who know how to swing a hammer," Katie added.

"Most Amishers are born with a hammer in their hand," her *Mamm* said, smiling.

After washing the soiled plates, Katie and Emma left for school and Ruth went up to her room. She reached under her mattress to retrieve the IPod and placed it into her apron pocket. This would be the last time she'd have to spend time alone with Jeremiah. Then she'd concentrate on other things. A pang of sorrow crossed her mind as she realized they might not speak again in private. If only...

"Come on, Ruth. We have to get over there."

"I'm coming." Ruth tucked a stray strand under her bonnet and went downstairs and out to the buggy where her brother had prepared their horse for the ride.

There were more people today and the weather was cooperating. Sunny and warm. Two of the men organized the group into teams. Some prepared the boards and studs and others began the task of measuring out the footers, having placed slabs of concrete down for the corner reinforcements, the day before. The sides were prepared on the ground and by noon two sides were complete and ready to raise, but they planned to wait until all four sides were ready to hoist. The men seemed exuberant at the speed with which the project was moving.

This time around noon, Priscilla made a point of heading over to tell the men it was time to eat. Ruth touched her pocket to reassure herself the music maker was still safe. She had wrapped it in tissues. But how would she give it back to Jeremiah if they were never alone? She had an idea.

When Jeremiah went through the line of food he looked over at her and tipped his straw hat. "Mornin' Ruth."

"Mornin' Jeremiah. Here have some extra biscuits." She lifted two biscuits with a paper napkin and as she handed them over she nodded at the food. "There's somethin' good and special for you." She looked up and he was staring quizzically at her.

"*Jah. Gut.*" He walked over to a tree and sat on the ground away from the others. She watched as he unfolded the napkin. He smiled and looked up at her, nodding slightly. Her suggestion to meet at three o'clock by the tub of water on the side of the house was written hurriedly on his napkin, but she could think of no other way to correspond.

After everyone ate and the little ones were settled together on blankets for rest time, the women cleaned up and three tables were set up for quilting.

"Come, Ruthie," her mother called, "you love to quilt with us."

"Not now, *Mamm*. I'm takin' a walk."

"Want company?" Waneta asked, drying her hands.

"Don't be offended, Waneta, but I just want to go off by myself for a few minutes. I didn't pray this morning."

Waneta nodded, smiling. "*Jah*, it's hard to find time some days. I'll see you later. I'll go help with the sewing."

It wasn't a lie, she hadn't prayed that morning, but she knew the implication was she was walking alone to spend time in prayer. Before the guilt became too heavy, Ruth made her way to a large boulder off to the side of the farmhouse, where she sat and really prayed. She named everyone she could think of and thanked God for family, friends, nature in every form, her good health, the health of her family, the sky, the birds–again, and finally she sighed and added "Amen," as she raised her head and opened her eyes. Jeremiah was standing in front of her, several feet away, respecting her privacy.

"I hope I didn't disturb you," he said. "It's not quite three yet, but I wanted to be sure I didn't miss you." He came and sat on the ground next to her.

"It's okay. I'm done now." She reached into her pocket and withdrew the IPod and batteries wrapped in the tissues and handed them over.

"You heard the whole thing?"

"*Jah*. It was wonderful-*gut*. Magnificent. The voices…" her eyes went up towards heaven, "sounded like angels. *Danki* for sharing with me."

"Do you want more?"

"Oh, Jeremiah, I could never get enough of beautiful music, but it's yours."

"I don't mind, really."

"No. It's okay."

"So you like Beethoven. He was going deaf when he wrote that symphony."

"No way!"

"*Jah.* Really. But it was all up here," he said as he touched his forehead. "He could hear it in his head."

"And his heart."

"*Jah*, there, too."

"If I never listen again, it will be in my heart." Ruth fought back tears finding their way into her eyes. To think she might not hear such sound again grieved her.

"During *Rumschpringe* you can listen. You're not yet baptized."

"*Jah.* I still feel guilty."

"You shouldn't feel guilty to listen to classical music. I'll sit with you a few minutes more. We're taking a little extra time for break. Your brother said a dozen more friends of his are planning to come by this afternoon. We want to get all the sides up today and the crossbeams for the roof. If we get enough help, we may get the main roof done."

"You are all working so hard."

"Hard, but fun. I love working with my brothers. I'll miss this part."

"Miss it?" Ruth looked into his sky-blue eyes. "Are you leaving?"

"I'm thinking about it, but I haven't made up my mind totally yet. Do you want me to stay?"

Ruth looked down. This was not something she wanted to answer. It might give too much away. "We'd all miss you. I know Emma would."

"Just Emma?"

"Katie, too."

"And?"

"Priscilla?" she looked over and noticed he was grinning.

"But not a girl named Ruthie?"

A laugh came from her. "*Jah,* she might too."

He placed his hand on hers as she stroked the grass.

"Are you serious about Josiah?" He was no longer smiling. *Oh, if he only knew.*

"No. Not yet."

"But you may *become* serious?"

"Jeremiah, I can't read into the future. He's a nice strong Amish man. I could do worse."

He withdrew his hand and plucked a few strands of grass, running them between his fingers. "You could. He is a good man. But you should keep your options open."

"Anyone in mind?" How brazen. She couldn't believe her own words.

"I think you know."

"How about you? What are your options? My sister?"

He looked startled. "Emma?"

"*Jah*, she's a fine woman. She cooks real *gut* and sews–far better than I do. And she–"

"Don't Ruth. You're making fun of me. You know I care about you."

"Oh, Jeremiah, don't." Ruth put her head in her hands and swallowed hard to keep the tears at bay.

"What did I say wrong? Ruth, I want to be with you more. I think about you all the time."

"Don't. Don't say any more." Ruth rose abruptly. "We can't talk again like this. Please don't try." She walked hurriedly toward the house. She heard him call her name, but she continued moving away from him without turning.

Instead of heading back to the porch and the other women, she entered the side door of the house and hid in the pantry away from the others. Her heart was in turmoil. It was true–he did care about her. Maybe even loved her. She couldn't deny her own feelings for him. They grew stronger each time they were together. But Emma, dear Emma. She couldn't hurt her sister by marrying the man Emma loved. Never. Her tears flowed silently and she held her skirt to her eyes until they ceased.

When she returned to the kitchen her mother looked up from the corn she was removing from the cob for corn pudding. "Ruth, you look awful. What's wrong?"

"Nothing's wrong."

"Come here. Let me feel your head. You look sick."

Ruth's sister-in-law, Hannah, heard the exchange and came over to Ruth to feel her forehead. "*Jah*, she feels warm. Go home and rest, Ruth. You don't want to give germs to anyone else. Especially the little ones."

"*Jah*," her mother agreed. "Take the buggy. I'll go home with someone else tonight. Go right to bed."

"But I'm not–"

"You're hot to the touch," Hannah started again. "Please, don't stay around. We have plenty of help."

"If you insist," Ruth said, actually relieved to be getting away from everyone–Jeremiah, anyway. "*Jah*. I'll go. *Mamm*, don't do too much."

"We won't let her, Ruth," Hannah said. "Now drink plenty of water and keep your room darkened."

Ruth walked over to their buggy and started toward home, without once looking back at the men. Her decision was final. Jeremiah was out of her life–forever.

Chapter Thirteen

Ruth snapped the buggy whip in the air and clucked to her horse to make him travel faster. Away from the crowd and away from Jeremiah. She knew this was final. She could no longer pretend it was friendship that drove her to seek him out. The look in his eyes–the soft tone in his voice. How long had she known he cared? Surely she hadn't imagined their moments together at the concert or the touch of his hand on hers. It was more than mere infatuation. How would it be if he married Emma and they were thrown together at family get-togethers? How could she bear knowing he was with her sister, loving her, laughing with her, siring her babies?

Ruth could encourage Josiah and end up in a loveless marriage. Maybe she'd learn to love him. She knew he'd remain faithful to her. He was a hard working man, fairly intelligent and pleasant to look at. Most important, he was a strong Christian. He had been baptized last year and was fully committed to the Amish way. Not all marriages are filled with romance and laughter. She observed far too many relationships that seemed dull and stagnant and yet somehow they worked. The children of those unions seemed to be well adjusted. Normal kids. So why did she want more? Why couldn't she just be content to have a union with a good man?

The tears came unbidden and she was glad her horse knew his way back. She could let him lead her without further thought. Two cars passed before she realized they were even behind her and she had no time to pull over on the shoulder. Fortunately no one was coming on the other side. Did it matter? An emptiness she had not known before enveloped her in its cold embrace.

Lord, have mercy. Help me through this.
Take away my love for Jeremiah. I feel so desolate–
so heavy in my heart. Why, Father? Why should he

have this effect on me? I pray for Emma. If her
heart desires a union with Jeremiah, I pray he will
learn to love her and forget me. I mean it, Father.
Well, help me to mean it. I want to. She's my dear
sister.

A honk from a van shattered her thoughts and her hands trembled as she realized how close the vehicle had been to her small buggy. At last she arrived home and made her way into the kitchen, dampened a clean towel and placed it over her swollen eyes. Her tears finally ceased and she went back out to unhitch the horse and remove the harnessing. It seemed strange to be alone. Too quiet. She began to sing a chorus from a familiar hymn, but her voice sounded strained and unfamiliar. Ruth remained outside and stood watching their dozen cows grazing in the pasture. So calm. Such uncomplicated lives. She watched the distant clouds against the horizon and felt peace flow through her. God was still in control even though her life felt totally at odds.

For supper Ruth ate an apple and cheese. She had no appetite, but knew she needed something. She put left-over food out for the barn cats and stood watching them gather. Soon she heard the crunching of the buggy wheels on the drive. Her father and Wayne greeted her and proceeded to the pasture to bring in the cows for their milking. A few minutes later her mother returned with her sisters. Emma ran over to her.

"Ruthie, *Mamm* said you were sick. What's wrong?" She placed her hand on Ruth's forehead. "You feel cool. I've been so worried about you."

Ruth felt her sister's love at her touch. "I'm fine. I wasn't sick really. Just had a few bad moments, is all."

"I'm thankful. Did you eat anything? We brought back some baked beans. Too many people brought them, so Lovina insisted we take some home for you."

"That's sweet, but no. I'm not hungry. I had some fruit."

Katie and her mother waved as they went toward the kitchen door and into the house. A few moments later her mother came out to join them. She reached for Ruth's forehead.

"*Mamm*, I'm fine–really."

"*Jah*. You look better. Maybe the sun got to you."

"Mmm. How is the barn coming?"

"Tomorrow they should finish the basic structure–if they get the men back. I counted eighty some workers at one point this afternoon."

"Wow! That's great."

"Jeremiah was there," Emma remarked. "Oh, I guess you know that. You were there earlier. He barely spoke to me. He was actually grumpy."

"Really? That's too bad."

"I saw Josiah, too. He was a lot friendlier than normal. He's not so bad, Ruth. You should think about him seriously."

You think about him. That would be a great trade. Ruth rebuked herself for her thought. "I'll give him a chance, Emma. I know he's a nice man."

"And Godly."

"Mmm."

Katie came over to them. "Wayne needs help milking. He hurt his hand at the barn building."

The three started walking toward the barn. "How did he hurt it?"

"I think he hammered his thumb instead of the nail," Katie said as they reached the door to the barn.

"He should let us do the milking and put cold water on it," Emma said as she led the way over to their brother.

"Here, we'll take over tonight," Ruth suggested when he turned to them.

"I'll be fine. I don't need girls to do my job."

Katie cuffed his ear. "We should let you do it then, silly."

"Come on, don't play big brother with us. Look at your thumb. The nail is blue," Emma remarked.

"*Daed* said I'll probably lose it."

"Yuch. Go show *Mamm*. It makes me sick," Katie said, averting her eyes.

Their father came over to them. "*Danki*, girls. Poor animals are late for their milking. They must be uncomfortable."

"*Daed*, we'll do the whole dozen. You look tired. Go relax," Ruth instructed her father.

"My girls are special. I'll take you up on it–only this once. I had the roof work with your brothers and their friends. My knees are feelin' it."

"Tell *Mamm,* she should rest, too," Emma suggested.

"*Jah*. She was limping pretty bad. She needs new shoes, and one with a lift. I've been after her for years now to spend the little extra money on herself. Ruthie, maybe you can talk her into going this week. She won't listen to me."

"I'll try to convince her, *Daed*. I could use some more fabric. I'm going to make pillows for Waneta for her wedding."

"*Gut*. See you later, *dochders.*"

After he left the barn, Emma dumped milk into a thirty liter container and perched herself on a stool by the next cow. Ruth sat at her right and Kate went to the other end of the lineup.

"So you're really going to make pillows for Waneta?" Emma asked.

"I thought she'd like them. I know she puts pillows behind her when she comes to our house. She has short legs."

"But you can't sew very straight."

"I'm better than I was, Emma. It doesn't take a whole lot of talent to sew pillows."

"If you need help, let me know."

"Humph." Ruth knew her sister was not trying to hurt her, but it still touched a chord somewhere and she could feel herself become annoyed. "*Danki,* but it won't be necessary."

"Are you going to be in her wedding?"

"I think so. She mentioned it many times before she even had a man to marry."

"But she hasn't said anything?"

"Not yet. She wants to wait until they publish their names next week. I can't believe it's October already."

"She tell you their date?"

"*Jah.* Second Tuesday in November."

"Emma let out a long sigh." I wish that was me and Jeremiah. I had so hoped."

"You don't know him well, Emma. He may not be what you think." Ruth pulled too hard on an udder and the cow let out a grunt.

"I know him well enough to love him. We've been friends forever."

"It's one thing to be a friend and quite another to be a wife."

"I think you're jealous he pays attention to me and not you." Emma's eyes shot over at her sister's.

"Don't be so ridiculous! I'm not jealous! But I think you've made a fool of yourself over him."

"Do you now? He touched my bonnet. Did he ever touch yours?" Emma stopped milking the cow, stood and placed her fists on her waist.

"Maybe you had a fly on your hat."

"No, he wanted to touch me. I thought he was going to kiss me."

"Nice men don't kiss women unless they are very, very serious and sometimes not until they marry."

"Well, he didn't, so I know he respects me too much to try. I know he wanted to."

"And how, pray tell, did you figure that out?"

"Emma, Ruthie, you're yelling. *Daed* will hear you." Katie put her finger to her lips as a warning.

"I wasn't yelling! Ruth was."

"*No!* You were *screaming!*" Ruth rebuked.

Katie shook her head. "I heard what you were saying and I think you're both wrong. I think Jeremiah likes Priscilla. They were talking a lot as we were leaving. You didn't see them, did you, Emma?"

"You're making it up."

"I don't lie!" Katie's voice rose.

"Shhh. Here comes *Daed*. Quick, grab a bucket." The three girls immediately took their stations by the remaining cows.

"I thought I heard some noise out here," their father said as he came through the door. "But everything looks okay. How many more to do?"

"We're about half way through, *Daed*," Emma answered.

"*Jah*. We're doing just great." Ruth looked over at her sisters and let out a giggle.

"*Mamm* is lying down. Come in quiet-like."

"We will," Katie said as she pulled an udder and a stream of milk splashed into the pail.

After he turned toward the house, the girls laughed together. "We can't let a man come between us," Ruth said softly.

"*Jah*. Sisters forever," Emma said, smiling. Katie nodded in agreement.

Chapter Fourteen

The men completed the major work on the barn the next day. Ruth worked non-stop, not even taking time to eat. As the women cleaned up the tables, her mother clucked at her. "Tsk. You'll get skinny like a scarecrow if you don't eat better."

"I'm really not hungry, *Mamm*."

"But you're feeling okay?"

"*Jah Mamm*, please."

"Okay, if you say so. *Daed* said you'd take me in town next week for shoes. I should have picked some up when we were there." They dumped the soiled paper goods into a can and headed back to the kitchen. Some of the women were wiping the tables. "It will be good to do something different anyway. This has been a hard week."

"*Jah*, I can't argue with that," Ruth agreed. "Everyone's tired out, but look at the barn."

"Ruth." A familiar voice came from behind. It belonged to Josiah.

"*Jah?*"

"Could I trouble you for a clean cloth? I got sawdust in my eye."

"Sure," she said as she went quickly to the kitchen drawer where she found the clean linens. She handed one to him. He took a cup of water, held his head back and poured the water across his right eye. "Ouch."

"Let me look," Ruth suggested as she pointed to a bench. "Sit and I'll look for it." She pulled down his lower lid. "*Jah*, I see something. Keep still." She took a corner of the towel and deftly removed the minute splinter of wood. "There. It's out."

"*Danki*. You should be a nurse," he said, smiling at her.

"Never. I don't like blood."

He laughed. "Neither do I, especially if it's mine."

Jeremiah came up from behind. "What's so funny?"

"Just a private joke," Josiah answered, tapping Ruth on the arm. "Nurse Ruth cured me from possible blindness."

Jeremiah's smile didn't match his eyes. His brows furrowed. "*Jah.* She's good at what she does."

"That she is." Josiah stood, folded the towel, and handed it back to Ruth.

Jeremiah moved on without looking over at Ruth and she felt deep regret that her life was the way it was.

"So, there are going to be the names published. You know Daniel Schrock is marrying Emma's friend, Abby." Josiah folded his arms and leaned against a tree.

"I heard. And Waneta and Jacob are marrying."

"Will you be in her wedding?"

"Probably. Nothing is definite." Ruth was aware that Jeremiah remained nearby, probably to eavesdrop, she thought.

"Jacob wants me to be in it."

"Oh. I forgot you were such good friends."

"*Jah.* Forever. I hope you'll be in it too. I'll make certain we sit together at the evening meal."

"Okay."

"Who knows? Maybe next year it will be us."

Ruth was stunned to hear how bold he had become. She noticed Jeremiah was still standing within earshot, scooping water into a cup to drink.

"I don't ... know."

"It would be pleasing to me, Ruth. You are a *gut* person and would make a wonderful-*gut* wife."

With this, Jeremiah tossed the water to the ground and stamped past them, without a word. His shoulders were tense and his jaw set.

"Jeremiah looks upset. I wonder why," Josiah remarked, following him with his eyes.

"Maybe his water spilled."

"Maybe. I must go help clean up. See you Sunday. Would you like a ride to church with me?"

"No. Maybe next time." It took every bit of effort Ruth had not to go to Jeremiah, but instead she focused her eyes directly on Josiah. Oh, if only she felt the same emotions for him.

"Ruth," her mother called over from the porch. "We're going home now. There are enough women left to handle things. Your *Daed* wants me to go home and rest."

"Let me say good-bye to my friends."

"*Jah*, but hurry. My feet are killing me."

On the way home, her mother mentioned seeing Josiah speaking with Ruth. "He's a nice man, Ruthie. You could do worse."

"I could do better, too, I think. I don't get any special feelings when I'm with him."

"Some women don't."

"But you, *Mamm*. Didn't you feel something exciting with *Daed?*" Ruth glanced over at her mother. Her eyes looked alivened from the memory.

"*Jah*, he was such a good man. His voice gave me bumps. And his eyes–they were like pools of water."

"See? Don't you want that for me?"

"*Jah*. I see what you're saying. Well, isn't there anyone else in your group you could love?"

Oh, yes. One very special man, but he's not mine to have. "I'll give it a closer look."

"Your sister thinks Jeremiah might ask her to be his wife. What do you think?"

Ruth kept her eyes steady on the road ahead. She was glad there was so little traffic. Her hand trembled slightly. "What do I know?"

"You see them together, *jah?*"

"To be honest, I think she reads way too much into every word or motion he makes. I think you should discourage her somewhat, *Mamm*. I don't want her hurt."

"Me, neither. I won't mention it again to her. Maybe if you don't want Josiah, Emma will give him a closer look."

"She keeps telling me how great he is. Maybe she should think about it." What a perfect solution, Ruth thought.

There was much to do the rest of the week at the farm since they had missed several days helping at the barn raising. Their soiled clothes had piled up and Ruth and her mother worked one whole day to catch up. The weather cooperated and the clotheslines were filled. Ruth enjoyed hanging clothes since it gave her time to be outside. Most of the leaves had fallen and her feet crunched over the dried colorful carpet as she moved along the line, organizing the socks by pairs and the underwear by family member. She sang as she worked. How she wished she could attend another concert, but she dared not go alone and going with Jeremiah was out of the question.

Her desire to know more of the outside world grew daily. Surely not everyone was immoral just because they didn't hold to the Old Order Amish. Sometimes she noticed the tourists when she went into town and many looked like nice people. They often smiled at her and most respected the Amish's desire not to be photographed–at least from the front. Sometimes she'd hear the click of a camera when she turned away. On occasion she noticed people whispering or pointing at her, making her feel like an animal in a zoo, but for the most part, she had positive feelings toward the English.

On hot days, Ruth sometimes wished she could put shorts on and a lighter top, but such dress was forbidden. *Rumschpringe* was the only opportunity there was to fulfill her curiosity. She wondered if Emma would go with her to a city sometime before her baptism, but Emma showed no curiosity about the English ways. She was quite content to live the Amish life without exploring the outer world. No, if she was going to go, it would be by herself.

That afternoon while helping her mother prepare supper, she mentioned her mother's need for shoes. "Let's go tomorrow, *Mamm*. We're finally caught up around the house and your limp has been getting worse."

"*Jah*, tomorrow would be *gut*. Do you need anything?"

"No. I have everything I need for myself, but I'll pick up some fabric for the pillows for my wedding gift to Waneta."

"Did she ask you to be in her wedding yet?"

"It's kind of understood. I'm sure I will be asked soon."

"Is she excited?"

"It's all she talks about. *Mamm*, is my sewing really so bad?"

Her mother laughed. "Of course not. You just need to shorten your stitches a little bit. Your sister likes to tease."

"I still like to quilt even if I'm not the greatest sewer."

"You do real fine, Ruthie. Don't you worry."

The next day, right after the noon meal had been served and the kitchen cleaned, Ruth hitched up the buggy and they left for Bird-in-Hand. While her mother picked out her shoes and waited for a lift to be inserted, Ruth walked down the sidewalk, retracing her steps from the day Jeremiah appeared and suggested the concert. She stopped at the same window. The bulletin for the symphony was still in the front and she looked at it, remembering the thrill of being present at the concert. She could almost hear the music and feel his hand on hers when she had that moment of panic. He was so sweet. He knew just how to calm her down. *Oh, I love him so.*

Ruth moved on and picked up a free tourist guide. She sat on a bench next to a shop while she read the brochure. *Sight and Sound* was performing *Noah's Ark* and Ruth gazed at the pictures. Goodness, those lions looked real. How exciting to go to a show like that. Would it be so wrong? After all, it was about the Bible. She was sure there'd be no cursing or nudity. She knew of a girl who worked for the company during her time of *Rumschpringe*. But that girl had left the Amish community. Though she hadn't been baptized and wasn't actually shunned, she still was talked about and her family rarely heard from her. Last she heard the girl had married and moved to Chicago.

Ruth looked up to see her mother walking toward her with deliberate steps. Mary grinned at her daughter. "Well?"

"Nice, *Mamm*. Do they feel *gut*?"

"Stiff. It will take getting used to, but my legs are about the same level now. See?" She stood still with her feet close together, standing more erect than Ruth had ever seen her.

"You look *gut*. Like a statue."

They laughed and headed to the fabric store. After selecting a yard of bright chintz, they returned to their buggy.

"We have to stop at the buggy shop. Hannah gave me some money. She wants your brother to pick up a thermometer. Anna's been sick and feverish and their other one broke. It will only take a minute. He doesn't have money with him."

Ruth shook her head and turned the buggy toward the shop. Would she see Jeremiah? Last time she was with him, he threw a fit. She had never seen him so angry before, or was he merely hurt? The timing had been poor. She never wanted to hurt him. Perhaps he thought she was flirting with Josiah, but that was the last thing on her mind.

When they pulled up front, Jeremiah was taking trash around to the back of the shop. He spotted them and turned away. Ruth felt her heart palpitate double time and told her mother to wait in the buggy while she took the money in for her brother. As she was about to enter the shop entrance, Mark came out to say hello to his mother and he called Jeremiah over.

"So let me see your new shoes," Mark said, smiling over at his mother.

"*Jah*. Wait till you see." She opened the side door, took his hand, and climbed down to the sidewalk. "Look." She stood motionless, heels together and arms extended in the air. "Your *Mamm* is like new!"

Mark and Jeremiah grinned at each other. "*Jah, Mamm*. You look twenty years younger. *Daed* will have to keep an eye on the other men."

They all laughed and Jeremiah turned to Ruth. "You look healthy today, Ruth. Your cheeks are nice and red."

Of course, I'm with you and that's how you affect me!

"*Danki*. I feel good."

"I guess I'll see you at Waneta and Jacob's wedding. You and Josiah." His mouth was turned up in a smile, though his eyes showed resentment. What was she to do? Break her sister's heart?

"I'll be there."

"I wonder who they'll seat me near, since I don't have a girlfriend yet."

"Maybe Emma."

Mark put his hand on Jeremiah's shoulder. "You'd be a welcome brother to our family."

Ruth's mother smiled. "*Jah*, you would."

"I've considered it," Jeremiah said, framing his words carefully. He looked over at Ruth and there was more expressed in his eyes than spoken. She knew he wasn't referring to Emma.

"We have to get back, Ruth," her mother interrupted her thoughts. "I'm making chicken salad for supper and I have to boil eggs."

"Did Hannah say how little Anna's doing?" Mark asked his mother. "She looked pretty sick this morning."

"She said she was feverish, was all. Keep your brother's baby away from your house till Anna's all better."

"*Jah*. I warned him. I think it's merely a bug. Mary and Sarah had it last week. You take care, *Mamm*, and stay home till everyone's well."

"I'm not scared of bugs. I'm more scared of thunder than getting sick."

"Hannah wants you to pick up a thermometer when you're done work. Here's money. I offered to buy it, but she said you wanted to pick up aspirin anyway." Mary handed over several bills folded neatly in half.

"*Danki*. I forgot to take money this morning."

Ruth looked over at Jeremiah to say good bye. His eyes were downcast and she wanted to run to him and hug him. Instead she said good-bye and walked around to the driver's side as her brother helped her mother into the buggy. Their horse pulled slowly away as Ruth looked through her rear-view mirror. Jeremiah was standing alone on the sidewalk, arms loose at his sides and hat lowered over his eyes. His mouth was turned down and her heart was sore.

Chapter Fifteen

The names of the betrothed were read on Sunday morning. There were five couples planning to marry in November and four more in December. Ruth would probably attend all of them, but her friend, Waneta's was the only one she would take part in. Waneta came by the day after to ask Ruth.

Ruth put her bucket and mop aside after scrubbing down half the kitchen floor to give her friend a hug. She put a kettle of water on the coal stove for tea. "You have to tell me everything. Did you make dinner for Jacob on Sunday? I know you weren't in church."

"*Jah*. He said I'm as good a cook as his *Mamm*."

"You must be real good. No one can make *schnitz* and *knepp* like she does. What did you cook?"

"Just chicken pot pie. The noodles were yummy."

"Not too gooey?"

"Nope. I was surprised myself, though I've made them dozens of times. So how are you and Josiah getting on?"

"I don't know what you mean. We're just friends."

"*Jah*. Just friends. That's not what I'm hearing, Ruth. I have you sitting next to him at the supper after the wedding and I put Emma next to Jeremiah. Next year maybe you'll have a double wedding."

Ruth put her head down as she felt her throat tighten.

"Ruth, what's the matter? Did I say something wrong? Doesn't Emma like Jeremiah anymore?"

"She does. I'm okay. Everything is fine." Funny, even though she was her best friend, Ruth had not shared her feelings for Jeremiah with her. What was the point? They were merely feelings. Not reality. Or were they?

"I think I'll have enough celery to make the creamed dish and still have leftover for the tables."

"You need any vases?"

"Probably. I'll let you know when we get closer. My uncle planted an extra row of celery, just in case. He does it every year."

"Well, I'll know where to go someday if we don't have enough," Ruth said, forcing a smile. "What should I bring to the wedding? Do you want me to make dessert?"

"Whatever you're good at," Waneta said.

"According to Emma, I'm not real good at anything."

"Don't be silly. I had your chip cookies last year and they were delicious."

"*Jah?*" Ruth grinned at her friend. "Then put me down for five dozen chip cookies and *Mamm* will bring her tapioca pudding if you want. Katie can help her."

"Great! I love hers. Can Katie do her brownies, too?"

"I'll ask her. She'll probably make an extra hundred for herself."

"Oh, she's not so heavy, Ruth. Go easy on her. She just likes to eat."

"That's the trouble. Eating's her favorite hobby. She put on five more pounds this summer."

"She's active, isn't she?"

"I guess. She rides her bike sometimes and she's teaching with Emma, you know."

"I heard. It's *gut.* When Emma marries Jeremiah, she can take over."

Ruth stood abruptly and spoke harshly to her friend. "Why is everyone so sure Emma's going to marry Jeremiah? He hasn't asked her yet and they don't really know each other that well."

Waneta's mouth dropped open. "Why are you mad? I thought it was pretty much a sure thing. Maybe I was wrong, but you didn't have to snap at me."

"Oh, Waneta," Ruth said as she sat back down, "I'm so sorry. I wasn't really mad at you. I think people are pushing them too hard, is all. I don't want to see Emma hurt if he's not interested in her. Have you ever heard him tell anyone he has his cap set for her?"

"Come to think of it, no. I go by what Emma tells me."

"See? She's dreaming it up in her head."

"How do you know?"

Ruth twisted a tassel of her *kapp* and looked down. "I just do."

"Ruth, are you interested in Jeremiah yourself?" Waneta's voice was low and she touched Ruth's hand.

"It's not that," Ruth began. "I can't lie. *Jah,* I like him–a lot. But I will not stand in Emma's way. She's so in love with him."

"But you don't think he feels the same?"

Ruth shook her head. "No, I don't think so."

"Oh. That ain't *gut.* Not at all. I don't know what to do about seating them together now."

"It's okay. I want him to like her. Go ahead and put them together. Maybe I'm wrong and besides, if God wants them together, it will happen. I don't want you to ever tell a soul what you know. I'll get over him. After all, it's not like anything was ever said, anyway."

"I won't speak of it again, Ruth. I'm sorry things aren't the way you want them to be."

"While we're talking private, I'll tell you something else you should keep secret."

Waneta's eyes widened and she leaned in. "*Jah?*"

"I'm thinking about leaving the community for awhile."

"By yourself?"

"Maybe. I'd rather have someone with me, but I have too many questions about my life here."

"Ruth, you never seemed discontent. What troubles you?"

"I'm not really sure. I think I just need to get away and do some thinking. I don't want to be baptized unless I'm absolutely sure of everything. I'd probably only be gone a few months. Waneta, I want to go to Philadelphia to the Academy of Music. I read about it."

Waneta let out a quick breath. "But why?"

"I went to a concert in Lancaster and it was unbelievable. The music was like angel music from heaven."

"*Jah?* When did you go?"

"Not long ago, but that's not the point. I'm thinking I'd like to learn to play a violin."

"But you can't. It's not allowed."

"That's one of the problems I'm having. I don't see anything wrong with playing a musical instrument. Some of the districts allow it. It doesn't seem evil to me at all. Just the opposite. In the Bible they played instruments, remember? And David sang."

"And danced in the streets, but the bishop–"

"I know, but he's so old, Waneta. Maybe he should reconsider some of the things he expects of his people."

Waneta sat back and shook her head. "You be careful, Ruth. A woman alone in a city? That scares me. I don't think you should go. Have you talked to your parents?"

"Only *Mamm*. I'm afraid to mention it to *Daed* yet. I'm still thinking about it. It may not happen."

"Well, I for one, hope it never does. I'd miss you so much."

"You'll be a busy married woman. You'll probably have a baby right away."

"True, but you're my very best friend."

"We'll always be friends."

"But if you go–"

"I would be surprised if I didn't head back home in time. After all, my family is here as well as my friends."

"*Jah*, that would be mighty hard to give up. Let me know what you decide. In the meantime, I won't share any of this–not even with Jacob."

"*Danki*." Ruth rose to pour the water in the teapot and the girls talked more about the wedding.

Ruth didn't see Jeremiah until the day of the wedding. It was six-thirty in the morning when she and Katie arrived at the Hershberger's farm and began arranging celery stalks in vases for the table decorations. When Jeremiah arrived, he set up the benches in the largest room with the aid of three other men. He barely nodded in her direction and she felt a flush rise up her neck. Turning away from his view, she busied herself with the celery after which, she and Katie folded paper napkins. Several other women arrived and there was activity in every room. Waneta was flustered, dashing back and forth between the groups of people preparing the dinner and those setting up. Jacob was no where in sight.

The aroma coming from the kitchen made Ruth's mouth water. Whole chickens with casseroles of bread filling were already cooking slowly in the ovens. Women came in with bowls of cole slaw and a couple of them were peeling potatoes for mashing later on. Ruth's mother, Mary, set her pudding aside next to Ruth's cookies and Katie's brownies and helped prepare the creamed celery. Emma was icing cakes and babbling to her friend Abby who was planning her wedding for December. It was a joyous time.

Ruth wore an old dress with an apron while she helped with the preparations. Waneta had sewn a light blue dress for her younger sister who was an attendant, as well as one for Ruth. She had made a navy blue dress for herself, unadorned as was the custom.

Checking the clock, Ruth realized she needed to change. She glanced over once at Jeremiah, who quickly put his head down as he re-arranged several benches, placing them closer together in order to add two new ones. His jaw was clenched and his cheek muscles appeared tense. When he was done arranging them in order, he left the house to help with outside work. They expected over two hundred people.

The groom arrived in a new black suit with a sparkling white shirt and a black bow tie. Josiah was dressed the same way, as well as another friend of the groom. They each wore a black hat with a three-and-a-half inch brim. High-topped black shoes completed their attire. The *Forgeher,* or ushers, who were married couples, helped to seat the many guests. At eight-thirty the service began. The congregation started off by singing. Ruth noticed Waneta and Jacob had already been escorted to another room by one of the ministers where they were to receive counseling.

Once they returned, a prayer was given and one of the ministers began his sermon. It went on and on. Ruth tried to concentrate on the message, but her thoughts kept travelling to the bride and groom, and of course to Jeremiah, who was in her range of sight. He looked handsome, his blonde hair combed neatly and arranged under his black hat. He was paying close attention to the minister's message and barely moved.

Finally, the sermon ended and the minister told Waneta and Jacob to come up front. He asked them several questions and they promised to care for each other through adversity, illness and affliction. He took their hands in his and wished them the blessing and mercy of God. "Go forth in the Lord's name. You are now man and wife."

Ruth felt a tear trickle down her cheek and she sniffed hoping to stifle any further tears from following. She was so happy for her friend, but a deep well of sadness filled her. She would never be standing there with Jeremiah. Could she handle watching Emma as his bride? *What choice do I have? Dear Emma.*

Chapter Sixteen

As soon as the ceremony was finished, the women began the final preparations for the wedding feast. While they worked and chatted in the kitchen, the men rearranged the benches forming tables and seating for the many guests. Ruth watched Jeremiah and Josiah work together to form the corner tables in the *"eck"* where the newly weds would sit with their attendants. There were too many people to all eat at the same time, so several seatings took place. Josiah was very attentive to Ruth's every need to the point where she wanted to scream. He watched her constantly. Even Waneta noticed it and whispered to Ruth once while he was busy talking to a friend that he treated her like a queen. Ruth would have preferred being treated like an adult.

After everyone had eaten, the hymn-singing began. The slower hymns were ignored for the occasion and the music was lively and uplifting. Only once did Jeremiah's eyes meet with Ruth's. His expression was one of sadness and Ruth felt a pull in her heart. Of course Josiah followed her around. Once he tried to take her hand, but she reached for her glass and took a sip of water, avoiding physical contact.

Ruth and Emma went for a walk to get some fresh air. The sky was a deep blue with scattered cotton puff clouds, which whisked across the horizon creating shadows on the distant hills.

"Waneta looks so happy," Emma remarked, walking with her arms folded across her chest, tucking a cape around her.

"*Jah.* She looks lovely. She'll be a good wife."

"And Jacob, a good husband. She's fortunate to be mated to someone like him."

"*Jah.*" They took a few steps before Emma continued. "What do you think about Jeremiah?"

Ruth turned to her as they walked. "What do you mean?"

"He's still so grouchy and moody. What do you think is wrong with him?"

"How should I know?" Jeremiah was not a subject Ruth wanted to discuss with Emma, or anyone else.

"Well, I don't know. I thought maybe there was talk. Maybe someone else noticed it."

"I have no idea."

"Josiah adores you, Ruth. He can't let you out of his sight. I'm surprised he's not right behind us."

Ruth took a quick peek back to see if he was following. Relieved to be alone with her sister, she let out a long breath. "He's on my nerves, Emma. I think he'd follow me into the outhouse if he could."

Emma let out a laugh. "*Jah*, you're probably right. I kinda wish someone liked me that much though."

"Maybe you should check out the other fellows. Maybe Jeremiah isn't interested in getting serious with anyone."

"You may be right, but I can't let him go. My mind is constantly on him. Jeremiah, Jeremiah, Jeremiah. I even dream about him. I'll give him time. He'll come around. I'll try to get him to talk to me about his problems. It always helps to open up to a friend."

"Mmm."

"*Mamm* is walking better now with those new shoes," Emma said as her pace slowed.

"What a relief to see her limp improve. She looks younger, even happier."

"She's still a pretty woman. You look like her, Ruth."

"*Danki*. My hair is darker than hers though. Katie's, too. You and Wayne got the pretty blond hair."

"*Jah*. Jeremiah could be our brother."

"Emma, let's talk about something else."

"Sorry, I didn't know he bored you so much."

"It's not that. I really get tired of hearing about him. There are other men in the world."

"Not for me, but okay, we'll talk about the trees. Look, nearly all the leaves are down. It looks so barren over on the hills."

"It does. Before you know it, it will be covered in snow."

"Ladies, wait for me," a familiar voice came from behind as Ruth's shadow appeared.

"Oh, no, let's head back," Ruth said softly as Josiah approached with his toothy smile.

Toward evening the tables were filled again with food and the bride and groom, their parents and some of the elderly Amish were served first. Macaroni and cheese, stewed chicken, fried sweet potatoes and platters of cold cuts were passed on to the others seated around the room. Desserts were plentiful with lemon sponge pies in abundance. Not only were there several decorated wedding cakes, but there was one purchased from a bakery with a tier.

Waneta had seated Josiah across from Ruth, and Jeremiah across from Emma. It was impossible to ignore Jeremiah now at such close proximity, so Ruth nodded and smiled. "*Hallo,* Jeremiah."

He returned her greeting with his first smile of the day. Fortunately, Emma was talking to her friend on her left, Abby, and didn't notice the exchange. Ruth feared her eyes might give her away. Conversation continued amongst the group and soon there was laughter and teasing and Ruth felt her stomach settle down enough to eat. An occasional butterfly fluttered through her when she caught Jeremiah observing her.

Once everyone had eaten, the cleanup began again. Ruth observed the older women showing signs of fatigue, so she and her friends did the major part of the work. When she was finished, she removed her soiled apron and replaced it with the one she wore at the wedding and avoiding Josiah, walked onto the porch to get away from the crowd. Within moments, Jeremiah joined her on the porch. They were alone and very aware of each other.

"I have a note for you, Ruth. Don't read it now and don't show anyone, please."

He placed it in her hand and stood gazing at her. She put it in her pocket and stood speechless. His strong features were enhanced by the moon's brilliant beams casting light and shadow on his face. His eyes appeared dark but gentle.

Katie barged out the kitchen door onto the porch. "*Mamm*'s tired, Ruth. *Daed* wants us to take her home now."

"*Jah*. Okay. Let me go say something to the bride and groom first."

Katie returned to the kitchen. Jeremiah placed his hand on Ruth's cheek. "*Gut nacht*, Ruth."

"*Gut nacht*. I'll read your note later. *Danki*."

She turned and went in to say good-night to everyone but there was a glow in her heart and a note in her pocket–both from the man she loved.

Chapter Seventeen

The ride home seemed interminable. Ruth touched her pocket, feeling the small square of folded paper under the fabric. All her resolve to not think about Jeremiah or have hopes were gone– swept away by an unread letter. Maybe he was leaving the Amish. Maybe he was moving to California. Perhaps this was his way of saying good bye.

"Ruthie, you're not even listening to me," Katie said, her puckered brows showing displeasure.

"I'm sorry, what did you say?"

"I said, all my brownies were eaten. Aunt Hannah said they were the best ever."

"*Jah.* I had one. She's right. I never tasted any better."

Katie grinned and nodded. "A guy's gonna be real lucky to get me for a wife."

"Whoa, aren't we conceited. A bit prideful, don't you think?" Emma asked with a chuckle.

"*Jah*, prideful alright, but true," their *Mamm* added. "You are a *gut, gut* girl, Katie. Just have to stop with the bragging."

"I didn't mean it to sound that way." Katie folded her arms, scowled and looked out the back window.

Once they got back to the house, Emma and Katie sat with their mother to chat about the wedding. "Aren't you going to join us, Ruthie?" her mother asked as Ruth headed toward the staircase.

"In a few minutes. I want to change and do a couple things."

Once in her room, Ruth closed the bedroom door and raised the wick on her lamp. She slipped out the note and read.

> *Dear Ruth,*
> *I would like to talk to you about something serious. We never seem to be alone. Please meet me tomorrow at noon in Bird-in-Hand. We can meet in front of the shop with the notice about the concerts.*

*Then I will treat you to lunch and talk to you. I will
be there and I hope you will be too. I know it is not
a long notice but I am hoping you will make it.*

Sincerely,

Jeremiah.

She read it again. *What could be so serious? Is he dying?
Oh, God, don't let that be the case. He's so young. No, maybe he
wants to talk about Emma. Do I want that? How will I ever get to
sleep tonight? How will I explain my trip to town–alone? Oh, my,
this is not easy. Maybe I shouldn't go. I have to. I don't really. But
I do. Ohhhhh.*

She tucked the note back in her pocket and sat on the bed to
think. She needed an excuse to go in town. Usually her mother
wanted to tag along, but she was so tired maybe she wouldn't even
suggest it. But if she does? *I'll cross that bridge when I come to it.
I won't mention it tonight. There would be too many questions. No.
I'll wait until tomorrow.*

She joined her mother and sisters and they sat and chatted
until nearly mid-night when *Daed* and Wayne pulled onto the
drive. After coming back home earlier to milk the cows, they had
returned to the wedding party and remained to help with the
removal of the benches and ended up talking with some of the
other men.

"I'm surprised to see you still up, Mary," their father said
as he entered the sitting room where they were gathered.

"I'm too wound up to sleep, plus I wanted to wait for you,
Leroy."

He came over and kissed the top of her head. "That was
nice. *Jah*, I'm pretty beat myself. It was a long day and now I have
three girls to marry off." He smiled at his daughters and Katie
giggled.

"Everything went smooth, don't you think?" Mary asked
her husband.

"*Jah*, perfect. The food was wonderful-*gut*. I ate three
bowls of your tapioca pudding."

"I didn't even get any," Katie complained. "But I had lots of pie."

"*Jah*, my little *wootzer*," her *daed* said affectionately.

"*Mamm*, you promised to talk to him about that word."

"Sorry Katie, I forgot. Leroy, Katie doesn't like you to call her that anymore."

"*Jah*? You too old for your papa to tease you?" he asked as he tapped his daughter on the head gently.

"I'm not a little piggy."

"It's just a joke, Katie. You are a pretty little thing–not a swine at all."

Katie stood and gave her father a hug. "I saw Skinny Abner looking at me lots of times. He smiled, too."

"Take your time, Katie. You're only sixteen."

"It's time to look, *Daed*. All my friends are talking about the boys now."

He shook his head. "Things don't change. *Jah*, I noticed your *Mamm* when she was about your age. Pretty girl she was, too."

"With my limp?"

"I didn't even notice your limp, Mary. All I saw was a lovely young woman with a beautiful smile. What your legs did was of no concern."

"I didn't think any one would want me–a cripple."

"You were never a cripple in my eyes. You still ain't."

"*Daed*, you're such a romantic tonight," Emma teased. "Must have been the cider turning hard."

"Weddings make me think back is all. *Jah* well, I think I'll turn in."

"I'll be right up, Leroy."

"Take your time." He reached for a lamp and made his way up the stairs.

Ruth looked over at her mother who was following him with her eyes. The love she held for her husband showed in her smile and expression. Even after so many years. That's what every woman hopes for.

"I guess we should head up," Emma suggested. "My feet are killing me."

"Wish we didn't have school tomorrow," Katie said, sighing. "At least it's Friday."

"*Jah.* That helps." Emma rubbed the soles of her feet and moaned. "I barely sat all day."

"Don't leave your shoes for *Mamm* to trip over," Ruth reminded her as she rose to retire for the night. Sleep? Probably not, but her body was exhausted from all the work she'd done.

Kate and Emma left for school leaving the newer buggy behind. Sometimes they walked when the weather was fair, but the mornings were chilly now and they had two buggies.

Ruth checked the clock a hundred times an hour. She'd have to leave by ten-thirty to make it to town by noon. She dusted the furniture, wiped down the jars of preserves they had done the week before and took them down to the coolest section of the cellar where shelves held a year's supply of food. It took many trips to complete her task. Meanwhile her mother was checking the sauerkraut which was in a huge crock in the pantry.

"*Mamm,* I need to leave for a while. I'm taking the buggy into town."

"*Jah?* You hadn't mentioned it. I hope you don't mind if I stay home, Ruthie. My legs are still wobbly from standing so much yesterday."

Ruth felt a sigh of relief forming inside, but she kept it silent and went over to her mother to give her a hug. "I understand, believe me. I'll be back shortly."

"What do you need?"

"Um. I want to check the general store for sales. Margie Stohl told me she got underwear half price last week." Yes, she'd check after seeing Jeremiah. That way it wouldn't be a lie.

"*Gut.* You can buy me three pairs if they're still on sale. Here, I'll get the money."

"I have plenty of money on me, *Mamm.* You can pay me back if I buy them."

"Okay. So have a nice time. Take the day off and *piffle* around, Ruthie. You don't get off by yourself very often. Even eat lunch out. Why not take a sandwich with you and find a park somewhere."

"That's okay, *Mamm*. I really must go."

Her mother nodded and returned to her chore as Ruth placed a fresh *kapp* on her head and checked her apron for cleanliness.

After hitching up her horse, Ruth made her way down the drive to the road leading to Bird-in-Hand. It was nippy and she tucked her cape around her for warmth. Her heart wouldn't behave and she felt it tripping along faster than the horse trotted. She could still change her mind about seeing Jeremiah, but it was as if she had no control over the events transpiring. Her mind said one thing and her body ignored it and here she was heading to see the man whom she loved.

At last she arrived in town and there were several spaces in front of the general store. She secured the horse and headed toward the shop where she was to meet Jeremiah. He was already standing there, leaning against a wall. When he spotted her, he stood straight, adjusted the rim on his hat and gave a wonderful smile which she felt down to her toes.

"You came. *Danki*, Ruth."

"You have me curious, Jeremiah."

"*Jah*, I figured," he twisted his mouth in a half grin and took her arm, leading her down the street. "Are you hungry?"

"I could eat, but I'm not real hungry yet."

"Neither am I. Let's walk first."

They walked toward the edge of town and Jeremiah pointed out a large flat rock where they sat next to each other, touching only with their clothing. Jeremiah took a stick and traced a circle in the dirt beside the rock, silent.

"You wanted to talk about something?" Ruth was frustrated. She still had no idea why he summoned her.

"*Jah*. I don't know how to begin. I guess it's...I need to talk to you about Emma."

Of all the subjects she didn't want to hear about, Emma was number one on her list. "Emma? My sister?"

"*Jah*. I don't want to upset you, but I'm tired of everyone trying to push Emma on me." He stopped tracing circles on the ground and tossed the stick to the side. "Emma is a nice person. She's a good strong Amish girl, but I don't love her and I never will."

"I see."

"Do you? Do you realize every time we see each other, you talk about her? It's like you want me to marry her someday."

Ruth couldn't respond. It would be a lie to say that's what she's wanted, but it was true she pushed him.

He continued. "Before I go any further, I need to ask you something and you must be very, very honest with me."

Ruth turned to face him. Her hands felt damp. She stared into his blue eyes.

"*Jah*. Go ahead."

"Do you love Josiah?"

Her answer could have been immediate. A negative response was on the tip of her tongue, but she held back slightly. "I don't as of now."

His posture became slightly more relaxed. "Are you thinking of marrying him?"

"Not really. Why are you asking me this?"

"Ruth, don't you know really? I'm in love with you. I have been for a long while now. Haven't you guessed?"

Now her heart was not only bouncing–it was singing! "I hoped."

"*Jah*?" His grin spread across his face. "You mean…"

"*Jah*. I mean I love you, too." Suddenly she pictured her sister and what this would mean to her. Ruth's joy of the moment dissipated and she put her hands up to her face, covering her eyes.

"Ruth, what's wrong? This should be a happy time."

She shook her head without looking up. "It can't be. I can't allow myself to love you, Jeremiah."

"Goodness' sake, why not?"

"Emma." She still kept her head down and fought the tears with her whole being, but it was impossible to keep them from flowing. She began to sob and she felt Jeremiah's arms go around her. His breath was warm upon her ear and she felt his rough cheek against her's. He lifted her chin and brought her lips to meet his. He kissed her tenderly. Even though she continued to weep he held her to him. "I love you, Ruth. There is nothing I can do about that."

"I can't love you. I can't hurt Emma like this. She's so in love with you. You're all she talks about."

"But I haven't done anything to encourage her. Why does she believe we will one day be together when I've never once mentioned love to her? Or anything else. Believe me, Ruth, I would not lead her on."

"I know. I know. She imagines things. I've tried to talk to her about it, but she won't listen. She builds everything up in her mind."

"She'll have to face facts, Ruth. We can't let her imagination ruin what we have together. I want you for my wife."

"Oh, dear Jeremiah. How I would love to marry you."

"Then we will marry."

"You don't understand. Not yet, we can't. I must somehow get Emma to think of someone else. I need time."

"How long? I want to start my home—my family."

"I don't know how long. You have to trust me. But until she releases her dream, we can not let our feelings for each other be known."

"That doesn't seem right! It's not honest. How will I be able to stay away from you?"

"You must."

"Ruth, you're being unreasonable." He moved away slightly and his eyes darkened.

"I'm sorry, but that's the way it has to be. Certainly you can understand—"

"I understand your love for me can't be much since you'd let a sister prevent us from being together. She needs to grow up and see reality."

Ruth felt anger surge through her. "You *must* have given her some reason to believe you–"

"*Nein* . Never!" He stood and paced back and forth, his hands formed into fists. He didn't look over. "Now what do you expect of me? I'm a man. I have needs and feelings. How long must I wait?"

Ruth stood up too, and her jaw tightened. "Maybe too long! Maybe I'm not worth waiting for. That's how it looks to me, Jeremiah. You should understand the situation I'm in. I love my sister. *Jah*, I love you too, but she's my blood sister. We are like twins. I simply can not hurt her. In time she will understand."

"And if she doesn't?" His eyes challenged hers.

"Then…then I don't know. I guess it's off between us."

"What kind of love do you call that? I thought you really cared about me."

Ruth could feel her eyes burn and her heart beat wildly. "I do. I really do care."

"*Jah*, just not enough. Come, we go back now. I'll still take you to lunch if you want."

"Not now. I couldn't eat with my stomach like it is. I'd *kutz* for sure."

He began walking quickly back to the center of town with Ruth trying to keep up. What should have been the most wonderful moment of her life, was the worst. Why couldn't he understand and be patient? Surely if he really cared, it would not present a problem. He had so little compassion. Did she really want a husband like that? Perhaps she'd been wrong about him the whole time.

Without a further word, Ruth went to her buggy, untied the reins and climbed inside. Her head was aching and there was a surreal feeling to the moment. She didn't look over at him while she backed up, but instead snapped the whip and headed home, heart broken and sick in her stomach.

Chapter Eighteen

"Ruth, you're back so soon. Did you buy anything?" Mary looked up from her sewing.

"No. I don't feel good. I'm going to lie down for a while."

"You look pale. Can I get you something to drink?"

"Maybe later." Ruth hung her cape on a peg and went up to her bedroom. She removed Jeremiah's note from her pocket and placed it under her mattress, lay down, and closed her eyes. He loved her yet he wasn't willing to wait for her. What kind of love is that? After all, Emma would eventually get over her feelings for him without the pain of knowing her younger sister had stolen his heart. Wouldn't she? Why was it so difficult for him to understand? Tears rolled onto her pillowcase and she reached for a hanky and wiped her eyes. She was sorry she told him she loved him if that was the way he was. Uncaring. She wouldn't marry him now if he begged her. At least she didn't think she would.

"Oh, Emma, Emma," she whispered aloud, "why did you have to imagine so much? Why couldn't you have looked for love with another man?"

After awhile, Ruth fell into a disturbing sleep. Images of Jeremiah and Emma laughing together and holding hands tore at her even in her dreams. Then a knock came on her door and Emma let herself in.

"Ruth, *Mamm* said you weren't feeling good. What's wrong?"

"I'll be alright soon. How was school?" Ruth blew her nose and sat up on the edge of the bed.

"Same as always."

"How about that boy who was having problems."

"Merv? He's not any easier. I may go visit his *Mamm* next week if his behavior doesn't improve, but I heard she's sickly."

"Mmm."

"*Mamm* said you went into town but came right home. Think you're getting a cold?"

"No, I'll be fine in a little while. I'm just real tired."

"In that case, I'll let you sleep. I promised Katie I'd help her bake cobbler. The apples were plentiful this year."

"Sounds good. Emma?"

"*Jah?*" she came over and took Ruth's hand.

"Emma, I love you."

"Ruthie, *danki,* you know I love you too."

"Sisters forever?"

"*Jah.* Sisters forever." Emma leaned over and kissed her sister on the cheek. "Now get some rest so you'll enjoy the apple cobbler tonight after supper."

As Ruth heard her sister go down the hall she closed her eyes. *It's just as well he's out of my life. I think it's time to go on* rumschpringe *and make some decisions about my future.*

Sunday was the alternate week when the families remained home and had private worship or visited with friends and family instead of communal worship. Ruth was relieved she wouldn't have to see Jeremiah or Josiah. At this point she was satisfied without any man in her life. After all, she was only eighteen– hardly old and on the shelf. The more she thought about leaving the area, at least temporarily, the more she was determined to do so.

Monday morning after her sisters had left for school and her father and brother were out in the barn working, Ruth asked her mother to sit and have coffee with her.

"Something on your mind, Ruth?"

"*Jah.* I've been doing a lot of thinking about my future *Mamm,* and I really do want to go off for *rumchspringe* by myself."

"*Ach,* Ruth, that's so dangerous. You have no idea what it's like out in that world."

"Neither do you. Maybe it's not so bad."

"I don't want you to go alone, Ruth. Your father would forbid it."

"But–"

"No but. There is one possibility though."

"What's that *Mamm*?"

"You could stay with your aunt."

"The one who left the Amish years ago? You rarely talk about her."

"Well, once in a while I hear about her. A letter or a word from another. She's still living in Philadelphia, I think."

"Do you have an address?"

"Somewhere. I'm sure I can find it." Her mother put her cup down and folded her hands in front of her.

"Do you think she'd let me stay with her?"

"*Jah*. She never married so she has no children. She'd probably like to see family. I've wondered if she'd ever regretted leaving."

"I don't even know her name or anything about her." Ruth pushed her cup aside and rested her arms on the table waiting for her mother to speak.

"Her name is Esther and she's seven years older than me. She left when I got polio. Your *oma* was very upset with her."

"Why would she leave at that time?"

"She was upset because there was a polio epidemic amongst our people. There was a vaccine available but the bishop wouldn't allow anyone to get it. She blamed the family for my illness and said our parents should have disobeyed him for the sake of the children."

"I see. It must have been terrible for you all to have her leave."

"I was too sick to even realize what was going on. I was not close to Esther anyway. She was twenty when she left."

"Had she been baptized yet?"

"No. She was supposed to get baptized in a few months, but of course that didn't happen."

"I don't think she'd want to have to put up with me, *Mamm*."

"That's the only way I'd allow you to leave. I trust she'd watch out for you. Blood is thick, you know."

"How well I know," Ruth agreed, thinking of her own relationship with her sister. "Do you think *Daed* would allow it?"

"I don't know. Why don't you ask him tonight? Unless he's too tired."

"Mmm. How would I get to Philadelphia? By bus?"

"*Jah*. I'm sure they have bus service from Lancaster. If it comes to that, we'll check. Ruthie, I'd miss you so much." Her mother's eyes filled and her shoulders shook as she lifted her apron to wipe them. Ruth went over and knelt by her chair.

"I'm sure I'd be back."

"That's what Esther said."

"*Jah*, but I'm different. I love the Amish life."

"Then why are you hoping to leave?"

"It's just to be sure. I want to hear more music and maybe even learn to play piano or violin. I have such a strong desire. I'd like to go to a movie and maybe even wear pretty clothes. I'm so afraid if I don't try these things, I'd regret it and someday resent my husband."

"If you feel that strongly, I'll support your decision, Ruth, but only if my sister will have you stay with her."

"How would I reach her?"

"Tomorrow I'll find her address and you can write to her. I don't have her phone number, though I'm sure she owns a phone. She went back to school, graduated college and even got another degree. Now she teaches at a university. She was always the smart one in the family."

"*Mamm,* you could have gone to college, if you'd wanted."

"Maybe, but I didn't have a desire for an education. I knew what I needed to know to run a home."

"And you run it very well, *Mamm*. You are a wonderful mother and wife. I'll always love you."

They held each other in an embrace for several minutes, each fighting tears. Finally her mother pulled back. "I'd better get the pork roast started. It will be noon before you know it."

"I'll get the potatoes from the cellar. *Mamm, danki* for helping me with this."

Her mother nodded, apparently unable to say too much as Ruth noticed her lip quiver. What was she doing to the family?

Was it fair to put her own needs ahead of theirs? She needed to pray extra hard before making the next move.

That evening, when her father had finished his supper, he sat in his easy chair to read the *Die Botschaft,* a weekly newspaper, which served the Amish community. His spectacles sat on the edge of his nose as he concentrated.

"*Daed,* how did your day go?" Ruth asked quietly.

He looked over the rims. "Why you asking?"

"Just wondered, is all."

He looked back at the newspaper. "Fine."

"It's getting cold."

"*Jah.*"

"Is it harder to milk?"

He put his paper down and removed his glasses. "What you want, Ruthie?"

"I guess...I wanted...well, I'm thinking about going away for awhile."

"That's nice. Where to?"

"Philadelphia."

"With friends?"

"Alone."

"*Nein.*"

"But *Daed,* I–"

"You cannot travel alone to a big city. That's out of the question."

Ruth's mother and sisters were motionless watching the exchange. Wayne was out in the barn checking his goats.

"Leroy, I thought Ruth might visit with my sister."

"We don't talk about her in this house."

"But–"

"Discussion has ended. Katie, get me another of those cookies."

"*Jah, Daed.*" She jumped up and went to the kitchen to fill a plate for her father.

Ruth looked over at her mother and then Emma, whose brows were furrowed.

Ruth picked up some mending and tried to concentrate. She sniffled several times before her father peered over his paper again. "Stop your sniffles. It ain't the end of the world."

"But, *Daed,* it would only be for a while. I want so much to see concerts and wear nice clothes and–"

"You wear nice clothes now, not those pieces of material only tramps should wear."

"Not everyone dresses like that," her mother asserted.

"You in favor of your daughter running off like this? You want to lose a daughter as well as a sister?" His voice was raised. Something Ruth rarely heard.

"I'm sorry I brought it up." Ruth stood and tucked her sewing in a drawer and started up the stairs. She heard Emma excuse herself too, as she followed Ruth to their room.

When they got there, Ruth closed the door and let out her tears.

"Ruthie, don't cry. *Daed* will change his mind when he has time to think about it. After all, our aunt wasn't baptized, so she wasn't officially shunned."

"Why didn't *Mamm* keep in touch? It's terrible not to care about your own sister."

"I think *Mamm* was only a girl when she left."

"True and she was sick at the time. Still."

"*Mamm* is agreeable to your going?"

"Only if I stay with her sister. She was going to give me her address, but now…"

"*Jah.* Not good timing now. Give *Daed* a chance to mull it over. He may change his mind."

"I doubt it, but I can hope. I need to get away, Emma. I'm not happy."

"I can see that, Ruthie. I'm so sorry. I wish there was something I could do."

There is. Stop wishing for the impossible. "I'll be okay tomorrow."

"*Jah.* Tomorrow's a new day."

The girls prepared for bed and Ruth geared up for another sleepless night.

Chapter Nineteen

Nothing more was said. For over a week Ruth moped around the house, fulfilling her duties without complaint, though she was cheerless. Her father appeared to be ignoring the situation, refusing to speak about it–even to Mary.

The Sunday arrived when the families were to gather at John Lapp's home. Ruth couldn't face seeing Jeremiah, but if she wasn't ill, she had to attend with her family. At the last minute she used a slight headache as an excuse not to attend. Her mother took her aside and asked if it was legitimate.

"*Jah*, it's not a terrible headache, *Mamm*, but a headache just the same. Please, I want to stay home."

Her mother sighed. "Your *daed* will not look kindly on this, but I will try to explain. Go rest then."

Ruth went back to her room and fell asleep briefly. When she awoke, her head felt better, so she suspected the headache was the result of her restless night.

After dressing, she went downstairs where she picked on fruit and left-overs to satisfy her hunger. Then she bundled up and took a walk around the edge of the yard. The frost had killed off the remaining flowers and the landscape was a dreary mix of browns and grays. She wondered if what she felt was depression. Amish people didn't speak of mental conditions. It was expected one would cope and with God's healing, move on–no matter what one faced. She had always believed it possible, but lately her mood swings and tears were frequent no matter how hard she tried to pray them away. Maybe she wasn't devout enough. Perhaps she no longer found favor in His sight. After all, wasn't she becoming too self-centered? Even Emma had hinted at that possibility, hurting her further, actually increasing her desire to leave.

Monday when she and her mother were finally alone in the kitchen, Ruth brought up the subject of her aunt.

"I did find the address, Ruthie, but with your father so upset about this, I haven't mentioned it to you. Last night though, for the first time, he told me he was re-thinking your request."

"Really? Why, do you think?" Ruth looked up from the bread board where she was kneading dough.

"He's concerned about you. We all see how sad you've become. It's not like you, Ruthie. You're normally such a cheerful girl."

"Do you think it would be alright if I at least wrote to her? If she doesn't want me there, I must either think of another way or give it all up." She pounded the dough and flipped it over into a layer of flour.

"*Jah.* Write and see what she says. She may not even write back, Ruthie. I just don't know what to expect."

"Could you write too? To kind of introduce me?"

Her mother stopped cutting carrots and looked over. "I'd love to start up a relationship, but maybe I'll let you be the one to break the ice. It's thick as an iceberg from our years of silence. I hope if you do go, you can help mend things."

"*Jah,* I understand. I'll write something tonight and then let you read it."

"*Gut.* Now once you get the dough rising, you can make pie shells."

"I don't feel up to baking a pie, *Mamm.* It's all I can do to make bread."

"I guess your *daed* will live with brownies. He doesn't want to get a pot-belly, that's for sure."

Ruth couldn't wait for evening to write. She finished her chores quickly and instead of mending a pocket on one of her aprons, she took a writing pad and pen and went to her room, making several attempts before settling on one. She read it over.

Dear Aunt Esther,

You don't know me but I am your niece. My mother is Mary. I know she was only thirteen when you left and I know you have not been back. Maybe you don't know I'm even born. I am eighteen now and I am not engaged so I am free to do my freedom time. I wish very much to come to Philadelphia and maybe hear an orchestra play. My father does not want me to leave but my mother says it would be okay with her if I stayed with family. You are the only family in Philadelphia so I was wondering if I could stay with you for just a little while until I am sure I want to stay Amish.

I do not eat much and I work hard. I could make all your meals and clean your house for you if I come. I have saved some money from selling pot holders and things at our vegetable stand and my mother said she would give me some more so I would not be a burden to you. If I come and you do not like me I will leave and go home. But I hope you would like me and let me stay just for a while. I think about music a lot and I wonder about many things. If I come to Philadelphia I will go to museums and parks and maybe wear prettier clothes. If I am too lonesome I will go home sooner.

Please do not worry if you say no I will understand. But I hope you say yes.

Sincere
ly, Ruth Zook

When she was satisfied, she took the letter down to show her mother. Mary sat in the rocker and put her reading glasses on. She rocked back and forth, nodding occasionally as she read. When she was finished she stopped rocking and folded it in half and returned it to Ruth. "It's *gut. Jah,* I like it. You leave her a choice. Now before you send it, we should show your *daed* and get his okay. It may take a few days. I've been working on him, but I may need more time."

Ruth nodded and tucked the letter in her pocket.

"Here Ruth, I made a copy of her address. I hope she's still living there. This was from a couple years ago." She handed Ruth a piece of paper torn from her grocery list with the address neatly printed on it. "There are envelopes in the desk drawer in my bedroom. Fill it out, but give it to me and don't seal it yet. I'm sure your *daed* will want to read it first." Ruth nodded and went upstairs to get the envelope. After filling it out she gave it to her mother.

"I'm nervous. I hope *Daed* isn't upset."

"He sees how you've been acting. Is there more here, Ruthie? Does any of this have to do with Josiah Stoltz?"

"What do you mean?"

"Well, he's trying so hard to have you like him, but I don't see signs you feel the same for him."

"Perhaps he's part of it, but certainly not all."

"Is there anyone else?"

"*Mamm*, I can't talk about it with you or anyone."

Her mother let out a long breath. "Then you pray, Ruthie. He hears and knows best."

"I do pray."

"Ruthie, will you take down the sheets now. They should be dry, for sure."

"*Jah.* And I'll make up the beds for you."

"I can do them."

"I know, but I'd like to. I haven't been much help lately." Ruth went over to the large empty clothes basket setting by the kitchen door and picked it up to take outside.

"Not true. You always help," Mary said as she checked the rising bread dough.

"*Mamm*, how will you manage if I do leave for a while?"

"Oh, *Dochder*, I'll do just fine. Your other sisters will help if I need it. They're home week-ends and every afternoon. Don't you worry about it–not one bit."

It was several more days before the letter was mentioned. After supper the family gathered for devotions. After prayer, Leroy cleared his throat and sat forward, elbows on his knees. "We have a family matter I want everyone to hear."

Ruth's palms immediately became damp. It had to be about her.

"*Jah, Daed*? What is it?" Wayne asked first.

"It seems your sister, Ruth, has decided to use her invisible wings to fly away from us. She says it's only for a while."

Emma exchanged glances with Ruth, but Katie's mouth flew open. "Ruthie, I knew you wanted to leave for awhile, but you never told me you hated being Amish."

"Don't be silly. I don't hate it! I merely want to see other things before I settle."

Wayne shook his head and looked down at his hands. "You may not want to come back," he said softly.

"*Jah*. You might want to live like the English." Kate looked horrified at the possibility.

"Not true. I'm almost sure I'll want to return. I just need to be absolutely positive this is the way I want to spend my life. Lots of teens leave for a while."

"*Jah*, and they don't all come back," Wayne said.

"There is a possibility that could happen, but very, very slight. I love you all too much to walk away for *gut*."

"What if you meet an English man and fall in love?" Kate was the practical one.

"I won't let that happen."

"But it could," Emma added. "Especially since you don't care about anyone here much. Josiah would marry you in a split second, if you'd have him and there's nothing wrong with him. Maybe you're too fussy."

Ruth felt her anger rise. "I am not fussy! I just don't want to enter into a marriage with a man I don't love. Would you?"

Emma looked at her sister. "No, I guess not. But of course I have Jeremiah."

"You don't have Jeremiah! No one has Jeremiah! Why do you continue to imagine he's in love with you?" Ruth stood at this point and walked back and forth.

"Stop this right now," her father spoke up. "There is no need to speak harshly to each other. I have made a decision and it is final."

Ruth caught her breath and stopped to stare at her father.

"Ruthie, you may go if your aunt will have you. I will not let you leave this home unless it is family you would stay with. Your *Mamm* told me about the letter and she had me read it. You may send it. If and when your aunt writes back, I need to read it also before I make the final decision." He sat back in his chair and placed his hands on the chair arms. "To the rest of you, your sister is free to make up her own mind. We can not keep our community pure if people join only because they feel they have to. It is voluntary and Ruth has questions. God will protect her, but it will be our job to pray for her every day. That is the end of this discussion." He picked up the Bible and cleared his throat. "I will end with the reading of Psalm one hundred."

Ruth barely heard a word her father spoke, as her mind tried to grasp what had transpired. She felt tremendous relief. Now she could mail the letter and her future would depend upon the answer she'd receive, so in a sense it was no longer her concern. God would lead her in the right direction. Of this she was sure. Later Emma and Katie wanted to talk to her about everything, but Ruth preferred not being questioned any further.

"*Daed* said that was the end of the discussion and until Aunt Esther replies, if she does, there is nothing further to say."

Katie looked at Emma and shrugged. "If that's the way you want it, so be it." She huffed and walked away. Emma gave a weak smile and went to fold towels.

Chapter Twenty

The letter was sent out the next day and after two days Ruth watched for the mail truck and met the mailman hoping against hope her aunt would write back immediately. After ten days, she gave up hope. Surely if she'd wanted Ruth to visit, she would have responded by now.

The days were growing shorter and the temperatures dropped to below freezing at night. It was early December. Time for her father and Wayne to work on repairs in the house and the out buildings. Of course the cows needed to be milked twice a day, and the goats and chickens needed to be fed and cared for as well. Life was difficult but no one complained. It was accepted as their way of life and it was Godly living. But oh, such hard physical labor.

No one mentioned that Ruth had not yet heard from her aunt. It was embarrassing and left her plans in limbo, since her aunt was her only hope of leaving. Perhaps her aunt didn't want to be bothered with her sister's daughter.

Church service was merely a requirement for her at this point. She dreaded seeing Jeremiah and they avoided each other even when they attended weddings of their friends. It was difficult not to think about him and Josiah was as annoying as a mosquito at night. He never lost an opportunity to talk with her or sit by her. She no longer accepted his invitations to go along in his buggy to the Sings or Frolics. She didn't want to hurt him, but he didn't seem to take the hint. Ruth even tried to get Emma involved, but she insisted Jeremiah would one day come around and ask her to marry him. Any time he smiled or nodded in her direction, Emma took it as a "sign." Ruth tried to convince herself that she had given up all hope of ever being his wife. She told herself she was over him, but her heart still danced when she observed his profile or heard his laugh. At night, before falling asleep, she'd say her prayers and end with, "Please help me not to think about Jeremiah so much," but that prayer went unanswered. Not an hour went by without her picturing him or hearing his voice. Hopefully, if she ever did make it to Philadelphia, she'd be able put him into her past, once and for all.

Since so much time had passed after sending the letter off, she no longer ran for the mail everyday, so she was surprised one Saturday when her father came in with a letter addressed to her. He handed it over without a word and returned to the barn. Ruth ran up to her room to read it in private.

Dear Ruth,

As you can see by the post date I did not get back to you as quickly as you would have expected. I recently moved and the letter had to be forwarded, which always takes time. I was both surprised and pleased to receive a letter from a family member.

Yes, I knew of your existence since I still hear from a friend in Lancaster County who keeps me up to date on the family.

I would be delighted to have you visit me and if things go as I expect they would, you may stay as long as you please. I'm assuming this arrangement has been discussed with your parents and they are agreeable.

Do you wish to come before the holidays? Please let me know so I can make my own plans. Normally I would be cruising this time of year, but due to a knee problem, which has been corrected, I was hesitant to make plans ahead of time. Therefore the only other potential problem would be an invitation I've received for the New Year's, which if I know ahead of time, I can cancel. I may celebrate with a few close friends in my apartment instead.

I am on vacation in December so I would have more time to visit with you and show you the sights of Philadelphia than I would once the spring semester begins.

*Please give my best regards to your family
and I'll wait to hear from you.*

*Yours
truly, Aunt
Esther*

Ruth held the letter in her hands, her heart beating wildly. Did she really want to do this? Her aunt sounded rather formal. Yes, she was willing to put up with Ruth, but it sounded as if she would have to alter her life for her niece. Or maybe she read too much into it. Maybe her mother would have more incite. After all, Esther was her sister. Ruth folded the letter and went downstairs to show her mother. Mary was baking holiday cookies with Katie who was babbling on about school and the "cute" little girls and the "annoying" little boys.

"I heard from Aunt Esther."

"*Jah?*" Her mother's brows lifted and her eyes showed surprise and a touch of fear. "So what did she say?"

"I'll let you read it."

"Can I hear it, too?" Katie asked, licking the spoon.

"May as well listen. *Daed* will want to see it later. Where's Emma?"

"She's in the cellar hanging laundry." Her mother wiped her hands and came over to Ruth. "Let's sit. My feet are tired."

She took the rocker and Katie and Ruth sat on the sofa opposite. Mary read the letter out loud slowly, looking up once in a while at Ruth. When she was finished, she laid it on her lap and leaned back in her chair. "So, she wants you."

"I guess. It sounded so formal."

"That's my sister for you. She thought she was better than the rest of us."

"Really? You never mentioned that before."

"Never felt a need to. But she has a *gut* heart. She'll treat you *gut*. She is pretty rich I guess. In material things."

Ruth noticed her mother's eyes register sorrow.

"*Mamm*, do you want to write to her yourself?"

119

"No. You do it. If you decide to go with her, you can find out what she thinks about me and the family. I'm curious to know if she regrets leaving."

Katie had been silent. Now she expressed her own feelings. "I think she sounds snooty. Maybe it's the way she says her words, fancy-like."

"You're being judgmental, Katie. We don't even know her. She is nice enough to offer her home to me. I'm going to accept, that is, if *Daed* agrees. What about the timing? Should I wait till Christmas is over?"

"It's up to you, Ruthie," her mother replied, but Ruth suspected she knew the answer her mother wanted to hear.

"I think I'll wait. I want to have Christmas with you–my family first."

Her mother smiled broadly. "*Jah.* I was hoping so. *Daed* will like you to be here, too."

"Me, too," Katie added and went over to hug her sister. "It won't be the same without you here, Ruthie. I hope you won't be gone too long."

"I think I'll be ready to come home by spring."

Mary rose. "Now, let's go check the cookies. I smell them. I hope they're not burning."

"I'll go help Emma with the laundry," Ruth remarked. "*Mamm,* you hold onto the letter so you can let *Daed* read it."

"*Jah.* I'll do that."

Ruth made her way down the steps to the basement. Emma was humming a hymn while she placed socks by pairs over the line. "So, you came to help?"

"*Jah,* although I see you're nearly finished."

"*Gut* timing, Ruthie."

"I got a letter from Aunt Esther."

"Oh, I'm happy for you, but sad for me. It took long enough."

"She had moved and it had to be forwarded." Ruth shook out an undershirt of her father's and laid it over the line next to the socks.

"Is she still in Philadelphia?"

"*Jah*. Fitler Square, it's called. Sounds real fancy."

"Whoa, you're going to be living like a princess, I bet you."

Ruth laughed at the thought. "I hope not. I want to live like I'm a regular English person."

"Not the immoral kind."

"No way. There are *gut* English too. I know a Mennonite family that lives next door to Methodists and they are nice people. They even helped when she had a baby. They brought meals and everything."

"I know. It's silly to think we're the only *gut* people on earth. God made so many people He must have made *gut* ones, too."

"I'm excited, Emma. I hope *Daed* won't say no."

"Will you leave right away?"

"No, I'll be here for Christmas."

"I'm relieved. It wouldn't seem like Christmas without you. Here if you carry the dry sheets upstairs, I'll bring up some jars of corn. *Mamm* wants to make corn pudding."

"Sure. Want me to help you make up the beds?"

"Why not? It goes twice as fast that way. The sheet on top has a hole in it though. I'll mend it first."

"I want you to read the letter, Emma, and see what you think about our aunt."

"You didn't like her letter?"

"It's not that. I want your opinion, is all."

They went upstairs and Ruth got the letter from her mother and had Emma read it. When she was done she placed it back in the envelope.

"Well? What do you think?"

"I'd be scared to stay with her. She sounds so...so formal. And all the parties."

"Maybe that's just the way she writes. She's a professor you know."

"What does she teach?"

"*Mamm's* not sure. Might be English."

"Wow. She must be smart. If you don't like her you can always come home."

"That's what I figure. I'm curious about her now. She's *Mamm*'s sister after all."

"*Jah*. Hard to believe. They're so different."

"But, Emma, maybe they're not. Maybe they've just taken different paths."

"Mmm. But no husband and no children. It makes me sad to think of it."

"Some women find happiness in other ways."

"Ruthie, tell me the truth. Could you be happy living all by yourself, forever?"

"I don't know. I've not been alone for more than an hour or two."

"And did you feel lonesome?"

Ruth thought back to the Sunday she stayed home from church and she nodded her head. "A little. But I'm not used to being alone. Maybe it's not so bad once you get used to it. Besides, we're never *really* alone. We always have God with us."

"*Jah*, true. Well, anyway, whatever makes one content. I know I need a husband and lots and lots of kids to be happy." *And Jeremiah for your husband. Oh, Lord, bring someone else into her life.*

Chapter Twenty-One

Before the family began their devotional time after supper, Mary handed the letter from her sister, Esther, over to Leroy. His eyebrows rose as he opened the letter and proceeded to read it twice in silence. Afterward he handed it back and looked at Ruth. "So, your aunt wants you to come. And you still want to go?"

"*Jah*. I do."

"When would you leave?"

"Probably after Christmas."

He shook his head and folded his hands on his lap. "Then you can make your plans."

Ruth wanted to jump up and run over to hug him, but that wasn't the way things were done. "*Danki*."

"Now I'll read from the book of Proverbs."

As Emma and Ruth put on their night clothes, Emma began to tear up. "I'll have to have Katie move in with me when you're gone. I don't want to be alone."

Ruth went over to her sister and embraced her. "I'll miss you so much."

"I'll miss you too. You're excited to leave though, aren't you? Is part of it because of Josiah?"

"No man would influence my decision that much. It's something that's been brewing in me for months now, Emma. I can't even explain it. Maybe it was the concert."

"Concert? You went to a concert?"

Oh, no, what had she done? She had not intended to speak of that day, especially with Emma.

"Uh, a long time ago I went without telling. It was in Lancaster."

"When was this? Who did you go with? Did *Mamm* know?" Emma's eyes were searing into Ruth's.

"I don't want to talk about it, Emma. It's not your business."

"I'm your sister–your best friend. Certainly I have a right to know when you go to a concert!"

"Please, don't push me! It's done."

"Who did you go with?"

"It's no one's business!"

"Well, if you act like that and keep secrets from me, maybe it's better you go to Philadelphia. Maybe you can get a job dancing in a bar!"

"Emma, what a horrible thing to say! How dare you!"

"I don't think I know you anymore. First off, I think you're jealous because Jeremiah finds me interesting and second, you don't have anyone except that little twit, Josiah, and he hasn't even asked you to marry him, and thirdly, you…you are too skinny!"

There was a knock on their door. Fuming, Ruth opened it abruptly to find her mother in her nightgown standing with a kerosene lamp in her hands. "Girls, we could hear you from our bedroom. What is going on?"

"Nothing!" Emma folded her arms, glaring at her sister.

"Absolutely nothing," Ruth added returning the look with a defiant stare.

Mary looked from one to the other. "You'd better behave and go to sleep. You both act like you're three-years-old and *Daed* is quite upset."

"Sorry," Ruth said, calming down.

"*Jah*. We'll go to sleep now. Sorry, *Mamm*." Emma looked contrite. When their mother left them, Emma whispered hoarsely, "You have a lot to explain, *little sister*."

"And you, *big sister*, will get no explanation from me." With this, they went to their beds, climbed in and turned their backs to each other. Ruth counted the days till she'd leave.

Things were strained between the two girls. Ruth offered no further explanation about going to a concert. Emma didn't ask again. One afternoon a week before Christmas, Emma and Katie came home later than normal from school. It was obvious to Ruth, Emma had been crying. Her eyes were red and swollen. Her sister heart went out to her and she forgot she was still angry with her.

"Emma, you've been crying," Ruth said softly, as she went over and helped her sister remove her heavy shawl.

"*Jah*. It's so sad. You remember I told you about a boy in my school, Mervin Kuhns? His mother was sick and he lost two sisters to the flu three years ago?"

"I do remember and I vaguely remember the family. They moved here right before their children died."

"*Jah*. Well, Katie and I went to see the mother to talk about his behavior problems. He doesn't listen well and disrupts the class. It makes it so hard to teach."

"You told me about him."

"It's real sad. His mother is terrible sick. She coughed the whole time and I saw her spit up blood. I think she's not going to make it even to Christmas."

Ruth moved over to the sofa and they sat together, Katie taking the rocker. Her eyes were puffy too.

"What about her husband? Did you see him?"

"*Jah*. He was there. He's so sad. You'd know him if you saw him, though they haven't been at service for the last year. She's been too sick."

"What's his name?"

"Gabe."

"Tall fellow, kind of lanky?"

"That's him. Nice enough looking, but so quiet. He hardly said a word. We had to leave. I couldn't bring up my problems with Merv when they're going through so much."

"Of course not. No wonder the boy is acting up. Not much of a life for him. Losing his *schwesters* and now maybe his *mamm*. Poor kid."

"*Jah*." Emma wiped her eyes. "I want to help, but I don't know what I can do."

"Do you know what's wrong with her, Emma?"

"Consumption. The doctor's been to see her, but she's too far gone. On the way out, Gabe said he'd be surprised if she made it to Christmas."

"My, how terrible. I hope you didn't get too close to her, Emma. Or you, Kate," Ruth warned as she turned from Emma to her younger sister.

"I didn't go in the room. I waited with Merv in the parlor," Kate said.

"*Gut.* And you, Emma, were you careful?"

"I went in her bedroom but I stayed a distance. Gabe warned me."

"Didn't they have another child?"

"*Jah*, a daughter. She's in my class too. Little Liz. She's only five and a sweetheart. Never gives me any trouble."

"Because she sits in a corner by herself and doesn't talk," Katie interjected.

"True. But she does her work real *gut.* She's a smart one."

"I think Merv is smart, too, but he doesn't seem to care," Katie added.

Ruth shook her head. "How can he care when he has so many problems in his home. Does he look after his little sister?"

"Oh, *jah.* He's wonderful with her. He takes her hand and walks her home. They live a mile from the school. He always puts a scarf around her head when it's cold. *Jah*, he's a *gut* boy that way.

"Girls," Mary came in from the outside bundled in a heavy shawl and a scarf. "Your *daed* wants you to bring in some greens for the house. Since Christmas is only a few days away, he wants us to decorate the house. He loves it when we fix it up to smell like pine. Look, I brought pine cones in."

"*Mamm*, I'll make a wreath," Katie said as she took the cones from her mother's apron and laid them on the long harvest table.

"*Gut.* Tomorrow I'm making candles. Ruthie, you help me, *jah?*"

"Of course. And Emma you can pop the corn for the strings."

"And I hear the cranberries are plump this year. It will be beautiful." Emma hugged Ruth. "And you'll be here with us."

Ruth laughed. "Whether you like it or not."

126

"Go help your *daed* now," Mary reminded them. "Emma, your eyes. Have you been crying?"

"I'll tell you later, *Mamm*. Right now I need to help *daed* with the greens."

"True. And I have to start supper. *Gut* thing we have leftovers tonight. I have so much to do. All the family and grand kids will be here Christmas in time for dinner. Hannah said she'd come early to help us cook. We're purchasing a huge turkey from the Stoudts' in Bird-in-Hand."

"They are the best, *Mamm*, and remember how good your soup turned out last year?" Katie reminded her.

"*Jah*. Your *daed* had four bowls one night. I thought he'd burst."

When the girls returned with the hemlock and pine branches, they laid them on tables and windowsills. The fragrance permeated the whole house. Ruth started singing carols and her sisters joined in. Even Mary added her voice, though she had trouble staying on key.

Their father removed his boots in the vestibule and then came in and took off his outer clothing. "It's getting mighty cold out there. Looks like we're going to get snow tonight. There's a haze around the moon."

"I hope it does snow," Katie said, grinning at her father. "I love to throw snowballs at trees."

"As long as you don't hit your old *daed*," he said, grinning back.

"*Daed*, I wanted to tell you something," Ruth started speaking.

"*Jah*? What is it?"

"I bought my ticket today for the bus trip to Philadelphia."

"Your *Mamm* said you were going to. When do you leave?"

"Two days after Christmas. I wrote to Aunt Esther to give her the time."

"What time does the bus leave?"

"At ten of one."

"We'll need to get you a ride in a car to Lancaster."

"*Jah.* I saved money for this, *Daed.* I have over a hundred saved."

"You'll need every penny. You can't go and not pay your way."

"I offered to clean her house and cook for her when I get there. I'm not lazy."

"That you're not. I know you'll work it out just fine. *Gut* for you both. I don't want to talk about your leaving now. We want to have a nice Christmas."

Ruth swallowed hard. Her father rarely showed his emotions. No, there was no need to talk about it once all the arrangements were made. It was too late to change her mind. But how long would she survive in the other world?

Chapter Twenty-two

"Here, Ruth, take the baby for me," Fannie said as she passed four-month-old Isaac over to her sister-in-law.

He gave Ruth a toothless grin and reached his hands out to her. "What a dear little *boppli*. You are so sweet," she crooned over her new nephew and nuzzled her nose in his neck. He let out a giggle.

"He's such a *gut* boppli," Fannie said smiling as she removed her outer clothing. "We have six inches of snow already."

"It's beautiful."

"*Jah*, but not too convenient. We walked over rather than slide on the road."

"*Gut* thing you live on the next farm."

"Abram went to the barn to see if *Daed* needs help."

"The cows have been milked and fed. I don't know why *Daed* stays out in that cold barn so much."

"Men. They like to be away from us woman folk, *jah*?"

Katie ran over and hugged her sister-in-law and tickled Isaac under his chin. "Oh, I want a dozen babies like him, Fannie."

"You'll change your mind when you see how much work they make," Fannie said, smiling.

"I'll hold him, Ruth, when you get tired."

"That may be never," Ruth answered, inhaling his sweet baby smell and kissing his head.

"Isn't it time for you to think about marrying, Ruthie?" Fannie asked as she removed her damp stockings and replaced them with dry ones from her apron pocket.

"Pretty soon. Did you hear I'm going to Philadelphia?"

"*Jah*. Abram told me." Her smile turned downward. "He's not thrilled."

"But I'll be staying with our aunt."

"She lives like the English now, right?"

"*Jah*, but she's a *gut* person."

"I hope so. Don't stay away too long, Ruthie. We want you back."

Ruth nodded and moved over to the coal stove with baby Isaac. She watched as Emma carved a large ham, and they talked with Hannah who was holding her baby, Sarah. Hannah's older girls, Anna and Mary were playing with Abram's son, Sammy, who just turned two. Katie sat on the floor with the little ones.

A buggy pulled up and Ruth's grandparents got out and left the horse tied up at the post by the porch. Everyone greeted them and *Oma* sat to watch the children play while her husband rocked nearby enjoying a plate of cookies.

Then Ruth's three brothers came up to the porch with their *daed* and removed their snow-covered boots before entering the cozy home. "It smells like heaven in here, *Mamm*," Abram remarked, kissing his mother on her cheek.

"*Jah*, I can smell the turkey," Mark said. "My stomach is grumbling like crazy."

"Wayne, check the fire in the fireplace and make sure the little ones are staying away from it," Mary said.

"I'll check, *Mamm*. When do we eat?"

"Soon. I let you know."

Katie held Isaac while Ruth prepared the potatoes, mashing them with fresh milk and butter.

Emma stirred the gravy while Hannah set up the long tables. The children sat at their own table, though not much food was consumed. Mary set up a carton with blocks to keep them occupied while the adults ate.

Ruth's father put his head down to say a blessing on the food and everyone followed suit. To announce the end of prayer, he shuffled his shoes on the floor. Soon everyone began talking as they passed platters of food around the long trestle table.

"We'll need another table built pretty soon," Mary said to her family. "Once my three girls are married and start their families, this one will be too small."

Leroy agreed. "We have time, though. Emma's not even got a man picked out yet and neither does our Ruthie."

Ruth noticed a blush rise from Emma's neck to her cheeks. "I thought I had someone, but nothing has happened yet."

"*Jah?*" her brother Abram looked at her with a grin. "So who's the lucky man you're hopin' to capture?"

"Never mind," Emma said looking down at her plate. "I didn't get cranberry sauce yet."

"Here," Wayne said as he passed it over to his sister. "Tell us Em. Who's the unlucky guy?"

Mark piled mashed turnips on his plate and passed the bowl on to his wife. "I bet I know. It's Jeremiah, *jah?* I see you chase after him."

"I don't chase men."

"*Jah,* you do."

"*Mamm,* make him stop," Emma appealed to her mother.

"He's only teasing. Emma has plenty of time for romance. She's busy teaching the little ones."

"So am I," Katie added. "They're a handful."

"Will you stay on teaching after Emma marries?" Hannah asked.

"Probably, but I'll need more help."

Anna ran over to Hannah, "Sammy knocked over my blocks. I had a big house."

"He's little, honey. Just build it again. Did you finish your dinner?"

"I'm not hungry."

"Try to eat something," she called out as Anna ran off.

"Give up, Hannah," Mary said, her lips forming a smile. "Somehow children that age survive even though they eat like sparrows."

"Birds eat a lot for their size, *Mamm,*" Wayne informed her.

"I know. I know. But *kinder* hate to stop to eat."

Baby Isaac began to cry from his carrier, wailing for his dinner. Fannie excused herself and took the baby into the quiet room to nurse him.

"So, you're headed to the big city," Mark said looking over at Ruth.

"*Jah.* I'm getting excited."

"What do you hope to discover there?"

"I'm not sure, but I know I have to open my eyes to the world before I make my final decision to stay Amish."

"I did the same as you know, Ruthie, but I stayed home while I went through my *Rumschpringe.* Why can't you do that instead?"

The family became silent while they waited for her answer. Forks scratched the plates and people shuffled their feet, but she knew their ears were on her. "It's something I need to do, is all I know. But I'm sure I'll be back soon. Probably by spring."

Her mother smiled weakly at her. "She might learn to play a piano."

There was silence again.

"I don't see what's so evil about playing a musical instrument," Ruth said defensively.

"*Jah*, you're probably right," Mark agreed. "It may be hard to learn and then never do again. Might be harder on you than not touching it in the first place. Know what I mean?"

"I guess so. I hope everyone will write to me while I'm gone."

Emma and Katie answered at the same time. "I will."

"*Jah* and I will, of course," her mother added, reaching for the applesauce.

"I hate to write letters, so don't look for one from me. *Mamm*, this is so *gut*," Wayne said, wiping his mouth with his napkin. "Best turkey we ever had."

"I think the boy is right," Leroy added. "And I can't wait to have pie."

"We have four kinds this year," Katie added. "I made the pumpkin and Emma made the apple."

"And what did you make, Ruthie?" her brother Mark asked.

"I don't do pies. So I baked more cookies."

"Ruthie would rather go to concerts than bake pies," Emma stated, looking across at her sister.

"Concerts? When did you ever go to a concert?" Abram asked, reaching for more cornbread.

"Enough talk about me. Tell me about Sarah. Has she cut any teeth yet?" Ruth asked Hannah, changing the subject abruptly.

"She has six teeth already."

"She'll need a dentist soon," *Daed* said, smiling.

"She bites me now. I need to wean her."

Mamm laughed. "She's ready to try a cup. We have extra goat milk."

Wayne's ears perked up. "Prickly gives tons of milk, Hannah. I'll milk her when Sarah gets hungry."

"*Danki*, Wayne. I'll take you up on it."

Ruth glanced over at Emma, who was staring at her. *Now why did she bring that up? And on a holiday, too? Did Emma suspect Jeremiah was somehow involved? That would not be good.*

"Are you going by bus to Philadelphia?" Abram asked his sister.

"*Jah.* I heard from Aunt Esther two days ago and she'll meet me at Sixteenth Street and Market. I guess it's in the center of the city."

"Are you scared?" Wayne asked.

"A little, but not too much."

"I'd be nervous," Hannah said. "Too many people all in one place."

"You be careful," Abram warned. "Don't talk to strangers."

"No. I'll watch myself and my aunt will take care of me."

"She's just a woman, like yourself. She'd be no help with gangs," Abram went on.

"Oh hush. Don't go scaring her," *Mamm* scolded. "It can't be all that bad. If it was, my sister would have returned to Lancaster County."

"Let's think about dessert," Katie suggested.

The family laughed and her mother shook her head. "We clean up first, young lady. Once we finish up, we think about more food."

"I can't eat another thing, *Mamm*. Let's wait till supper for dessert," Emma suggested.

"*Gut* idea," *Daed* agreed. "Anyone want to go for a walk in the snow?"

"I'll go," Wayne responded.

"Guys, let's all go out and throw snowballs. We'll have a contest," Abram suggested.

All the men went outside as the women began cleaning up from dinner. It was a pleasant time and Ruth tucked her memories away in her memory bank to feast upon in lonely moments. She feared there could be many such occasions.

Around midnight, after the family left, Emma and Ruth worked together in the kitchen, putting away the pots and wiping down the counters before heading for bed. At first they spoke only when necessary. When finished, Ruth placed her damp dish towel over a rack and removed her apron. "I guess I'll go to bed now. See you later."

"I'll be up in a minute. I want to look out first. It's still snowing hard."

"*Jah.*"

"I hope your bus trip won't be cancelled."

"It's a couple days away."

"I know. Look, Ruth, I'm sorry I mentioned the concert today. It slipped out by mistake."

"Mmm."

"Really. If you want to keep secrets, that's up to you."

"You don't have to know every single thing I do. I have my own life."

"As you're proving. It hurts me when you leave me out of things. We've always been so close."

"I know, and I'm sorry you feel left out. It wasn't important. Someday I'll tell you the whole story, but right now, I prefer not to."

"Ruth, is it because of who you went with?"

Ruth felt her heart jump. "What do you mean?"

"Like would I be upset if I knew?"

"You're fishing, Emma, and I've already told you all I'm going to say on the subject. Now I'm going up. Please turn the lamp down when you come up."

"I see. That's how it is. Okay, don't expect me to write to you. After all, why should I confide in you?"

"If you don't want to write? Fine with me! I'm going to be too busy to answer anyway."

"That's the way you want it?"

"That's the way it is." Ruth headed up the stairs, consciously walking softer than her heart desired. It would have felt so good to stomp with all her might. She did her toiletry quickly and slipped into bed only moments before her sister entered the room. Not a word was spoken. Philadelphia was looking better every day.

Chapter Twenty-three

One more day at home before Ruth would begin her venture into the outside world. There wasn't much packing to do. She had only four dresses, four small capes and five aprons to take as well as her prayer hats, several black caps and an extra pair of black shoes. Ruth rolled her underwear and black stockings, setting them at the bottom of the suitcase. She decided to wear her high-shoes since there was over a foot of snow. In lieu of a coat, she set aside her triangular woolen shawl, which proved adequate in most temperatures. She would definitely need that.

Looking around her room, she observed it as if for the first time. How long before she'd see it again? She packed her Bible, a notebook, which contained the addresses of several friends and family members and added a pen. She nearly forgot to take her hairbrush and comb. She placed them on her chest of drawers to be packed the next day.

Emma came in while she was folding her dresses.

"How was school?" Ruth asked quietly as she tucked the sleeves of a dress into the folded garment for easier packing.

"Busy. Merv and his sister weren't in school, but a neighbor of theirs came by to tell us they might be back next week. Their mother is worse."

"Such a shame. I remember her more now. Why did they move here from out of state?"

"I heard they didn't have enough land where they were but they were able to sell it at a high profit to some builder or other. They came here and bought property from the grandparents of Happy-Horace Lapp."

"So, are you still thinking you won't write to me when I'm gone?"

Emma smiled and tilted her head. "I might. If you want me to."

"I'd like that."

"You start though. I'll wait to hear how you're getting on with our aunt. I can't wait to learn all about her."

"She may have a photo. Would you want one?"

"I don't know how our bishop would feel about me owning a photo. Better not."

"*Jah.* You're right. Well, I think I have everything ready. *Daed* said tonight most of the family will be by to pray for me."

"*Gut.* What time are they coming?"

"*Mamm* said about six-thirty. That way they can eat first and still be home in time for the little ones to get to bed on time."

"Isaac will probably be walking by the time you return."

"Probably."

"And maybe I'll have a real boyfriend. Maybe Jeremiah. But you don't believe that will happen, do you?"

"Don't be silly. If not Jeremiah, than someone. You are such a *gut* person and pretty, too. A *gut* cook as well. You have much more to offer than I do."

Emma sighed. "I hope I marry soon. I'm tired of teaching."

Katie came into the bedroom and flopped on the bed. "You taking a quilt with you?"

"No. *Mamm* says Aunt Esther will have lots of bedding."

"Probably so. She'll probably have lots of everything. I bet she has a fancy television."

"*Jah,* I bet you're right," Ruth agreed. "I hear there is bad stuff on the television. Murders and naked people."

"I doubt that's true," Katie said. "People make up things like that."

Emma broke into the discussion. "Micah was on *rumschpringe* last year and watched a lot of television, and he said sometimes it was real disgusting."

"But I bet he watched it anyway," Katie added. "He thinks he's Mr. Wonderful."

"He's creepy," Emma stated. "Almost as creepy as Josiah."

"I thought you liked him so much. You wanted me to marry him." Ruth put her hands on her hips.

Emma laughed. "He's *gut* for you, just not for me."

"*Jah,* creepy!" Katie agreed and made a scary face.

"Get out. I have to finish packing. You two are silly as gooses."

"Geese." Katie corrected her, grinning at her sister's mistake.

"Okay, as geese." They laughed together and after a few minutes, Emma and Kate left Ruth alone to finish her packing.

Supper was quieter than usual. Ruth complimented her mother on the stew. Katie had made chocolate pudding, one of Ruth's favorites. Her father was unusually somber and added little to the conversation.

When they finished their meal, Mary suggested Ruth sit and talk with Wayne and her *daed* while her sisters helped with the clean-up.

"*Jah*, sit with us, Ruthie," her *daed* called over.

Wayne was whittling a small shovel for his young nephew while her father sat rocking, a newspaper unfolded on his lap.

Ruth took her place next to her brother. "Looks *gut*, Wayne. Sammy will love it."

Her father peered over his glasses at her. "So, Ruthie, you have everything you need?"

"I think so, *Daed*. I don't need much."

"Take some food with you tomorrow. You might get hungry on the way."

"Maybe an apple."

"You have to promise to be careful in the city."

"I'll be fine, *Daed*."

"Don't overdo your freedom."

Ruth looked at his expression as he spoke. There was fear in his eyes, something unusual for him.

"I will be careful. I know there are bad people out there, but I will not speak to them."

He nodded and looked down at his folded hands.

"You can always come home. Anytime. I will give you money tomorrow only to be used for a bus ticket home–when you're ready."

"You don't need–"

"I'm doing it, Ruth. Remember, things are merely things. It's loved ones who count. What we have here can't be bought."

"*Jah*, I know." Tears formed behind her lids, but she restrained them.

"When it's all over on this earth for us, it will be the mark we leave that counts—not the money in the bank. God sees our mark. He knows our hearts. Temptation is great in the English world. They don't even know they sin against God."

"I want to leave a *gut* mark, *Daed*. I just want to see the other way before I commit."

Her father shook his head, his mouth drawn down. Wayne had stopped carving to watch his sister.

"Please don't worry about me. I'm strong and I love God and will not dishonor Him."

"That's all I need to know. It's time for everyone to come for our prayer. You can finish cleaning with your sisters now."

Ruth rose, went over to her father and leaned down to kiss his cheek. "I will miss you, *Daed.*" He nodded and wiped his eyes.

Promptly at six-thirty, her brothers arrived with their families and then her grandparents drove up in their buggy. Once everyone greeted each other and the littlest ones were distracted with a few toys, the family formed a circle and Ruth's father led them in prayer.

> *Dear Father in heaven,*
> *Tomorrow our Ruthie leaves us for a little while. She is a gut girl, but she will be with people who don't know You, so we ask You to keep her safe. Keep her well. Guide her, Father in every step she takes and bring her back to us soon. In Jesus' name.*

Ruth's brothers added prayers, even Wayne who said, "and make Ruthie sad so she'll come home faster."

Ruth smiled as she continued to keep her eyes closed. She held Katie's hand on one side and Emma's on the other. When Wayne made his appeal, Emma squeezed Ruth's hand.

Once the prayer ended, it was quiet as people reached for hankies and tissues. While it was not unusual for teens to go through the *rumschpringe,* they usually remained at home. For a single girl to actually leave the family was rare and Ruth knew her parents were being tolerant of her decision.

"I want to add, before everyone goes home, I love each one of you and I know I'll return soon. I hope some of you will write to me. *Mamm* has my address."

"We will," Hannah responded. She reached for Ruth and embraced her. "We'll be praying every day for you."

Mark joined them, placing his arms around her. "Everyday, Ruthie."

As each of her loved ones came forward, she received more loving hugs and words of affection.

Her grandmother had tears streaking her face as she hugged Ruth. She had difficulty speaking, but stood several moments before releasing her granddaughter. "I'll write to you."

"Danki, Oma."

Mark was hanging back supposedly to help his grandparents, but he caught Ruth's eye and motioned toward the quiet room. While her grandmother was wrapping some cookies to take home, Ruth followed her brother and stopped once she entered the room.

"I have something for you." He took a small package wrapped in a small grocery bag and handed it over to her. "It's from Jeremiah. He told me not to let anyone else know about it."

Ruth's face burned as she took the article and placed it in her pocket.

"One other thing, Ruthie, he wants you to wait until you're on the bus before opening it."

She nodded.

"Do you have a message for Jeremiah?"

She shook her head no.

"I think he would like you to write."

"There's no point. Thank him for the gift, whatever it is, but I won't be writing to him. I don't think, anyway."

"I'll tell him. He doesn't talk much, so I was surprised when he gave me this."

Ruth remained silent.

"So, I guess I go now. One more hug for your brother, Ruthie, and we see you soon."

After another hug, he joined the others who were getting ready to leave.

After the last person had left, Ruth sat down with her immediate family.

"So, we should turn in now," her *daed* said. "Tomorrow will be busy."

"*Jah*. I'm real tired tonight. More than usual," her mother added.

Once in her bedroom, Ruth allowed her tears to flow. Emma added no words, but held her sister closely. Ruth felt her sister's tears on her own neck and pushed back gently. "I'm not going to my execution," she said. Her voice shook as a small smile escaped her lips.

"*Jah* well, you're right. I should be happy for you, but my heart is heavy, Ruthie. Please write tomorrow night after you get to our aunt's home and tell me everything. Maybe I'll feel more at ease once I know everything is *gut*."

"I promise to try. I might be too tired, though. Now let's get some sleep."

Emma rose and made her way to her own bed. "*Gut nacht*, Ruthie. I love you."

"*Gut nacht*. I love you, too." Ruth lowered the lamp and lay in bed. Jeremiah's gift sat in the pocket of the apron she planned to wear the next day for the trip. Why couldn't he leave her alone?

Her homemade quilt comforted her as she pulled it under her chin, rubbing the soft worn edge as she always did. *Life will be different, that's for sure.*

Chapter Twenty-four

Leroy rode along with Ruth in the rented car. Bob, the driver, chatted pleasantly, but Ruth and her father said little. Mary hadn't slept well and stayed back to rest, but Ruth knew down deep it was because she hated 'good-byes' and avoided them when she could.

The bus was right on time. Her father carried her suitcase over to the bus driver, who was stacking the luggage into the carrier section of the bus. Then he stepped back onto the sidewalk and stood, hat in hand, as she climbed aboard. Ruth took a window seat and waved to her father as he nodded, stern-faced and cheerless. It nearly broke her heart. She was relieved when the bus finally took off.

As difficult as it was to say good-bye to her family, she was excited, knowing the next weeks or months were going to be filled with adventure. An elderly woman sat next to her. She greeted Ruth and then opened a copy of <u>People</u> magazine. Ruth looked out the window, watching the lovely snow-covered landscape pass before her. The bus was filled. There was an elderly Amish woman sitting toward the back of the bus. They had nodded to each other as they boarded, but had not spoken.

After about fifteen minutes passed, Ruth removed the small wrapped package from Jeremiah and took off the two rubber bands holding it together. There was the IPod he had loaned her with a piece of paper, folded into a neat square underneath. She bit her lip as she opened it to read.

> *Dear Ruth,*
> *I hope you have a safe trip to Philadelphia. I wanted you to have this IPod so you would not get bored on your bus ride. I do not want it back. I added pieces by Rachmaninoff and Chopin and Verdi. I think you will like them all. We seem to like the same kind of music.*

I am sorry for the way I acted the last time we were together. I was unfair to you and to Emma. Perhaps we can be friends again when you come back. I would like that. I hope you have a nice time and don't get into any mischief. Ha. Ha.

Your   friend,
Jeremiah

It certainly wasn't a love letter, she thought, disappointed in the content of his note. *Friends. Jah, we'll be friends!* Her anger receded as she turned on the music and placed the earplugs into her ears. She shifted the music button until she heard unfamiliar music. It was piano music by Chopin and very beautiful. She leaned back in her seat and listened while watching the scenery change. Her heart was beating rapidly and she wasn't sure whether it was caused by the trip or the note. Should she have expected more from Jeremiah? They had parted on such a bad note. What could she have hoped for? He had not even come over to her at the last Sing. Instead, he had stood alone all evening barely speaking to his friends. She had spotted him watching her once, but she laughed and carried on as usual, more to impress him with her indifference than because she was happy. No, she wasn't the least bit happy, but things were about to change. New people and new experiences. That's what she needed at this point in time. She closed her eyes and prayed to God for her family. She prayed her parents would not remain sad and in time, she would want to return home.

After stopping twice, the bus finally pulled into the terminal. It was five minutes late. How would she recognize her aunt? They hadn't even discussed that. Of course her aunt wouldn't have a hard time finding her. Her clothing was a dead give-away, and the only other Amish lady was at least seventy.

As the driver unloaded the luggage, an attractive woman in a stylish navy coat came up to her. "Ruth?"

"*Jah*, I'm Ruth Zook."

"I'm your Aunt Esther. Welcome to Philadelphia." She had a warm smile and extended a well-manicured hand to her niece.

Ruth shook it gingerly, hoping she wouldn't knock off one of the nails.

"Do you have much luggage?"

"Only one suitcase. I see it coming."

"How was your trip?"

"*Gut.* The scenery was nice. Ah, here comes my case. I'll get it."

They walked together to the parking lot and her aunt headed toward a shiny beige car which said *Ultima* on the back. It looked as if it had recently come off the assembly line. Her aunt pushed a button on her keys and the trunk popped open. "You can lay your suitcase in there," she suggested and afterward started up the engine. Ruth got in the passenger side and managed to get her seat belt on. It slid on far easier than the one in the taxi.

"I moved three months ago. I'm not at Rittenhouse Square anymore. I have a nice view of the Schuylkill River from my apartment. I think you'll like it." Esther pulled out of the parking lot and headed west. Ruth looked out at the pedestrians walking along, burrowed in their winter attire. There were mounds of blackened snow in piles off the roads. Fresh flakes meandered from the sky, melting as they landed.

"It's a big city for sure."

"Yes," her aunt said as she smiled over at her. "We call it a neighborhood city. I've lived here so long, it's really home now." She seemed to hesitate before speaking again. "How is everyone at your home, Ruth?"

"Fine. My brother's wife had a new baby in August. He's real cute."

"I'm sure." She drove a minute before adding, "I wondered if you wanted to buy some new clothes tomorrow."

"It would be fun. Is it a bother?"

"No, of course not. I figured you'd want to go shopping."

"I always wanted to wear jeans."

Esther looked over and smiled. "Well there are plenty of stores that sell jeans."

"*Jah?* And maybe a pretty dress with flowers."

"That may be harder to find, but we can look." They drove to the next intersection. "I've hit every red light there is," her aunt mentioned as she came to a stop on Walnut Street. "We're almost there."

"Wow, you're close to the stores."

"Yes, and everything else. It's very convenient. I can even walk to the university if I have to."

"Is it safe?"

"Perfectly. At least during the daytime."

"*Daed* warned me about walking at night."

They were quiet for a few minutes. Ruth glanced over at her aunt who was stopped at another traffic light. She looked younger than her fifty-one years. She had auburn hair, which she wore straight and long–past her shoulders. Her profile was refined. It was difficult to tell if she wore make-up in the poor lighting.

"Here we are. I'll park first and we'll go in through the front lobby."

Ruth looked up at a huge modern apartment complex, several stories high. "It's huge," she said under her breath.

"Oh, yes, I guess it is. I'm on the fifth floor. Great view."

Ruth got out of the car and waited for the trunk to pop open. She removed her suitcase and they walked to the entrance, which led to a huge lobby filled with potted plants and tropical trees resting on a colorful marble floor. The front of the building was made up of tall glass windows and at one end of the vast lobby there was a counter with a manager and a uniformed concierge.

Ruth had to consciously close her mouth.

"Hello, Miss Miller," a voice at the desk called out. "I see you found your niece alright."

"Yes. Come over, Ruth, and meet the manager. Ruth, this is Dave Russell. Dave, meet my niece, Ruth Zook. "

He extended a warm hand of welcome. "Hope you enjoy your stay here in the city of brotherly love."

"*Jah*, I like it already." She suddenly felt self-conscious of her clothing as two of the tenants walked by whispering and smiling.

On the way up in the elevator, Ruth was silent. When the doors opened she stood motionless. "We're here, Ruth," her aunt said.

"Already? I didn't even feel it move."

Her aunt laughed. "It is a smooth ride."

Ruth followed her down a short hallway where the entrance to her apartment was enhanced by an attractive paneled door, painted a cream color with white woodwork. Esther unlocked the door and turned a switch by the molding. The whole apartment lit up. At the end of the room were ten-foot windows. White sheers graced the multi-panes and deep burgundy wallpaper covered a three-foot deep cornice. Matching decorator pillows nestled on off-white sofas. The carpeting was lush beige and Ruth, who had removed her shoes immediately, felt she was walking on fresh grass. "Oh my."

Aunt Esther smiled over at her. "I've only been here a few months. I still need more lighting."

Ruth walked over to the coffee table made of cherry and ran her hand over the smooth surface. A fern sat in the center next to a small carved bird. One corner of the room was set up for dining. A glass-topped round table was surrounded by four cherry dining chairs. A crystal bowl sat in the middle of the table.

"I'm afraid you'll be sleeping on the sofa, Ruth. I have only one bedroom."

"That's fine," she said softly, drinking in the beauty.

"Let me have your shawl. You can keep it in the front closet by the door." She walked over and opened the closet door and folded the shawl over a wooden hanger. "I put extra hangers in here for your dresses. If you need more space, let me know. And the chest to the right of the windows has two empty drawers for you."

Ruth nodded and smiled shyly. Her aunt was rich.

"I'll show you my room," Aunt Esther said as she walked toward a doorway opposite the kitchen. The room was as large as the living area. The white spread was quilted and she had several colorful pillows lying on top. A long dresser with a marble top took up most of a wall. A huge gilded mirror stretched the length of the dresser.

Ruth caught her reflection in the mirror. She was startled to see herself. She looked so out of place in this grandeur. Like a character out of a history book. Why had she come here? She should have known she'd never fit into this world.

"Ruth, it's alright." Her aunt came over and put her arm around her shoulders. "You'll get used to being here. It's a bit of culture shock, I'm sure."

"*Jah*, I mean yes. I feel like I'm a fish out of a lake."

"We'll get you some clothing tomorrow. It may help. I'd like to buy you some clothes."

"I brought some money for my expenses. I don't want–"

"Please. I want to do something for you. You're the only family I've seen since…"

"You're very kind, Aunt Esther."

"Do you want something to eat? I have sliced ham and cheese and I bought some rolls at the bakery."

"*Jah*, I could eat."

"Do you drink milk? I bought some."

"*Jah*. Yes."

"Good." She led the way into the kitchen. It shocked Ruth to see how small it was. Apparently the English didn't cook the same way as the Amish. Her kitchen back home was four times the size.

"Now here is where I keep the dishes," Aunt Esther said as she opened a cabinet. "And the silverware is in the drawer next to the sink. I want you to feel at home and help yourself to anything I have." She leaned down and opened another cabinet. "Here are my canned goods. There's tuna and peanut butter as well as other things you might like."

"*Danki.* Thank you."

Her aunt brought out the food and Ruth made her own sandwich, using one of the rolls, and poured herself a glass of milk. Esther made herself one, too, and they sat together at the glass table. Ruth bowed her head first as was her custom. When she finished she looked up to see her aunt staring at her.

"I'd forgotten about praying for my food," she said wistfully. "Next time."

"I didn't bring my quilt."

"I have lots of warm blankets. I keep the temperature around seventy. Do you feel chilly?"

"No, not at all. Our house is never this warm in the winter, except by the coal stove, of course."

"I remember winters as a girl. Yes, I was cold–especially going to bed. Those sheets felt so frigid on my feet. I never want to be that cold again."

"*Jah.* I bet."

After putting their plates in the dishwasher, Esther made up the sofa with sheets and blankets. Ruth helped tuck in the corners of the top sheet. They felt like satin, they were so smooth. She glanced out the window at the city lights. She could barely make out the river in the dark. "Is that the Delaware?"

"No, it's the Schuylkill River. It runs into the Delaware."

"Does it freeze for ice skating?"

"Maybe once in ten years. It flows too quickly. I can take you to an indoor rink, if you'd like."

"It's okay. I'm not a good skater, anyway."

"Have you ever played tennis? We have indoor courts nearby."

"No, but it would be fun to learn."

"You'll need to have shorts or a short skirt. What size do you wear? Size four?"

"I don't know. I sew all my own clothes."

"Of course, I should know that. Well, I'm a six, so maybe my shorts would fit you. We'll check it out. It's too early for bed. Would you like to watch television?"

"I don't see one. Where is it hidden?"

Her aunt laughed. "It's in the entertainment center in the corner over there. Just open the two doors."

Ruth did as she was told and a large flat screened television sat waiting to be turned on. "Take the remote and press 'power'."

Ruth pressed it and in a moment a clear picture came on of a high speed chase in Harrisburg, taken from a helicopter. "I don't know why they bother chasing those cars," her aunt said. "Sometimes innocent drivers get hurt. You have the local news channel. Do you want to see the food channel?"

"They have one just for food?"

"A couple. Here let me check." Ruth handed her the remote. "Yes, here it is."

Ruth sat on an upholstered armchair and gaped as a woman not much older than she was, flipped a cake out of a pan. "Here is the TV guide, Ruth, so you can watch whatever you want."

"It's amazing. I've seen sets on in the stores, so it's not like I didn't know about them, but I've never really watched anything before. The bishop says terrible things come across the sets and it could cause one to sin."

"He's right, Ruth. You're better off not watching much television. I usually try to catch up on the news and sometimes an old movie will come on that I want to see, but I'd rather read most evenings. Do you read much?"

"Not too much. I usually sew at night."

"Oh yes, that's right. I've forgotten so much." Esther looked down at her manicured hands and folded them together. "Do you have anywhere special you'd like to go?"

"Not really, but a friend of mine went to see Betsy Ross's house and said it was cute."

"We can go there. And of course, there's the Liberty Bell."

"*Jah.* That would be fun. What I'd really like to do is go to a concert. Beethoven would be nice."

Her aunt's eyes grew wide. "Really? Do you know much about Beethoven?"

"I know he was deaf when he wrote his last symphony."

"That's right. Have you heard any of his music?"

Ruth reached into her pocket and withdrew the IPod. "A friend gave me this. And he put all Beethoven's symphonies on it plus some Chopin nocturnes and even some other composers' music. I listened to it all the way here on the bus. It's beautiful music."

"I'm impressed. I didn't think it was allowed."

"Well, since I'm old enough for *rumschpringe*, I can listen."

"Yes, you're right. But after you're baptized…"

"I don't think it's so wrong to like music, do you?"

"No, I don't. Not that kind of music. A lot of music today, however, is bad, not only to your ears but to your spirit."

"That's what *Mamm* says, too."

"She's a smart lady."

"*Jah*, she is. She thinks you're smarter than her, though."

"No, maybe I've had more education, but I'm no smarter. Sometimes, I think the opposite." Her eyes seemed to wander back to another time. Ruth noticed there was sadness in her expression and wondered what she was thinking.

They watched a cooking show and when it was finished, Ruth asked if she could take a bath since she felt uncomfortable after traveling all day. Her aunt showed her how to turn on the water and control the temperature. She handed Ruth a set of plush white towels and a washcloth for her exclusive use. Even her own soap. "Do you need shampoo?"

"Oh, I forgot to bring it."

"No problem. There is shampoo and conditioner on a shelf as well as a new deodorant. Help yourself. I have several calls to make, but I'll see you before we turn in. I hope you'll like it here, Ruth."

"I know I will. Thank you for all your trouble."

"You are no trouble, believe me," Esther replied, smiling tenderly at her niece. "Tomorrow we'll have a wonderful time together."

"*Jah*, I believe so," Ruth said.

She could barely sleep thinking about her upcoming adventure with this lovely lady she called her aunt.

Chapter Twenty-five

Ruth awoke around six. Since it was still dark out, she turned on a light. How simple. Merely press a button and there was light to read by. She heard the heat check on. It seemed like a dream. Ruth dressed in a navy blue dress and put on her apron and cape. After twisting her hair into a bun, she placed her white *kapp* on top and let the streamers hang as was her custom. She looked in the mirror in the bathroom and stared. An Amish girl stared back. It would feel strange to wear jeans and a sweater like she'd seen the tourists wear.

Ruth tip-toed into the kitchen and poured herself a glass of orange juice. She took out some paper she'd brought with her and started a letter to her family.

> *Dear Mamm, Daed, Emma, Katie, and Wayne,*
>
> *I had a good trip on the bus, but was tired from travel. Aunt Esther was right there to meet me. She had no trouble picking me out. Ha. HaHer apartment is so beautiful. She must be very, very rich. The windows almost touch the ceiling. The ceiling is so high. Daed, you would not want to build such a house. I took a bath in her great big tub. I could almost swim in it.*
>
> *Today we are going to go shopping. She wants to buy me something although I would rather pay for it myself. I woke up early and she is still in her bedroom. Now I am going to read my Bible and say my prayers, but I wanted to let you all know I am fine.*
>
> *Love, Ruth*

Ruth sealed the envelope, placed a stamp on the corner and laid it aside while she read from her Bible. She had only the book of Revelation left to read. Each year she started at Genesis and read the entire Bible. By New Year's Eve, she expected to be finished with Revelation at which time she would start all over.

After Ruth finished her reading, her aunt appeared in a terry robe. Her hair was hanging loosely about her shoulders. She looked younger than her years even without any make-up.

"Good morning, Ruth. Did you sleep well?"

"*Jah*. It was so warm and comfy. I had some juice already."

"Oh, good. Would you like eggs this morning? I also have a couple boxes of cereal."

"Do you have oatmeal?"

"Yes. I'll get it out for you." Her aunt glanced over on the table where the letter stood. "Ah, I see you've already written to the family. Good. I'm sure they're concerned."

"A little maybe, but because I'm staying with you, they allowed me to come."

"That's nice to hear. I'm the black sheep in the family, you know, so it's good they trust me with their daughter."

"*Mamm* wants to talk about you more than *Daed*. She said you weren't close growing up. I guess because you're older and she was sick and all."

"True. No, we weren't really close. How about you, Ruth? You have two sisters, right?"

"*Jah*. Emma, who's two years older and Katie, who's two years younger."

"And you're eighteen now?"

"Almost nineteen. My birthday is April tenth."

"Well, if you're still here, we'll have to celebrate."

"Mmm." Ruth wondered where she would be come April. It seemed like a long way off, but time went quicker the older she became.

After they ate together, her aunt sat having a second cup of coffee. "Let's discuss your clothing. New Year's Eve, I'm having a few friends over to help celebrate. Even though we live casually most of the time, we dress rather formally for New Year's, so I'd like you to pick out a special dress for the occasion. Would you be comfortable with my idea?"

"If it's not too expensive."

"Ruth, I have no children and all my family is in Lancaster County, as you know. I make a nice income and I'd really appreciate it if you'd let me indulge you while you're here. It would give me great pleasure." She reached over and touched Ruth's hand gently.

"I guess when you put it that way, I have little choice," Ruth replied with a wide smile.

"Good. Now let me shower and dress and then I'm taking you to a very special place."

It was flurrying as they drove to a parking lot in the center of the city. The traffic was heavy being a Friday. People bustled about, arms loaded with packages and plastic shopping bags. Crossing the street was a major event. You needed eyes surrounding your head. Ruth's aunt took her by the arm at one point and pushed her quickly across Market Street to a large old building which was made of stone. "This is the old Wanamaker Store. It was taken over by Macy's years ago."

"It's really big," Ruth said with awe as they entered the building. She stopped and stared. "Oh, my goodness. I don't believe this is real."

The huge expansive interior was surrounded by several levels of ornately decorated balconies. At the end of the Grand Court, as her aunt called it, was an enormous blue Christmas tree with thousands upon thousands of twinkling lights. Above the tree, creating a drapery effect, were strings of colorful lights and character images. The most spectacular of all was the organ music which filled the entire cavity of the department store. Music from a real pipe organ was something Ruth had heard discussed, but never imagined seeing. She was unable to speak and her aunt stood next to her and smiled.

Busy shoppers passed by, occasionally bumping into them, but Ruth was aware of nothing but the scene in front of her. If this was the only place she went to during her *rumschpringe,* it would be quite enough to last a lifetime. The organist was playing Christmas Carols. Not the Frosty snowman type, no–"Oh, Holy Night," "Silent Night," "It Came Upon a Midnight Clear," and other familiar carols. Ruth's heart was pumping along with the music. She glanced over at her aunt. "I can not believe this. No one will believe me."

"But you'll remember it."

"Always."

The concert continued for a few more minutes and when it ended, Ruth and her aunt walked around the first floor. Ruth stopped at the famous eagle which graced the center of the store on a high platform and she let out a long breath. "Wow."

"When you're ready, we'll go to the junior department and then the misses."

"That would be *gut*."

They took the elevator to the dress department. It was all a bit overwhelming. Most people barely gave Ruth a glance, but the children seemed fascinated by her appearance. Ruth smiled at them and one little girl grinned back and scooted behind her mother's coat.

Once they found the right department, they started rummaging through the racks. "How do you like this dress?" her aunt asked, holding up an aqua chiffon garment with layered tiers.

"I think it's beautiful, but the top is too low."

"Oh, I hadn't noticed. You're right." She put it back on the rack and shifted a few more to the side. "I guess most of them are rather daring."

"I see one I like," Ruth exclaimed, taking a black silk dress with a high neckline and long sleeves from the row of garments.

Her aunt laughed. "I thought you wanted something bright and colorful."

"Oh, I did. You're right. I'll look some more." She selected a light green dress and an off-white dress with lace overlay."

"That could pass as a wedding dress," her aunt commented.

"Oh my, it's too fancy for sure. And the price-tag! Goodness, I can't believe such prices. I can sew five dresses for what it costs for one. Let me check the rack over there with the sale dresses."

"I don't want you to worry about price."

"No, but I see a pretty one with colors." She walked over and pulled out a paisley silk with shades of rose and green and touches of beige. "What do you think? You like it?" Ruth held it against her front.

"I do. Your hair goes well with it, I think. Do you want to drop your hair down in the changing room and we'll see?"

"Should I?"

"Well, aren't you going to wear it down from now on?"

"I didn't think about it, but why not?" Ruth grinned at her aunt. "*Jah*, why not look like English for a while. What harm can there be?"

The dress fit perfectly. It had a V-neck, but it didn't show too much and her aunt said she could add a small safety pin from the back of the material so nothing would show. It fit snuggly in the waist and the fabric dropped gracefully to mid-calf length. The image was flawed by her black stockings and high shoes. Ruth took them off and stood barefoot while her aunt un-twisted her long golden brown hair and allowed it to fall gracefully to just above her waistline.

"You might consider cutting it a little," she suggested as she removed a brush from her purse and smoothed out the snarls.

"Emma's hair is prettier. She has curly hair."

Esther smiled at her through the full-length mirror. "Your mother had curls when she was young."

"*Jah*? It's gotten thin through the years, I guess."

"It doesn't help to keep it so taut." Esther stood back. "There. Look at yourself. You're stunning."

A flush went up Ruth's neck and covered her cheeks at the compliment. "I don't want to be proud."

"Of course not, Ruth. I'm sorry, I guess I meant you've hidden your beauty. You do want the dress, don't you? Or we can check other racks."

Ruth turned sideways and peered at herself in the mirror. She turned completely around quick enough to cause her skirt to flare out. "I love it, Aunt Esther. It feels so wonderful-*gut*."

Her aunt nodded. "Good. Now let's buy you some pretty heels to go with it."

"I've never walked in heels. I hope I don't fall down."

"We won't buy spikes. A medium heeled shoe would complete your outfit."

"This is fun," Ruth said as her aunt helped remove the new dress.

"We'll head for the shoe department. You'll need everyday shoes too. Maybe some sneakers. Do you ever go for a run or a hike?"

"Only if my brothers chase me."

Her aunt laughed. "I used to run every other day before I went to work. But since I hit fifty, I walk more than I run. It keeps me from gaining weight and is good for my bones."

"*Jah*, you have a nice figure. Not fat or flabby."

"Thank you, Ruth. I'll go pay for the dress while you finish dressing. Meet me at the check out."

They found some lovely two-inch brown suede heels, which picked up colors in the dress, as well as a pair of running shoes, and her aunt bought her three pairs of panty hose. Then Esther purchased two pairs of jeans and a white heavy pull-over sweater plus another top with long sleeves and a boat neckline in teal blue. "You look so good in blues, Ruth, with your lovely hair and complexion."

"Thank you. I feel like a princess. You're way too good to me."

"I'm having a ball. Thanks for letting me do this. Are you hungry yet for lunch?"

"I could eat something."

"They have a café on the third floor terrace. Unless you're looking for a large meal."

"Oh, no, a salad or sandwich would be fine."

Ruth felt conspicuous in her plain clothes and wished she was wearing a pair of her new jeans to fit in with the young crowd. She had put her hair back into a bun and covered it with her *kapp*.

After they ate, her aunt insisted on purchasing a winter coat for her. It was camel hair and had a belt. She bought her a matching hat with a brim and kid gloves. "We forgot to purchase boots for you. Let's go back to the shoe department."

"Can't I wear my old ones?"

"You can, of course, but I was thinking of dressier boots with a heel. How did you feel walking in your new heels?"

"Okay. It takes some practice, I think, but I feel so...so cool."

Her aunt laughed and patted her shoulder. "You look 'cool' young lady."

Around four they headed for home and Ruth spread all her new garments out on the sofa. She went from one to the next, touching the fabrics and exclaiming over the colors. "I don't know what I'll do with all these when I go home."

"Maybe you'll decide to be 'English' like me," her aunt said with a twist of a smile.

"I don't know. It's possible, but I really can't say."

"Of course not. I was kidding. If you decide to return to Amish ways, I'll donate them to a worthy cause. In the meantime, I want you to enjoy them."

"I will." Her aunt was sitting across from the sofa and Ruth went over and knelt on the floor next to her. "You are so kind. I can never repay you."

"I feel repaid just to have you here. My sister's child." Her eyes became moist and Ruth rose and sat next to her embracing her in her arms.

Neither of them were especially hungry that evening, so they ate bowls of chocolate ice cream.

"I feel so naughty," Ruth said, smiling.

"Sometimes ice cream is the only thing I crave. So would you like to watch television or read? I have cards if you want to play rummy or anything."

"Actually, I think I should write in my journal before I forget anything."

"I didn't know you kept a journal."

"I started one the day before yesterday. I want something to read someday when I'm old–to remind me of this special time in my life."

"Good idea. I'll get my latest journal and join you."

Her aunt put a Braham's string quartet on and they sat together quietly, enjoying their special time. Around ten, her aunt turned in for the night and Ruth followed suit, after a long relaxing bath. When she dried off, she looked in a drawer for hair-cutting scissors and carefully removed about a foot of her long tresses. "*Jah*, better now," she said to her reflection. She smiled and went to bed.

Chapter Twenty-six

The next day Aunt Esther took Ruth into center city again. Ruth wore her sneakers and a pair of jeans with her new sweater and coat. She avoided wearing her *kapp,* but left her hair in a familiar twist.

They decided to see the Liberty Bell and Independence Hall first. "This is where the early settlers debated and adopted the Declaration of Independence, Ruth, as well as the Constitution."

"I remember learning that in school and now I'm seeing it for myself. Actually, some of the younger children in our area came here by bus last year."

"It's good they learn their history. Let's walk over to Carpenter's Hall next where the first Continental Congress met in 1774. We can go to the Betsy Ross home after lunch if you want. It's not a long walk. Then I'll show you Elfreth's Ally, but right now we should look for a place to eat."

They walked off the main mall area and found a restaurant where they split a pizza. "I eat pizza sometimes at home," Ruth said. "We have to go to town first, though. *Mamm* won't make it. She says you have to be Italian to make good pizza."

Esther laughed. "Probably true. This is excellent. Are you having as much fun as I am, Ruth?"

"I've never had so much fun, Aunt Esther. My journal is not going to have enough space."

"We can't see everything in one day. I want to take you to see the 'Love' sculpture and Franklin Institute. But if we have time today, since we'll be near Christ Church, we'll stop there for a few minutes. It's a very early church."

"We have many more days before I go home, I'm sure. I was thinking, I need to find a job, even if it's part-time. Do you have any ideas?"

"You don't have to, you know."

"I do. I really don't feel right not to carry my weight. Besides, when you're teaching again, I'll be bored with nothing to do. Your apartment is wonderful, but it wouldn't take me long to clean it."

"Well, maybe I'll check at the university."

"I could work in a kitchen. I wouldn't mind cooking. Or in a nursery for babies."

"Let me ask around when I get back to teaching. In the meantime we have over a week together first. Maybe we'll drive one day out to the main line and I'll show you some nice small towns."

"Sounds like fun. I want to see everything."

"I haven't forgotten about the concert. I'll check that out, too."

After they ate, they walked block after block, Esther giving an informative talk as they went. Ruth was surprised at how knowledgeable her aunt was about the history of her city. It was amazing how quickly Ruth got into being a regular tourist. She felt inconspicuous in her new clothing and enjoyed wearing sneakers.

Around five, they went back to the car and drove home. She spent another evening penning her thoughts with music playing in the background. The Amish way looked less enchanting each day. Ruth decided to wait until she heard from home before writing again. She thought less about Jeremiah, though her conscience bothered her. She needed to send off a thank-you note. After all, he had parted with something very special when he gave her his IPod, which now sat in a drawer unused.

After breakfast the next day, Esther sat with her second cup of coffee at the glass table while Ruth looked through a poetry book she found on the coffee table.

"Today I need to start preparing for the New Year's party, Ruth. I can't believe tomorrow night ends another year. The time goes faster all the time for me."

"I'd love to help with the cooking."

"Super. We'll work together. I have all the ingredients purchased already. We're having *hors d'oeuvres*, *quiches* and *petit fours*. Nothing special. 'Picking food' I call it."

"I don't know how to make *petit fours*. I don't even know what they are."

"They're delicious little cakes, but I purchase them already made. They're in the freezer. Don't let me forget to take them out early tomorrow."

"I'm not sure about making *hors d'oeuvres*, either. Are they hard?"

"Not the ones I make. I confess, Ruth, I don't enjoy cooking much. I buy a lot of prepared dinners from a small deli near the university, or I go out to eat. Let me get out my recipes and you see which ones you'd like to help me with." She got up and opened a drawer in the kitchen and removed several recipe cards with handwritten instructions. She sat back down at the table and handed Ruth the cards. Ruth decided she'd make the crusts for the *quiche* and help with the finger sandwiches.

They worked all afternoon, chatting about anything and everything. Ruth shared stories about her brothers and their little ones and talked about Emma and Katie. Esther seemed interested in hearing about her family and asked questions as they went along. While Ruth rolled out the pie dough for six *quiches,* Esther began making the fillings. The aromas coming from the oven made Ruth's mouth water. Though she didn't care much about cooking at home, this was different. Why, she couldn't explain. Maybe it was because she was doing it with her aunt. She had many aunts at home in Lancaster County, but compared to her Aunt Esther, they seemed boring and old-fashioned.

After a light supper, Ruth forced herself to write to Jeremiah.

Dear Jeremiah,

Mark gave me the IPod the night before I left. I really appreciate your thoughtfulness. Danki.

I am having a wonderful time visiting my aunt. She bought me new clothes and I saw the liberty bell and lots of other things.

I hope you are well.

Sincerely,

Ruth

She folded the letter and sealed it.

There, that should do it and I hope he and Emma get together, because I'll never be his wife. Maybe I won't be anyone's wife. Maybe I'll be like my aunt and have a real *life.*

The next morning she took the letter downstairs and mailed it in the lobby. She was wearing a pair of her new jeans and the white sweater. Her aunt had convinced her to let her hair hang loose and even suggested a touch of lipstick. The manager looked up when she came out of the elevator and stared at her. "Miss, are you looking for someone?"

"No, it's me, Esther Miller's niece."

His smile spread across his face. "I never would have guessed it. My, you're a beautiful young lady."

"*Danki,* I mean thank you. Here, I need to mail this."

"I'll take it for you. The mail was already delivered so it won't go out until the second of January. But I was sorting today's mail and I believe...yes, you and your aunt each got some mail." He handed her a short stack of first class mail as well as advertisements.

Ruth nodded and smiled, feeling terribly self-conscious after his remarks. When she got back in the apartment, she gave her aunt her mail and then opened a letter from her sister.

> *Dear Ruth,*
>
> *We miss you already. We got your letter and it sounds like you are having fun. I am writing back the very next minute. Mamm was real quiet after we read it. I think she's sad you are away and maybe a little scared. Like you might not want to be Amish again.*
>
> *I have sad news. Merv Kuhn's mother died yesterday. We will go to the funeral, of course. I haven't seen Merv or his sister. I don't want to go over there since I don't know them that well. But after the funeral in a couple weeks, Mamm's going to have them come for dinner or supper. Maybe on a Saturday.*

*Wayne fell off his bike and bruised his face.
He is lucky he didn't break something.* Daed *was
not happy because he was late coming home from
his friend's house and Daed had to milk the cows by
himself. Now Wayne is not allowed on his bike for a
long while.*

*The other news is about our Bishop King.
He had a heart attack and is in bed. Everyone is
upset. I will let you know if he dies or gets better.*

Say hallo *to Aunt Esther and write again
soon.*

Love, Emma

Ruth placed the letter into her pocket as her aunt came into
the living room from her bedroom.

"Ruth, do you want to shower or bathe first? It's getting
late."

"When are your friends coming?"

"Not until around nine, but it's already eight o'clock."

"I'll shower after you, it's faster than a bath."

"I'll fix your hair for you if you'd like."

"*Danki,* I mean thanks. I'd like you to."

After they were each showered and partially dressed her
aunt brushed out Ruth's hair while blow drying it. She turned the
brush a certain way which gave her hair an attractive upward tilt
and moved the center part, keeping it undefined, off to the side.
"Like it?" her aunt asked through the mirror.

"*Jah.* It doesn't look like me."

"Wait till I put some eye make-up on you and a touch of
color in your cheeks."

"My. I'll feel like a new Ruthie."

"Maybe you're *becoming* a new Ruthie." Her aunt had a
pensive expression. Ruth wondered if she missed not being a
mother. She seemed so tender-hearted.

After Ruth put on her dress and stockings, her aunt put a
linen cloth around her shoulders and applied light make-up, adding

a touch of lipstick at the end. "There. How's that?" Ruth turned towards the mirror as her aunt removed the cloth.

"Wow!"

"Yes, 'wow' is right. You look fantastic! Now I have to get dressed myself. Don't wipe your mouth. The lipstick has to set a minute."

While her aunt was getting dressed, Ruth walked around the living room admiring its beauty. Her aunt had lit several candles and put on classical music. Everything looked perfect. The food was all prepared and just needed to be heated up. When Ruth had asked how many were coming, her aunt said, "Oh, between thirty and forty."

Ruth's stomach was doing flips all day. This was almost a test. Could she pass for a regular person? Did she really want to?

The intercom phone went off and Esther called out from her bedroom. "Get that, Ruth. It's probably a guest."

She relayed the man's name and was told to send him up.

Soon there was a gentle knock on the door and when she opened it, the most handsome man Ruth had ever seen was standing there with flowers in his hand.

Chapter Twenty-seven

"Hello! And who are you?" the handsome stranger wiped his feet and entered the vestibule. He handed the flowers to Ruth and took off his overcoat.

"I'm Esther's niece."

"She never told me she had a gorgeous niece. Where has she been hiding you?"

Ruth heard her aunt come through the living room. "Darrel, I should have known you'd be first to arrive."

"I just met your amazing relative."

"Yes, Ruth, this is Darrel Storm. He lives in the next apartment building. Darrel, meet my niece, Ruth Zook."

"So, you never told me about her. Here are some roses for my favorite neighbor." He handed Esther the bouquet, kissed her on the cheek and went over to the hall closet to hang up his coat and scarf. "Your aunt and I play tennis. Do you play, Ruth?"

"Not yet, but I'd like to learn."

"So where do you live?"

"I'm from Lancaster County."

"Amish country and your name is 'Zook.' Huh, you wouldn't pass for Amish, I'm afraid."

Ruth laughed and covered her mouth. "Oh, but I am. I'm only visiting my aunt for awhile."

Esther smiled as she put her arm around Ruth's shoulder. "I hope she'll stay for a long while. We're having so much fun getting acquainted."

"I hope she stays too. I can't believe you're Amish. You're so beautiful. I never saw an Amish woman dress like this."

"*Jah*, well, I never did either," Ruth said with a smile. "I'm on my *rumschpringe*."

"Oh, yeah. Freedom march sort of?" he asked.

"Sort of."

"I thought you were bringing a date," Esther said to Darrel.

"Thankfully, she had to cancel. Her dog died."

The intercom went off again and Esther answered it. "Oh, send them up. Thanks Dave. Yes, I know she's beautiful. And no, she's not married. You're a little old for her, aren't you?" She laughed, adding, "No, I don't have any more hiding in my apartment. Yes, Happy New Year's to you, too. You know most of my friends–please send them up when they arrive."

"Dot and Murray are headed upstairs. I'd better get the punch going. Ruth, you entertain my friends while I prepare the drinks."

"Don't you need my help?" Ruth asked, nearly stuttering.

"She doesn't. Believe me. Your aunt can do just about anything she sets her mind to. You should see her back-hand."

"I heard that Darrel. You're not so bad yourself," Esther called out from the kitchen.

A knock on the door and the Klinger's arrived. Soon another knock followed by laughter. Ruth opened the door to six new faces. They all acted surprised to see her answer the door and she stammered out her name and relationship, trying all the while to remember names and attach them to the smiling faces.

By ten, there were at least thirty people celebrating. A few of the finger foods were placed around the room and everyone had either a punch cup or a tall glass with some kind of liquid. Ruth suspected there was alcohol, but no one acted inebriated. She discovered the majority of guests were middle-aged fellow professors from the university.

Darrel followed Ruth around as she passed out the cheese and chips. After replenishing the plate with more cheese, Ruth stood in the kitchen for a moment with Darrel. "Don't you have anything better to do than follow me around?" she asked, stifling a grin.

"You're the only person under forty in the whole place. Besides, I'm hoping you'll accept a date with me, after you get to know me better."

"*Jah*? Would I be safe?" she gave him a slightly crooked smile.

"Do you want to be?"

Oh, dear, she hadn't expected that. "*Jah*. I do." Her smile dropped.

"Too bad. Okay, I'll be on my best behavior."

"So do you work at the university too?" Ruth asked him, changing the subject.

"Nope. I'm an attorney with Hill & Daniels in town. Heard of them?"

"Afraid not. Don't forget I'm just a poor stupid Amish girl."

"No one can say that about you. I haven't actually talked to someone Amish. Tell me about your life."

"You don't really want to know."

"I do. I'm serious. I think it's fascinating. You don't use cars, do you?"

"We don't own cars but we can ride in them."

"Ah. And your clothes," he mentioned, scanning her from her heels to her flowing hair. "They don't look like these."

"No." She laughed and shook her head. "They are very plain. The plainer the better. And I like to look plain."

"Impossible! You could never be plain. How come you're not married? Don't the Amish marry out of grammar school?"

"Not that early. But by sixteen or seventeen, you—"

"I'm almost afraid to ask, but how old are you?"

"I'm eighteen, almost nineteen."

"Like eighteen-and-a-half?" he winked at her and she wanted to swoon. He was like a movie star, even though she knew very little about movie stars.

She blushed and looked down.

"I don't mean to tease. I'm twenty-four. Am I too old for you?"

"Well, we're not engaged are we?" She was amazed at their repartee.

"Not yet." He turned around looking for someone. Spotting his hostess he called out, "What about dance music, Es?"

"You can change the music, Darrel. You know where I keep my collection."

"Wait right here." He went over and changed from classical to fifties-style dance music. Some of the others called out and teased him about his choice but soon three couples began to sway with the music, taking small steps to avoid a collision.

"Sinatra," he said when he returned. "Ever dance to his music?"

"I never danced at all. I have no idea how."

"It's simple. Here, follow me." He put his left arm around her waist and lifted her left hand into his right. Ruth felt her blood pressure go through the roof.

"Now, try to relax. That's it. Move your right foot when I move my left." He took a step and she followed suit. He moved again and she copied his action. "See? Now you can say you know how to dance."

Ruth laughed and looked down at their feet, trying to mimic his moves. After several minutes, she felt her body relax and they began to work as a unit. "You pick up quickly, Ruth. You're doing great. Now stop looking at your feet and look into my eyes and feel the music. You're getting the hang of it. You have beautiful eyes. Like pools of water."

"Uh, oh, I think you're flirting with me."

"You think right. Do you like it?"

"I...I don't know."

"Does it frighten you to be in my arms–almost a stranger?"

She stopped and moved away, dropping her arm from his shoulder. "Why did you ask that?"

"I'm sorry. I didn't expect you to react like that. I'm afraid I tease too much. Let's start over."

"I think I'd like something to eat."

"It's almost midnight. Do you want to wait? Only ten minutes."

Ruth had heard about the custom of kissing at midnight and it made her nervous. On the one hand, she found herself attracted to this man, but she felt uneasy about his boldness. No, a kiss would not be welcome.

"I'm really hungry. I'll be back." She walked into the kitchen and tried to relax. Her breaths had become quick and shallow while they danced. She was uncomfortable with the feelings she had when his arm was around her and the smell of his after-shave lingered in her mind. Only Jeremiah had ever made her feel like this. Ruth reached for a watercress tea sandwich and stuffed it in her mouth. Certainly he wouldn't want to kiss her with a mouth full of food. A few minutes passed and she peeked out. Darrel was talking with a man named Gary in the corner. Esther had the television on and there was a view of New York City with a huge lit ball on a tower or something. People were counting down to the big moment as the numbers flashed on the screen. "Four - three - two - one! Happy New Year!"

People started hugging and kissing and she noticed Darrel looking around the room. He spotted her and walked toward the kitchen. She had swallowed her sandwich and before she had time to think, he had his arms around her and his mouth on hers. While not unpleasant, it was still not wanted. It was over before she had time to react. He released her and wished her a Happy New Year. "I think we're going to get to know each other real well before this year is over," he said under his breath. Her heart was pounding but whether it was from desire or fear, she knew not which.

Around two-thirty, the last of the guests left the apartment and Esther slipped her heels off and sprawled out on a chair. "Let's relax a minute, Ruth. I'm exhausted."

"*Jah*, me too." Ruth followed suit by removing her shoes and sat on the sofa.

"Did you have fun?" her aunt asked.

Ruth nodded, but looked down at her lap. "Most of the time."

Esther frowned. "What happened the rest of the time?"

"I don't know how to answer."

"Was it Darrel? He can come on rather strong, but he doesn't mean anything by it. He's really quite harmless."

"I hope so. He gave me a kiss at midnight."

Her aunt looked relieved. "Is that all? Oh, Ruth, in our society a kiss on New Year's doesn't mean anything. He kissed me too."

"Like he did me? Like so hard and all?"

"Well, probably not quite the same. I'm old enough to be his mother. No, he kissed me lightly, more like a peck."

"It was not a peck with me, Aunt Esther. More like a marriage kiss."

"Oh dear, I'll have to talk to him. He doesn't understand the Amish lifestyle. Don't be too hard on him, Ruth. He's quite an amazing young man. Aside from his skills in tennis, he's a promising young attorney with a good firm. He has an excellent future and he seemed quite taken with you. You never know."

"I'm not looking for a boyfriend, Aunt Esther. I just had my heart broken by a young man who I fell in love with. I don't want any romance right now."

"I see. I'm sorry you broke up. Want to talk about it?"

"I'm so tired. Maybe tomorrow."

"Of course. I don't mean to pry. I suppose we should turn in. You can use the bathroom first. I'm going to clean up a little more before turning in, though. I hate the thought of facing all this in the morning."

"Let me do it, Aunt Esther. You get ready for bed. I want to, please."

Her aunt patted her on the shoulder as she headed toward the bathroom. "You are a doll, and yes, I'll take you up on it. Thanks, Ruth. See you sometime in the morning. Not too early and by the way, Happy New Year.

"*Jah*, to you, too." Ruth picked up dirty plates from the coffee table and made her way toward the sink, reflecting on the evening and her midnight kiss.

Chapter Twenty-eight

Ruth awoke at nine thirty to the aroma of fresh coffee. Her aunt was already sitting quietly at the table reading a journal and having her second cup of java. "Good morning, sleepyhead," she said, as she smiled at Ruth, who rose and stretched her arms.

"My, I hardly ever sleep in this late."

"What time did you finally get to bed?"

"I was in bed by three-thirty, but I couldn't sleep. Too wound up, I guess." Ruth reached across her bed and put on a bathrobe her aunt had loaned her, poured herself a glass of orange juice and sat at the table.

"I had trouble myself. I need this," Esther said, pointing to her mug. "How about you? Do you ever drink coffee?"

"I have, but I prefer tea. Herbal tea."

"I have some in the cupboard. Do you want me to put water on?"

"Thanks, but I think I'll take a shower. Do you have plans today?"

"I thought I'd leave it up to you. It's a holiday so I imagine a lot of places will be closed."

"Maybe I'll relax instead. I need to catch up in my journal and with my devotions. Unless you want to go somewhere." Ruth sipped at her juice.

"I'm content to relax. There's *quiche* left over for supper."

"Sounds *gut*. I didn't eat any last night."

"So how did you like my friends? Other than Darrel, I mean."

"They seem nice. I didn't talk too much. I guess I felt out of place."

"Oh, Ruth, you were fine. Most people would never guess you were Amish."

"I'm not sure that's a *gut* thing. I'm feeling a little overwhelmed."

"Ah, I guess you are. Darrel didn't help any. I have to speak to him about his behavior."

"Oh, please don't say anything to him. I'm sure he didn't mean to upset me. I'm just not used to men being so forward."

"Tell me about the man who broke your heart."

Ruth pushed her hair out of her eyes and folded her arms. "His name is Jeremiah. He's twenty and he's a buggy maker. In fact he works with my brother, Mark, in Bird-in-Hand. Anyway he confessed to loving me."

"Is that a bad thing?"

"No, if there are no obstacles."

"But there are?"

"*Jah*. Emma. She loves him and she thinks he cares about her."

"Oh, that is a problem." Esther spread cream cheese on her bagel. "Want the other half, Ruth?"

"No, *danki*."

"But Jeremiah doesn't love her back, is that it?"

"*Jah*. He says he has no interest in her at all, but how can I love a man who my sister loves without hurting her too much?"

"Maybe you need to have an honest discussion with her and explain the whole thing."

"She would only accuse me of being jealous or stealing him. It was easier to pull away from the whole situation."

"So that's why you came here?"

"Only partly. I've been restless for the last year or so. I'm not sure about a lot of the Amish ways. Like music, for instance. I see nothing wrong with classical music."

"Mmm. How well I know what you're going through."

"Aunt Esther, are you glad you left?"

Her aunt turned her coffee mug around a couple of times, staring at the brown liquid. "Most of the time. Sometimes though I think it was a mistake. Every one has to make up his or her own mind. It's not an easy decision."

"I pray about it a lot but one minute I'm sure I'll remain in this society, and the next minute I yearn to be home, living a simpler life."

"You haven't given it sufficient time, Ruth. You need to relax and allow yourself to live this way for awhile before you can make an intelligent decision. I wanted so much to finish high school and go to college. It was always my desire to one day teach. I thought about teaching in the Amish school, but I needed more. I love what I do."

"Were you ever in love?"

She nodded and her lips turned down. Ruth was sorry she'd asked.

"Only once. I met a man at the university–a fellow student working on his Master's Degree in English Lit, as I was. We started seeing each other after class. We went out steadily for two years." She stopped and took a sip of coffee.

"Were you engaged?"

"No. He came from high society and when I met his family and they found out my background they did everything in their power to break us up."

"And he listened to them?"

"Not at first, but they set him up with a young woman who was part of their country club set. She did everything she could to attract his attention. Called him constantly. I tried to tell him, but he couldn't believe anyone would be so conniving. Eventually he got tired of hearing me, I guess, because we stopped going out and eventually I read about his engagement in the paper. He didn't even have the decency to tell me in person. It blew my mind. I've dated a few times since, but quite frankly, I don't care anymore. I have lots of friends and my profession keeps me busy. And now," she said with a strained smile, "I have my niece–for a while anyway."

"You're such a nice person though. I'm sure you could have a happy marriage with a *gut* person."

"Ruth, there comes a time when you realize you're better off on your own. Not everyone mind you, but that time has come for me. I'm not unhappy, really."

She rose from the table, putting an end to further conversation, and took her plate and cup into the kitchen. "I'll hold off on running the dishwasher until you're done showering."

"Okay. I'll go in now." Ruth knew it had been difficult for her aunt to tell her story. She never mentioned her relationship with God, if she even had one. Maybe someday she'd share more. At least she had opened up about her past. Ruth considered it a privilege to be her confidante.

It was a relaxing day. They talked at length, but the subject matter remained light. Then her aunt watched a news show while Ruth read from the book of Revelation. Much of it she found difficult to understand, though she'd heard many sermons where the ministers attempted to interpret it.

When the show was over, her aunt turned off the television and turned to Ruth. "I see you're reading the Bible. Do you read everyday?

"I try to, though sometimes I miss. I make it a goal to read through the whole Bible every year, so some days I read for an hour or so."

"That's very commendable." Esther sat back in her chair and folded her arms. "I used to read it."

"Not any more?"

"Not since I made the decision to remain in Philadelphia."

"Don't you believe in God any more?"

She let out a sigh. "I go back and forth. Sometimes I'm sure he exists, but other times…"

"He does, Aunt Esther."

Her aunt smiled over at her. "You sound very sure."

"I am. I feel his presence in my soul." Ruth put her hand over her heart. "He answers my prayers."

"All of them?"

"In time, though I don't always like His answers."

Her aunt seemed amused at her response. "I don't think it helped that I lost the only man I cared about to another."

"Have you forgiven him?"

Esther looked up. Her brows rose, as she paused. "I guess I have. Perhaps there is a small part of me that still holds onto my 'righteous' anger, if there is such a thing."

"I shouldn't talk. I'm still angry with Jeremiah for not being willing to wait for me. I had hoped he would understand my feelings. I mean how could I possibly hurt my sister by dating him?"

"But you still love him?"

Ruth looked down at her open Bible. She closed it and set it on the table next to the sofa. "I do. I don't want to, but I know if I'm honest with myself, my feelings haven't changed. I try not to think about him. It makes it easier, I guess."

Her aunt nodded. "Strange you asked me about forgiveness. I've almost enjoyed these years of feeling betrayed–as if somehow holding on to my hate would be justified. Perhaps I need your prayers, Ruth."

"How about your own?"

"He wouldn't hear me anymore. I've turned my back on Him."

"But He hasn't turned from you. He still loves you."

A tear rolled down Esther's cheek and she reached for a tissue and wiped it away. "I wish I could believe that."

"Do you want to pray together?"

"You mean now?"

"Why not?"

"I...I wouldn't know where to begin."

"I can start and if you want, you can add something."

She nodded and came over to the sofa to sit beside Ruth. They held hands and Ruth began to pray.

"Heavenly Father, first dank...thank you for putting us together, my Aunt Esther and me. Thank you for her opening her home to me. Lord, I know there is purpose for us to be together. I hope you show us soon what that purpose is. Please be with the family and keep them well and happy.

"Father, my aunt was badly hurt years ago. As You know, the man she loved broke her heart. She has held on to a little bitterness in her spirit and she wants to let it go. Please take it from her and give her peace and help her to know You love her and want her back. Please be with Jeremiah

and keep him safe and maybe if Emma still loves him, you can have him love her back. God, you are so gut and care so much for us. Thank you."

They were silent for a few moments with their heads still bowed. Then her aunt began to pray.

> *"Lord, forgive me for staying apart from you these long years. I've known down deep You were always there and I've grieved You by turning away. Lord, as Ruth said, I know there is a purpose for her to be here. Perhaps a double purpose. I know you only hear the prayer of a righteous person and I'm so far from righteous. I've lived my life for my own pleasure, avoiding your voice. I want that to change now, Lord, but I cannot come before You with a clean heart until I release all my anger and hate. I do that now, Father. I no longer want to cling to the sin of anger and un-forgiveness. I place myself in Your holy hands and beg for Your mercy. Amen."*

Ruth looked up at her aunt and released her hands. Esther reached for another tissue and held it to her eyes. No one spoke. At last her aunt let out a sigh and whispered. "Thank you, Ruth. I know peace will follow in time."

"*Jah.* It will."

Esther rose and walked over to the stereo. "Shall we play the ninth symphony of Beethoven?"

"That would be real nice."

"I have a surprise for you," she said as she returned to sit beside Ruth. "Next Saturday night we are going somewhere special, but I'm keeping it secret until then. You can wear your pretty dress again, though."

Ruth's eyes lit up with anticipation. "I can't wait!"

Esther smiled, reached over and hugged Ruth. "You are a blessing from God."

"He has blessed me, Aunt Esther, by bringing you into my life. Maybe you can go back with me for a visit in the spring."

"Maybe. I'm thinking of writing again to your mother. I can use the excuse I want to tell her how you're doing."

"You don't need an excuse. *Mamm* would love to hear from you. She told me herself."

Esther's eyes widened and she smiled broadly. "Then I'll do it. I'll write and see if she would open her house to me in the spring for a short visit."

"*Jah*, do it. I'll tell her how kind you are and how you miss her."

"Good. I'll start a letter this very minute while you read. Before I change my mind."

Chapter Twenty-nine

The weather was cooperating with deep blue skies and mild temperatures. The next several days Ruth and Esther managed to visit all kinds of landmarks and nearby towns. Esther insisted on purchasing more clothing, which included a purse, dress slacks and two silk blouses. She suggested a trip to a beauty salon, but Ruth was reluctant to cut more of her hair. Instead Esther shaped it and then helped her style it.

On Friday, Darrel called and talked for several minutes with Esther, who was in the living room, reading the newspaper. After chatting a few moments, she turned the phone over to Ruth. She whispered, "I've set him straight. He promises to behave."

"*Jah*. I heard." Ruth took the phone.

"Hi, gorgeous. Oops, I mean Ruth."

"*Jah*. It's me. Miss gorgeous." She could play his game.

"I want to take you out to dinner. How about Saturday night?"

"Oh, I couldn't possibly. Aunt Esther is taking me somewhere as a surprise."

"Hmm. How about the following Saturday night instead? I promise to be a good boy and not do anything to upset you."

"No kissing."

"You're a refreshing spirit. You say it like it is. Okay, no kissing, unless you ask me."

"Ha! No chance of that." She realized she was grinning into the phone. It was kind of fun to tease.

"So do I get a 'yes' or a '*jah*' about dinner?

She giggled. "I guess a '*jah*'. Should I wear jeans?"

"Not unless you want to go to McDonald's."

"I don't care. Wherever you want." Ruth sat on a chair across from her aunt and smiled over at her.

"I'll take you to my favorite Italian restaurant. I assume you like Italian food."

"I like pizza. That's all I've ever eaten of Italian food."

"This will be a treat for you. Casual dress is fine, but jeans? Eh, maybe not."

"Okay. What time?"

"Seven?"

"*Jah*, but that's kind of late, no?"

"Not in the city, but if you want to go earlier…"

"No. When in Rome, right?" She heard him laugh.

"Now where did an Amish girl ever hear that expression?"

"I think I read it once. Anyway, I want to be like a Philadelphian–for a while."

"Great. I'll pick you up at seven, a week from Saturday."

After she hung up, she handed the cell phone back to Esther. The newspaper remained on her lap, but Ruth knew she had been listening to the whole conversation.

"So I'm going out for dinner with Darrel next Saturday night."

"That's nice. He should be a perfect gentleman. I threatened him he'd better be or I'd sic the whole Amish community on him."

"It's okay. I know how to step on a guy's feet if he gets fresh."

Her aunt shook her head as she placed the paper on the table. "What a great idea. I'll try to remember that one."

"Do you date at all?"

"Last year I dated a history professor from school for a couple months, but he was quite boring and I preferred remaining home alone."

"Maybe you should come along with Darrel and me."

"I don't think he'd appreciate that too much," Esther said with a lop-sided smile. "Although I met his father once and he wasn't bad."

"Single?"

"Yes, divorced."

"Not *gut*." Ruth scowled and shook her head.

"It's not, but it is common, Ruth. To find a single man my age who hasn't been divorced or widowed is rare."

"Widowed, is okay. He couldn't help that, but divorce…"

"I know how the Amish feel about that. Oh, well, we shall see. Want to listen to Vivaldi?"

"Oh, yes, I love *The Four Seasons.*"

Esther let out a laugh.

"What did I say?"

"You said 'yes' without even thinking. Not '*jah*'!"

"Oh, my, I'm losing my Amish talk. They won't let me come home," Ruth said as she smiled. "Next you'll have me saying 'good' instead of '*gut*'! What will the world come to?"

Saturday they stayed in the apartment and Esther ran a wash. Then Ruth vacuumed the whole apartment while her aunt dusted. The oven was self cleaning, so Ruth skipped that chore. They took turns in the bathroom preparing for the evening. Ruth suspected the surprise was musical in nature. She wore her New Year's Eve outfit and her aunt added a gold chain and matching bracelet. "Just a loan, of course," Ruth said as her aunt attached the clasp. "I've never worn jewelry. It's beautiful."

After eating supper, they drove down Walnut to South Broad Street and her aunt pulled into a special parking area. "I reserved parking, too, to make it easier," she remarked as they exited the car.

The Kimmel Center stood before them and Ruth's jaw dropped as she looked at the splendid architecture of the heavily glassed building. The lighting of the glass curved roof added to the dramatic architecture. "Looks like a place to grow plants," Ruth remarked.

Esther handed her tickets to an usher and they were shown to their seats in the second tier. Ruth's heart palpitated from excitement. She opened her program to discover the Philadelphia Orchestra was playing "Beethoven's Fifth Symphony."

"Oh Aunt Esther! I can't believe it. I listened to it only two days ago."

"Really? When did you play it?"

"I listened on my IPod when I couldn't sleep. It's so beautiful." Ruth leaned toward her and hummed the first four familiar notes.

"That's it, my dear and you are about to hear it live."

The musicians began to arrive on the stage area and tune up. The first violinist, the concert master, played the first note and everyone tuned up according to their instrument. It was even more fantastic than the time she heard the Lancaster orchestra. Ruth moved forward in her seat and watched, awe-struck. At one point she turned and grinned at her aunt, who was enjoying Ruth's reaction. "Aunt Esther, do you play any instrument?"

"No. I'm sorry to say, I don't know how to play anything. I never had an opportunity. You can't count the five or six chords I learned to play on the guitar."

"I would love to play a piano or a violin someday," Ruth said wistfully.

Her aunt nodded and looked down at her program. Perhaps she didn't believe that day would ever arrive, but Ruth held onto her hope.

Soon there was a hush over the audience and when the conductor came across the platform, there was enthusiastic applause. He lifted his baton, held the eyes of his musicians, and with the drop of the baton, the marvelous notes exploded on the scene. Ruth was mesmerized. She wasn't even aware of time passing. Sometimes she closed her eyes and allowed the music to sink into her soul. Other times she watched the bows in unison as they stretched across the strings of the instruments. She thanked God for this moment in time. And she thanked her aunt in her heart for making it possible.

During intermission, they walked around the lobby area. Ruth was aware of several men's attention on her. She caught them watching her and was embarrassed by their stares and smiles. It did not go unnoticed by her aunt, who leaned over once and said, "you're quite the object of male admiration." Ruth flushed and wished for a moment she was protected by her *kapp* and apron.

Once they were re-seated, the music began again and she was transported back into her other world of music.

On the way home, Ruth thanked her aunt with enthusiasm. "I'll never forget tonight–or you, Aunt Esther."

"Then it was worth every cent. I'm sorry I'll be returning to the university in a couple days. What will you do all day while I'm gone?"

"I need to look for work. Of course until I find something I'll clean and cook for you. Just leave a list of what you want done and–"

"Oh, goodness, that won't be necessary. Whatever you want for dinner will be fine with me. I'll leave grocery money and you can walk to the market if you need anything. As far as cleaning, you can wait until Saturdays and we'll do it together. The place stays pretty clean."

After parking the car, they walked into the lobby. Dave Russell called out to Esther. "You have some mail here, Esther."

"Oh, yes, we forgot to pick it up. Thanks, Dave." She glanced at the personal letters as they took the elevator. "You have a letter from home," she said as she handed it over to Ruth.

Once they settled in, Esther went into her bedroom to change into night clothes, while Ruth opened her letter from Emma.

Dear Ruth,

How are you? I hope you are enjoying everything. It sounds like your New Year's was more exciting than ours. We went to bed around ten. I was bored and besides as Daed *says, the cows don't know it's a holiday.*

Bishop King is in the hospital. He may need surgery on his heart. Everyone is upset and we had a prayer hour last night at Schrock's farm, which turned into three hours!

Katie has a bad cold and so she stayed home so the kids wouldn't get it at school.

The other news is about Jeremiah. He was not at the services last week and someone said he has moved. I asked his friend Ben and he said he went to Ohio. I think he has family there. I was upset at first but I have kind of given up on him. I

182

think I might like Seth Detweiler. Do you remember him from the next district? He moved in with his brother Aaron and now goes to our Sings. He smiles at me a lot so I know he likes me. He has big brown eyes and a cleft in his chin. Really cute. And Josiah flirts with me now that you're gone. So I have two guys to choose from. Josiah went a whole evening without talking about cows! I'm going to a Sing with him next week.

Mamm *and* Daed *said* hallo *. All Katie does is blow her nose and Wayne is still not riding his bike so he's grouchy. I miss you.*

Love, Emma

PS - Say hallo *to our aunt.*

Ruth read the part about Jeremiah again. So now her sister was over him. How quickly her feelings had changed and Ruth had been so concerned about breaking her heart. It wasn't love at all—merely infatuation. What a fool she'd been. And now Jeremiah was gone and she had no way to contact him. She still felt anger at his unwillingness to see her position about waiting for Emma to change her feelings. As it turned out, it wouldn't have been long at all. Did he care so little? What should she do? Probably nothing, since he had her address if he cared.

What a strange turn of events.

Chapter Thirty

The first day Ruth was alone, the time dragged. She vacuumed and scrubbed the bathroom, changed the bedding and ran three washes. It was only ten o'clock. She put tea water on and turned on the television, but quickly turned it off when the screen showed a woman scantily dressed leaving a bar after someone was shot. That was a world she wanted no part of. After she turned off the television, she read two chapters from Genesis and said her prayers. After a cup of tea she paced back and forth for a few minutes. It was cloudy out, but feeling the need for fresh air, she put her coat on over her jeans and sweater and donned her new hat. She walked down to the park area near the river. Others were walking dogs, pushing strollers or rollerblading. Ruth picked up speed, ending up in a slow run. It felt good to exercise. She and her aunt had run together two days before, but she had gotten winded after only a mile. Funny, she thought she was in good shape, but she wasn't used to actual exercise. On a farm, one didn't need to *try* to exercise. The days were filled with physical activity.

As she ran, Ruth thought about home. She pictured her room with her favorite quilt, her dresser, and her braided rug she had helped to make. She could see her mother as she rolled out pie dough and could hear her father as he asked how she felt each morning. Their lives were difficult and yet simple. It was clear what was expected of you. The community worked well because people filled their roles and understood their place in their closed society. It was a Godly world, fulfilling, and rewarding. But there were no violins. And now no Jeremiah.

When she got back to the apartment the phone was ringing. She picked it up and answered breathlessly, "*Hallo.*"

"Ruth, it's Darrel. How are you doing?"

"Good," she responded, purposely using the *D.* And you?"

"I'm fine. Listen I was having a cappuccino at this little café near my law firm and the owner mentioned needing someone part time to wait on customers. I thought about you."

"Really? Could I walk there?"

"Well, it's about a mile, I guess. Yeah, you'd be alright in nice weather anyway. What do you think? Do you want me to give you her number?"

"Why not? I think I could do that."

"I'm sure you could. I know you merely want something part-time for some change money. Then you can look for something better if you stay on."

"Thanks for thinking of me. Let me write down the number and the owner's name."

She wrote it down and thanked him again before hanging up. Then she called the owner, Terri Sharp, who seemed interested and asked her to come in for an interview. Ruth wrote down the directions and headed over after adding lipstick and brushing her wind-blown hair.

The café was on a corner, quaint with green and white striped awnings and Ruth wondered if they served outdoors in good weather. Inside, about a dozen small tables were scattered about, and there was a counter where a woman was serving coffee to three young women sitting on stools. She looked up and smiled at Ruth.

"Hi, I'm Ruth Zook, the girl who just talked to you on the phone for the job?"

"Right. Excuse me ladies. Enjoy your coffee. Ruth, want to follow me?" Ruth walked behind the woman to the other side of the room where she motioned for Ruth to take a seat at a small table. Terri sat across from her and asked a few pertinent questions.

"I have to tell you before you decide if you want me, I may only be here till some time in the spring."

"Oh? Then you're moving?"

"Perhaps. I'm from Lancaster County and I'm basically visiting my aunt for a while."

"Oh right. Darrel mentioned you're Amish. How interesting."

"We're not afraid to work, I promise you that."

Terri, about fifty years old with bleached yellow hair, smiled at Ruth. "That would be a refreshing change. You have the job if you want it."

"*Jah*, I mean yes. I'd love it. Can I start tomorrow?"

"Sure. Be here by six. Wear solid colored slacks and something white on top. The sweater you have on would be fine."

"And sneakers? Can I wear them instead of heels?"

"Whatever is comfortable. You'll be done work by two most days and you'll get half an hour for lunch. Bring your own. I'll need you Tuesdays through Fridays. I have enough help on week-ends. I'll pay you every Friday when you're done work. Agreed?"

"Yes. Do you need my social security number?"

"I'll give you a form to fill out and you can bring it in tomorrow when you come to work. Any questions?"

"You'll train me, right?"

"Sure. I'll be here tomorrow and Wednesday. You'll be on your own by Thursday. I have to leave town for a couple days, but I'll return Saturday."

"You mean I'll be working all by myself Thursday and Friday?" Her heart jumped at the thought.

"Oh, Billy, my son will help out. He comes in every day at noon to clean up the dishes and stuff. He knows how to do everything."

"Phew! Had me scared for a minute." Ruth followed Terri back to the front where she handed Ruth the papers to fill out. "See you tomorrow."

Ruth was so excited. When she got back to the apartment, Esther had already returned from her day at the university. When she came in the door, Esther came right over to greet her. "Ruth, I've been so worried about you. Where have you been?"

Ruth explained and Esther gave a sigh of relief. "I purchased a cell phone for you this afternoon when I couldn't reach you on the house phone. You have to carry it with you at all times. You're in a city now, Ruth. You can't be too careful."

"Wow! My own phone!"

"Now let's sit on the sofa and I'll teach you how to use it."
Esther showed her how to enter phone numbers. "Of course, your
family doesn't own a phone, but do you have an emergency
number of a neighbor or someone?"

"*Jah*...yes. I'll put it in my phone like you showed me."
Ruth reached over and hugged her aunt. "*Danki.* Thank you so
much."

"Now, I'll put the number of my cell phone in for you as a
speed dial." She explained the simplicity of speed-dialing and they
worked together on ring tones. Ruth was delighted to find
Pachelbel's Canon as one of the tones.

"I wish I had someone to call," she exclaimed.

"How about Darrel? He said you were going out with him
next week-end."

"*Jah.* Should I? Won't he be working?"

"I doubt it. It's nearly six."

"Good. Okay." She poked in his name and it dialed up.
When he answered she felt foolish for having called. "Hi, it's me.
Ruth."

"Oh hi, Ruth. What's happening? Still on for Saturday
night?"

"Yes. Uh, I just got a cell phone and I wanted to try it out."
Honesty was always the best policy, right?

His laughter came over the line and she felt chagrined for
making the call. *He'll think I'm childish,* she thought.

"Well, it works! Congratulations."

"Oh, dear. It was silly of me, right?"

"No, it was sweet. Thank you for thinking of me. You can
call anytime."

A smile spread over her face. "*Jah?* That's nice of you,
Darrel. I'll try not to bother you at three in the morning."

"Much appreciated. I made reservations already at the
Italian place, remember? They have a downstairs for dancing, so
bring your dancing shoes."

"I can barely walk in my fancy heels, but I'll try."

"That's all I can ask."

There was a moment of awkward silence.

"I got the job, Darrel. I start tomorrow."

"Good for you. I think it will be fun for you."

"I hope so. Well, I guess I'll say good-bye," Ruth said.

"Thanks for calling. See you soon," Darrel responded.

After they hung up, Ruth looked over at her aunt who was spreading frozen fish on a small cookie sheet. She smiled at Ruth. "You've made quite an impression on that young man. He mentioned getting together for tennis some evening and actually suggested bringing his father along for me."

"But I can't even hold a racket."

"I explained you'd never played, but he didn't seem to think it mattered. Apparently his dad used to play a lot, but hasn't done much in the last few years, so we'd have an array of players."

"And I'd be the worst."

"We don't take it seriously, but how about if I take you to the indoor court tomorrow after work and I'll show you a few pointers."

"I think that would be *gut*...good. I watched people play one time and it looked hard."

"To be really good, yes, but to play for fun, you only need to know how to lop the ball over the net."

"It sounds like fun. I was thinking after I get money from working, I'd like to rent a violin and take some lessons. Do you think I'm being foolish?"

"Not at all. I think it's a wonderful idea. I know a music store that would rent you one and teach you at the same time. It isn't far from here."

"You have everything in Philadelphia. It's a wonderful-*gut* city."

"We do have everything, unfortunately that includes crime and drugs."

"But if you look on the bright side–"

"Yes, and you're teaching me to do just that. I hope you like frozen cod. I have salad to go with it."

"I never had frozen cod or frozen anything, but I know I'll like it."

"I purchased ice cream for dessert. It's not homemade like you're used to, but it's pretty good."

"I love ice cream. Any kind. Poor Katie does, too. She likes everything fattening."

"And it shows?"

"Yes. Hey, I said it without thinking! *Yes!* It's too bad because she's getting fat."

"What a shame. Some people gain more easily than others."

"Oh, Katie works for every pound she adds, believe me— that's for sure. But *Mamm* says not to tease her, so we try to look the other way."

"Ruth, sit a minute with me. The salads were pre-made and the fish takes a few minutes more. I want to ask you something."

"You seem troubled Aunt Esther. Have I done something wrong?"

"Oh, no, Ruth. It's...I've hesitated asking about my mother."

"*Oma?*"

Esther shook her head. "How is she?"

"She's good. We celebrated her seventieth birthday recently and she had a wonderful time."

"Does she ever mention me?"

Ruth pondered the question a moment before answering. "Only one time in my presence. She sounded real sad. It was on *your* birthday last year and she said she wished she could call you. *Mamm* said she should, but *Oma* just shook her head."

"I'm so sorry I hurt her. I should not have left when I did. She was having such a hard time dealing with your mother's illness, and your Uncle Josiah was sickly at the time. I was selfish to think only of myself."

"Maybe you should write to her. In fact, you did send a letter to Mamm, didn't you?

"I chickened out, Ruth. I have written to my mother in the past, but I never hear a word back. Maybe if the next time you write home, you could mention me and see if anyone responds. I was planning to write on my own the other night, and I even

189

started writing a couple of times, but I never really got up my nerve."

"I'm going to write home tonight. You could even add your own message, if you want."

"Better you do it for me this time. Then we'll see."

The buzzer went off on the stove and Esther rose. "Time to eat, Ruth."

After dinner Esther showed Ruth how to play Scrabble and then Ruth wrote a short note to the family before retiring for the night. Tomorrow was her big day. Her first real job.

Chapter Thirty-one

Ruth barely slept past five o'clock due to her excitement about having a job. She showered, made herself half a sandwich and washed an apple for her lunch. By the time she was ready to leave, her aunt had risen and was starting the coffee.

"Now, ask questions if you don't understand. Some people assume you know more than you do."

"I wonder if she realizes I haven't made fancy coffee before. Even your pot–I wouldn't know where to begin. I'm so nervous."

"You'll do fine. You can call me if you wish. Leave a message if I don't answer. I may be in the middle of teaching."

Ruth tied her hair back and wrapped herself in her new coat. It was frigid out and she dreaded the walk, but her aunt had given her a woolen scarf, which she twisted around her neck twice. She walked quickly and arrived earlier than she anticipated.

Terri nodded to her as she came in and told her where to put her things. The room they used in the back was small and cluttered with magazines, cartons, and catalogues. When she returned, Terri showed her how to start the regular coffee, then went through the procedure for the various specialty coffees, while she raced around the room, placing napkins on tables and checking salts and peppers. "We have a small limited menu. Check it out when you have a chance. Ask questions if you need to."

Ruth felt herself perspire and her hands shook slightly as she took notes.

The first customers arrived and Ruth watched as Terri took their order. Ruth made a mug of hot chocolate while Terri poured a cup of regular brew for a customer. A middle aged man ordered a croissant, which Ruth placed on a dish to serve. By noon, she was fairly comfortable and more confidant than she thought possible. Everyone had been pleasant and she had no trouble making change. Her experience at the produce stand back home had trained her somewhat to deal with the public.

Around one o'clock, she turned to find Darrel seated at the counter. "Hey, pretty girl. You look very official. How's she doing, Terri?"

"Great! Give me the Amish anytime, Darrel. They know how to produce."

Ruth was pleased at the accolades and smiled at them. "It's not too bad. It's actually kind of fun."

"Whew, how's that for a change," Terri said. "Where's that kid of mine? He's late."

The place was packed and Ruth barely had time to smile at Darrel. After making a cappuccino for him, she attended to her other customers. When she returned to the counter, Darrel was no where in sight, but tucked under his mug was a twenty dollar bill. It embarrassed her to receive such a large tip and she intended to return it to him Saturday night.

As Ruth was leaving for the day, a red-haired man about her age came through the back. Terri introduced him as her son. He nodded and tied an apron around his waist to begin clean-up.

When she got back to the apartment, Ruth counted all her tips. She had made forty dollars, excluding the twenty from Darrel. That plus her pay would help her feel independent.

She showered and took a nap. When her aunt arrived home they sat for a few minutes. "First, tell me about your job. Did you enjoy it?"

"After I got over the shakies. I was a wreck at first, but by the time I left, I felt pretty good about it."

"I'm glad. It takes time to learn a new job. I know you'll be wonderful. It will get easier every day. Let's just have sandwiches before we go to the court."

After dining on tuna salad sandwiches, Esther loaned Ruth a tennis outfit, which was slightly large. Ruth wore her jeans on top for warmth as they headed for the courts. When they arrived, Esther took a pail of tennis balls and handed Ruth an extra racket she had brought along. "Before we use the balls, let me show you how to hold the racket and do the forward swing."

Ruth mimicked her aunt and soon felt comfortable swinging the racket. After a dozen swings using the balls, she finally connected and sent one over the net. "Wow! That felt good."

Esther worked with her niece for two hours teaching Ruth the basics. "We'll hold off on the serve and back hand. Continue to concentrate on what you're doing. I think you're a natural, Ruth."

"It's so much fun."

That night Ruth wrote to her mother.

Dear Mamm,
   I am learning to play tennis and Aunt Esther says I'm a natural. I am not being vain, I hope, but I think I did okay for the first time.
   I also have a job. I waitress at a cute coffee house right near by. It is only about a mile away and I walk. It is not full time, but that is okay with me. It gives me some spending money and I do not want to take from my aunt, though she is very generous and seems happy to buy me things. I have nice clothes to wear—even jeans.
   Aunt Esther would like to write to Oma, *but she says when she has,* Oma *never writes back. Do you think she would this time? Aunt Esther says she is sorry she left when she did. She sounds real regretful and I think* Oma *should forgive her.*
   Philadelphia is big and has lots of places to visit. You would like the parks. Maybe you could come see us here with the family. I will help pay for a driver. It would be much fun.
                                             Love, Ruth

Thursday went well and Billy arrived on time. He barely spoke, but he helped when they became overwhelmed with customers. Friday went better than she expected since Billy came in early to help organize. No one waited too long for service and business slowed down enough for Ruth to leave at three. She came home exhausted, but happy for a job well done.

On Saturday Ruth received a letter from her mother.

Dear Ruth,

It was nice to hear from you. It sounds like you are having a good time. I saw people play tennis and it looks very hard. You must be smart.

I am glad you found a job near by. I hope the people are nice to you.

I talked to Oma *and she said she would answer a letter from your aunt, but Esther should write first. She got sad when she talked.*

Katie likes teaching better than she did. Emma is trying to help the little boy and his sister who lost their Mamm. *Lots of problems. We will invite them here soon for a meal, but the* daed *needs time to grieve first I believe.*

Wayne is riding his bike again but it is very cold and some days he does not ride. His goats are good.

Emma likes a new boy. I think he likes her too. They laugh a lot after church. I thought she liked the Jeremiah boy but now he is gone and she seems happy anyway.

Your daed *said hi and sends his love. We all do. We miss you lots.*

Love, Mamm

Ruth pictured her mother writing her letter, bent over the kitchen table with her reading glasses perched on her nose. She'd probably have her shawl on to keep away the draft and *Daed* was most likely reading in his chair. The aroma of rising bread seared Ruth's memory and she yearned to be with her family again, even if it was just for awhile.

"Ruth, sorry to interrupt, but I'm leaving for a friend's house. I just wanted to remind you about your dinner date."

"Oh," Ruth returned to the present and smiled at her aunt. "Have a good time."

"I will. You, too. Make sure you have the key to the house on you. I may be late."

"I keep it with me whenever I leave, but thanks for reminding me."

"Ruth, Darrel is a nice young man, but he's used to a totally different life-style. Don't be too shocked at some of the things he says."

Ruth nodded. "So far I think I've kept him in his place," she said, giving her aunt a perky smile.

"Good for you. See you tomorrow."

Ruth prepared for her date by changing to dressy grey slacks with a black silk blouse. She wore her hair loose and used make-up the way her aunt had shown her. Subtle, but a bit on the glamorous side. She smiled at her reflection. "Keep your head on your shoulders, Ruth. Don't let this man give you sweet-talk," she said aloud as the intercom went off.

As they drove toward the restaurant, Darrel looked across at his passenger. "You look stunning tonight, Ruth. Probably too good for this restaurant."

"I merely have slacks on."

"On you, they're not just slacks."

"Oh, here we go. My aunt warned me about you," she remarked, grinning over at him.

His eyes returned to the road and he stopped at a red traffic light. "She did, huh? And what did she warn you about?"

"That's between us. I guess for me to keep my eye on you."

"Well I have my eye on you, so we'll be even. And how did work go?"

"Oh, work. That reminds me. I have twenty dollars for you."

"That was for the great service."

"All I did was give you coffee."

"But it was presented in such a professional manner and with such a sweet smile. I insist it was worth every penny."

Ruth laughed and shook her head. "At this rate, you'll be a poor man, for sure."

The restaurant parking lot was filled with expensive cars and the waiters were all dressed in black and white outfits. They were seated at a corner table in a low-lit room. The white linen tablecloths were spotless.

"Do you want wine?"

"I don't drink, but you can have some."

"Thank you," he teased, "but it's not necessary. Water will be fine."

"Will you order for me? I haven't eaten any of these dishes. I wouldn't know what to get."

"Surely you've eaten veal."

"*Jah*...yes, but only once in a while. Maybe chicken would be better."

He ordered chicken parmesan for her and chicken Marsala for himself. "You can taste mine when it comes and if you prefer it over the parmesan, we'll switch."

"It will be fine, Darrel, I'm sure. I eat almost anything. In the Amish home you do not complain. You eat what is put before you."

"I hear the food is pretty good."

"*Jah*, I mean yes, it is, but rather fattening."

"You don't have an extra ounce on you."

Ruth was glad the lights were low as she felt a blush rise on her neck. "I'm lucky I guess. I don't gain easy."

Ruth loved her meal and exclaimed over the crusty bread. "Just like home."

"Do you miss your home," he asked as he sat back waiting for *tiramisu* and coffee.

"When I have time to think about it."

"Is there anyone in particular you miss?"

"Oh, my sisters Emma and Katie, of course. And my parents and my brothers and their families and of course my grandmother and my–"

"Whoa!" Darrel let out a chuckle. "I guess I meant a friend. A male friend. Were you going with anyone?"

"No. I had a crush, but Emma liked the same man, so I stopped caring."

"Just like that? You can turn off your feelings that easily?"

"Well, if there is no future and you know it, why would you allow yourself to dwell on it?"

"Good question. It's really hard for most people to switch their feelings on and off that easily."

"Like my aunt's lamp, you mean."

"Yeah. Like that."

"Okay. I admit it was harder than that."

"Do you write to him?"

"Only once."

"Did he write back?"

"I think I'd rather talk about something else. Why don't you tell me about your girlfriend. The one with the dead dog."

"Who is that?"

"New Year's. The girl with the dead dog."

"Oh, right. We don't see each other anymore."

"Ah, the light switch went off?"

"I guess you could say that. Right now I'm not serious about anyone. If I was, I wouldn't be sitting here with you."

"Good. So you're not a two-timer."

"You know some pretty worldly terms, young lady. No, I'm not usually a two-timer."

"Tsk. Tsk. Sounds like sometimes you are." She tilted her head and winked at him. He reached over for her hand, but she reached for her water glass and took a sip before he was able to touch it.

"I remember the part about 'no kissing' but I don't think you mentioned no touching."

"We are only friends."

"Friends can hold hands."

"That's not the Amish way."

"But you're not living like the Amish right now."

"I think I'll always be Amish inside."

Darrel sat back in his chair and folded his arms. He looked across at Ruth, his mouth drawn and brows raised. "Then I guess there isn't much hope for me."

"Why? Can't we be friends?"

"Oh, yeah, we can be friends, but I was hoping for a lot more?"

"Like marriage?" Certainly he can't be serious already.

He laughed and shook his head. He leaned on the table on his forearms. "Not exactly."

"What then?"

"You are naive, Ruth. Don't you understand anything about the dating process?"

"I know you need to get to know someone well before thinking seriously, but we don't believe in physical things. Is that what you're referring to?"

He tilted his head and smiled, mischievously. "You're on the right track."

"I made it plain–no kissing. That includes a whole lot of other stuff, Darrel."

"Well, you've set me straight, Ruth. I appreciate your honesty. Here comes our dessert now."

"Hope I have room for it." She smiled over at him, reached across the table, and patted his hand. "Now be a *gut* boy." She knew she had hurt him, but she needed to set boundaries–even for herself.

Chapter Thirty-two

The following Saturday, Esther took Ruth to the music store near the apartment. Ruth's eyes became saucers as she looked at the many pianos on display.

"May I help you?" an elderly man asked as Ruth fingered the keyboard on a small grand.

"Actually, I wondered about violin lessons," Ruth ventured.

"We teach violin, yes. Are you a beginner?"

"*Jah.* I don't even know how to hold a violin."

He smiled and nodded. "We also teach piano."

"But I have no where to practice. I figure with a violin, I could rent one to keep at home."

"That can certainly be arranged."

While Ruth followed the man to the back of the store, Esther took a guitar and strummed a couple chords she had learned years before.

Ruth signed up for her first lesson for the following Monday and the gentleman presented her with a practice violin that was affordable to rent. After Ruth paid for three lessons and a month's rental, he gave her an instruction book and a case for the instrument. "Don't be discouraged if you have problems. Once you're shown, you'll be fine."

"I hope so," Ruth said as she took the handle of the violin case. The salesman walked over toward the door with them.

"Oh, *danki*…thank you."

He smiled and waved as they made their way to the car.

"Aunt Esther, did you learn guitar? I heard you play something."

"Oh, I only know a couple of chords. I never really got into it. I'm not terribly musical, I'm afraid."

Once they got back to the apartment Ruth removed the precious instrument and attempted to play a note. As the bow went across the strings, a weird assortment of sounds registered and she squealed. "It sounds horrible."

Esther laughed. "Pretty bad, but he warned you. You may want to wait. By the way, Darrel wants us to play some tennis next Saturday. Are you up for it?"

"Maybe, if we could have one more practice first. I don't want to be horrible."

"I don't see why not. How about Monday after I come home from work?"

"Good."

"So I asked Darrel how his date went with you."

Ruth held back a grin. "What did he tell you?"

"He said he had a nice time."

"That's all?"

Esther smiled and tilted her head. "He said you put him in his place."

"*Jah*, I did. He probably won't call again."

"On the contrary, he seems fascinated by your rejection."

"I didn't reject him, just his plans."

Esther laughed and walked into the kitchen to start supper. "It's the first time I've seen him like this. He usually has two or three women hanging all over him."

"Not *gut*. It's not the Amish way."

"No, not my way, either. It will be fun to see you two in action when we play tennis."

"Is his father coming?"

"He plans to. Hope he isn't too professional. My serve leaves much to be desired."

Ruth helped by making turkey patties and she fried them while her aunt set up the table and tossed the salad.

"I wrote to my mother last night," Esther said while reaching for the salad tools. "It wasn't as hard as I expected it to be."

"I'm glad."

"I didn't mail it, though."

"Why not?" Ruth looked over at her aunt, who looked hesitant to answer. Then Esther let out a sigh. "I'm not sure, but I'm going to mail it Monday."

"Monday, for sure?"

"For sure," Esther assured her. "Ruth, are you any closer to making a decision about where you will live permanently?" She handed Ruth the salad dressing for the table.

"Not really. I love my job and the idea of playing a violin. And I love being here and getting to know you better. Your home is beautiful, Philadelphia is fun, but I think about my family a lot and I get real homesick. Mostly at night, when I try to sleep."

"You still have plenty of time to decide. Take all the time you need. I was only wondering."

"Maybe if things were different with the man I loved..."

"I don't think you've stopped loving him, have you?" She looked over at her niece as Ruth turned the burgers.

"I don't know. I want to stop, but the off switch is broken a little bit. His face creeps in on me or his laugh. He took me to a concert in Lancaster and opened my eyes to what is out there in the non-Amish way of life. I have him to thank for that."

"Is he still living Amish?"

"I don't know. He has left the area."

"And you don't know where he is?"

"I heard he was in Ohio with family. I'm guessing he got my letter, but he hasn't written back."

"Did you include this address?"

"I did. But then there's Emma, though I think she's over him."

"I thought you said she's seeing someone else."

"That's right. It leaves the door open for me now with Jeremiah, but the door leads no where. I can't find the door."

"I'm sorry, Ruth. It must hurt." Esther put the salad on the table.

"I don't dwell on what can not be. I leave it in God's hands. He knows far better."

"You're a wise woman for your age. Shall we have our salads while the burgers cook? I'm famished."

Ruth nodded and they sat together as Ruth poured dressing over her salad.

"Shall we say grace?" Esther asked. Ruth nodded and they each prayed silently.

After a few mouthfuls, Esther wiped her mouth with her napkin and looked over at her niece. "Speaking of God, I bought myself a Bible yesterday."

"You didn't have one?"

"I left it in Lancaster."

"So now are you going to read it?"

"I've already started. I'm reading the New Testament first. I'll get around to the earlier books later. I wanted to read Christ's own words."

"*Jah.* Seems like a good place to start. I just started the Old Testament again. There is so much in Genesis."

"It is good. I remember some of the stories."

"They are true, you know."

"I realize that now. As a child I believed, just because my *Mamm* said they were true, but as an adult I realize they are actually historical."

"If you ever want to study together, I'd be happy to share what I know."

"Thanks, maybe in time. Better check those burgers. I think they may be burning."

They were caught in time. Ruth brought them back to the table and laid a plate in front of her aunt.

"Delicious," Ruth said, after sitting down and taking a bite, "if I'm not being too prideful." Some feelings never left her.

"Well, God made the food, the devil made the cook," Esther teased.

"Oh, my!"

"Sorry, Ruth, It's just an old saying."

Monday morning finally arrived. Ruth was excited as she watched her violin instructor, a middle-aged woman with a narrow and proud face, position the instrument on Ruth's shoulder. "Now take the bow and hold it this way. Gentle. Let the strings do the work."

It took several tries before Ruth put the idea into practice. She worked steadily for an hour and then went home, feeling more inadequate with each step. If only she had started as a young girl, she'd probably be good by now. How proficient can one get in only a couple of months?

Ruth decided to practice before her aunt returned from work in order to spare her ears. Once the sound came through rather pleasantly and Ruth was elated. She stood in front of the mirror to make sure she was holding the violin correctly. Even if she didn't learn to play well, she felt satisfaction in attempting it. Nothing ventured - nothing gained, she remembered hearing once and it made sense.

Ruth went down to check on the mail and the manager, Dave, handed her a stack. "Looks like you're a popular young lady," he said.

"Probably most everything is for my aunt," she said as she headed toward the elevator, rummaging through the different shaped pieces of mail. She caught sight of one in Jeremiah's handwriting. Her heart began to pound. She almost feared opening it. Perhaps he was ill–or married.

Once in the apartment, she sorted the mail and took her letter from Jeremiah over to the sofa where she sat down to read it.

> *Dear Ruth,*
>
> *By now I guess you know I have left Lancaster. I am in Ohio. My grandfather had surgery for cancer and he is still very ill. They do not hold out much hope for his recovery. It saddens me very much. He is a good man and he suffers now. My grandmother tries to smile a lot, but she is crying inside for sure.*
>
> *I miss Pennsylvania and especially you. How are you? Do you want to stay in Philadelphia? Have you made any English friends? Is your aunt a good person?*
>
> *See, you need to write to me to answer all my questions. But my most important question is this. Do you miss me?*
>
> *Please write soon. Yours, Jeremiah*

Ruth read it over, letting her eyes feast on the second paragraph. *Oh, yes, Jeremiah, I miss you. I miss your voice–your laugh–your smile–your touch. Oh, how much I miss you.*

But how much should she tell him in a letter. Was he like Darrel with more than one girl interested at a time? He would be sought after by the single girls in Ohio just like he was in Pennsylvania. Why would he hold on to his interest in her unless he just likes collecting girls? Then again, maybe he still cared. More than that, he could still love her. She wondered if he'd come to Philadelphia if she asked him. Of course, she wouldn't do that. No, she felt too vulnerable to ask. He might say no. If God wanted them together, nothing could keep them apart. She prayed fervently for His will to be done in her life and Jeremiah's. And she hoped His will matched up with hers.

"I'll do the serving for you," Darrel told Ruth when she explained she had no idea how to serve in tennis.

"I serve coffee real good, but no tennis balls," she said.

Darrel's father, Martin took his racket and swung it several times in the air. "I bought this yesterday. Today's the big christening."

Ruth noticed her aunt seemed slightly nervous, laughing too easily and talking too quickly. She was surprised this self-confident professor could be thrown off by a man.

Martin was handsome like his son and had an engaging smile. Esther had mentioned he'd been divorced for almost a year. He owned his own business on the Main Line, selling computers and other technological items.

"Think we can take them on, Esther?" he asked, giving her a crooked smile, similar to his son's.

"We have a slight advantage since Ruth has never really played."

"But look at our ages compared to them."

"Goodness, I don't consider myself old."

"And neither do I. You look about forty."

Esther smiled and added, "try fifty-one."

"You wouldn't know it."

"Hey guys, do you want to play tennis or stand around complimenting each other," Darrel teased.

Ruth would never have spoken to her father the way Darrel spoke to his dad. Things were way different here, and yet she didn't detect any disrespect on Darrel's part.

They volleyed for several minutes and then played an easy game. Darrel was very patient and instructed Ruth throughout the game. When they were done, the four of them sat at a refreshment area and drank iced tea. Darrel purchased a bag of cookies and passed them around the table.

"Not like my Katie makes," Ruth said, nibbling a chocolate chip one.

Martin looked over. "You have a cute accent. Where are you from, Ruth?"

"Lancaster County. I'm Amish."

"Amish!" He turned to his son. "You didn't tell me that." He began to roar with laughter, as Darrel raised his shoulders in a shrug.

"What's so funny about that?" Darrel asked.

The women watched waiting for an explanation.

"My son–with an Amish girl? That's too rich." He turned to Ruth. "My dear girl, you are out with the original party guy. I hope you can keep him in his place."

"*Jah.* I do the best I can."

"Wait, you were Amish, too, weren't you?" Martin turned to Esther, who was obviously uncomfortable with the discussion. She twisted her paper napkin in her hands and cleared her throat. "I was, yes. It's really not as quaint as you seem to believe. Most of the Amish, though not educated beyond the eighth grade, are very intelligent. They have chosen to separate themselves from the rest of us. It's a conscious decision. Their faith means everything to them."

"I'm sorry I responded like I did," Martin said softly. "Of course I didn't mean anything derogatory." He turned toward Ruth. "Please forgive my reaction. Why wouldn't my son date you? You're a fine girl, lovely to look at and very intelligent."

"But I can't serve tennis balls," she said, lightening up the mood.

Darrel looked across at her and caught her eye. He approved.

Nothing more was said about Amish life and the discussion turned to political issues. When Ruth returned to the apartment with her aunt, they chatted a few minutes before turning in. Ruth's muscles ached, but it was a good ache. She'd accomplished something. She'd actually gotten some balls across the net with her forehand swing.

Chapter Thirty-three

The next day Esther sat with Ruth to watch the news. She put it on mute when the advertising started and looked over at her niece. "Did you have fun playing tennis?"

"*Jah*, it's a fun game, even though I wasn't good at it."

"Practice. That's all it takes. We can go a couple evenings a week if you want."

"Maybe. I'm learning so many things. Now that I've had my violin lesson, I've been practicing when you're not at home."

"I don't mind if you practice when I'm here."

"You would, for certain, if you heard my squeaking. I'm getting a wee bit better though."

"Through practice. Anything you want to get proficient at, needs repetition."

"And dedication," Ruth added.

The news came back on and they watched the latest weather report. The central states were having a blizzard, but so far it looked like Pennsylvania might escape the heaviest part and merely receive a dusting. Esther turned off the television.

"It's almost March. You seem to be fitting right in with the English ways, Ruth."

"Funny, I think about home more all the time," Ruth commented. "Maybe I should take a visit."

"I'm afraid you won't come back." Her aunt looked down at her hands and twisted her gold bracelet several times. "I'd miss you terribly." She looked over at Ruth. "I shouldn't say that. I don't want to be part of your decision-making. At least during our time together we've become close and I hope you'd pay me an occasional visit if you go back."

"Oh, Aunt Esther, of course I would. You have been wonderful. Besides, I haven't made up my mind. I would not only hate to leave you, but I like my job and I'm so excited about learning the violin. I'm going to go twice a week for lessons if my tips stay so good."

"That's smart. When will you let me hear you?"

"When I'm good enough not to hurt your ears," Ruth answered, smiling at her aunt. "It may be sooner rather than later, if I practice more."

"And Darrel?"

"*Jah*, what about him?"

"You two seem to hit it off. Are you interested?"

"As a friend. Nothing more."

"Think your relationship could change?"

"I think he's a wild person. Too many women in his past."

Esther sighed. "You may be right, but he hasn't gotten fresh with you, has he?"

"No. He's been the perfect gentleman so I'm not scared to go out with him or play tennis like we do. He is entertaining."

"And very handsome and interested in you."

Ruth shook her head. "I'm a novelty. He probably thinks if he charms me enough, I'll break down and fool around."

Her aunt laughed. "You seem to know men pretty well."

"*Jah*, I've heard so many stories, you can't believe. And how 'bout you? His father is pretty nice, too."

"He is. He wants to take me out to dinner next week-end."

Ruth smiled over at her. "Are you going?"

"I think so. I told him yes."

"He seems really nice–especially to you, Aunt Esther. I think he likes you a whole lot."

"Do you?"

"*Jah*, I looked at his eyes when you were at the net playing tennis and he had a nice smile and watched you real close."

"Maybe he only wants to suggest ways to improve my backhand."

Ruth wagged her head back and forth. "No way. I know when a guy is looking and liking someone. Believe me."

"Well, time will tell. Think I'll turn in early to read."

"*Gut nacht*, Aunt."

"*Gut nacht*, dear. That felt good to say. Sometimes I miss hearing the old dialect."

The four played tennis twice a week now and usually went out afterwards for something to eat. Nothing lavish, but it was a pleasant time. Tennis had replaced her aunt's exercise of running. It was bitter cold out. Two other evenings a week, Ruth went with her aunt to practice. Her game was improving steadily and she could now serve, though she had not developed speed. Her aunt assured her it would come in time.

Afternoons, before her aunt got home, Ruth practiced faithfully on the violin and her teacher commented at how quickly she had improved. She actually played "Three Blind Mice," without error. When she was done practicing, she listened to the classical radio station or played her IPod. Sometimes, when she did, she'd picture Jeremiah and her tears would surface.

One day when she returned from work, the manager handed her the mail. "It's supposed to warm up next week."

"Good. I'm ready for spring."

"Are you going home for a visit?"

"I'm not sure yet. I want to, but I have a job now, you know."

"So your aunt told me. Good for you. Looks like you got news from home."

On the way up the elevator she checked and sure enough there was a letter from Emma, one from her sister-in-law, Hannah, and one from Jeremiah. Her heart took a sudden leap when she noticed his handwriting. When she got in the apartment, she sat on the sofa and forced herself to read the ones from Emma and Hannah first, saving the best for last.

She opened Emma's.

Dear Ruth,

I am sorry I do not write more often. It has been so busy at school and I am tired at night. Mamm is tired too. I know she misses you a lot. We all do.

I went to a Sing with Josiah Stoltz. I know all he talks about is cows, but he is cute and he is smart, though he acts like a dummkopf *sometimes.*

No one hears from Jeremiah. I do not miss him even a little. It's funny, I thought I cared more than I do.

The bad news is Bishop King died a few days ago. Everyone is very sad. He was a good man even though many people thought he was too strict. Now we need a new bishop and everyone is whispering about who it might be.

Say hallo *to Aunt Esther.* Oma *talks about her now. Not like bad.*

Do you like your job? I bet you are real good in tennis. It looks very hard. I like badminton better, I think.

Love, Emma
P.S. Abby is in a family way. She is happy.

Hannah's letter was brief, but she gave Ruth an update on all the family. She mentioned she was pregnant and this time they were hoping for a boy since their other three children were girls.

Now she slid a letter opener under the flap of Jeremiah's envelope and cut through the top.

Dear Ruth,

Why have you not written? Are you so busy? No time for old friends?

I got a note from my mother and she said Bishop King died. That is too bad. He was ninety-four years old though, so he had a good life. That's what I think.

I am working extra hard now. My two uncles help too, but they have their own farms to manage so I do most of the heavy work. I can not believe my grandfather did so much work. His cancer is out of control now. They just try to keep him comfortable. My grandmother stays by his side all the time. She is a good woman. The ministers pray a lot and come by to talk, but he is too weak and can only listen. I wish I could play him some music to help him, but I can not. He would not think it right.

Do you listen to the IPod? What is your favorite piece?

Please do not stay angry (Amish should not stay angry) and write to me. Soon.

Sincerely, your friend,

Jeremiah."

Ruth tucked the letter back in the envelope and held it in her hand. She should write. What did she have to lose? After all, they were friends–had been for years. What's the harm? With his grandfather on his death bed, shouldn't she write to let him know she is thinking of him and praying? She had added his grandfather to her prayer list. After reaching into the desk drawer for some stationery and a pen, Ruth sat back down as her cell phone went off.

"Hi Ruth, It's Darrel. What are you doing?"

"Nothing much. Aren't you working?"

"Had a case in court and now I'm free for the afternoon. Wondered if you wanted to go to a museum or something. I'll take you out to dinner, too."

"Wow, sounds like fun. How soon?"

"Can you be ready in half an hour? The museums may close early."

"Sure. Even sooner. I was going to practice the violin, but it can wait."

"I'll be there. Wear comfortable shoes."

Ruth took the stationery and put it back in the drawer. *Tomorrow,* she thought, and went to fix her hair and change her blouse to a fresh one. She left a note for her aunt and within minutes, the intercom buzzed and she went down to meet Darrel, handsome in his business suit. He beamed when he spotted her and she was glad she had said yes.

They decided on the Philadelphia Museum of Art, though Ruth forgot how many artists portrayed their models without clothing. She passed over those quickly, feeling her face flush. She

211

noted Darrel fighting a smile as she quickened her pace, but he didn't say a word. Her favorite artists were the early Renaissance painters, especially the ones who concentrated on Christ. She wondered why it wasn't wrong to have a painting, but it was a sin to allow your picture to be taken. Surely, if cameras had been invented when Jesus was alive, some one would have taken his picture. Then everyone would know for sure what he looked like. She mentioned it to Darrel.

"Maybe it's better this way," he said. "You can picture him any way you want to. Even change his ethnicity, if you want."

"Maybe."

"Need to rest for awhile?"

"I'm okay, but that bench looks like it needs us." Ruth took the end seat and Darrel sat next to her. "This is fun. Thanks for bringing me. I don't understand the real modern ones though."

"I doubt any one does, really. It doesn't take much talent to throw globs of paint on a canvas."

"*Jah*, you are right."

"How's the violin coming?"

"*Gut*. Good."

"You can say it in the Pennsylvania Dutch. I think it's cute."

"I feel silly here in a big city, dressed as an *Englisher*, even dating a regular man, using the old language."

"Do you like dating a regular man?"

Ruth twisted the free gallery brochure in her hands. "I guess that's what I'm doing, isn't it?"

"I guess so." He grinned at her and reached over to put his hand on hers. It made her uncomfortable, but it didn't seem too forward. It had the feeling of friendship, so she left her hand under his.

After a couple of minutes they went on to the gallery of impressionism. "I like these, too," Ruth said standing in front of a Renoir.

"Yeah, they are wonderful. So are you, Ruth."

She stopped moving and tried to think of a response. Finally, she uttered a *danki* and moved on.

After having dinner at a Japanese restaurant, Darrel drove her back to her apartment. He walked upstairs with her and she used her key.

"Isn't your aunt home?"

"No, she was meeting a friend for dinner. Do you want to come in for a couple minutes?"

"Why not." He removed his suit jacket and loosened his tie before sitting on the sofa. "So are you going to play something on the violin for me?"

"Oh, no. Not yet. All I can play is "Three Blind Mice" and "Are You Sleeping.""

"Not ready for the concert hall, yet?" he teased. "Well sit and tell me about your job."

"Like I said at dinner, not much to tell. Billy barely speaks to me, but he barely talks to anyone. He cleans good though."

"Glad he doesn't give me any competition."

"Oh no. Don't worry about him." Ruth realized too late what she had said. She didn't want to encourage the man. It wouldn't be fair. Her heart still belonged to Jeremiah and would remain so, that was for sure and for certain.

"I never dated anyone like you," Darrel said softly. "I can't get you out of my mind."

"But we are so different."

"Does it matter?"

"I...I don't want anything more than friendship."

"Ever?"

"I didn't say that. Someday, maybe." She pictured Jeremiah and remembered his hands on her as she nearly fell from the buggy that Sunday. And his sweet lips on hers.

"I guess we'll leave it there," Darrel said, his voice displaying disappointment.

"I do like you, Darrel. Don't think I don't."

"Enough to take it to the next step?"

"What do you mean? What is the next step?"

He leaned over and before she had a chance to move away, his lips were on hers. She was so shocked she merely moved back and stared at him. His kiss had been gentle, but not without passion and it had given her strange feelings. Desire. Unwanted desire. She pulled back.

"*Nein.* I can't do this. We aren't married."

"Ruth, Ruth, people don't have to be married to enjoy being together and showing affection."

"*Jah*, but it could lead to more."

"True. I guess that's what I hoped would happen."

"Maybe we should not be alone again. Maybe neither of us should want that."

"I'm sorry if I offended you. I'll be more careful in the future."

"I think we should just play tennis maybe."

"If that's what you want, Ruth."

She detected a tone of regret. Was he willing to proceed on her terms?

"Wow, it's getting late. I need my beauty sleep." He rose and reached for his jacket. "Thanks for going with me, Ruth. I had a great day."

"*Jah*, me too. *Danki.*" She walked to the door with him, locking it after he left. She touched her lips where she had felt his and felt shame. *I should have seen it coming. Maybe that's what I wanted to happen. Oh, Jeremiah, what now?*

Chapter Thirty-four

"Mary, another cup of coffee before I go to the barn." Leroy pushed his empty plate, which had recently contained bacon and eggs, off to the side.

"I get it. Want a sticky bun with it? Fresh from the oven." Mary rose and headed for the stove to take a bun from the hot pan. After placing it in front of her husband, she removed his soiled dish and set it in the sink before sitting next to him at the table.

"*Jah*, why not?"

Leroy sipped the hot liquid slowly as Mary sat patching a pair of work pants for Wayne. Leroy spoke in quiet tones. "Bishop King was a fine man. A Godly soul."

"*Jah*, he was."

"He was loved. A lot of people will show up at the funeral."

"I know. He was loved indeed. He'll be hard to replace."

"The ministers are holding a meeting in a few days to discuss it. In the meantime, Bishop Kapp from the next district will take care of things."

Mary made a knot and broke the thread with her teeth. "Seems like a lot of work for one man."

"It's his duty, Mary. It's God's will."

"I know. If one of our ministers becomes Bishop, he'll have to be replaced, *jah*?"

Leroy sipped his coffee and nodded. "It would be *gut* to have a younger man as bishop. We need to change some simple things to the *Ordnung*."

"I'm surprised to hear you say that, Leroy."

"We're losing too many children to the English way. I don't talk about electricity, but maybe a phone nearby would be *gut*."

"*Jah*. Maybe Ruth could play her violin in her room."

"We shall see. I saw Jeremiah Fisher's *daed* yesterday at market. He's building a *dawdi haus* for his *mudder*. We're getting a group together to go help next week."

"Did his *daed* pass away yet?"

"No, but it won't be long. Poor man suffers terrible. Hopefully, the good Lord will take him soon–just like the bishop."

"Will you need the womenfolk to prepare meals for the bishop's funeral?" Mary asked her husband as she put the needle in her pin cushion and laid the slacks aside.

"Most likely. I'll know more later. Daniel said he'd come by and let us know."

"I can make extra bread today, just in case."

Leroy rose, placed the mug in the sink and headed for the door.

"You gonna be warm enough, Leroy?"

"*Jah*, it's up in the fifties today. Glad to see spring coming."

"Now with the bishop gone, when will we have communion service?"

"Soon. Next Sunday. Did you hear any more from Ruthie?" Leroy asked.

"Emma hears more than me. She reads her letters to me."

"When is she comin' home?"

"She doesn't talk about it yet." Ruth's mother lowered her head to avoid showing her pain.

"*Jah*, well. She needs to be sure, that's for certain. Do you miss her, Mary?"

"Now what do you think? Of course, I miss her. Now I know how my *Mamm* felt when my sister left. It breaks my heart."

"*Yah*, me, too." Leroy tapped his wife gently on the shoulder and left for the barn.

Two days later, Mary's parents came for the afternoon. Her father, Amos, went searching for Leroy while her mother, Carrie, sat at the quilting frame to add some stitches. Mary sat across from her.

"So what do you hear from Ruthie?" Carrie asked. "Is she ready to come home?"

"*Nein.* Not yet. She has a job."

"Doing what?" Her mother looked up from the quilt.

"She works in a coffee house and serves food."

"So she works with English."

"I guess so."

"No problems?"

"Ruthie wouldn't tell me if she did, you know that, *Mamm.*"

"Mmm. Esther wrote me a letter."

Mary stopped sewing and raised her head. "*Jah?* Did you write back?"

"Not yet, but I will. She broke my heart, Mary. I hope and pray your Ruthie doesn't do the same to you. Maybe Esther will tell her she made a mistake."

"Maybe she didn't. Think of that?"

Carrie's eyes met Mary's and her mouth fell open. "I think she's sorry. Otherwise, why is she writing me again?"

"You are her *Mamm.* You don't stop loving your *Mamm* just because you leave the Amish way."

"I don't know, Mary. Maybe we should hire a driver and go see Ruth and Esther."

"*Jah?* You'd go there?"

"I have money aside. We could be back the same day."

"What about *Daed?* Would he go too?"

"I didn't ask him yet. Maybe we go just the two of us." Carrie stopped sewing and looked over at her daughter.

"Leroy would have to know," Mary said softly.

"*Jah*, and so would your *daed*, but I think it would be better if it's only the two of us the first time."

"Mmm. Hand me the scissors, *Mamm.* Let's plan a day to go. Emma can write and find out when they would be home. I miss my *dochder* so much."

"*Jah.* Daughters are special." Ruth's grandmother wiped her eyes and re-threaded her needle.

Chapter Thirty-five

Work had been extremely busy and when Ruth returned to the apartment, she lay on the couch and listened to music from her IPod. It brought back memories of Jeremiah and their moments together. She wondered if she'd ever see him again. After listening to Mozart for awhile, she turned it off and removed the stationery from the drawer for the second time. This time she would write the letter, even before practicing her violin. The day before her instructor had given her "Amazing Grace" to play, and though she was anxious to attempt it, she was more concerned about writing to Jeremiah. Ruth sat a few minutes, pen in hand, before she started her letter.

> *Dear Jeremiah,*
>
> *I hope you are well. I hope your grandfather is not hurting too much and your grandmother is not getting too tired. It is a hard time for your family. I am sorry.*
>
> *I am making nice friends. A couple anyway. I play tennis two times a week at night and I work at the coffee place but not hard. Today was hard though. Too many people. I came home and listened to Mozart on the music maker you gave me. It made me relax some and now I am writing to you.*
>
> *You asked if I am ready to go back to Amish ways. I miss my family much but I am not ready. My Aunt Esther is a good woman. She reads her Bible now. She loves me and I know she would be happy if I stay with her.*
>
> *I am sorry about the bishop. Now they will need a new bishop. Maybe he will think different about some things. Things that bother me and make it hard for me to settle on Amish right now. Like my violin. I am not good yet, but I love to make the*

music come out of it. I do not think it is a sin. Do you? I think about the concert you took me to sometimes. It was one of the most wonderful gut days in my whole life.

You asked me if I miss you. Jah. I do. Maybe we will someday see each other again. Maybe God will make it happen.

Emma likes Josiah Stoltz who used to like me. I am glad. I want her to marry and be happy. Josiah may be the man for her. He was not for me, though.

I am going to be nineteen on April 10. Only two weeks away. I am getting old. Ha. Ha.

Your friend,
Ruth Zook

Ruth read it over and placed it in an envelope and then opened her violin case, gently removing the instrument and the bow. She was improving so much her teacher was amazed. It pays to practice, she thought to herself as she attempted the new music. It was not that difficult to read the notes and the haunting sounds of the violin filled the apartment. Not realizing the time, she was startled to see her aunt standing in the hallway listening to her. She stopped abruptly.

"Please go on."

Ruth completed "Amazing Grace" and then set the violin in its case.

"I can't believe you play so well already. You have a natural talent."

Ruth blushed at the compliment. "*Jah*, well. God gives talent. It will not make me proud."

"Of course not. I enjoyed listening though," her aunt said as she set her purse down in the hallway. "I brought the mail up with me. Emma wrote to you." She handed Ruth the letter as she headed toward her bedroom. "I need to get my slippers. I have new shoes on and they're killing me."

Ruth read the letter from her sister.

Dear Ruth,

How is everything going in Philadelphia? Hope you like your job. It sounds like hard work, especially serving Englishers. Do they complain a lot? I heard they like everything perfect.

Mamm *and* Oma *want to come to see you. They will hire someone to drive them so he can come right to your apartment.* Oma *wants to see you and she wants to see Esther. I hope it will be okay with her. Katie and I want to come, too, but* Mamm *says she may want to come alone with* Oma *the first time. I don't know why, but if she does want that, she probably has a good reason. Daed said okay. She has money saved but* Oma *will pay for the ride. Please write back soon so they can make plans. It would probably be a Saturday since you will not have to work that day. I think you said Aunt Esther does not work on Saturdays either. Am I right?*

I went to a Sing last week with Josiah. He has a good voice. Not as good as Jeremiah, but he can carry a tune gut. *He held my hand one time. He is strong. I can feel it in his hand. I like a man to be strong. Do you?*

You can send your letter to me or Mamm. *We read each other's letters.* Daed *went to a meeting where they talked about getting the new bishop. They will have another meeting. It will be one of the preachers. I hope it is Luke Schultz. He smiles a lot and I think he would be good. He's only forty, though.*

Happy birthday if I don't write again soon. I hope you have a cake. Maybe Aunt Esther will make one. I love you and miss you. Our room is so empty now. I use your pillow when I read and it makes me so sad.

Love, Emma

"Aunt Esther, wait till you hear this." Ruth walked over to Esther's bedroom where she was changing into tennis clothes. "Oh, I forgot we play tonight."

"Are you too tired? We can skip it if you'd like."

"I'll be fine. I rested. But you need to read the letter from Emma. Here." She handed it over and Esther sat on the edge of the bed to read it.

"Oh, my." Her eyes teared up. "I can't believe it. I'll see my mother again after all these years. Thank you, God, for answering my prayer." She allowed her tears to flow and Ruth sat beside her, surrounding her with her arms.

"See? She still loves you. A mother loves forever."

"Yes, and so does a daughter."

"I want to write back tomorrow. We should pick a Saturday in April," Ruth suggested.

"Yes, we'll check the calendar tonight and decide. Oh, Ruth, what will I say after all these years?"

"I guess just say what's on your mind. It will be awkward maybe, but not for long. God will help you with your words."

"Yes, He's faithful...even when we're not."

Ruth played tennis poorly. She was still fatigued from her busy day at work, so Darrel suggested his father and Esther play a game while he took Ruth for ice cream. Esther smiled broadly and waved her racket. "Have fun, guys. Take your time, but don't forget to come back."

"Ah, now you'll *really* have to work for points," Martin, said to Esther with a grin.

"You're on," Esther replied, smiling back.

Darrel drove a few blocks to a popular ice cream parlor where they split a large sundae. "I'm glad I didn't try to eat one of these all by myself," Ruth said.

"They are huge. I could do it, but better for my heart if I don't."

"I got a letter from my sister back home today. My mother and grandmother are coming for a visit soon. Only for the day."

"Sounds nice. Have they been to Philadelphia before?"

"I think my mother was here years ago, but not my grandmother. She's never been anywhere outside of Lancaster County."

"What a shame."

Ruth looked up, her eyebrows arched. "Why is it a shame?"

"That she's never been anywhere. Done anything."

"Oh my, I don't think that's the case at all. What reason did she have to leave her home? After all, she had everything she needed right there."

"Ruth, you sound so defensive. If that's the case, why are *you* here?"

"That's different."

"How so?"

"Things have changed. There's more to do now."

Darrel took a spoonful of ice cream and held it to his mouth before speaking. "Aren't you glad you've seen some of the world's greatest art? And heard some of the finest music known to man? Would you have wanted to die without ever experiencing those things?"

"No, but I'm different."

"Your grandmother is a woman, probably much like you when she was young."

"No. I'm sure she never wanted more than to be a wife and mother and a Godly woman."

"You know that much about the woman's mind?"

"Well, she never complained. She always had a smile and a good word for people. If she was unhappy, she hid it."

"I'm not trying to be argumentative, Ruth, I want you to understand she sacrificed a lot by remaining Amish, whether she ever realizes it or not."

"I guess I know what you're trying to say. Maybe you're right. Now that I've been to the museum and the concert hall, should I be satisfied to return to Amish ways or should I want even more? Like travel to London or Hawaii?"

"You're the judge of that. If you stay," he reached across for her hand, "you may find everything you want right here."

"Everything and everyone?"

"Perhaps. You should give me a chance to prove it."

"Darrel, could you ever be faithful to one woman?"

"If that woman was the love of my life."

"It would be risky for a woman to assume she would be able to hold a man's love forever; especially when he had proven to be a lady's man."

"You don't hold back any punches, do you?" he asked with a crooked smile.

"I believe in honesty."

"At any cost?"

"Most of the time." She looked down at her sundae and took a nibble.

They were silent for a few moments. Ruth cut the top strawberry in half with her spoon and slid half to his side of the dish. Then she took a large mouthful and savored the fresh-churned vanilla ice cream. It was almost as good as her *mamm's*. "This is delicious."

Darrel removed his hand and nodded. "You know how to change the subject as well."

"I like being with you, Darrel. I really do, but I don't see a future for us. Our lives are too different. I will probably go back to Lancaster County by the end of the summer."

"What's keeping you here, then?"

"I'm not sure. Music. Art. My job. My aunt."

"Not me?" His eyes seared into hers.

"I would miss you, *jah*–if I left."

"Ruth, I don't know what's come over me, but I really do care about you. I really want you to keep an open mind and see me more often. I won't try to become intimate, I promise."

"I believe you. You wouldn't get far, anyway," she said with a quirky grin as she raised one brow.

Darrel laughed out loud. "How well I know. I have no desire to get a black eye."

The subject turned to his law practice and he told her about a case he had been following in the newspaper that had reached his firm. "I hope I get the file. It could make a difference in my career. Good exposure, especially if I win the case."

"Is it so important to you?"

"Well yeah. Doesn't everyone want fame?"

Ruth laughed and shook her head. "See? We are like oil and water. Never to mix."

After finishing the ice cream, Darrel paid and they drove back to the courts to pick up his father and Esther. When they went in, they were just finishing up a game. "This woman is good," his father remarked, shaking his head. "I nearly lost."

"Watch out. Next time, I'll do even better," Esther commented. "My backhand was off."

"Shall we go get something to eat?" Martin asked the group.

"We just gorged ourselves with ice cream, Dad, but we can sit with you if you want."

"Why don't we go back to our place," Esther suggested. "I have pizzas in the freezer."

"Sounds good. Everyone up for that?" Martin asked the others.

Ruth nodded and Darrel slipped his arm around her waist. "I'm game."

"And I'm not fair game," Ruth whispered to him as she removed his hand.

"Oops, sorry," he said, feigning forgetfulness.

After the pizzas were devoured, they played Monopoly for two hours. Ruth yawned as she checked her watch.

"I guess we'd better head for home, Son," Martin said.

"But I just put hotels on Boardwalk and Park Place. No one's landed yet."

Esther laughed and slid her chair back. "I'll hold the board until next time."

"That's alright. I'm merely kidding around. Yeah, it's getting late."

"I wanted to ask you to come on the 10th for a birthday party," Esther said to the men as they headed toward the door.

"You're having a birthday?" Martin asked Esther.

"No," Esther replied, reaching for Ruth and putting her arm around her. "My dear niece is turning nineteen. We'll have supper followed by cake and ice cream. How about it?"

"Aunt Esther, it's so sweet of you." Ruth rested her head against her aunt's. "Thank you."

"We'd love to help celebrate," Darrel said quickly. "What time do you want us here?"

"How about seven?"

"You can count on it. Of course, we'll see you both before then. Tennis, anyone?" Darrel took a swing with an imaginary racket.

"Let's do it again next Tuesday evening. I've got a tremendous amount of paper work this week. End of semester and all coming up," Esther said.

"That's fine. I'll call to confirm, Esther. Thanks for a great evening," Martin said as he leaned over to Esther and kissed her cheek lightly. Her smile was radiant.

Darrel put on a light jacket and touched Ruth's nose with his finger. "See you, Ruth. Don't work too hard."

"I won't."

After they left, the two women shed their shoes and sprawled out on chairs before heading for bed.

"It looks like you and Darrel's father enjoy each other's company a lot."

"I think you're right. He's a very nice man and interesting to talk to. I've dated men who bore me stiff."

"*Jah.* I had a guy do that. All he talked about was cows."

Esther laughed. "Oh, that would be dreary. What about you and Darrel?"

"We're good friends."

"Martin seems to think there is something more going on."

"He's wrong. I don't love him, Aunt Esther."

"But maybe he's falling for you."

"I hope not. I don't want to hurt him. I've made it clear we can see each other as long as it doesn't go further than friendship."

"And he's okay with that?"

"He has no choice. It's that, or nothing."

Esther laughed at her comment. "You are a strong-willed young lady. Most women your age would be drooling over that young man. He's got it all–looks, charm, money."

"*Jah*, but that's not what's important. What about his heart? How does he stand with God? How much does he care about others? Would he always be faithful? Those things are what I look for in a man."

"I see, and Jeremiah fills that description?"

Ruth became somber. "I think so, but I'm not sure anymore. I need to see him again before I know for sure."

"Does he mention getting together with you at all?"

"He hints at it. But he's all the way in Ohio and he works all the time, helping his grandfather on the farm. His grandfather's dying, remember?"

"Yes, I do. Very sad. Jeremiah's a good person to drop everything to go help family."

"*Jah*. I like that about him. Maybe some day…"

"And in the meantime, we'd better get some sleep. It's midnight already and we have to get up early." They both rose from their seats.

"You're right. *Gut nacht*, Aunt."

"*Gut nacht*, Ruthie," she responded as she hugged her niece.

Chapter Thirty-six

Ruth finished twisting her hair into a bun. No point in shocking her mother and grandmother immediately. It was enough for her to be dressed in jeans and a casual sweater. She knocked on her aunt's bedroom door. "They should be here soon."

"I'll be ready in a minute. Oh, Ruth, come in and help me." Ruth opened the door to find her aunt standing by the closet, pushing dresses along the rod. "I don't know what to wear. Everything looks so bold...and almost garish. What do you think? Should I wear my black slacks and a white blouse?"

"You look good in black."

"I can't believe how nervous I am. It's so ridiculous."

"No, I understand."

"Well I don't. Okay, I'll change. Thanks, Ruth. Would you check the pasta? It should be done."

Ruth went to the stove and checked to make sure the pasta was cooked through. It was slightly *al dente*, the way Esther preferred it, so Ruth poured the spaghetti through the colander, placed it in a large ceramic bowl and ladled sauce on top to keep it from sticking. Her aunt had made the sauce earlier and Ruth was responsible for the dessert–a chocolate *mousse,* which now looked ridiculously rich next to the spaghetti and meatballs.

Her aunt came out fully dressed, and plumped up the cushions on the sofa and chairs for the second time. She checked the pasta and tasted it. "Good. I hope they like it."

"*Mamm* has never had spaghetti. She's in for a treat."

"Or we'll be passing the salad around twice."

The intercom went off and Esther gave permission for them to come up the elevator. She waited by the open door to receive her family. Ruth stood behind her and noticed her aunt's hand shake as she held the knob. The elevator doors drew open and the two Amish women emerged, carrying packages. They stood silent for a moment before making their way over to Esther and Ruth.

"*Wilkum*," Esther said in her childhood accent. Her eyes glistened with unshed tears as she led them into the foyer. Mary and Esther's mother, Carrie, laid their packages on the floor and Carrie extended her hands to her daughter. Esther took them gently in hers and met her mother's eyes. Then she surrounded her mother with her arms and they embraced, weeping in silence. Mary came over to Ruth and took her hand as they watched mother and daughter share an emotional reunion.

After several moments, Esther released her mother and turned to Mary, embracing her sister as well. Ruth felt her throat constrict as she tried to hold back tears, but such happy tears should be released. She allowed them to flow. Soon all the tears were replaced by laughter and words of endearment spoken in their familiar German dialect. Esther conversed so easily. It surprised Ruth that after all those years, she had not forgotten.

"Let me look around," Mary said as she moved from the foyer into the main living room. "Oh, my. You are very rich."

Esther laughed slightly. "I'm very comfortable."

"It is very beautiful, *jah*?"

Ruth's grandmother, stood next to her and whistled through her teeth. "My daughter is a fancy woman with an education." There was a hint of pride in the statement Ruth realized, but how could she not be pleased that her daughter had accomplished so much?

"I'll show you the rest of the apartment and then we can sit and talk." Esther opened the door to her bedroom and the four of them walked inside.

"*Jah*, I wouldn't want to get up from a fancy bed like that," her mother responded. She walked to the bed and pushed on the mattress with her hand. "Too soft. It could hurt your back."

"So far I'm doing alright, *Mamm*," Esther said, amusement peeking from her eyes.

"We brought you some goodies from home," Mary said as they finished their tour. "Katie made cookies and Emma baked an apple pie from last fall's apples." She took them out and laid them on the counter. "How do you manage in such a tiny kitchen?"

"I'm afraid I don't do much cooking."

"*Gut* thing. It would be hard."

"Is anyone hungry yet? Lunch, or I should say, dinner, is ready anytime."

Her mother nodded. "I could eat. What did you make? It smells *gut*."

"Spaghetti and meat balls, plus a salad."

Mary and her mother exchanged glances. "Sounds real wonderful-*gut*. Right *Mamm*?"

"Oh, *Jah*. I never ate such things. It will be fun to try something different."

"Now you sit down at the table and we'll bring things out." Esther motioned to Ruth who took a pitcher of water and filled their glasses.

"Look at your fancy bowl," *oma* said, touching the edge of the cut glass piece. "I would be scared to death to use it."

"I don't usually put anything into it," Esther replied as she brought two bowls of pasta in and laid them on their dinner plates. "Do you want your salad at the same time?"

"Whatever the custom. We don't know your English ways, *dochder*."

"Well, Ruth, why don't you bring the salad bowl out and people can do their own thing. Your plates on the left are for salad."

"Lots of fancy things. I feel kind of funny," Mary said lifting a sterling salt shaker.

"Please don't," Esther said almost apologetically. "As you may remember, I've always liked things of beauty."

Oma nodded. "*Jah*. I remember. You used to draw pictures of little girls with lace and big fancy hats on them. I kept one."

"Really?" Esther looked over at her mother as they seated themselves.

"Oh *jah*. I have other stuff too. I did not forget my *dochder*, even if she forgot me."

"I never forgot you."

There was silence–an uncomfortable strain, almost tangible. Ruth looked over at her aunt and noted the struggle in her eyes. Things were not right.

Esther lowered her eyes and the others followed suit. After prayer they began eating. Ruth passed the Italian bread.

"*Jah*, well. I like the spaghetti. The bread is different. Not like mine," *Oma* commented.

"The Italians make a crispier crust," Ruth said, trying to keep the discussion off personal things.

"Yes," her aunt added. "In Rome, the bread is so delicious. That and a cup of strong coffee with cream makes a great start to your day."

"*Jah*." Mary cut her pasta up into tiny pieces. "So, Ruthie, how do you like your job?"

"*Gut*. The lady who owns it is nice to me."

"And you make enough money to help out?"

"Oh, she doesn't have to help with the expenses," Esther broke in.

"Sure, she does. That's the Amish way. No one eats if they don't work. Unless they are old or sickly." Mary nodded over at her mother who agreed.

"I'm learning to play the violin," Ruth said with a forced smile.

"*Jah*, Emma told us. She read your letter. Are you *gut* yet?" Mary looked over as she spooned the tiny pieces of pasta into her mouth.

"She is," Esther answered for her. "I'm amazed at how much she's learned in such a short time. Even her teacher–"

"We heard."

"I play tennis, too," Ruth added, hoping something would take the edge off the guarded questioning.

"It is *gut* for you to play a sport, I guess," *Oma* said. "Now that you don't get exercise any other way. On a farm you get all the exercise you need."

"Speaking of farming," Esther chimed in. "How is *Daed*?"

"*Gut*."

"Does he know you're here?"

Oma looked at her with furrowed brows. "*Jah*, I wouldn't come without telling him."

"Did he want to come, too?" Esther asked, Ruth seeing hope in her eyes.

"He is going to wait till you come home for a visit."

"Pass me the salad, please," Mary asked. Ruth handed her the bowl. "*Danki*."

Mary put a small amount on the plate and cleared her throat. "Emma wanted me to ask you this, Ruthie. Have you any men friends?"

Ruth swallowed a piece of her bread, selecting the right words before answering. "*Jah*, a nice young man who helps teach me to play tennis."

Oma's eyes went up and rested on her granddaughter's. "He is your age?"

"A little older. We're good friends."

"Be careful, Ruthie," her mother warned. "English men want more from their friends than our Amish men."

Esther broke in. "Darrel is a real gentleman. You don't have to worry about him. His father, too, is very polite."

Oma looked over at her daughter. "Is he a married man?"

"He was." Esther glanced at Ruth, who rolled her eyes in her direction.

"Widower?"

"Actually, no. He had a very bad marriage. His wife was–"

"Tsk. No excuse. Ruthie hand me the butter again."

Things didn't seem to improve much as they completed the main course. Ruth stacked the dishes in the sink while Esther put the coffee on and took in the desserts. "Ruth made a wonderful chocolate *mousse*," she said as she put small dishes out with a serving spoon.

"*Mousse?* Like the animal?" *Oma* asked, amusement on her face.

"No, it's a French word for pudding."

"*Jah?* Call it pudding then. *Nein*, I will stick with the apple pie."

"Me, too," Mary said, adding, "the pudding looks *gut*, but I love apple pie best in the world."

As they sipped coffee with their dessert, Esther asked if they wanted to visit a museum or drive through the city. They decided to remain at the apartment since time was a factor.

"Our driver will return for us soon. We told him three o'clock," Mary said.

Ruth glanced at her watch. It was already two, but unexpectedly, she felt relief. Only one more hour of this torture.

"So, how is Emma getting on with Josiah Stoltz?" Ruth asked her mother.

"They get along pretty *gut*. He is a nice boy. You could have had him yourself, Ruthie."

"*Jah*, you would have liked that, but he bored me silly."

"Well your *daed* didn't talk much to me when we were courtin', but he was a fine man."

"I know," Ruth said as she poured more coffee in her cup.

"So, Esther," Mary looked over at her sister. "You like being a professor lady?"

"I love it."

"What do you teach again?"

"American literature."

"Mmm. It pays pretty *gut*?"

"Yes, I'm fortunate."

"But you never married." Mary's mouth was drawn.

"No."

"Did you have chances?"

"I...I was in love once, yes."

"You miss not having *bopplies*?"

"Sometimes, of course. We make choices in our lives. Are there things I've missed out on? Yes, but can't you say the same for yourself? I've been very fulfilled living here in Philadelphia. I attend concerts and plays and I have many friends. The restaurants are excellent and I work out at a center."

"And church. Do you attend church?" her mother asked.

"Not yet."

"How many years and you haven't found a church?" Mary clucked her tongue.

"Mary, please. This should be a time of reconciliation. Not an inquisition." Esther's expression was frozen, the earlier smiles seemed forgotten.

"*Jah*. I'm sorry. You are right. I want us to write and keep in touch. It is sad we have grown so far apart."

Oma put a hand on each of her daughter's arms. "No more questions. We do what we have to do. Our hearts lead us in different directions, but we can still love."

"Yes," Esther said pensively. "And see each other more often. We can't let so much time go by."

"You are right," *Oma* responded. "I was wrong not to write you back."

"I understand."

"I don't think so. I was so hurt, Esther. And so concerned about Mary. I needed you at that time."

"I know. I know. Can you forgive me?"

"*Jah*. I have no choice but to forgive. I did it a long time ago, but I couldn't write back. I am not sure why, but I would try and end up not sending it. I should have. Can you forgive me about that?"

"Of course, *Mamm*." They held each other's hands. Esther's phone went off and she reluctantly walked over to answer it.

"No, I don't want a new credit card." She hung up abruptly.

"See why we don't like phones?" Mary said, her lips lifting slightly.

"I think you have the right idea," Esther said with a forced smile.

"Ruthie, we brought you a little something for your birthday," her mother said. "But don't open it yet. Wait." She went to the alcove and picked up a small bag, handing it to her daughter.

"*Danki*. You didn't need to do that."

"*Nein*, but we wanted you to have something."

The intercom went off and Esther walked over. It was the driver who chose to wait for them in the lobby.

"We mustn't keep him waiting. He will charge more," *Oma* said as she arranged her shawl and headed for the door. She stopped and looked over at Esther and reached out her arms. Esther went immediately and held her close. "Thank you for coming. I'll write soon, but I expect an answer this time."

Then Ruth hugged her mother and grandmother. She watched as her mother and aunt embraced briefly. Once the door closed behind them, Ruth looked over at her aunt, who let out a long breath. "Phew, that was something."

"*Jah.*"

"On a scale of one to ten?"

"Maybe a six?"

"More like a five-and-a-half. Oh, Ruth, I'd hoped for so much more."

"But it's a beginning. The door is open now."

"Yes, and I will keep it open this time. Let's eat some *mousse*," she said as she put her arm around her niece and headed to the messy kitchen.

Chapter Thirty-seven

Due to an extremely busy week, Ruth and her aunt cancelled their tennis dates with Darrel and his father, though Esther did accept Martin's invitation to dinner one night. While she was gone, Ruth practiced on her violin. She ran her scales and tried a couple techniques her instructor had shown her. Sometimes, when she closed her eyes and drew the bow across the strings, she pretended she was playing for Jeremiah. She pictured him smiling at her, humming along with the music. She could almost hear his tenor voice joining hers. How could she give up her violin? And why should she?

While Ruth enjoyed her time alone, it left her with too much time to think. After she put the violin back in its case, she sat back and listened to the distant flow of traffic from the incessant traffic, barely audible through the thick window panes. She closed her eyes and pictured her bed with the quilt against her cheek, the sound of Emma's light breathing and the occasional bark of a dog. She could smell the lung-cleansing breeze from their window and the faint scent of the rich overturned soil of their fields. Then Jeremiah's laugh—

Enough!

Ruth forced her mind to return to the present and paced the floor, reprimanding herself for her indulgence. Then she heard the turn of a key as Esther entered the apartment. *Thank goodness.*

"Ruthie, it's me." Esther entered the room glowing from her evening with Martin. After several minutes discussing their day and Esther's date, they prepared for the night.

On the way back from work the following afternoon, Ruth stopped for the mail and then headed up to the apartment. There was a new letter from Emma. She told her how much their mother and grandmother had enjoyed their visit. She also said the new bishop had not been selected yet and there was much talk among the men folk as to who it would be. Then she mentioned that some of her students continued to be difficult, especially the boy who lost his mother over the holidays.

>Mamm *had the father and his two children over last week for supper.*
>
>*Their poor* daed *looks so sad. He doesn't even see his* kinder *right now through his grief. I tried to talk to him about it, but he just looked away .I'm afraid I didn't help much.*
>
>*I hope you like the birthday present we sent. We all had a hand in it, even Wayne. I still miss our talks and my hair is all snarly at night. Katie hurts worse than you do when she combs it out.*
>
>*Write back soon.*
>
>   *Love, Emma*

Ruth didn't hear from Darrel all week-end, which bothered her ever so slightly. Her aunt spent Saturday at the university catching up on her work and later met Martin for dinner. Ruth could play the violin all evening if she desired to, since she wouldn't hurt any one's ears but her own. In reality, she had improved so much, the squeaks were all but gone and she was gaining speed on her runs. This time Ruth didn't allow herself thinking time. She read from her Bible instead and got half way through Leviticus.

When she arrived at work the next day, she discovered the café owner, Terri, had fired her son for showing up inebriated. In his place, she had already hired a young woman around twenty, who she planned to train as a server. Deb Greenley was intelligent and attractive with straight black hair and jade green eyes. She and Ruth hit it off the first day and during a slow period, Ruth learned she also played tennis.

"With the weather so nice, we could play at a park, Ruth," Deb suggested. "Of course, we still have our jobs."

"It would be fun. I need to work on my game. I am still, as you say–lousy."

Deb laughed. "I love your accent."

Later while Deb was wiping the counter and Ruth was taking an order, Darrel came in dressed in a grey suit with a red tie. He really was quite handsome. He chatted with Ruth and reminded her he would be over on the tenth to help celebrate her birthday. After finishing his cup of coffee, he checked his watch. "I have to get back to the office. New trial coming up and I need to prepare. See you soon."

As soon as he was out the door, Deb motioned for Ruth to come over to the counter. In a low voice, she asked who he was. "Ruth, that man is gorgeous. I know I've seen his picture somewhere. Maybe in the Philadelphia Magazine. Yes, it was! I remember now. He's one of the city's most eligible bachelors! And you're dating him?" Her eyes were brilliant circles.

"We go out sometimes, sure. But it's not what you think. We're just friends."

"Come on, girl. Only friends? Through choice?"

Ruth laughed. "In a way. Okay, I choose it that way."

"You're out of your mind. Don't let that one get away."

"If it's God's will, it will be done."

"Well give God a break and help Him out."

"Girls, there are two new customers. Let's cut the gossip," Terri said as she worked on her books at an empty table nearby.

Esther spent part of each evening on the phone with Martin. Ruth was amused at her aunt's girlish laughter.

The night before the party, the two sat together before heading for bed.

"You spend a lot of time now with Darrel's father," Ruth mentioned.

"I guess I do. He's so much fun to be with and so knowledgeable. He was considering a run for the state legislature last year."

"*Jah*? He changed his mind?"

"For now. He knows a lot about politics."

"And you like to talk about that?"

"Of course. Doesn't your family ever discuss worldly events?"

"Once in a while. I heard about nine-eleven. That was terrible. I even went to a store where I could see pictures of the buildings as they collapsed. Of course, it was a week later for me. But presidents and elections - no, we are not interested. Of course, it's not the Amish way."

"Another reason I'm glad I left."

"Aunt Esther, here it is April and I still don't know what I should do. How will I ever make up my mind?"

"Sometimes, it takes one incident to push you to one side or the other."

"Is that what happened with you?"

She nodded. "It was when your mother came down with polio. Someone had told us we could get vaccinated earlier, but the bishop wouldn't hear of it. Then a neighbor's five-year old came down with it. He was permanently paralyzed. I begged my mother to let the rest of the family get the vaccine and she said God would protect us."

"And He didn't."

"No. Your mother was so sick. I was angry and I accused *Oma* of being a bad mother for not protecting her children better. It was not a pretty scene. She actually told me to leave and stay with an aunt, but I had been contemplating leaving the Amish anyway. This gave me the boost I needed."

"And you have no regrets?"

"I'd be lying if I told you I never look back and wonder, but all in all, it was the right decision for me. That doesn't mean it would be the right one for you. You simply have to weigh everything and maybe it will appear obvious after something happens that you least expect."

"Maybe a bolt of lightning will hit me on the head."

"Oh, Ruth, don't say that!" her aunt exclaimed. "I know you're kidding, but what a ghastly thought."

"I know this is personal, but what about you and Darrel's father?"

"You mean are we serious?"

"*Jah.* Do you think it's love?"

"On my part, I think it is. He mentioned moving in together but–"

"You wouldn't!" Ruth's face paled.

"Of course not. That's not going to happen. Marriage or friendship, but not a tawdry affair. Actually, he said he was joking, but who knows?"

"I'm glad Darrel doesn't talk like that."

"I think you've set him straight, Ruth. His father said he hasn't seen his son carry on before about a woman he's never…well, never been intimate with, I guess you could say."

"Oh, this English world. This may be the tipping point."

Esther laughed and patted her on the arm. "Darrel is a good catch. Don't dismiss him from your mind."

That Friday was Ruth's birthday. Deb found out and lit a candle on a cupcake while she, Terri and some regulars sang to her. Ruth was touched by their thoughtfulness. She still hadn't opened the present from home and decided to wait until evening when the men arrived. It would be more of a celebration.

When Ruth got back to the apartment, she showered and changed into a casual jade green dress, which she had purchased with her own money on a clearance rack at Macy's. It showed her slim figure to its advantage and she loved the feel of the soft neckline against her skin. After drying her long hair, she applied a modest amount of make-up and trimmed her nails, before adding a clear gloss.

Her aunt changed into a pair of off-white slacks with a colorful silk blouse of beiges and shades of rose. "Do you want to borrow any jewelry, Ruth?"

"That would be fun."

"Come on, let's check out my jewelry box." They went into Esther's bedroom and she took down a case with several drawers and they went through them together.

"Gold goes well with your dress. Here's a brooch. Try it on."

Ruth did as she suggested and looked in the mirror. "I think I like it better plain."

"Maybe, what about–" The intercom interrupted her and she went to answer it.

"Ruth, they're here already. So much for jewelry."

When they entered, Darrel was holding half a dozen helium balloons, all decorated differently, but all saying 'Happy Birthday'. His father had two gifts wrapped with giant bows. One was about a foot long and the other was larger–oblong and fairly narrow.

"Oh, what fun!" Ruth ran over and took hold of the balloons. "I never had a balloon. They are so cute."

Darrel smiled at her and took the packages from his father's arms. She was relieved he didn't attempt to kiss her, though his father leaned over and pecked her cheek and afterward went over to Esther and kissed her lightly on the mouth. He stood there with his arm around her aunt. "You girls look beautiful tonight."

"You mean every night, Dad," Darrel added as he took off a light jacket and sat on the sofa. Ruth joined him. Martin and Esther sat across from them on the other sofa.

"How soon do we eat?" Darrel asked. "I'm starving. I didn't have time to eat lunch. I did run into the café earlier, but you had already left. The new girl, Deb, was there. She seems pretty efficient."

"She is. I like her a lot. She's not lazy like Billy was."

"Well, to answer your question about dinner, the roast should be ready in about fifteen minutes."

"So did you help, Ruth?" Darrel asked, turning to her.

"*Jah.* Yes. I peeled the potatoes."

"And Ruth made the bread."

"Sounds good," Martin said. "It's been ages since I had homemade bread. So how are you doing with your violin?"

"I'm getting better all the time. I love to play."

"Why don't you play for us tonight?"

"Yeah, great idea," Darrel added to his father's request.

"Oh, I don't think I'm ready for a recital yet. Please give me a little more time."

"I guess we'll have to," Darrel said, smiling. "I don't want to force you. Why don't you open your presents while we wait."

"Should I? Okay. My *Mamm* brought one with her when she came. I'd like to open that first if it's okay. I'm so curious."

"Yes, of course, open it." Martin reached around Esther's shoulders and drew her closer to him.

Ruth rose and walked over to a chair and reached behind it for the present from her family. She opened it slowly and smiled. It was a plaque for a wall, decorated with *distelfink* birds and the word, *"Willkommen"* painted in blue lettering. "Oh, I love it," Ruth said. "Let me see their note. *Jah.* My *daed* cut it out of wood, my brother Wayne smoothed it down and put the hook on the back and Emma and Katie painted the design. Oh, and *Mamm* cleaned up their mess." She grinned at her guests, who appeared amused at her excitement.

"Now mine, Ruth," her aunt went into her bedroom and brought back a large box decorated with silver paper and a pink bow. When she opened it, Ruth caught her breath. It was a beautiful sweater she had seen when they shopped together. It was navy blue with trim of white fur. "Oh, thank you so much, Aunt. I love it."

"Dad's next." Darrel handed her the longer package and it turned out to be a new tennis racket.

"Now if it's too heavy, you can exchange it," Martin said. "I'll give your aunt the receipt in case you're not happy with it."

"It's wonderful!" She stepped back from the group and swung it back and forth. "Here's my new serve." She tossed an invisible ball in the air, stared at the ceiling for a good five seconds and then swung with all her might, whishing the racket through the air.

"Marvelous. It went a country mile," Martin said. They all laughed.

"And now mine," Darrel said as Ruth returned to the sofa.

There was a small box wrapped in tissue in a larger box. "I didn't want it to get lost."

A small diamond pendant on a sterling chain rested in a jeweler's velvet box. "Oh, my! This is way too much. I can't possibly accept this." She attempted to hand it back.

"Ruth, it's the English way. We like to show those we care about how much we like them. You must keep it. Unless you want to insult me."

"I wouldn't do that, goodness me. Thank you, Darrel."

"Do I get a kiss for this?"

"Now Darrel, don't ask for a reward," His father said.

"I'm just teasing. No strings attached. May I put it on for you?"

"*Jah*. Please." She felt the warmth from his hands on her neck as he worked the clasp open.

"There. Let's see. You couldn't have picked a better dress for it. It drops just below your throat. I picked a diamond because it's your birthstone."

"I didn't even know that. I picked a *gut* time to be born, *jah*?" Ruth self-consciously reached for her neckline and felt the drop diamond on her bare skin. She looked over at Darrel, placed her forefinger against her lips and passed a kiss over to his lips.

"The roast should be ready. Let me check." Esther headed for the kitchen. "Does anyone want something to drink?"

"We're fine," Martin spoke for his son as well as himself.

"I want to help you, Aunt Esther."

"Can you make gravy?"

"Oh, *jah*. I need an apron though."

"Ruth, I don't even own an apron. What about one you brought from home?"

"Sure, why not?" Ruth returned with one of her spotless white aprons from her past life and put it on over her dress.

Darrel followed her into the kitchen. "Look at you. You are so adorable." He took both her hands in his. "You really are Amish in that."

"*Jah*, but where's my heart?"

"I wish I knew." When her aunt turned away, he leaned over and gave her a light kiss on her cheek. She blushed, dropped her hands and went over to the stove to stir flour into the meat drippings.

After the meal they sat around and listened to some light jazz, while discussing everything under the sun, including politics.

"So I may run in the next election. My friends are pushing it," Martin remarked.

"It takes a lot of money, doesn't it?" Esther asked.

"Yes, that's one of the problems. I don't know how many would support me. I need to send out some feelers. Being a business leader, I have plenty of leads."

Ruth and Darrel were sitting next to each other on one of the sofas with her aunt and Martin relaxing on the other one, when the intercom went off.

Esther rose and headed for the front door. "I wonder who that could be. I'll go see."

Darrel was telling a joke he had heard over the radio and was about to give the punch line when Esther came back into the room. "Ruth, it's a man named Jeremiah Fisher. I told him to come up."

Ruth felt her face flush. How could this be?

Chapter Thirty-eight

Ruth rose from her seat and headed for the front door behind Esther, unable to believe this was happening. Surely her aunt misunderstood. Jeremiah was in Ohio. Why would he come here without letting her know? By the time they reached the door, they heard a knock. Esther opened it and took a step back. Jeremiah stood motionless for a moment while Ruth moved closer to him. "Jeremiah, I can't believe you're here."

"I knew it was your birthday." He had on a black jacket over a white shirt and the black trousers all Amish men wore. He removed his straw hat, held it in one hand, and clutched a package in the other.

"Please come in," Esther said. "We were just celebrating. So nice of you to come by. Oh, by the way, I'm Ruth's aunt. Call me Esther." She headed toward the living room with Ruth and Jeremiah following right behind. Darrel and his father stood and Esther introduced them. Ruth couldn't speak; she was still stunned, but she took note of the cool exchange of expressions between Darrel and Jeremiah. She was aware of their backs stiffening and their eyes appeared icy. Though the words sounded cordial, she could sense tension, which emanated throughout the room.

"So how did you get here?" Ruth asked Jeremiah as he sat down in a chair next to the sofa where Esther returned to be near Martin. Ruth sat on the other sofa again, leaving a space for Darrel. She hoped he'd sit at the other end, but he sat nearly touching her.

"I took a bus." He appeared to avoid Darrel by looking directly at Ruth.

"Are you going back today?" Ruth asked, fearing the answer. Could she find a way to be alone with him? She wanted so much to talk to him privately, but it looked impossible with the others there.

"*Jah*. I have only about two hours to see you. You all," he added, moving his arm in an arc to include everyone.

"Well, we will have to make them memorable then, won't we?" Esther said enthusiastically. "First, let me get you something to drink. We have coffee, lemonade, water–"

"Water will be just fine, *danki*. Thanks." Jeremiah looked down at his shiny black shoes as he turned the rim of his straw hat. He had the package on the floor next to the chair. "So, Ruthie, how are you doing?"

"Oh, *gut*. I like my job. Lots of good tips."

Darrel had been silent, but he joined in. "Of course, with your charm."

"*Jah*, she has charm, alright."

Silence.

Ruth attempted another subject. "I'm learning to play the violin."

"*Jah*. That's *gut*. I bet you play nice."

"And I'm teaching her to play tennis," Darrel said with a weak smile pasted on his face.

Jeremiah looked over at him and nodded. "Is she *gut*?"

"Sure is. She's got the perfect athletic body for tennis."

Ruth felt her face heat up from embarrassment. "It's fun to play."

"I bought her the new racket over there," Martin said, pointing to the corner of the room where the racket stood against the wall. Jeremiah looked over and nodded, his jaw firmly clenched.

"How is your grandfather?" Ruth asked, feeling her underarms become damp.

"Not *gut*. He hasn't much time left. The Lord will take him home soon, I hope.

"How old is he?" Martin asked.

"He's seventy-one. Ever so strong until the cancer struck him down."

"Yeah, that can be brutal. So are you a farmer?"

"Not really. Right now I'm handling my grandparents' farm for them, but I'm a buggy maker."

Darrel let out a sudden laugh. "Seriously? They still have buggy shops?"

Jeremiah frowned. "*Jah*, there are thousands of Amish families that need them. We provide a modern version. Much safer than the old ones."

"I'm sorry, I didn't mean to laugh," Darrel replied. "It seems unfathomable to me that people anywhere still depend on buggies for transportation when cars are so available."

"It's a choice we Amish make. We do not like the English ways."

"English? How about the Americans?" Darrel sat forward and laid his elbows on his knees.

"We call anyone who isn't like us, English," Ruth explained. "Some call you 'yanks', but in Lancaster County we say 'English'."

"I see."

Jeremiah looked over at Ruth and smiled. "I see you have your hair down long."

"I do, but I cut off over a foot."

"Wow! It's pretty. So do you like wearing clothes like that?" Jeremiah nodded toward her.

"I do, Jeremiah. I like nice colors."

"You look nice."

"She's gorgeous." Darrel stood up and went into the kitchen area. "I'll help myself to more coffee, if that's okay."

"Sure," Esther answered. Darrel returned and sat back down.

"So how long have you two known each other," he asked, looking over at Ruth.

"Forever, *nein?*" she said with a grin as she turned to Jeremiah for confirmation.

"*Jah*," he said, smiling, "we were little *kinder* when we met."

"*Mamm* said your family is building a *dawdi haus* for your grandmother," Ruth said.

"*Jah*. She doesn't want to leave Ohio, but my brothers there have too many kids and not much room. She will do better in Pennsylvania, that's for sure."

Ruth turned toward the others. "A *dawdi haus* is an attachment to a house or a separate building for parents when they need help."

"Interesting," Martin said as he covered his mouth, stifling a yawn.

"Well, maybe we should have the birthday cake now," Esther suggested.

"Do you need help, Aunt Esther?"

"Nope, you stay there with your guests. I'll only be a minute."

"So, have you been back to Lancaster County?" Darrel asked Jeremiah.

"Not yet. Later when my grandmother is ready to come east, then I will return."

"What about her farm, Jeremiah?" Ruth asked.

"My brothers will farm it. They need all the acreage they can get. Land is so expensive now and with their big families, they need more and more."

"Do any of your people go to college?" Martin asked.

"Once in a while, someone will go on to school. Most of us stop at eighth grade and just learn more in our homes. There's much work to do at home."

"Sounds like you're missing a lot," Darrel said as he leaned back in his seat.

"Maybe it seems so to people like you. We don't need a lot to be okay. A *gut* wife and a nice house, lots of *kinder*, and of course God. That's what we want in life."

"In that order?" Darrel pushed.

"Well, *nein.* God would come first."

"Then the wife?"

"*Jah.*" Jeremiah looked down at the glass of water in his hand. His light complexion, only slightly tanned from the spring sun, took on a rosy hue. His hat sat on the floor.

Ruth felt her stomach flip. She wanted so much to reach for his hand.

"Happy birthday to you," her aunt began the song and everyone joined in as she brought the decorated cake into the room and set it on the glass table. There were nineteen candles lit. Ruth was about to blow them out when Darrel stood up and took out his cell phone. "Wait, Ruth, I want to get a picture."

"No. No pictures, please," she said abruptly. "I'm sorry, Darrel, but that's not the Amish way."

"Look at you. You're about as Amish as Madonna." He laughed at his own joke, but it was lost on Jeremiah.

"Madonna? Jesus' mother?" he asked.

"Holy cow! You've never heard of Madonna? The singer?"

"Look, Darrel, I hate to tell you this, but we don't care about your singers and super stars. We–"

"Oh, let's cut the cake now. So who wants ice cream?" Esther asked quickly.

Ruth blew them out and Esther handed her a knife. She began cutting pieces and laying them on plates, wishing the night was over.

"Here let me help," Darrel said as he came over to the table and carried two plates with forks over to his father and Jeremiah.

"*Danki.*" Jeremiah took the plate as he avoided Darrel's eyes.

"Wait, did you want ice cream first?" Ruth asked.

"I'm fine," said Martin.

"*Jah*, me too."

"Well maybe I'll have a scoop," Esther said as she went to the freezer. "How about you, Ruth?"

"Cake will be fine, Aunt. Thank you."

They ate in silence and Esther offered them seconds. No one took her up on it.

"You don't look like your niece," Jeremiah said as he smiled over at Esther.

"I'm sorry to hear that," she returned.

"I'm sorry. I didn't mean to hurt your feelings," Jeremiah continued. "You just have different coloring."

"True." Esther took another bite of cake, while everyone ate silently.

Ruth looked over at Jeremiah. "*Mamm* and *Oma* came out to see us."

"*Jah*? That's *gut*. It was a long time."

Esther nodded. "Too long. Way too long."

"Now you can go to see them," he added.

"I believe I will. Ruth will want to get back once in a while to visit them, too, I'm sure," she added.

"Aunt, I haven't made up my mind yet about leaving the Amish way."

"Oh, I kind of thought you had," she answered. "I shouldn't have said anything."

"I don't see how a girl like you could live like a nun–"

"Oh, she wouldn't live like a *nun*," Jeremiah cut in with a grin. "Far from it!"

Ruth wanted to sink through the floor. "Oh, mercy," she said under her breath.

Darrel continued, "I guess 'nun' was the wrong word. Like a pilgrim? Is that better? I guess you don't realize, Jeremiah, how quickly she took hold of all our ways here. She goes to concerts and shopping malls and–"

"*Jah*, but I went to a concert with Jeremiah, too. I do things like go in shops at home and I even play an IPod." She looked over at Jeremiah, who nodded and grinned.

"*Jah*, she knows her composers now."

"This is delicious cake, Esther," Martin said. "Did you make it yourself?"

"I'm afraid not. I cheated and bought it at a bakery near by. They make marvelous sticky buns, too."

"*Jah*? My *Mamm* makes great sticky buns," Jeremiah said. "I eat three at a time with butter."

"Oh, Jeremiah, you make me hungry for them," Ruth said, smiling at him.

"They're fattening," Darrel added.

"*Jah*, most *gut* things are," Jeremiah agreed. "Will you play your violin for us, Ruthie?"

"Oh, I'm not very good really."

"Please, Ruth. You've gotten so much better," her aunt said. "Play the one you were working on, 'Amazing Grace'."

"We'd love to hear you," Darrel added and his father nodded in agreement.

"Well, if you promise not to laugh at me," Ruth said as she went over to the closet to reach for her violin case. It took a minute to tune it up. She stood off to the side and began. It even sounded good to her own ears. She was surprised, with the mixed audience she had, that she could play anything at all. When she finished, they applauded.

"Really nice, Ruthie. *Danki*."

"You're incredible, Ruth. You've only taken a few lessons," Darrel said.

"Amazing. You must have natural talent. Anyone in your family musical?" Martin asked.

"I don't know. My *daed* sings nice. We don't allow musical instruments."

"Seriously?" Darrel's mouth dropped open.

"I told you that, didn't I?"

"If you did, I don't remember. Tough on people like you, Ruth, who are gifted and love music."

"*Jah*, well. Things may change." She laid the violin down next to the tennis racket and asked Jeremiah about the Bishop. "Have you heard whether our district has chosen a new bishop yet?"

"*Nein*. Too bad Bishop King died."

"*Jah*, very sad."

"But he was real old."

"*Jah*. In his nineties."

"Well, Ruth," Darrel broke up their little private dialogue, his eyes darting from Jeremiah to Ruth. "How about seeing what your friend brought you. That is for Ruth, I assume," he added, pointing to the box on the floor with a ribbon. It was about the size of two shoe boxes.

Jeremiah nodded and handed it to Ruth. "Here, Ruthie, I hope you like it."

Ruth removed the ribbon and pulled off the lid to the package. "Oh, Jeremiah, it's beautiful." Removing a rectangular wooden box with small brass hinges, she ran her hand over the smooth wood surface. "Did you make it?"

"*Jah*, just for you. I got the wood from that old cherry tree at Boot-Ben's place. Remember we used to climb it?"

"Oh, *jah*." Ruth smiled at the memory. "I'm surprised he let you have it."

Jeremiah laughed and shook his head. "He's too tight to do that. I had to give him a buggy whip for it."

Darrel cleared his throat. "Now you have a place to keep the diamond pendant I bought you, Ruth."

Her hand went to her throat. She had totally forgotten. "No, it's for my *Biewel*, my Bible."

"No *gut* Amish girl wears jewelry," Jeremiah said, his jaw set in a firm line.

"I guess you don't think Ruth is good then, is that it?" Darrel looked over with a direct challenge in his words and demeanor.

"I did not mean Ruth. She is very *gut*. While she's here, she can do things like that. She can wear jewelry and have her hair all fancy, but when she comes to her senses and returns to Amish, she won't want any of the stuff you people make into gods."

"Listen here," Darrel rose and took a step closer to Jeremiah, who also stood as he folded his arms across his chest, with his muscles flexed.

"No, you listen. I see what you are doing. You are after Ruthie. I know it in my bones. You would turn her into a movie star or something. Then one day you'd get tired of her and end up hurting her. Ruthie is too smart for you, though."

"Please, *Jeremiah—Darrel!* This is my birthday. I don't want you two arguing. It's my life. I don't know what path I'm going to take, but it will be *my* decision and I don't need to have you two trying to figure it out for me."

"Bravo," Martin broke in. "That's what I like. A girl with *gut*s. Now how about a second piece of cake and we can all settle down and behave like adults."

Jeremiah was breathing hard, but he backed up and sat down, gripping the arms of the chair. Darrel left to use the bathroom and Ruth went to cut another piece of cake. Her hand shook as she returned the plate to Martin.

"Honey," he said, "Don't let anyone upset you. You're too young to make up your mind about anything. Enjoy the time you have in Philadelphia. There's still a lot we want to show you."

Ruth nodded and looked over at Jeremiah. He had picked up his straw hat and was turning it around by the rim. He didn't look back at her and she felt deep sadness. If only he had called. Somehow she had to let him know she still cared.

Darrel walked back in the room and Jeremiah rose. "I guess I'd better get going. I have to walk over to the station."

Everyone stood. "Let me get you some cake to take back with you," Esther suggested.

"No, *danki*. I will pass on that. Take care, Ruthie."

"*Danki* for the box. I really love it."

He nodded and then turned and shook Darrel's hand. "Take care of Ruthie."

Ruth stood immobile as he followed Esther to the door and left.

"So, maybe I'll take you up on the ice cream," Darrel said cheerily to Ruth. "Make it a double scoop."

Chapter Thirty-nine

After Darrel and his father left, Ruth helped her aunt clean up the dishes. Ruth went through the motions, barely able to concentrate. The evening played out in her mind.

"Ruth? Are you okay?"

"*Jah.* I guess so."

"That was obviously the Jeremiah you told me about."

Ruth nodded.

"He seems like a nice young man. I'm sorry you didn't have a chance to talk to him privately. I was going to suggest you take a walk together, but with Darrel sitting there..."

"I know. It would have been difficult. It's okay."

"I'm afraid they have no love for each other–those two."

"Mmm. I hate it when things are said real hurtful."

Esther dried her hands. "I know. It was uncomfortable for everyone. I think we can sit a few minutes and talk, unless you're too tired to stay up."

"I'm not ready to sleep yet. I doubt I'll be able to sleep at all."

They walked over to the sofa and sat down. "Did it help to see them together?"

"How do you mean?"

"Well, their differences. It was like watching people living in two different centuries."

"Jeremiah is a very smart man. Just because he doesn't have a fancy degree–"

"Ruth, please. You got this all wrong. I'm not putting Jeremiah down in the least. Don't forget I lived Amish for twenty years. I know the people well. What I was trying to say is, you could see the effects of the different cultures. I wondered if it helped you any with your final decision."

"I don't know. I need to pray about it and ponder it in my mind. So many feelings I have. They are both *gut* men, I think anyway. I don't know Darrel real well to know his heart."

"But you think you know Jeremiah's heart?"

"*Jah.* I think so. But after tonight, I don't think he will ever come to see me again. Why would he? I didn't know how to act. I was sick in my stomach. If he had called, maybe we could have seen each other and talked about things. It would have been better."

"He wanted to surprise you."

"*Jah*, that he did, for sure."

"The Bible box is lovely."

"*Jah.*" Ruth picked it up off the coffee table and opened it. After closing it, she ran her hand over the surface, admiring the cherry finish. "It must have taken him a long time. It's so perfect."

"Maybe you should write to him."

"I think so, though I'm not sure. He didn't even look my way when he left. He was real hurt, that's for certain."

"Well, maybe seeing them together was God's will for you. Maybe this will be your turning point."

"Maybe. I guess I'll turn in. I need to say my prayers, Aunt Esther. They will take a long time tonight, I'm afraid. Thank you for the party."

"It didn't quite come off the way I had planned, but life's little surprises…"

"*Jah.* You can say that again, for sure."

Several days later, while Ruth was at work, Darrel called to remind her about their tennis date. She hesitated before accepting.

"Had you forgotten?" Darrel asked.

"No. I'm afraid the time has gone so fast lately, I just forgot it was tonight. We'll meet you over there."

"I'd like to take you out afterward to meet friends of mine. They invited us to their home for dinner."

"Oh. If you want me to go."

"I wouldn't have asked you if I didn't."

"I'll have to come home first to shower and change."

"That's fine. You can go back with your aunt. I'll clean up at the tennis club to save time and pick you up later. Wear the green dress you had on the other night. You look fantastic in that."

Ruth smiled into the phone. "Thanks. Okay. See you later."

Deb had overheard her conversation as she was wiping down a table. "Is that the hunk who came in to see you? Darrel?"

Ruth nodded. "We're playing tennis tonight."

"He came by one day when you had already left. We had a nice talk. He's a brilliant attorney from what I've heard."

"He's that famous?"

"I told you, he's in magazines and everything. You may be hooking the big one if you play your cards right."

"You talk funny, Deb, like I was fishing."

"Girls, check and see if the sugars are on the tables. And Ruth, I don't like you taking personal calls while you're working."

"Sorry, Terri, I forgot to turn off my phone. I made it quick."

"Okay. You're both pretty good about it."

It got busier as the morning went on and before she knew it, it was time to leave.

When she got back to the apartment she picked up the mail. There was a letter from Emma. She took off her shoes before sitting down to read.

Dear Ruth,

I have big news for a change. It is about Daed. *He was chosen by God to be a minister for our district. He was real quiet when he came home. He was not acting proud to be chosen.* Mamm *put her arms around him and said God chose him because he is a very* gut *man. I agree. The new bishop is the man I wanted. Luke Schultz is his name. He told the men he hoped to make a few changes and he asked them to give suggestions. They will meet once a week to talk.*

Mamm *said to ask about violins and she wonders if you could keep yours.* Mamm *said you love to play it and would be so sad to not play it again. I think she is scared you will stay in Philadelphia for music. I told her it was silly to think you love music more than your family. That is true, Jah?*

I hope you had a nice birthday. Tell me about it. Do you go out with people your age? Have you met any Amish people?

School keeps me real busy. I am glad I have Katie there. She helps me a lot. Your nieces and nephews are growing big. You should come and visit us even if you go back. Everyone asks about you and we pray for you every day. Sometimes I pray you will come home soon, but I also add if it is God's will. But I am hoping it is His will for you to come home.

Josiah is always trying to hold my hand. He wants to kiss me. I let him one time and now he thinks he is my owner. I am kind of sick of him and his cows. But no one else looks too good right now. I do not even think about Jeremiah any more. I guess it was not real love. I bet he is married in Ohio.

I have to go now and help Mamm *with supper. She said to say* hallo *and give you her love. So I just did.*

Love from me, too. Emma

Ruth put the letter in a drawer with her others. So, her father was now a preacher. He'd be good, she was sure of that.

She wondered how she could have allowed Emma to determine her future. Here she was totally over Jeremiah. How fickle. Now she's tiring of Josiah, too. Oh, why hadn't she remained in Lancaster County and continued to see Jeremiah. Was it too late now? She didn't like the way he and Darrel had nearly come to blows over her. What was she? A piece of chattel? A possession? She could feel the blood rush to her face. What nerve! Maybe she'd stay single and be a waitress forever. That would show them both!

Lord, settle me down. It's not good to feel anger. They are both gut *men–just a bit too possessive. Most women would love to have my problems. I just get more confused all the time. Please guide me.*

Ruth reached for her Bible. Usually as of late, she thought of the violin first, but today she knew she needed to get back in the Word. Maybe that was why the Amish frowned on instruments. Maybe they take over in your mind and you end up thinking more about the music than about God. She read three chapters in Deuteronomy and then prayed for all her loved ones, including Jeremiah. She added Darrel and his father before ending her prayer. When she finished, she practiced on her violin.

When the four finished playing tennis, Ruth went back to get ready for her dinner date with Darrel. Her aunt showed her a trick with her hair, to keep it from going in her eyes. "You won't even see the bobby pin," she said as she slipped one in place, "because this part will hide it." She draped a lock of hair down to the side. "Like it?"

Ruth looked at her image in the mirror. "*Jah*, it looks okay. *Danki.*"

"Have a nice time. I wonder if there will be other guests there."

"I don't know, but my stomach is jumping around. I hope I do okay."

"Ruth, of course you will. Be yourself and everyone will adore you."

"I hope so."

Soon Darrel arrived and they drove out of the city to a town called Villanova. The homes kept getting larger and more ostentatious as they turned down one street and up the next. "Wow, they must be billionaires," Ruth said.

"Rich, but not quite that rich. Forrest is a partner at the firm I'm with. He has a lot of influence."

"And his wife?"

"Well, they aren't officially married, but her name is Francine."

"They live together?"

He looked over at her and frowned. "It's common practice today, Ruth. That's the real world."

"Oh. I guess God has changed then." She couldn't keep the sarcasm from her voice.

"Times have changed. I doubt your God cares one way or the other."

"My God? Is He different from yours?"

Darrel ignored the question and looked straight ahead, his mouth in a frown. "Here we are." Darrel pulled into a circular drive and stopped at the entranceway.

When they rang, a man in a servant's uniform opened the door. "Good evening, Attorney Storm. Nice to see you. Every one is in the living room."

"Arthur, this is a friend of mine, Ruth Zook. This is Arthur Moore. He's been with my friends for five years now."

"Six. Nice to meet you."

"*Jah*, me too." She put her hand out and he shook it, eyebrows slightly raised.

Darrel led her into the huge living room where there were three other couples. The men stood as they entered and she was introduced to everyone. It was overwhelming to try to remember everyone's name and look relaxed. She felt anything but and wished she had refused to come.

"Sit here next to me," Darrel said as he found a vacant love seat.

"You have a beautiful home," Ruth said to her hostess, Francine.

"Thank you. We enjoy it. So are you from the area?"

"*Nein*. From Lancaster County."

Francine looked over at Darrel, quizzically. "*Nein?* Are you from Germany?"

"Oh, no. Not *nein*. I forget sometimes. I am Amish."

There was dead silence throughout the room. Then Forrest let out a whistle. "I'll be. I never saw an Amish girl look like you. Where did you find her, Darrel?"

There was restrained laughter throughout the group and Ruth felt like an object being stared at. Was this going to be the tipping point?

"She's mine, guys. Don't get any ideas."

"Pardon, Darrel," Ruth stated before she had time to think, "I am not anyone's–just God's."

"Oh, I didn't mean–"

"No, we certainly didn't mean to suggest–"

"I think it's wonderful to be Amish. Think of the money you save," a redhead in a purple dress said.

"Right. And you get to eat fresh food from your garden," someone else offered.

"Not to mention you don't have to pay taxes."

"Actually, we pay income tax."

"Really? I didn't know that," the man next to the redhead said.

"Ruth is learning the violin. She plays real well considering she's only taken a few lessons." Darrel took hold of her hand and squeezed it gently. She felt slightly reassured by his gesture.

"Wonderful," Francine said. "We must hear you next time."

"And we're into tennis." Darrel glanced over to smile at Ruth.

"Tennis? How marvelous," one of the women on the other side of the room said. "We definitely should all get together for a mini tournament."

"Oh, I'm not very *gut* yet."

Ruth noticed people exchanging glances.

"I mean *good* yet," she added quickly.

"Oh, '*gut*' sounds so cute, doesn't it Forrest? Don't change on our account."

"Don't you 'outen the lights'?" a man from the long sofa asked. "You know, when you want to turn them off?"

Darrel broke in. "I think we're making Ruth uncomfortable. Let's talk about something else, shall we?"

"Oh, sorry Darrel. It's not every day one meets a real Amish person, especially with the town's most eligible bachelor," Francine teased.

The conversation turned to some legal cases the firm had taken on and Ruth felt her heart settle down to a slower beat. She kept her hand in Darrel's grip and was aware he had become her protector. She looked over as he spoke animatedly about his latest trial and she compared him to Jeremiah. Both were handsome men. Both strong and possessed self-confidence. One was English and already a success in the world; the other was Amish and concentrated his attention on his family and friends. And God. Where did Darrel stand with God?

"Dinner's ready, ma'am," a young woman in a black uniform with a starched white apron, announced.

"Thank you, Martha. Shall we?"

Francine stood and everyone followed suit. "I put place cards around to simplify things. Boy, girl, boy, girl."

Ruth was relieved to see she was seated next to Darrel. On her other side was a man named Jim. He re-introduced herself to her and gave her a genuine smile. Jim was in his fifties and had a prominent nose and a bristly mustache, which distracted from his other features.

The servant brought everyone a bowl of cream of asparagus soup and small homemade wheat rolls. Ruth checked around to see if she was using the correct spoon. She was reassured and took her first sip, which burned her mouth, but she took a quick sip of her ice water to neutralize the effect.

Half way through, Jim asked if she had graduated college yet.

"Actually, I never went to college."

"Oh, I see. Do you plan to attend?"

"No, I don't think so. I'd have to graduate from high school first, I imagine."

"Of course, that's true. How far did you get?" He took his roll apart and buttered half.

"I finished eighth grade. After that, I taught for a year."

"You taught without a teaching degree?"

Ruth thought he would choke on his soup.

"In the Amish society, we don't believe you need more education. Most of our men farm or work manual labor jobs. The women stay home and raise their familes. That's the way it is."

"I think I can understand why you're in Philadelphia now. No one can blame you for wanting to leave that kind of life."

"Oh, I'm not sure I'm staying here. There are many things I love about the Amish life."

"Really? Like what?"

Ruth realized the other conversations had ceased and she was the only one speaking. Their heads were turned to hear her response.

"First, we all believe in the same things. Everyone believes in Jesus as the Son of God. We do our best to please Him by living according to Biblical values."

"You mean stoning the kids who talk back?" one of the men asked, creating a few laughs.

"No. We don't do that, but we do believe in discipline. Not cruelty. I was never spanked, but my brother was once when he did something really bad. Family is everything to the Amish and divorce is not allowed."

"Whoa, that would be a problem," the red-head in the purple dress remarked.

Ruth was uncomfortable. She felt she was being ridiculed. Darrel's hand reached for hers under the table. "They have very strong values. I don't think we should go any deeper into Ruth's culture. She has yet to make a decision about remaining Amish or leaving. It's a tough decision for someone to make. Her family will not accept her if she leaves."

"Well, they don't shun you, Darrel," Ruth corrected, "if you haven't gone through baptism yet. But you are right, for certain. Things are never the same once you leave for good. My aunt is a professor at the University, but she hadn't seen her mother for over twenty years."

"How sad," Francine said.

"*Jah*, it is sad. I love many things about the English way. I love music, especially classical, and I like the clothes–some of them anyway, and your houses are pretty and I can wear my hair any way I want."

Francine covered a smile and glanced over at Darrel. "Darrel, do you plan to take up farming?"

"Francine, that's enough," Forrest said, glaring at her. "Let's have the next course. Martha," he called out to the woman serving, who was standing by the buffet. "Please serve our guests their salads."

The conversation did not return to Ruth or the Amish way, much to her relief. Darrel was quiet for the rest of the dinner, but kept one hand on hers throughout most of the meal.

After they finished eating, everyone collected in the library where the men went to one end to discuss case histories and the women sat on an assortment of chairs and a sofa. Ruth had never seen so many books in one place. She heard libraries had a lot, but this was a private home. Her eyes drank in the mahogany wood paneling and the rich Oriental rugs, which graced the hardwood parquet floors. She hoped they would leave soon, but Darrel seemed in no hurry and appeared to enjoy the company of his friends.

The other women discussed designer clothes and society galas leaving Ruth's mind to wander. If she ended up with Darrel, it would be like this. These are the people they would associate with. Rich people. Maybe even godless.

She was startled out of her reverie by Darrel's voice. "Ruth, are you ready?"

She didn't realize an hour had passed from the time they left the table to now. "*Jah*, I am."

"I'm beat. I think we should head home."

Ruth stood and then went over to thank her host and hostess. Francine leaned over and pecked at each side of her face, without touching. "I hope we didn't make you uncomfortable, Ruth. You are a lovely young woman and I hope we'll see more of you."

"*Danki*, I mean thank you. Dinner was very good." Ruth secretly patted herself on the back for remembering the '*D*' sound in good.

Darrel was silent throughout most of the trip back, but as they drew close to the apartment building, he stopped the car in the lot and put his arm out to draw her closer to him. "Ruth, I'm so sorry you were made to feel like a spectacle. I was so ashamed of my friends."

"It's okay, really. They were nice people. They just don't understand the Amish way."

"You handled it so well. I should have known better than to put you through that. Forgive me?"

"There is nothing to forgive."

"Ruth, we *are* from two different worlds, but I find you enchanting. More than that, I'm falling in love with you. It's crazy I guess. I don't mean that to sound like it did. Any man would love you. I know Jeremiah does."

"*Jah*? You think so?"

"It was pretty obvious. How do you feel about him?"

"I liked him a lot once, but now I think it's over. Maybe we never did have anything really. I'm so confused."

He smiled at Ruth, leaned over and pressed his mouth against hers. She didn't draw back, but felt pleasure in his touch and his masculine scent. "Darrel, I'm so confused. Help me."

He continued to hold her. He kissed her cheek and then her ear. She suddenly realized she was being tempted and it frightened her. She pulled back. "No, Darrel, please. You are tempting me."

"Oh, Ruth, I love you. I want you."

"Please take me home. This is not right."

"Is it really so wrong? When two people care about each other like—"

"No, Darrel. It's all wrong. I don't like the feelings I'm getting. Please."

He moved back and started the car. "I'm sorry, Ruth. I'll try to behave. You don't make it any easier, though. You're so desirable."

"I don't see a future for us. You know we see things so differently, and one of us would have to give up a great deal. I don't know if that would be fair to either of us."

"I know you're probably right. I can't give you up, though. Please let's continue as we have. As friends. I won't talk about my feelings again and I promise not to kiss you without you wanting me to. Can we do this?"

"*Jah*. I think it would be *gut*–good. As long as you hold to your promise."

"You say '*gut*' anytime you want, Ruth Zook. I adore it. Now let me get you to your apartment before I break my promise."

Chapter Forty

It was late April now and things between Ruth and Darrel had remained on friendly terms. He no longer spoke of love and she avoided his touch. He was still a temptation to her. While she enjoyed his company and found him very attractive, she did not believe it was love on her part, which made it all the more disturbing to get such strong feelings and desires.

One day, she and Deb were working together. There was no one else to serve, so they sat down to chat. "Let's play tennis after work," Deb suggested. "It's a gorgeous day out there and I'm sick of being stuck in here."

"Why not? I'll need to run back to get changed and pick up my racket and balls. I can meet you at the outdoor courts you told me about."

"Great. Uh oh, here comes the boss lady. Let's look busy."

"Girls, it's so slow today; do either of you want to leave early?"

"Why don't you go, Ruth? You have farther to walk to get home. We're meeting after work to play tennis, Terri."

"Sounds like fun. So do you want to leave now, Ruth?"

"Sure, if you don't need us both."

The walk back to her apartment filled her with joy. A slight breeze combed through her hair and the scent of fresh flowers reminded her of home. Miniature arrangements in window boxes and urns in front of homes and shops showed caring hands had arranged them. Tulips bursting in primary colors and the scent of spring made its way through the prevailing dusky odors of humanity's dark side of the city streets, giving new hope for the emerging spring. Ruth pictured her father and Wayne planting and hoeing. This season was such a busy time for farmers. She missed picking the early lettuce and peas. Even as a young child, she enjoyed the vegetables–watching them grow and helping her mother shell the peas and wash the early asparagus. Spring meant life on a farm. New life, as animals procreated their offspring.

At four, Ruth met Deb at the courts, but they had to wait before a court became available. "Let's sit on that bench," Ruth suggested, pointing to one in the warmth of the sun.

"Sure. Guess who showed up looking for you?"

"Not Darrel."

"One and the same. I told him we were playing tennis here around four and he said maybe he'd join us and bring a friend. How about that?"

"I guess it's okay. I hope his friend isn't super good."

"Wait, there's a court. Let's volley before they get here to warm up. If they don't show in a little while we can play a set."

Deb led the way to the vacated court and Ruth took the shady side and began to send balls Deb's way. She returned all of them and when Ruth congratulated her she mentioned she played for her college team.

"I didn't know you even went to college," Ruth said as they stopped long enough to sip some water.

"Oh, look, there's Darrel with another guy. He looks cool, too. Love his thick dark hair. And look at his muscles."

"Oh, Deb, you shouldn't look at things like that."

"Ruth, you're a riot. Over here, guys," Deb called out and the men headed over toward them. Ruth recognized the man from the dinner she went to, but couldn't recall his name. She wondered if he was married.

"You remember Frank Lewis from the other night, Ruth, don't you?"

"*Jah*. Hi, Frank."

Everyone introduced themselves and they went on the court to practice. It was a mellow exchange until Frank and Deb decided to take on Darrel and Ruth. Deb had the first serve and the fun and games were over. She walloped the ball with such force, Ruth's swing was three seconds late. Deb switched sides and Darrel missed the first serve altogether. "Phew, you didn't warn us you were a pro."

Deb laughed. "Not really. I just have a good serve." Ruth noticed she not only served well, but she played every move like an expert. It was an easy win for Deb and Frank and after two sets they decided to go out for burgers. Ruth called her aunt to tell her she wouldn't be home for supper. She mentioned Darrel had brought a friend and that they had played doubles together.

"Sounds like fun. Thanks for calling, Ruth. It was considerate of you. That's something I love about you. You think of others."

Darrel treated and after eating, they had a discussion about sports. "So where did you learn to play tennis so well?" Frank asked Deb.

"My family belonged to a country club on the main line and I started tennis lessons when I was about ten. My first year in college I played on the team, but I'm too busy now."

"Where do you go?" Darrel asked.

"I've been going to the University of Pennsylvania–pre-med, but I took a semester off because I needed a break. I work part-time at the café so I don't go crazy."

"Pre-med, that's quite an undertaking," Darrel said, looking over at her with a smile that gave Ruth a pang of jealousy.

"It's not that bad, really. You're a lawyer, right?"

"We both are," Frank answered.

"Well, I couldn't begin to study law. It's not my thing. But even as a kid I enjoyed looking at biology textbooks my older brother brought home. I couldn't wait to dissect my first frog."

"Eee. I could never do that. The day we did an earthworm in class, I got sick to my stomach," Ruth commented.

Darrel laughed. "A farm girl like you? I'm surprised." Turning back to Deb, he asked her how far she was in her pre-med.

"One more year. I've already started applying to med schools."

"Let me know if you want a connection to Temple Med. I have a friend in admissions."

"Really? How sweet of you." She patted his hand. "Give me your card, Darrel, and I'll keep it handy."

"I don't have any with me, but I'll drop one off at the café."

"Or give one to me," Ruth suggested. "I'll pass it on."

"Oh, right."

"Anyone want ice cream?" Frank asked. "There's an ice cream parlor down the street."

"Sure, why not?" Darrel said as he pulled the chair out for Ruth and took her arm.

When Ruth returned to the apartment, her aunt was resting in her bathrobe, reading a book.

"So how was your tennis match?"

"Deb is fabulous. She put the rest of us to shame."

"Really? I thought Darrel could hold his own."

"He played a good game, but she beat us with her serve. It was so fast, it was scary."

Esther laughed. "Martin left about an hour ago. Since you weren't coming back to eat, he came over and we split the steak I had planned."

"*Gut.* So it didn't get wasted."

"No. Then we played chess. He's so quick and I'm so slow. It was embarrassing."

"Teach me sometime, would you? Jeremiah plays with his *daed,* but I never learned."

"Speaking of Jeremiah, have you written yet?"

"I keep putting it off, but tomorrow I go in late to work, so I'm going to definitely write."

"You haven't heard from him?"

"No. I didn't think I would. He was not too happy when he left. I thought I'd know by now whether I was going to return or not, but I'm no closer than I was to making a decision."

"No hurry."

"*Jah,* but it's not fair to drift along. *Mamm* stressed the importance of getting baptized."

"I haven't been baptized."

"Oh, my, you'd better. Maybe we should go to a church Sunday and get you started."

Esther smiled. "Actually I checked on a church up the road to see what time their service began."

"A *gut* church?"

"A Christian friend of mine from school loves it there. She said it's a strong Bible believing church and the pastor gives an excellent sermon. Would you go with me?"

"I would! I miss having church. What time would it be?"

"They have a nine o'clock service and another at eleven. So let's see if we get up early or not."

"*Gut.* Maybe I'll ask Darrel if he and his father want to come."

"Good idea. I haven't talked to Martin about church. Maybe they belong to one already."

"I don't think so. I need to talk to Darrel about his faith also. It's important to me and I don't want to start caring about him too much if he doesn't believe."

"Ruth, do you think you already care too much?"

"Aunt Esther, I'm ashamed to say I think about him a lot, but it is not so *gut* what I think. He is very handsome and strong and charming. He kissed me and it felt way too exciting. It scared me and I try to keep him away from my lips."

"Oh, Ruthie, what a predicament."

"Are you laughing at me?" Ruth pouted as she looked her aunt squarely in her eyes.

"No, not at all. It really is a predicament to be your age and feel things strongly and have to curb all those feelings and thoughts."

"Even with Jeremiah, I had feelings and thoughts that were not real holy, but I always figured in my heart that he would one day be my husband, and so it didn't feel so sinful as when I think about Darrel. Should I stop seeing him even as a friend?"

"As long as he respects your feelings, Ruth, I think it's alright to continue as his friend."

"He promised to behave."

"Then give him the benefit of the doubt. You never know, you may one day feel more than friendship toward him."

"You're right and he is not pushing me."

"I'm glad to hear that. Now I think I'll turn in. I'm pretty beat tonight. Glad you're home safe and sound."

"*Jah,* I'm real tired, too. *Gut nacht,* Aunt Esther."

"*Gut nacht.*" This had become their every night exchange. A touch of the Amish not to be forgotten.

Chapter Forty-one

Ruth looked for every excuse not to sit down and write to Jeremiah. She spent extra time reading her Bible and praying and was about to practice the violin when she scolded herself and reached for writing paper instead.

Dear Jeremiah,

It has been lots of days since I saw you and I am ashamed for not writing sooner. It was such a surprise to see you and I know you paid a lot of money to come for such a short time. Every day I look at my present you gave me and feel sad that I could not spend more time with you—even alone like I wanted. It was hard to do that. I did not want to be rude to my friends. That is all they are.

Spring is nice here but not so beautiful as in Lancaster County. I miss the rolling hills and the smell of fresh turned soil. I miss the lowing of the cows and the rooster telling me it's time to get up. I miss my Mamm *and* daed. *I miss Emma and Katie and Wayne and of course all my brothers and wives and children. So you can see I miss lots of things about home.*

I hope you can understand me and why I wanted to be a regular Englisher *for a little while, but in my heart I think I am still all Amish. I wish I could say for sure that I will come home. Maybe you can help me figure it out. Music is special and I listen so often to the music you made for me, but there is so much more that I love. God is my first love. I feel His love for me and I know He will help me understand myself soon.*

My job is still very busy, but it is gut to make a little money so I do not become a burden to Aunt Esther.

I hope your grandfather is not suffering too much. It is hard to watch someone suffer. I pray for your grandmother, too. I can not imagine what it would be like to lose a husband you've shared your life with. I know I would be so sad.

Today I go to work later than usual. That is why I am writing to you. I wanted to say thank you again for the beautiful Bible box and I think of you every time I see it. I picture you and me as kinder climbing the tree. Remember how we ate so many cherries I turned green? And you teased me about looking like I ate green grass?

So I guess I am going to tell you something. I miss you most of all. I picture you in my mind and it makes me smile, but then I open my eyes and you are not there. That is a sad thing for sure.

I am planning to visit my family in two weeks. It is my Katie's birthday and she wrote to ask me to come home. I am homesick anyway and it gives me a reason to visit. I will stay a week. I told my boss and she said it is okay. Now it is your turn to write.

Ruth hesitated, wondering how to sign off. "Sincerely" sounded too cold, but "love" was too revealing. So she settled on "Yours, affectionately," and sealed it in an envelope to mail.

Around eleven, Ruth made it into the coffee shop where Deb was already working. Terri was behind the counter. Ruth smiled as she tied her hair back and washed her hands. "Have you been busy?" she asked Deb, who was washing a few mugs.

"Pretty busy."

"What do you want me to do first, Terri?"

"I guess you can grind some more hazelnut beans. We're low."

Three people came in and sat at a table and ordered lattes. Ruth went behind the counter to fill their order. Deb seemed to be avoiding her and there was nervous tension in the air when she or Terri spoke to her.

Around two o'clock, Terri asked Ruth to come back to the storage room. "Ruth, I hate to do this, but I'm going to have to let you go. Business has gone down and well…Billy has straightened himself out and uh, Deb has promised to stay until the next semester starts. I won't need another wait person."

"But I was here first," Ruth said, feeling her throat begin to tighten.

"Yes, but you may leave at any point. Deb told me how you probably will return to your home in Lancaster County."

"But I'd give you notice."

"I'm sure. And then you want a week off–"

"I can cancel that."

"Ruth, I'm sorry. Really. I'll pay you for a week's work."

"Not if I didn't earn it. When should I leave?"

"Let's call today your last day." Terri reached in her desk drawer and pulled out a check already made out."

"Okay. I tried to do a *gut* job."

"You *were* good. Really."

"*Danki* for hiring me." Ruth put out her hand. Terri shook it, reached over and hugged her briefly.

On the way out, Ruth stopped to say good-by to Deb. "I guess you know I'm not coming back."

"Terri told me. I didn't mean to steal your job, Ruth. Really."

"That's okay. We can still play tennis together, right?"

"Oh, sure."

"Want to play after you are done work tomorrow?"

"Uh, actually I have plans for tomorrow. Maybe some other time. How about if I call you?"

"*Jah*, sure. See you soon, Deb." Ruth walked out quickly before the tears forming would make their way down her cheeks. She left the café and began her walk home. There would be other jobs. She was getting bored anyway.

Aunt Esther was already home when she arrived at the apartment. She was plumping up the pillows on the sofa when she looked over at her niece. "Ruth, what's wrong? Have you been crying?"

"A little bit. I lost my job today."

"No! But everything was going so well."

Ruth explained about Terri's decision and allowed her tears to flow. "I can't stay here and make a problem for you."

"Ruth, truly, you are no problem."

"I feel so useless. Aunt Esther, without an education like you have, there is not much for me to do in a city. No one cares I can quilt and tend gardens. Everyone in Philadelphia is so much smarter than me."

"Not true, but why not study for your GED?"

"What is that?"

"A test to get a diploma from high school. You probably know most of the answers already, but it would give you the degree you need and you could go on to college. I can help you there. You can be anything you want. You have the brains. Perhaps you could get a teacher's degree and teach in the Philadelphia schools or out on the main line. Or you could take up nursing. I think you'd make a marvelous nurse; you're so caring."

Ruth shook her head vehemently. "But I don't desire any of those things."

"Let's sit and talk." They went over to the sofa and sat down. "What do you want, Ruth? What is your heart's desire?"

"It's to be married to Jeremiah and bear his children and live near my family and hang my sheets in the sun and laugh with friends at quilting bees." Ruth was crying as she spoke and Esther put her hands on her niece's.

"Then that's what you should do."

"But I don't know if Jeremiah still cares about me. I was so mean not to follow him out when he left the apartment. He must think I don't care."

"How could you do that with your other guests there? Really, you did the right thing."

"I sent him a letter today. Maybe he will write back."

"Do you want to go home, Ruth?"

"At least for a visit. My heart is so heavy."

They embraced and Ruth noticed her aunt was weeping quietly. Finally, her aunt moved away and attempted a smile. "I've known all along you would eventually leave."

"It's not final, but it's the way I'm leaning."

Esther nodded. "I understand. All I want is for you to be happy."

"I know and I want you to know I love you, Aunt Esther. I will always remember the wonderful times we had."

"I wanted to share something, Ruth. Martin has asked me to marry him and I said yes."

"Oh, I'm so happy for you!" Ruth squeezed her aunt's hand. "I knew you were in love. He is a nice man and he loves you so very much. I know you will be happy. Maybe you'll have a baby!"

Esther laughed. "I don't think so, not at this stage of life. It would be a miracle birth. No, we are content just to have each other."

"When will you marry?"

"Probably not until December sometime."

"Ah, a Christmas wedding. That will be beautiful."

"I hope you will be there."

"Nothing could keep me away. And *Oma* and *Mamm* will come, that's for sure."

Esther smiled and nodded. "I truly hope so. Now let's go out to eat for a change. My treat."

"*Jah*, I could eat a giant cheeseburger with French fries and a milkshake."

"That sounds like McDonald's."

"*Jah*, that's for sure."

Chapter Forty-two

Ruth called several help wanted ads, but they had either been filled or were too far away from the apartment. Strange, somehow she felt relieved. She wondered if God wasn't trying to wean her away from her life in Philadelphia, by closing doors to her employment efforts. Or was she looking for an excuse to leave? She took out her violin and worked on a passage which required some intricate fingering and was pleased she was mastering the three stanzas. She put the violin back in its case and headed out toward the music store.

She took her last scheduled lesson and gave back the rental violin, explaining her job loss. Choking back tears, she asked if they had any for sale that were inexpensive. Even the cheapest one they had, was too dear. Ruth had saved a hundred and ten dollars, but she needed to keep some for emergencies.

As she left, her teacher came over to her. "Ruth, you've accomplished so much in such a short time, don't give it all up. Maybe after Christmas we'll have some violins on sale."

"Thanks. I will miss my lessons."

"Here, take this instruction book with you and when you buy a violin someday, you can teach yourself some of the techniques I was planning to show you."

"Oh, but I don't have—"

"No, no. This is a gift. It has been a pleasure to have a student who practices!" Her teacher handed her the book and placed her hand on Ruth's upper arm. "Come back and play for me some day."

"I hope I can do that. Thank you again. And if I stay and get another job, I'll be back for more lessons."

Once she arrived home, she found a note from her aunt saying she was going out for dinner and a show with Martin, but Darrel would stop by to keep her company. Ruth felt a pang of apprehension. She knew it was time to make a decision and she hoped God would help her make the right one.

Around eight, Darrel showed up with a carton of peach ice cream he purchased from a local creamery. They sat at the table eating generous scoops and sipped water. "Delicious. Almost like homemade," Ruth said.

"They do make it there. Use all the real ingredients, I've been told."

"*Jah*, you can tell."

"So, what's going on? Your aunt said you had news. Good or bad?"

"I guess she meant about losing my job."

"Oh, that. I already knew about that."

"Who told you?"

"Uh...let's see. Oh, it was Deb."

"You went in to find me?"

"Actually, Deb offered to teach me how to serve better, so we played tennis last night for awhile. I think my serve did improve."

Ruth lowered her head. She did not want him to see her frown at the mention of Deb. And really, why should it distress her?

"So since I have no job and my sister is having a birthday soon, I think I'll take a bus back home next week and spend time with the family. I may not come back."

"Is that what you want?"

"*Jah*."

"And what about us?"

"Are we an 'us'?" she asked, looking across at him.

"I was hoping."

"Darrel, let me ask you a question and I want the whole truth. What do you think about God?"

He let out a hesitant laugh. "I'm afraid I don't give him much thought."

"But you *believe* in Him?"

"I guess so, most of the time. Look, Ruth, I want to be totally honest with you. I don't see many signs of there being a God. Not one who is caring, anyway. I lead a good life so if there's a place called heaven, I'm sure I'll make it."

"You don't know you are a sinner?"

"Have I cheated a little on my income tax? Or maybe told a lie or two? Of course, who hasn't? But I've never murdered anyone or stolen anything. No, I don't think I'm a sinner."

"A lie is a sin, or cheating the government. You have to realize, Darrel, every one is born with a sinful nature. It's only through Christ we are made right with God. Through the blood shed on the cross, He took everyone's sin on himself. Now we can be pure in front of God, because we're forgiven."

"Ruthie, that sounds interesting. Really. I'm just not ready to go that route. Maybe when I'm old and retired I'll have time to look into it."

"That's scary. You could have an accident tonight on the–"

"I guess I'll take my chances. It's sweet you believe all that though. I respect you for it."

Ruth looked down at her hands and asked God silently to help her with the words that could make a difference to Darrel. "I will pray for your salvation, Darrel."

"That would be nice. You will be back, won't you?"

"I can't say for sure. I know I can not go on without a job to help pay with the expenses. Besides, I need to make up my mind."

"And you're leaning toward the Amish lifestyle?"

"I think so."

"I can't believe it. No electricity, no cars, no concerts, nothing but hard labor! Why would you even *consider* going back?" Without waiting for an answer he leaned over and drew her closer to him. "Besides, you know I love you. Apparently, you don't feel the same."

"I'm not sure what I feel for you. I know I like you very much and I have to admit you are a temptation to me, but I look at the long term picture, and you're not part of it."

Darrel stroked her cheek with one hand as he reached for her hand with his other. "Why do you say that?"

"Darrel, come on. Look at us. You're a fancy lawyer, rich, handsome, girls drooling over you. I'm an eighth grade graduate, poor by comparison, I don't even talk right with your friends. They find me amusing. Would you find that 'cute' in five years or just embarrassing? You need a woman of sophistication, someone intelligent enough to know what you're talking about when you discuss your job."

"Ruth, you're every bit as intelligent as any of those women. You'd catch up in no time and you can get a degree in anything you want."

"That's a problem right there. I don't want a degree. I don't want to leave my children to be raised by strangers. Don't you see? I want to marry and have children and take care of a home and a husband, and I don't care if we're rich with money. We'd be far richer with the love we'd share."

"I see. You make life with me seem rather shallow."

"No. You're a good man, but I don't know if I'm just a novelty to you. I'm probably the first girl who told you 'no' about certain things. Maybe I'm even a challenge."

He dropped his hand and stared at her. "You don't really believe that."

"Well? I don't know. Ask yourself if there's any truth to it. And then there's the God issue."

"I'd go to church with you and you could raise the children, if we had any, any way you wanted and if you didn't want to work, that would be fine."

"And my lack of education and funny speech?"

"Ruth, I don't know what to say. Maybe you're right. Maybe in time we'd pull apart. Perhaps our differences are too great."

"You need someone–like Deb. She's pretty and smart and knows how to act at your cocktail parties. No one would stare at her and think how quaint she talks."

"I don't think–"

"No, it's true."

"There's more here, Ruth. It's Jeremiah, isn't it? You two are in love."

"I...I'm not sure about my feelings or his. But he would understand the Amish way. He wouldn't laugh at my 'quaintness' and he's a strong believer in God." Ruth reached across and put her hand on his arm. "That's important to me, Darrel. He would be the spiritual leader of our home. I need that."

"Well, at least you're up front about this. I admire you for being so honest, but it hurts. More than you realize."

"I'm sorry, Darrel. One other thing before we part tonight, I want you to take back the beautiful pendant you gave me."

"No. That was a gift. Please, take it to remind you of me once in a while."

"You know I can not ever wear it again."

"Give it to your aunt if that's the case. Please."

"Very well, I will." Tears began to surface in her eyes and she wiped them with her hand.

"Oh, Ruth, is there any chance you'll change your mind?" He wrapped his arms around her and held her close. She wondered if she ever would.

"Don't ask me. This is not easy for me either. I do care, more than you know, but I'm trying to prevent us from doing the wrong thing."

He released his arms from around her and moved back. "I think I'll leave now Ruth."

"Are you angry with me?"

"Not at all. I know you're probably right about everything. I'll never forget you. You're the sweetest girl I've ever met as well as beautiful. And there's not a mean bone in your body."

"And you've been a gentleman and very kind and I will always remember you, too. But it would be better if you left now, before I change my mind," she added smiling through her tears.

They walked together to the door and he turned and lifted her chin and kissed her tenderly. "*Gut nacht*, Ruth."

"*Gut nacht*, Darrel."

She closed the door behind him and wept.

Chapter Forty-three

An hour later when Esther returned from having dinner with Martin, Ruth was sitting with only one low light burning. "Ruth, I didn't see you there at first. Are you okay?" She set down her purse and removed her shoes before taking a chair across from her niece.

"I guess so."

"You've been crying. What's wrong?"

"I said good-by to Darrel."

"As in, 'not going to see you again' good-by?"

Ruth nodded. "It was hard. He's such a nice person and I didn't want to hurt him."

"But you've decided you don't love him."

Ruth turned on another light. "*Jah*. There was no point in leading him on. I've made a decision about leaving, Aunt Esther."

"I was afraid of that," her aunt said, leaning back in the chair. She looked over and waited.

"It took a tipping point, like you said it might."

"What was that point?"

"Losing my job. I feel it was God's way of nudging me into a decision."

"I see. And when do you want to leave?"

"I think Saturday."

"That's only the day after tomorrow."

"*Jah*, I know, but now that I've decided, I'm more homesick than ever and I don't want to get confused and wonder if I'm doing right. Aunt Esther, I hope you understand. I have loved living here and getting to know you. It's not like I'm never going to see you again. This way, you can visit the whole family at the farm."

"I know." She reached for a tissue from her pocket and blew her nose. "I think I always knew you'd decide to go back. I probably should have returned myself."

"But you made a good life for yourself. A productive life."

"I gave up a lot, too."

"Now you have Martin. He's a good man and will make you happy."

Esther looked up and smiled. "Yes, I believe you're right. I've never met a man like him. He's generous and kind and constantly puts others ahead of himself. He was interested in attending church with me. I'm sorry you didn't get to go, but I'll write and tell you all about it."

"I'd like to hear."

"Have you heard from Jeremiah?"

"I forgot to check for mail."

"So did I. Maybe I'll go back down. There was no one at the desk when I came in.

"I thought he would have written by now," Ruth remarked. "Let me go check."

There were several bills and advertisements, but no personal mail. When Ruth walked back in, Esther was in her bedroom on the phone with Martin, so Ruth read the Bible and said her prayers. Even though she felt distressed at hurting Darrel and leaving her aunt, she felt peace in her decision to return.

She scheduled her return bus trip at a convenient time for her aunt to see her off. Since there wasn't time to notify her parents of her early arrival, she made arrangements for the family driver to meet the bus in Lancaster and take her to her farm. Hopefully, she'd be home before supper. Her sisters should be home from teaching by then.

Esther sat in her favorite chair, sipping her coffee while Ruth made the call. When she hung up, Esther looked over at her. "The family doesn't know you're coming early?"

"No, but it will be fun to surprise them, *jah*?"

Esther smiled. "They'll be so excited. Your mother has written me a couple times you know. She often mentions how much they miss you. It actually made me feel a bit guilty."

"It was always my decision. You were just there to be a support. I feel peace, Aunt Esther. I know now this is the right decision, even if it doesn't work out with Jeremiah."

"If there's peace, you know you've made the right choice. We have one more day before you leave. When I get back from school, we should spend the time together."

"*Jah*, that would be special. I will pack everything up ahead of time to be ready. Of course the bus doesn't leave until the afternoon." Ruth hugged herself in her bulky knit sweater, which she wore so often. "I will miss my beautiful clothes. What will you do with them?"

"This may sound crazy, but I'm going to keep them. I may even wear them. We're almost the same size."

Ruth grinned. "*Jah*, that would be so neat. I would like to see you wearing that green dress. It would fit real *gut*. Oh, I have the diamond pendant for you, too. I tried to give it back to Darrel, but he wouldn't take it. He suggested I give it to you if I don't want it. So I will leave it on your dresser tomorrow."

"Ruth, that's so sweet of you. Will you miss not being able to wear jewelry?"

"Truthfully? I felt kind of funny with such an expensive object hanging on me. I won't miss the jewelry, but the jeans? *Jah*, I'll miss them."

The next morning Ruth pressed the outfit she planned to wear home. It was her newest pale blue Amish dress and apron. Her cape was light enough to wear and she decided on a black *kapp* for travel. All her letters were tucked in the suitcase next to the wooden box Jeremiah had made. When she was done reading her Bible, it would go in the beautiful box also. She looked around and tried to memorize every detail so she could re-live some of her special moments with her aunt.

When her aunt returned early afternoon, she had a large carton with her. She set it down next to the sofa and called Ruth from the kitchen. Ruth wiped her hands from washing her lunch dish and came in to obey her aunt.

"This is for you, Ruth." She pushed the package over to her niece.

"For me? Oh, my, what is it?"

"You could open it."

Ruth broke open the top of the carton and peered inside. "A violin? Oh, my!" She removed the violin case and opened it to discover a beautiful new instrument. "My goodness, this is so wonderful-*gut*! I can't believe it! My own violin and look at it. It is like a real concert one." Ruth removed the bow and lifted the violin, placing it on her shoulder, tightening the strings first. She drew the bow across the strings and played the stanzas she had mastered. The sound was superior to her practice violin and it brought tears to her aunt's eyes.

"You will be able to continue playing, won't you, Ruth?"

"I have prayed for that change to come to our district. Some are loosening up a little bit. *Daed* is a minister now and he and the new Bishop talk about things. Until a decision is made, I will keep it under my bed and maybe once in a while I can play a little bit so I don't forget. I don't want to sin, though."

"Dear Ruth, you are such a sweet person. I hope you'll be happy."

Ruth put the violin back in its case and clamped the bow in the top. "*Danki*, Aunt Esther. You can't believe how happy I am right now." Ruth leaned over and kissed her aunt on her cheek.

"So, are you pretty much ready for tomorrow? If so, we can do anything you want with the rest of the day."

"Maybe we can go to that flower place you talked about?"

"Longwood Gardens?"

"*Jah*. You said it was real nice."

"Good idea. Let's go soon though. It will take a little while to get there. It should be beautiful this time of year. Spring is my favorite season."

They spent the rest of the afternoon walking through the marvelous gardens at the arboretum. There were blankets of colorful tulips, flowering azaleas and across the meadows of the thousand-acre property, the dogwoods and flowering cherry trees added their brilliant pinks to delight the viewer. It was truly a feast for the eyes and Ruth exclaimed her awe at God's creation. Esther removed a camera from her purse and asked Ruth if she could take one picture of her in front of a willow tree, fresh with fragile leaves.

"*Jah*, that would be okay. I'm not yet baptized," she reminded herself. A woman was walking by with her young son and offered to take a shot of Ruth with her aunt and they stood, arms looped together for the picture.

After they left Longwood, they stopped at a restaurant in Chadd's Ford and then headed home. As Ruth made up her bed on the sofa, she realized she would be spending the next night in her own bed. She smiled to herself, picturing the surprise in store for her family. She was excited now and eager to return. Yes, this was the correct decision. She knew it in her heart as well as her mind.

Chapter Forty-four

After donning her Amish outfit and tucking her hair under her *kapp*, Ruth ate a light breakfast before heading to the bus terminal.

It was difficult to say good-by to her aunt. They hugged and parted after confirming their mutual desire to get together often. Ruth promised to attend the wedding, though she dreaded seeing Darrel again, who would probably be with another woman. She reminded herself she no longer cared, but perhaps a part of her would always care.

Ruth waved from her window seat as the bus slowly took off. She noted her aunt's eyes were brimming with tears, as were her own. After her aunt was out of sight, Ruth sat back and tried to calm her stomach, which was doing somersaults from nerves. In time it settled down and she watched the passing scenery with praise in her heart for God's wonderful creation. Spring was bursting forth. May was her favorite month on the farm and she began picturing the clapboard farmhouse and the massive red barn. She could practically hear the lowing of their cattle and smell the fresh grasses.

When she arrived in Lancaster, Bob, the driver was there waiting. He was talking with several taxi drivers, but when he spotted her, he headed over to help carry her luggage to the car. Ruth carried her violin herself, protecting it as a mother would a new infant.

"How did you like living in the big city," Bob asked as he pulled out of the lot.

"It was fun, but I missed this area."

"Yep. Can't beat it for beauty."

"*Jah*, and not so much traffic."

The closer Ruth got to her home, the more excited she became. She could feel her heart palpitate when she was a mile away. When Bob pulled onto the drive, Ruth saw her father and Wayne grooming a horse in front of the barn. When he heard the car pull in, he and Wayne turned and walked toward the front.

"Oh, my Ruthie is back," she heard her *daed* say as he quickened his pace to reach her. Ruth ran to greet him. Wayne let out a hoot and the next thing she knew, her mother came out from the house and hugged her daughter. Katie and Emma heard the commotion from the hen house and joined the happy group. Tears and laughter encircled her and she knew beyond a doubt that she had made the right decision. One can not turn away from the shared love of close family. Possessions pale in comparison.

The driver got paid and Wayne carried in her suitcase. "What's in this thing, Ruthie?" He held up the violin case.

"What do you think, silly? A violin."

"Uh, oh. I best put it under your bed," he said with a wink.

Her father shook his head. "That's my Ruthie."

"You look *gut*," her mother said, holding Ruth's hands in hers and stepping back. "You gained weight?"

"*Nein*, she's still skinny," her *daed* answered for her. "Come, we have tea together–all of us. Just like we used to."

"*Gut*, I'll hold off supper for an hour or two then," Mary said as she put an arm around Ruth's waist and they headed to the kitchen.

The family discussed everything and everyone. Ruth got an update on each of her nieces and nephews and she heard about the troubles and successes at the school house. Emma seemed eager to talk about her job and Katie complained about gaining weight. Nothing had changed and for this she was thankful. After their noon meal, Emma and Ruth took a walk together.

"I heard Jeremiah is back from Ohio now that his grandfather passed on," Emma said out of the blue. "His grandmother is living with the family now in their *dawdi haus.*"

"*Jah*? Have you seen him?"

"No. I heard it from Mark. Jeremiah will be working again at the buggy shop."

"But you're totally over him now, right?"

"Oh *jah*. For a while now. He was cute, but that was it. He was too grouchy."

"You know of course I've always liked Jeremiah."

"*Jah*? My goodness, Ruth, why didn't you tell me?"

"Because you were all mushy about him and I didn't want to hurt you."

"Did he like you too at some point?"

Ruth nodded. "I believe so."

"Well, did he tell you so?"

"I'll be frank with you. I love Jeremiah and for a while anyway, he felt the same way, but he came to see me on my birthday in Philadelphia and things changed."

"He did? All the way to Philadelphia? He must care a lot. Why do you think things changed?"

"I'm afraid his feelings were hurt. I had no idea he was coming, and I was celebrating with a male friend, his father and my aunt so I couldn't talk to Jeremiah alone. He got the impression that I was more interested in the English life than Amish and when he left it seemed to be over. My heart was breaking, so I wrote and tried to let him know I still cared, but he didn't write back."

"You're going too fast. Who was the male friend?"

"A neighbor of Aunt Esther's."

"Young?"

"*Yah*, and handsome and rich."

"Oh, my. But you didn't like each other?"

"It's a long story, Emma. We dated, yes, and he liked me more than I liked him."

"Why didn't you write more about him?"

"I had to figure out my own feelings first. I couldn't get Jeremiah out of my mind, but now I've given him enough encouragement. If he still cares at all, it's up to him. As a tennis player would say, 'the ball's in his court now'."

"Maybe he didn't get your letter. He was grieving for his grandfather, that's for sure."

"Maybe. That's what I'm hoping."

"I feel terrible that I ruined things for you. My mouth is too big. I should have kept quiet about my feelings and you probably wouldn't have even left."

"Not true, Emma. I needed to explore the other world. I feel so good about my decision now and if I hadn't lived with Aunt

Esther and seen for myself, I might never have settled down in my mind."

"I hope that's true. I really have been childish over this whole thing. What are your plans now about Jeremiah?"

"I know I should wait for him to make the first move."

"But if you know you hurt him, even though you wrote, maybe you should not be prideful and go talk to him about it."

"Maybe, you're right."

"I am right. Believe me on this one, Ruthie. Swallow your pride."

"Okay. I'll take the buggy and go over tomorrow to his farm house. I need to know one way or the other. I think I'll be able to tell if he still cares by how he greets me."

"You will be surprised. Church service is there tomorrow, so you'd see him anyway! He will be surprised, too, I betcha."

"Oh my, now I'm really nervous. I'll see him anyway then, even if I changed my mind! Let's talk about something else before I *kutz*."

"*Jah*, tell me about the violin."

"I love to play, Emma. I can show you how to do it, if you want. Not that I'm some kind of expert, but I can play a few pieces now. Of course, I don't know if I'm allowed."

"Ruthie, you may have permission to play it at home, where no one can hear, of course. This new bishop has newer ideas."

"*Jah*? that would be great. It gives me much pleasure."

"I would like you to show me how to play it."

"*Jah*, but it takes a lot of practice to get *gut*. I'm not that *gut* yet."

Wayne rode his bike around the neighborhood informing the extended family about Ruth's return. That evening her brothers showed up with their families and their wives brought salads, casseroles and of course, pies, to help with the celebration. Ruth told them all about her job, her trips into the city and Longwood Gardens. She did not mention Darrel. What was the point?

By the time she prepared for bed, Ruth was exhausted, but she was unable to sleep more than four hours. Her anticipation at seeing Jeremiah the next day filled her with hope, as well as trepidation. Which way would things go? She prayed over and over for the same outcome. *Please, Lord, let him be the one.*

Ruth took extra care dressing Sunday morning. Emma chattered away while Ruth smoothed out her hair to wrap it into a bun. "I'll miss having my hair loose," she told her sister. "There were things I liked about the English way."

"*Jah*, you look so pretty with it down. But that's vanity, Ruth."

"I know. All the same."

"Girls," her mother called up, "We're heading over with Wayne. You two take the other buggy. *Daed* harnessed him up for you."

"Save us seats, *Mamm*," Emma called down.

As they drove over in the buggy, Ruth's heart beat rapidly. The horse's hooves clopping on the asphalt pavement were music to her ears and the familiar sights made it seem she had never left. When she pulled up, she spotted Jeremiah motioning to the buggies ahead of theirs to pull over to an area cordoned off for the church service.

"He doesn't know we're here," Emma said looking over at her sister who was holding the reins. "I'm going to get out here so you can surprise him." Emma disembarked and smiled over at her sister. "Hope it goes real *gut*."

"*Jah*, me too."

She was the next one in line and at first Jeremiah motioned for her to drive the buggy to an empty space, but when he realized it was Ruth, he stopped and gaped. He removed his straw hat and stared at her.

Ruth smiled. "Aren't you going to say '*hallo*'?"

"Oh, my. I think my eyes are playin' tricks on me. Is this the girl I saw in the big city with long hair and diamonds?"

"*Jah*. It's me, but now I'm me again. Just a plain Amish girl."

He looped the reins over a post and held out his hand as she stepped from the buggy. "Ruthie, you look so *gut*. I'm sorry I didn't write. My grandfather died and things were all confusing, but I thought about you every single day and hour. We must talk after the service. Please don't go home right away after we eat. Maybe we can go for a walk, *jah*?"

"Of course. I hope the preacher doesn't talk for three hours."

"It might be your own *daed*. What then, Ruthie?"

"Oh, then I'll signal him that people are sleeping and he'll shorten it." They laughed together and it felt so right to be there with him.

He took her hand and they walked over to the large sitting room where the benches had been set-up. "Sit in the next room where I can see you, Ruthie. I don't want you out of my sight."

"Never?"

"Never again."

The music was a salve to her spirit. She felt the presence of the Holy Spirit through the music, the words, and the prayers. Her father was not selected to speak that morning and the preacher who gave the sermon held it to two hours.

When it was over, many of her friends gathered around to hug Ruth and she gave a brief summary of her months away. Then her friends joined the other women prepare for the meal as the men rearranged the benches for eating. Jeremiah helped for a few minutes, but then motioned to Ruth to go outside.

He took her by the arm and steered her out to their herb garden behind the barn. There was no one in sight. Without a word, he drew her into his arms and kissed her tenderly over and over, caressing her back. "Oh, Ruthie, don't ever leave again. Please tell me you are here to stay."

"*Jah*, I want to be baptized. I have made up my mind. I am Amish in my spirit and Amish I will remain."

He continued to hold her and he kissed the side of her forehead. His voice became a whisper. "You will be my wife, Ruthie?"

"Are you asking me to marry you, Jeremiah?"

"*Jah*, I believe I am."

"Then I believe I will accept the offer."

"Ruthie." He bent down and kissed her again. "You have made me the happiest man in the whole world. Let's keep it to ourselves for a little while so we can enjoy it privately."

"I like that. *Jah*, it will be our secret and we can wait to tell our family in the fall."

"*Jah*, and be married in November. Can you be all ready by then?"

"Oh, I believe so, Jeremiah. I've been waiting for this day my whole life."

"And I've been waiting for you, my dear love."

Eventually, they walked back to the house, hand-in-hand, to join their family and friends.

After the meal was served, Ruth stayed near Jeremiah and he took her hand. "I'm holding on to you, Miss Zook, so you can't get away."

"*Jah*. I was afraid some nice *gut* Amish girl would win your heart in Ohio."

"Oh, there were many trying. I had to hold them off with a rake."

"I believe you."

"But what about your friend Darrel?"

"What about him?"

"He was in love with you. I know it. I could see it in his face. What did he say when you told him you were coming home."

"He wasn't real happy but he must know down deep that we are from two different worlds."

"So he told you he loved you?"

They stopped walking and leaned against a rail fence, facing each other.

"*Jah*."

Ruth watched as Jeremiah's jaw tightened and his eyes darkened.

"Jeremiah, I never told him I felt the same. Because I didn't. I've never stopped loving you. Not even for a minute."

"Ruthie, Ruthie, I prayed all the time that you would love me and we would marry."

"I prayed it too."

"I guess He got tired of us praying about the same thing over and over and said, 'okay you two.'"

Ruth laughed and leaned against him, surrounding his waist with her arms. "I'm so glad I got fired. It hastened my decision."

"*Jah*? Why was that?"

"I saw it as a sign from God. He was closing doors for me and opening my heart to be home. I was so homesick."

"*Jah*, and lovesick for me, right?" Jeremiah looked into her eyes. "You looked so pretty with your hair down long. I wanted to run and grab you when I saw you. My heart broke when I saw you wearing that necklace Darrel gave you."

"I no longer have it. I tried to give it back but he wouldn't take it so I gave it to my aunt. She's marrying Darrel's father, probably in December."

"So you want a double wedding?" he teased.

"I thought you said November."

"I would marry tomorrow if I could. It will be hard to wait. I have *gut* news, though. I will have my own place by the time we marry. It's the house my uncle lived in before he went to Ohio. It needs a lot of work, but it will keep me busy which is a *gut* thing. I'll take you to see it whenever you want."

"How many bedrooms?"

"Six."

"Wow. That means we can have many *kinder*."

"*Jah*. Six boys and six girls would be nice."

"It would, but I'll take whatever the Lord gives us."

"Maybe we will have a year all to ourselves first. It would be nice."

"Maybe. I didn't sleep *gut* last night, Jeremiah. Now that I have seen you, I feel calmer inside. I was afraid you were still angry with me."

"Not after reading your letter. I read, what do they say, between the lines and you sounded like you still liked me."

"*Jah*, a lot."

"My *daed* is motioning us to return. Remember our secret."

"Can I tell Emma? We are like twins."

"If she can keep it to herself."

"Jeremiah, when people see us together every chance we have, it won't stay secret very long."

"*Jah*, true, but I still like the idea of just you and me knowing how much we feel."

"Then, husband-to-be, that is the way it will be."

"You are very obedient," he teased. "Now I order you to kiss me one more time before we join our group."

"An order is an order," she said lifting her lips to his. Her dreams and prayers were being answered. Her life as an Amish wife and mother was about to begin.

Epilogue

Ruth looked out at the light snow falling. It was the first snow of the winter and the landscape took on a white coating signifying to Ruth, her own purity. She felt joy in knowing she could present herself to Jeremiah as a virgin.

It was perfect for her wedding day. None of the wedding guests had far to go. She and Jeremiah would remain in her parents' home the first night so they could help the family clean up the next day. Such was the Amish tradition. They chose a Thursday to wed and most of the preparation was done the day before with many helping hands. It was a joyful time for the whole community. The harvest had been plentiful this fall and now several weddings were scheduled for their district during the months of November and December.

Previously, she and Jeremiah had spoken at length to the Bishop when she told him about her violin. He had smiled and nodded. "I don't think that is sinful, Ruth. But you cannot play it at a service. You know that."

"I will play only in my home and I will play *gut* music."

"I'm sure you will. I always wanted to learn the organ."

"My goodness. I heard an organ at a big department store in Philadelphia. It was like being in Heaven."

"*Jah*, I can believe that."

It was only six in the morning and a few helpers had arrived. Her *daed* and Wayne had already milked the cows and fed the animals.

Ruth took a long bath in privacy and then dressed in a new violet colored dress she had sewn herself for the ceremony. All her clothing was new, but she planned to wear her wedding dress again, for church later on. There would be no frivolous waste in her Amish home.

Emma sat behind Ruth on her bed to comb out the snarls. "I will miss this, Ruthie. It was hard when you were away. At least I can see you when I want to now."

"*Jah*, and you can still fix my hair once in a while."

"Katie is so excited. She'll probably marry before me."

"I doubt that. You can have a husband easy. You are a wonderful-*gut* person."

"No one yet has taken my heart. I'm sorry I made such a fuss over Jeremiah. I know it was baseless now looking back. He never did anything to encourage me."

"We won't talk about that again. It was *gut* for me to go away and I feel God wanted me to be with Aunt Esther. It was a way to bring the family together. We will all go to her wedding next month."

"I'll get to meet the man who gave you the diamond."

"Don't get any ideas." Ruth pulled away from the comb. "Ouch! Why did you do that?"

"Sorry, just an accident," Emma said with a grin on her face.

Mary came in the room and looked at her daughters. "Ruthie, you are glowing. You look so happy. God is *gut*."

"*Jah*, all the time."

"Now let's put your *kapp* on. Are you almost ready? Nearly everyone has arrived. There must be two hundred people downstairs. Some even standing against the walls."

"Oh, my. My stomach just jumped upside down. Is Jeremiah here yet?"

Mary nodded. "He's pacing back and forth like a cow in labor."

Emma laughed. "Wait till his wife is in labor!"

"Not so fast, Emma. I don't even have a husband yet."

"*Jah*, but in a couple hours, you will."

Ruth went downstairs and Jeremiah went over to the staircase to take her hand. "You are a lovely bride, Ruthie. I'm such a fortunate man. God has blessed me."

People turned around and her friends smiled and waved. One of the ministers called Ruth and Jeremiah into a separate room where he talked about the importance of marriage and the requirements. While they were there, Ruth could hear the people as they sang hymns.

Ruth looked over at Jeremiah during the discussion and he smiled back and winked at her while the minister was searching for a verse to read. When they were finished they went out to the sitting area and joined the others for prayer and scripture reading. Then a long sermon was given. So long, Ruth had to stifle a yawn several times. Finally, it was over and she and Jeremiah went forward where they made vows to each other. Then the bishop pronounced them husband and wife and offered a blessing. Her father gave a brief message and Jeremiah's father added his good wishes. Ruth had never felt such happiness. Her heart sang praises to her Lord.

Ruth and Jeremiah were being surrounded by their family and friends, receiving hugs and kisses and well-wishes, when Ruth's eye caught sight of a woman dressed in English clothing appear at the open doorway with a man in a navy suit holding her arm.

"Oh, my! It's Aunt Esther and Martin!" Ruth broke through the crowd and reached her aunt who stretched out her arms to embrace her niece. "This is so *gut*–so wonderful-*gut*! I had no idea you were coming."

"We didn't tell anyone, Ruth. I wanted to surprise you. Oh, my, you look so radiant. Let me look at you. Absolutely beautiful."

"Yes, she is," Martin said as he leaned over to hug her. At that, Jeremiah came across the room to greet them.

"I'm so glad you made it here. It means a lot to us. May I call you Aunt Esther, too?"

"Of course. We're all family now."

"My Ruthie's a real 'knock-out,' *yah*?" His grin displayed his perfect white teeth and his eyes sparkled as he put his arm around his bride.

"That she is," Martin said as he looked over at Esther. "Runs in the family."

"Oh, my," a voice came from behind Ruth. "It's Esther! *Oma* come see your daughter." Mary took her sister in her arms and tears ran down her face.

"I couldn't stay away on such a special day, Mary. I hope it's okay."

"My goodness. Is it okay? Of course! We would have asked you to come, but we didn't think you would."

"Well, I'll be," *Oma* said as she stretched out her arms to her daughter. "You made it. Our Ruthie's day will be complete now." Mother and daughter embraced. As Esther broke out of her mother's arms, she saw her father standing several feet away, watching. She walked slowly over to him and stretched out her arms. Her father blinked several times and wiped his eyes against his sleeve before reaching out to his daughter. They held each other closely.

"I missed you, Daed."

"*Jah.* You should have. We had broken hearts, Esther, but now maybe we can mend them together."

"I'd like that, *Daed.* I truly would."

Some of the other relatives came forward to greet the prodigal daughter. Leroy stood back until the others moved away before coming forward. He patted Esther on the arm. "It's *gut* you came. Too many years have passed. Your family has mourned for you, Esther."

"Thank you, Leroy. You're a good man. Mary has had good fortune to have you for her husband"

Martin approached the couple. "Please meet my fiancé, Martin."

The men shook hands as Ruth joined them and looped her arm through her aunt's. "See? God had a purpose in bringing me to Philadelphia."

"I believe you're right, Ruth. Yes, much good came from your visit."

At last the signal was given to begin the meal. The tables formed a "U" shape with the *eck,* or corner reserved for the bride and groom. Ruth sat at her husband's left and the single girls were seated at Ruth's side, while the single men sat by Jeremiah. The bride and groom held hands so as not to be separated.

There were so many people attending that the tables had to be set and re-set to provide for all the guests. All the women worked. Katie and Emma along with their aunts and sister-in-laws did most of the running about, but in spite of all the activity, things went smoothly. Roast chicken with filling and mounds of potatoes, mashed with farm fresh butter and milk poured forth from the kitchen as the women worked tirelessly.

Abby was large with her expected baby and talked excitedly about the change in their lives. "It's due in January," she added.

"You're big enough you may be having twins," Ruth added.

"That would be fun. Will you help me, Ruthie, if I do?"

"You know I will."

Waneta was standing with Ruth and Emma as well. "I have a confession," Waneta said with a huge smile. "You too?" Ruth asked, patting her friends expanding tummy.

"*Jah*. I guess no one's surprised. We're so excited. It should come in April, maybe on your birthday, Ruth."

"I hope it does. We can have a double birthday every year."

After the meal, the young people gathered separately and the young men flirted with the single girls and sometimes they sang together. All the while, the older women busied themselves preparing for the supper.

Ruth noticed Emma was talking with her student, Mervin Kuhns, the boy who had lost his mother months before. The boy's father, Gabe, stood with his arm around his son's shoulder, nodding at something Emma was saying. Ruth thought she noticed a sparkle in her sister's eyes and wondered if it might be for the attractive young widower. Or perhaps she was merely delighted to see her student behaving well. The other child in their family, Liz, who looked about six, ran over to her father along with Mark's daughter Anna. Ruth walked over and joined the conversation. Liz looked up at Ruth in awe. "You are the bride, aren't you?" she asked.

"Yes, Liz and someday you will be a bride too."

Liz looked over at her father. "I have to take care of my *daed*. I don't want to get married."

Her father laughed. "You'll change your mind, little one. Your *daed* can take care of himself, that's for sure."

Emma laughed and patted Liz's head. "You'll want lots of children someday."

"No," the child said. "They're too much work." The adults laughed and then Ruth excused herself. She looked around and spotted Jeremiah watching her with a smile. She went over to him and took his hand in hers. He leaned over to whisper in her ear, "I wish everyone would leave. I want you to myself."

"*Jah,*" she whispered back. "We should have run away like the English do." He squeezed her hand and kissed her on the cheek. "We'll have wonderful memories of today to cherish." She nodded in agreement and said a prayer of thanks in her mind to God for bringing them together. Her many prayers were being answered.

Esther and Martin left around nine after receiving promises from the family to attend their wedding in December.

Finally, by eleven, the guests had departed and the family went to bed, leaving the exhausted couple to themselves. Emma was sharing Katie's room, leaving Ruth's bedroom for her and her new husband. Jeremiah pulled Ruth over to the sofa where they sat for awhile, discussing the day.

"It went so well, don't you think?" Ruth asked her husband.

"*Jah.* Only there were so many people here I didn't get to be with my wife enough."

"But we have a whole life time to spend together now."

"Oh, Ruthie, I am so happy I could burst."

"Don't do that, Jeremiah. I'd have to find me a new husband."

He chuckled and squeezed her shoulder. "I guess we should turn in, *jah*?"

"I guess so. I'm pretty tired."

"But not too tired?"

"You have something in mind?" she asked coyly, running her hand against his rough chin.

"*Jah*, as a matter of fact, I do."

"Then we should begin our life, husband. I love you."

"I will always love you, Ruthie, till the day I die."

"*Jah*, me too."

They walked up the stairs together to begin their life as husband and wife, with God as their partner–a constant presence in their home.

THE END

31918387R00171

Made in the USA
Lexington, KY
30 April 2014